HUGO

HUGO

Alfred Shaughnessy

TABB HOUSE

First published 1994
Tabb House, 7 Church Street, Padstow, Cornwall PL28 8BG

Copyright © Alfred Shaughnessy 1994

ISBN 1 873951 12 4

Typeset by Exe Valley Dataset Ltd, Exeter
Printed by BPC Wheatons Ltd, Exeter

1

ON that warm June afternoon in 1918 the battles were raging so fiercely on the Western Front across the Channel that the distant rumble of gunfire could be heard in Kent. But Charnfield Park, nestling in a hollow at the foot of the Dorset downs, seemed light years away from the nightmare world of war.

The only sounds to be heard on the broad gravel terrace in front of the Cardwells' ancestral home were the far-off croaking of a pheasant in the woods, the buzzing of bees in the herbaceous borders and the gentle sigh of a breeze agitating the tall beech trees in the park.

At the back of the terrace stood the old stone south wall of the Elizabethan manor house, with its winter irises, clematis and japonica, its mullioned windows and curved gables. Round the corner the vast windows of the Great Hall looked east towards the distant killing fields of France and Flanders.

Around mid-afternoon three adult figures could be seen moving slowly along the terrace, preceded by a small child, dragging behind him a toy horse which toppled over every few yards, causing the three-year old to toddle back with a happy laugh to put the painted wooden animal back on its wheels. In these fumbling efforts the small boy was assisted by his nurse, Nanny Webster. She was a woman of uncertain age with a healthy, weather-beaten complexion, dressed despite the warmth of the day in a grey flannel uniform and bonnet.

"Poor Dobbin," Nanny said, helping her charge to right the creature after its third fall; "we mustn't pull him along too fast, must we, or he'll go on falling over and hurting himself."

"Poor horsie," gurgled little Hugo Mayne, pausing to pat Dobbin on the rump before tugging at the string once more and continuing on his way.

1

"Shall we stop and sit down for a while?" a voice behind them said. "You must be getting dreadfully tired."

"Yes, I should like to rest," Richard now said, "just for a while."

Rosemary Cardwell, a tall, delicate-looking woman, wearing a straw-coloured shantung dress with a natural wide-brimmed straw hat on her fair hair, made a beautiful picture in that setting, while she looked towards her husband who had paused for a moment. Richard Cardwell, who was thirty-four years old, was of medium build with dark hair and a trim moustache. He was wearing an open-necked shirt, flannels, bedroom slippers and was leaning on a stick. A painting by Sargent would have perhaps done justice to that scene: a handsome couple, and their child, their stake in the future, with the crown of his inheritance, the House, behind them.

Richard had inherited his 1,400 acres in 1908 on the death of his father, the thirteenth Baronet, who had been a Conservative Member of Parliament, briefly holding office under Arthur Balfour. Before then, through twenty or more generations the Cardwell family had planned and acted in order to secure their estate, to husband it through lean years and to advance at moments of success. All that had led to this beautiful summer day of 1918. But perhaps the zenith was already passed; anyone looking closely would have seen that Richard Cardwell was breathing heavily while the set expression on his pale, patrician face suggested a man in some pain; and anyone acquainted with the family would have known that Hugo was not Richard's son.

Richard had come to England on leave from the trenches in March 1915 to visit Rosemary Mayne, whom he hardly knew. She was the recent widow of a brother-officer in his Battalion and seven months pregnant. After a piece of shrapnel from a shell burst had pierced Lieutenant Robert Mayne's lungs during a night raid on the enemy trenches and sent him off to join the Glorious Dead, his company commander, Richard Cardwell, who was due for some leave, had been assigned by the commanding-officer the unenviable task of calling on the bereaved Mrs Mayne at her home at Godalming in Surrey to tell her how bravely her husband had died. The encounter resulted in an emotional bond between the pair and it quickly developed into a deeper relationship.

In early May, soon after Richard had rejoined his regiment in

France, little Hugo was born to Rosie Mayne posthumously. In the following June, Rosie, whose weak lungs had been causing anxiety since she was a child, contracted tuberculosis and her doctor advised a long spell in a sanatorium at Banchory in Aberdeenshire. She had let her home in Surrey and spent the first year of her widowhood in Scotland, depositing her baby son and his nanny with her parents, the Brandons, at their Wiltshire home, Lainby, near Chippenham.

NOW Rosemary called ahead to the Nurse. "Don't wait for us, Nanny, we'll catch you up."

Nanny Webster looked round. "Very good, Lady Cardwell."

"Sir Richard's done well today, hasn't he, Nanny?" said Rosemary, asking for confirmation of her hopes. "All the way from the gatehouse."

"Yes, but he mustn't overdo it."

"No, he mustn't."

"Nonsense, Nanny," Richard cut in, "I'm as fit as a flea". He was lowering himself awkwardly onto a seat facing out across the park. Rosemary sat down beside him. Little Hugo, Nanny and Dobbin continued to the end of the terrace where Rosemary could see Nanny pick up the toy horse and, taking Hugo's hand, lead the child down some steps and out of sight towards the herb garden.

After a while Richard took another deep breath and said "Must do a bit more each day or I'll never get rid of this damn stick."

A momentary silence fell, while the mild breeze stirred the brim of Rosie's hat. Watching her husband's faraway expression, Rosie wondered if he was still re-living the horrors of the trenches, or simply wondering about Charnfield's future after the war when he could once again live there and continue running the estate.

"Is it still very painful to walk, darling?"

Richard looked up at his wife and noticed that her rather hollow ivory cheeks were a little flushed.

"A bit, but it's worth it to get round the old place and see everything, while I can."

Rosemary suddenly looked anxious. "How do you mean, 'while you can?'"

"Before my sick-leave expires and I get posted back."

3

Rosemary stared at her husband in horror. "Not back to France, surely?"

"That's where the battalion is, darling," Richard said.

"But they can't expect you to go back to the fighting before your wound's properly healed!"

"They will, if they're short of officers. But it could be over before then. The Huns are still advancing. It's in *The Times* today. They've taken Soissons now and reached the Marne".

"Oh, God, if this push can only end it all, before you have to go . . ."

Rosemary bit back her words, for she was anxious to avoid betraying her anxiety on this warm, peaceful afternoon. To have lost one husband at the Front, and now . . .

Glancing at Richard, seated beside her, she remembered how those long, lonely months at the sanatorium in Scotland had been relieved by his passionate love letters from the Front, most of them scribbled in pencil on message paper with the censor's stamp on the envelope. By July, 1916 Richard was back in England instructing on an Infantry Course. In a reply to Rosemary saying she was much better and would soon be discharged from the sanatorium, he had written from Pirbright Camp:

My Precious Darling,

I am counting the days before my vision of you comes true, with your adorable face veiled and your slender body wrapped up against the cold, appproaching me down the platform at Euston Station. For I shall, of course, be there to welcome you home, and shower you with kisses.

If your mother agrees, I shall go to collect little Hugo and Nanny and bring them up to London with me to meet your train. Then we can all motor back to Lainby together . . .

Rosie always found it strange that Richard, who was oddly shy and conventional in conversation, could write with such passion and depth of feeling in a letter.

As Richard continued to sit in silence, looking out across the park, Rosie remembered their subsequent courtship. Whenever Richard had leave from Pirbright she would travel up to London from Lainby and they would dine together and go to the theatre or dance afterwards at the Grafton Galleries. Shortly after a Zeppelin raid, in the back of a taxi on one such evening, Richard asked her to be his wife and, as the taxi rounded Hyde Park Corner, she had managed to whisper "Do you really mean it?" before dissolving into tears of joy.

The wedding had taken place quietly in November, 1916 at the little Norman church at Lainby. The young widowed bride was given away by her father, Lord Brandon, and Richard was warmly welcomed by Rosie's family who saw in him a secure and happy future for Rosie and her fatherless child.

In March, 1918, three weeks after being posted back to France, Richard was caught by a hail of bullets from a German machine-gun which shattered his left thigh-bone and narrowly missed his abdomen. A month later, after a delicate operation at a Base Hospital near St Omer, he was shipped back to 'Blighty' and, towards the end of May, had been finally discharged from a Military Hospital in Aldershot to spend his sick leave at home . . .

"How he loves that horse." Richard's voice jolted Rosie out of her day-dreaming.

"Hugo? Yes. Doesn't he?" Instinctively Rosie took Richard's hand, squeezing it tightly. "He loves his home too," she murmured. "Our lovely home."

"Good," Richard said, mildly embrarrassed, and added, "It's not such a bad old place. I just hope old Robert would have approved."

Rosie raised her husband's hand and pressed it to her cheek. "If Robert could look down on us from up there, wherever he is," she said quietly, "I think he'd be very happy to see his wife and son so well looked after."

Rosie let go of Richard's hand, for he was struggling to his feet now, anxious to cut short what was developing into an uncomfortably emotional scene.

"Come on. Let's go down and see old Cooper in the walled garden before he goes back to his cottage for tea."

"Sure you feel up to it?"

"Yes, if we go slowly."

Rosie got up, handed Richard his stick and took his free arm, and they moved off again along the terrace.

"Mrs Cooper has had good news about their boy," she said. "You know that his ship was torpedoed off the Irish coast?"

"Yes, you told me. What news of him?"

"The Red Cross have written to say he's a prisoner-of-war somewhere in Saxony. It's a wonderful relief for them."

5

"It must be," Richard murmured weakly. "Let's hope he'll be home soon, and all the prisoners-of-war and the troops; everyone."

"It won't be long now," said Rosie with a deep sigh. "I feel it in my bones."

AS the rockets, fire-crackers and Roman Candles exploded in the sky above Charnfield, showering down myriads of many coloured sparks, the small, pale face pressed against the window of the day nursery was intermittently illuminated by each succeeding flash. Hugo's eyes were shining with excitement at his first experience of a firework display. It was happening in the lower meadow across the trout stream and close to the Home Farm. Richard had given his consent for fireworks on the estate in celebration of the Armistice, although he and Rosie had themselves gone up to London for the two days, November 11th and 12th, to celebrate with friends.

Even though the nursery window was closed against the cold November night air, and as much as the recent display excited him, Hugo was not too keen on the loud bangs outside and duly kept his hands pressed to his ears.

Between the loud explosions and the popping, crackling sounds in the sky above, Nanny was attempting to explain the reason for this pyrotechnical display. "The war is over, you see dear, and the Germans have been defeated and England is celebrating. It means that little boys' and girls' daddies won't have to go on being killed at the Front. We must thank Jesus in our prayers tonight for sparing them and . . ."

Another massive explosion outside, every bit as noisy as the heaviest shell burst on the Western Front, rapidly put an end to Nanny's remarks. Hugo reacted by bursting into tears of fright, scared by a sound loud enough to penetrate his blocked up ears. Nanny, also mildly shaken, decided it was time for bed. Hoping the fireworks would soon be over and a period of quiet would allow the child to sleep, she led her charge, still snivelling, along the passage into the night nursery where words of comfort and a mug of hot chocolate soon had him relaxed in his little painted bed.

After he had said his prayers and Nanny had left him alone with a little night-light glowing in its saucer on the mantlepiece, Hugo lay on his back, clutching his toy dog Pip, pondering the strange remark Nanny had made about little girls' and boys' daddies not being killed any more. He knew about animals dying; one of Uncle Richard's dogs, Toby, had died not long ago and Nanny had told him that when people died they went to heaven, and he knew about animals being killed. The memory of the awful discovery that Jack the under-gardener drowned Pansy's kittens made him shudder; but he was too young to grasp the fact and to know that his own father had been killed three years and eight months before, while he was still secure in his mother's womb.

ROSIE and Richard were standing on the doorstep of Jack Mitchell's house in Connaught Square waiting for someone to open the door in answer to the bell. To Rosie it seemed that no one was ever going to let them in; it felt to her that she had been waiting for hours – but she would rather have died than admit how tired she felt.

All over London the streets were filled with people celebrating the coming of peace. Every pub was full to the brim. Londoners were aimlessly wandering about the town singing, cheering and shouting with joy. In Picadilly Circus taxis, trying to get through the surging crowds to reach the theatres with their well-dressed smiling occupants, were constantly held up by the dense press of revellers, some of them attempting to climb onto the roofs for a free ride through the crowded streets. Even in a quiet backwater like Connaught Square Rosie and Richard could hear singing and cheering coming from Marble Arch nearby.

At last a parlourmaid, wreathed in smiles, opened the door.

"Good evening, Wilson," said Richard, who was a frequent visitor to the house, while Rosie added "Isn't it exciting news? Peace at last!"

"Oh, yes, m'lady!"

As they entered the front hall a murmur of conversation and laughter could be heard coming from the drawing-room on the first floor.

Lieutenant-Commander Jack Mitchell, an old school friend of Richard's, had been on leave from the Navy just a week when the news of the Cease Fire came through from France. He and his wife, Eve, had decided to gather together a dozen of their closest friends and have an Armistice Night party. The plan was to serve soup and hot punch at their house and then to go down to

Buckingham Palace to join the cheering crowds who were calling for the King and Queen to appear on the balcony.

As Richard and Rosie walked into the crowded room, Jack spotted them. "Come along in, Richard me old son of a gun, and get some hot punch down yer and yer good lady, eh?"

When Richard asked Eve what her husband thought about the Armistice, she murmured "Poor Jack. The thought of being back at his desk in the City again fills him with gloom. He's going to miss the Navy."

"I think we're all going to find it hard to readjust," said Richard. After about an hour of chatter and refreshment Jack organized his party into the three taxis he had assembled at the front door and they set off for the Mall. They left their taxis in Constitution Hill and walked down to mingle with the mob in front of the iron railings of Buckingham Palace.

Whether it was due to her fear of being crushed in the huge crowd or to the damp, foggy air that night, Rosie was suddenly convulsed with a terrible fit of coughing. It seemed to be uncontrollable and unstoppable, tearing at her lungs. There was little Richard could do for her. They were wedged between total strangers in a thick block of humanity; people of all ages, classes and nationalities, wildly cheering and waving small Union Jacks.

Holding onto Rosie tightly, Richard spotted a burly policeman a few yards off and managed to call out to him "Officer, can you help me to make way for this lady? She needs to get out of this crush. She's not well."

One or two people attempted to make a gap for Rosie and a member of the Mitchells' party, seeing what was happening, also tried to help clear a way but was soon separated from her in the crush. After a brief struggle Richard managed to get Rosie to within reach of the burly policeman.

"If I can just get her clear of this crush, Constable . . ." Richard held firmly onto his wife, who was still coughing in violent spasms. The crowd continued to surge round them, pressing hard on their arms, elbows and backs.

"'Ang on, sir, I'll push a way through; just follow me, lady." The constable did his best to cleave a passage through the crowd for Richard, who kept his arm protectively round Rosie to ward off the crowd. It was slow going, but at last they reached the edge of the crush and Richard saw the constable ahead of them signalling to a St John Ambulance team which had set up a tent just inside the railings of Green Park.

Inside the tent Rosie made a partial recovery, with the help of a St John nurse who plied her with hot tea. There was no chance of finding the rest of the party now, so Richard decided to get his ailing wife home to their flat in Bryanston Square as soon as possible.

"Think you could manage to walk up to Piccadilly?" he asked her. "We'll never get a taxi here."

Rosie nodded, holding on tightly to Richard's arm as they set off slowly across the grass towards a bus stop by a gap in the railings. Mercifully a crowded bus came along almost at once and Richard helped her up the step.

Inside, an Irish drunk shifted in his seat to make room for Rosie, winking at Richard as she sat down. "Been celebratin' too much, is it, the poor lady? Not surprisin' tonight with the peace and all!"

Richard smiled wanly at the man, moving across to stand protectively in front of his wife, in no mood for jokes.

Rosie was still shivering with shock and distress when they alighted in the Edgware Road to make their way home on foot.

"If things don't improve," said Richard later, when Rosie was safely tucked up in bed with a hot-water bottle, "we'll have to send you back to that sanatorium."

"No, please don't, Richard; not back there. I couldn't bear it!" Rosie dreaded a return to the gloom and isolation of Banchory in the Scottish hills, surrounded by people dying of T.B.

"Might be the best thing, darling, until your lungs are really clear."

"But I want to be down at Charnfield with you, helping to run things."

Richard moved to look out of the window at the glowing night sky over the jubilant capital. "I can manage," he assured her.

Rosie had to speak softly for fear of starting up her cough again. "In any case, I couldn't possibly take Hugo up to that sanatorium with me and I don't want to leave him again."

"What's that?" Richard turned away from the window, unable to hear what she was saying, and came back towards the bed.

She repeated her remark in a hoarse, grating voice that seemed to hover on the edge of another severe coughing fit.

"Don't try to talk, darling," her husband said, sitting on the bed beside her.

Rosie reached out and took his hand. "What kind of a useless wife have you married, if every time I cough I have to go rushing off to Scotland?"

She managed to get her way about the sanatorium but Richard insisted that she must go straight back to Charnfield the following morning and stay in bed there for the time being.

CHRISTMAS that year for the Cardwells was a quiet one. Richard had to cancel his customary Boxing Day shoot and another one some days later after news was received that Rosie's father Lord Brandon had suffered a heart attack in a taxi on the way to his club and had died a few hours later.

There was no son and heir to inherit Lainby and as Lady Brandon was well over sixty common sense demanded that she should move into a flat in London. She would then be free to see more of her daughter and grandchild whom she could visit in Dorset.

SO it was that Lady Brandon was staying at Charnfield for Hugo's fourth birthday on May 19th, 1919. She was, therefore, a party to the big secret of Hugo's birthday present which Richard and Rosie had planned to give him after tea.

Rosie always had breakfast in bed, brought up on a tray by her lady's maid, Saunders, while Lady Brandon preferred to have hers downstairs. A discussion between Richard and his mother-in-law on the merits of scrambled eggs was interrupted by Hugo's sudden appearance with Nanny in the doorway.

"We were just going for a walk down to the lake to feed the ducks, Sir Richard. Good morning, Lady Brandon."

"Good morning, Nanny, and good morning, birthday boy," said Lady Brandon. "Come here and give your Granny a kiss."

Hugo obliged. Then Richard said "I'd rather, if you don't mind, Nanny, that you didn't go to the lake this morning. The point is we . . . thought we'd all go down there this afternoon." He turned to Hugo and added "Mummy would like to go too," then to Nanny, "so perhaps just round the garden this morning."

Nanny suddenly caught on and glanced knowingly at Richard and Lady Brandon, who was nodding mysteriously. She looked down at Hugo. "Come along, dear, we'll see if we can find some

10

wild flowers to pick in the paddock this morning and go to the lake this afternoon."

Nanny took her charge off and his grandmother, buttering herself a piece of toast, remarked "He's growing fast."

"He is," said Richard, "in every way. Bright little chap as far as I can see. Takes in everything you tell him and asks endless questions."

"Rosie was very bright at that age, you know, and filled with curiosity. Do you know, when she'd been at school for only a year, Harry used to grumble that he was constantly having to rush to the bookshelves for the encyclopaedia to look up answers to her questions."

There was a short pause, while Lady Brandon stirred her coffee. "Poor Harry," she went on in a flat, unemotional voice. "He'll miss Hugo's school days. He'd have loved to go down and watch his grandson playing cricket."

"Yes, he would have, wouldn't he?" Richard poured himself another cup of coffee. Then he added "I'm sure we're right to put him down for Stanborough House. They teach the Classics very well, I hear, and there's an excellent cricket master; chap called Wooldridge. Former county player."

"I don't know the school but I'm sure you and Rosie will make sure the child gets a thoroughly good education," Lady Brandon said.

"You can depend on that," said Richard, resuming his seat.

"BLOW hard, go on, blow."

Hugo filled his cheeks with air and puffed with a violence that almost caused him to fall off his chair at the nursery table.

Three of the four candles on the cake went out and Nanny moistened her forefinger and thumb to pinch out the fourth, to shrieks of delight from Hugo. Next, the little boy cut his cake with Nanny's hand helping to guide the knife. Rosie, Lady Brandon and Richard were offered a slice each which they nibbled at diffidently while Nanny and Hugo pulled a cracker. The resulting bang, unlike that of the fireworks on Armistice night a few months earlier, had no effect on Hugo who took it in his stride, laughing and wanting to pull another one instantly.

But Nanny said "We must go down to the kitchen now and thank Mrs Walcot for making you such a nice cake, mustn't we?"

11

She was already starting to pick up the remains of the crackers and clear the nursery table of the tea things.

"Then down to the lake," Rosie said.

"That's right," Richard murmured with a conspiratorial wink at his wife.

A WEEPING willow tree overhung the water and a slight breeze was rippling the lake and bending the tree like an old umbrella caught in a squall when Richard led Hugo by the hand down the rough path to the water's edge.

The boy had been told to keep his eyes closed until further orders so that the full visual impact of his birthday treat would provide the maximum thrill. "I can't see," Hugo cried, his voice shrill with excitement.

"You're not supposed to, darling, not yet," said his mother, who was following a few paces behind with Nanny and her mother. They reached a spot by the lakeside where Richard stopped.

"Keep 'em shut, Hugo, there's a good chap, and just turn round. Now you can open them. There!"

Hugo opened his eyes and stared for a few seconds in unbelieving rapture. A few yards from the lakeside path and under the cover of the trees surrounding the lake stood a little cabin, constructed of pine logs. There was a small window on either side of the front door, which was three steps up with a little porch. The sloping roof was made of old tiles and a small chimney protruded from the back. The whole cabin measured no more than ten by eight feet square and was eight feet tall, providing just enough headroom for an adult and plenty for a child.

Hugo recovered from his initial stunned surprise and turned to Richard. "Can I go into it?"

"That's the idea, old boy. It's for you."

Hugo ran quickly towards the cabin, up the steps and stopped at the front door, hesitating.

"Go in; the door's not locked."

In a flash Hugo was inside, looking round him in ecstasy. Richard, Rosie and Granny followed. Nanny remained for a moment behind. Then she followed the others in, at a discreet distance.

Young Jim Cooper, safely back from the war and Mr Keegan,

the estate carpenter, had secretly built the cabin for Master Hugo. The front part was bare and unfurnished but for a small table and two chairs. Through an arch in the partitioning wall was a tiny kitchen with a sink and an old stove with a pipe going up through the roof.

"A real stove, you see, for cooking on. It's a wood burner, so you'll have to collect your own fuel from the woods."

Richard opened the small iron door of the stove and closed it again. When Rosie took Hugo's hand, it was trembling with excitement.

"You'll be able to come down here and picnic in it, won't you?" she said.

"Fry sausages and things," Richard added.

"And invite your old Granny to tea," said Lady Brandon.

"As long as we're careful to see the fire's put out when we leave," warned Nanny.

"Will I be able to sleep in here?" Hugo asked.

"At night? All by yourself?" Lady Brandon sounded alarmed.

"I can't see why not," said Richard. "Damn good fun and a lot more comfortable than a canvas tent. Besides, we don't want him to grow up into a mollycoddle."

There was a sudden silence, broken by Nanny who said, "What do we say to Uncle Richard and Mummy?"

Hugo caught on at once. "Thank you, Mummy and . . . thank you Uncle Richard." He kissed his mother and went up to Richard who put a hand on his head and ruffled his hair. "Can I stay and play in it now?"

Rosie said "Of course, darling. Nanny will show you how to collect wood and lay the fire."

"I don't think we'll lay the fire today; just pretend," said Nanny quickly. Her remark, ostensibly addressed to her young charge, was intended for Rosie. Perhaps she could foresee long days and nights in the cabin by the lake with Hugo wanting to cook and sleep in it. He must be allowed to develop an adventurous spirit, of course – as any boy should – but she was responsible for him.

FOR much of the following winter Rosie did not feel well enough to entertain and very few guests were invited to Charnfield. This suited Hugo pretty well for he had Mummy and Uncle Richard all to himself.

When he wasn't curled up on Rosie's bed reading to her – he rather fancied himself as a reader now and could not wait to show off his skill – he was pottering around Charnfield with Nanny, well wrapped up in a huge scarf, tweed coat and cap and little boots and gloves. Together they peered into every potting shed and greenhouse down by the walled garden, every loose box in the stables as well as the tack room, the garages and lofts and outhouses around the perimeter of the house. Occasionally, if it was too wet or foggy to venture out of doors, Hugo would accompany his stepfather round the house to visit the Long Gallery, the billiard room, the library, some unused bedrooms in the East Wing and a couple of secret passages, one of which led down to a small, dark room about seven feet square. Here, Richard explained to the wide-eyed child, a seventeenth century ancestor, Sir Matthew Cardwell, had given shelter to a Royalist spy on the run from Cromwell's men.

"They hid the wretched fellow under the floorboards for several months. Must have been a bit cramped for him, eh? The servants took him food and drink in baskets during the hours of darkness, to keep him alive, you see."

Hugo was also shown a tattered flag on one wall of the library, the remnants of a Company Colour carried at the Battle of Fontenoy by another Cardwell ancestor who had served with Marlborough in the Low Countries.

Armed with all this exciting and dramatic information, which he only half understood, Hugo would run breathlessly upstairs to recount it all to his mother where she lay in bed, weakly smiling against her pillows, until the time came for Hugo to say goodnight and accompany Nanny up to the nurseries at the top of the house.

By the Autumn of 1920 Rosie was up again and Hugo was a regular visitor to the hall after tea. As soon as Page the butler and Robert the footman had cleared the tea things and folded away the table, Nanny would appear with Hugo clutching a game to play with or a book to look at. In Nanny's view, a child ought to be capable of amusing himself at all times and should not rely on his parents to entertain him. Thus she made sure that Hugo was equipped, in case Sir Richard and Lady Cardwell might be too tired or pre-occupied to play with him.

Exactly forty minutes later to the second Nanny would re-appear to collect the boy and his belongings with the same

14

unvarying remark. "Time for bed. We must put our things away now, mustn't we?"

At this Hugo's face would fall, for he enjoyed those after-tea sessions, lying on his tummy in front of the log fire playing Snakes and Ladders or turning the pages of some comic book or one with pictures of animals or ships. Sometimes Rosie would lift her son up to sit beside her on the sofa and go through the books with him, explaining things. Or Richard would tell his small stepson to place the Snakes and Ladders board on a low table by the sofa and challenge him to a game. At other times Hugo would lie gazing into the fire, when the logs had burnt sufficiently low to make glowing caves and palaces of pulsing, fiery light.

When Richard first noticed this, he found the boy's absorbed intensity disturbing, but after the door had closed on Hugo and Nanny that evening and he mentioned it to Rosie, she replied: "Darling, you must allow children their dreams," and he had bowed to her superior knowledge of the infant mind.

It was during one of his after-tea visits to the Great Hall that Hugo wandered off while Rosie and Richard were discussing their engagements for the following week.

On a table by the window a large, glossy illustrated book had caught the boy's eye. Impulsively he attempted to lift it off the table but its weight caused him to turn round for help. "May I look at this, please?"

"What is it?"

Rosie glanced over to Hugo and saw the child wrestling with a heavy book of illustrations. She knew that it would crash to the floor. "Richard!" she called for help.

At the same moment Hugo cried out "I can't hold it . . ."

Richard jumped up and hurried across the room as fast as his stiff leg would allow, too late to prevent the book from hitting the floor with a dull thud.

Hugo burst into tears of shame and humiliation. "I'm sorry, Uncle Richard," he wept, as his stepfather retrieved the book, which was mercifully unharmed, and replaced it on the table.

"I only wanted to look at it," Hugo sobbed, running instinctively to his mother for comfort, "because it's all about our house with lots of pictures."

Within minutes Rosie had wiped away Hugo's tears and the little boy was blissfully lying on his stomach by the fire once

15

more, turning with breathless care the pages of the book in question: *Charnfield And Its Treasures* by Edith Walker.

Page after page of photographic plates of Charnfield revealed to Hugo's delighted recognition the exterior of the house in which he lived, shown from every angle, with its stables, ornamental gardens and the lake. There were also interior photographs of many of the rooms, and long paragraphs of text about the architectural features of the house and its complement of fine paintings, statues, busts, porcelain vases and other precious items.

Hugo was totally engrossed by the book, sometimes looking up to ask his mother a question about some picture or ornament in its pages. Sometimes Rosie was uncertain of the answer and would consult her husband.

Richard would then look at the book and say, "That's the Rubens in the Long Gallery," or "Yes, nasty looking snakes aren't they?" and add, for Rosie's benefit, "Those twin-serpent candelabra used to adorn the dining-room table on formal occasions in my grandfather's day but they're put away now in the cellar; much too ornate for nowadays and devils to keep clean."

Hugo turned another page and came across a full-length oil portrait of a Georgian squire.

"That's my great-grandfather, painted by Sir Joshua Reynolds," Richard explained. "Funny-looking chap. He was High Sheriff of the County. Look at his red nose. Much too fond of his port."

"What's port?" Hugo enquired.

"Never you mind, old chap." Then, with a wink at Rosie he added "You'll find out one day."

Noticing with some pleasure the child's rather precocious interest in the house and its contents, Richard said "Let's go and have a look at my great-grandfather, shall we? That chap there. We'll go upstairs and find the real picture."

Hugo jumped to his feet with excitement and was just taking Richard's hand to be led up to the Long Gallery when Nanny came round the screen from the steps down into the Hall.

"There's Nanny," said Rosie, lowering her petit point and removing her glasses. "I'm afraid it'll have to wait until tomorrow."

But Richard saw no reason to disappoint his stepson. "We're

16

just off to look at a picture in the Long Gallery," he said. "You go on up, Nanny; I'll bring him to the nursery directly."

Nanny deferred to her employer with mild annoyance. She felt this was an infringement of her authority over the child but she suppressed her feelings and said "Very well, Sir Richard," adding as a face-saver, "just this once."

Rosie said nothing but tactfully concentrated on her needle-work.

LEAVING the lighted hall to climb the broad wooden stairs that stretched up into the gloom of the first floor, Hugo felt increasingly excited. The carved banister posts were too tall for him to reach the wide rail that they supported so his stepfather had taken a firm hold of his hand. Hugo tugged it impatiently. At the top of the stairs and round a corner the Long Gallery stretched away into darkness. Richard turned some electric switches on the wall and lanterns hanging from the ceiling sprang to life, casting pools of light at regular intervals along the passage, where yards of carpet ran past high oak presses and marquetry chests into the distance, while on the walls ancestral figures stood out, each lit by its own spotlight. Richard led Hugo past men in ruffs with dark clothes and beards and women with large filmy lace wings that framed their pale faces and with high-piled hair in which were looped strings of pearls. Hugo was fascinated by these strange people and their rich clothes but Richard led him on, to stop in front of a portrait that was larger than the rest. This was of a man who looked somehow more alive than the others, although his clothes were plainer.

"There he is," Richard said, in front of the Reynolds portrait.

Hugo gazed up in awe at the elegantly dressed Sir Peter Cardwell. "Did he live in this house?" he asked.

"He did indeed, and his father before him and his grandfather. They're probably all still here, wandering about the place as ghosts."

Hugo shivered at the thought of ghosts. But he could see in his imagination the Long Gallery where they were standing filled with 'picture people'. This was his name for all these funnily-dressed people from the olden days who adorned the walls here and in other parts of the house. He now knew the names of some of the makers of these oil-painted portraits: Gainsborough, Kneller, Lely, Hoppner, Lawrence. Their subjects were men

17

dressed in knee-breeches and satin coats with three-cornered hats and ribbons with medals and orders and spy-glasses round their necks, bowing and gesturing; and ladies in huge bulging dresses with bows, cooling themselves with elaborate fans; and, of most interest to Hugo, children hand-in-hand or with their arms round each other's necks, or playing with dogs or rabbits or looking at birds in circular wire cages.

After looking at the Reynolds portrait Richard took Hugo to the Grand Drawing-Room, which was seldom used now. There, Richard showed Hugo the Rubens he had found in the book downstairs, and Hugo was fascinated by the blueness of the sky and the puffiness of the rosy clouds from which rays of light came down towards the almost equally puffy pink-armed, pink-cheeked women in the picture.

There were also an early eighteenth century harpsichord and a glass case containing some priceless old manuscripts.

"Look what funny writing they did in those days," Richard said, pointing to a letter written in 1688.

Hugo tried unsuccessfully to decipher the spidery handwriting while Richard told him that it was a letter from Mr Cross, the bailiff at Charnfield, reporting to the owner of the day details of the arrangements for bonfires to be lit in the park to celebrate the arrival in England of William of Orange and Mary to claim the throne. "They came from Holland to become King and Queen of England," Richard explained.

Before they left the drawing-room, Richard showed Hugo the Grinling Gibbons wood carvings on either side of the great fireplace.

Hugo felt with his small delicate hands the finely-carved leaves and birds and sheaves of corn. "They're like real birds," he cried out in wonder, while Richard looked at his watch and decided that it was time to take Hugo up to bed.

A few minutes later, as Nanny finished darning a pair of Hugo's socks, Richard came through the nursery door to hand over a very flushed, excited little boy. When Nanny put him to bed Hugo's thoughts were far away, his mind awash with the world of paintings and beautiful furniture and the vast, empty rooms of Charnfield, a world seemingly miles from the familiar, hum-drum nursery he was used to, with Nanny sitting at her darning, the small fire in the grate and all his childish toys. That night Hugo felt very grown-up, and with reason, for on that

18

autumn evening in 1920 something important had happened to the five-year old boy. A seed had been sown in the mind of Master Hugo Mayne that was to take root and flourish over the years to come. Two seeds, to be exact. One was a general feeling for works of art and an appreciation of beauty. The other was a passionate love for Charnfield, his home, with its history, its beauty, its treasures and all that in his mind it stood for.

2

"THAT'LL need one more coat, I reckon," said young Jim Cooper, standing back to inspect his work. "How are you going on, then, Master Hugo?"

The early spring day was dying fast, the light fading in the clear sky. Rooks were cawing high in the tall trees of the surrounding woods. The boy paused in his painting to look up.

"Look, Mr Cooper, I've finished this bit," he called out.

Jim Cooper, son of the old Charnfield gardener, who had survived the war with the Merchant Navy, was back working on the estate now as under-gardener and odd-job man. He it was who had helped Keegan, the estate carpenter, to construct the cabin and was now busy painting it. Richard had left little Hugo to help Jim paint the door and window-sills while he and Rosie walked together round the lake to discuss a letter Richard had received that morning from his old friend Jack Mitchell.

Mitchell had written

This chap I know, Gordon Adams, is a very experienced white hunter and he'll fix up everything for us. We could sail in early October on a P & O boat. It's a fine sea voyage, through the Straits into the Med., through the Suez Canal and into the Indian Ocean to Mombasa. Then by train to Nairobi and on to camp from there. I know you'd enjoy it. The sea voyage is splendid and the African climate is very bracing. Also, it would make a change for you, besides which you might bag a lion or a rhino. Talk to Rosie about it and see what she feels. I'd suggest her coming out too, but I'm not sure going on safari wouldn't be a bit too much for her; all the walking and camping out – not to mention the heat and the old mosquitoes buzzing about.'

Richard paused to put Jack's letter back in the pocket of his tweed jacket, while his wife thought about their old friend.

Jack was a short and stocky man with a weather-beaten face. A year older than Richard, his father had been an Irish immigrant to Canada, his mother Scottish. The family had settled in New Brunswick at the turn of the century and much of Jack's boyhood had been spent on the Eastern seaboard of Canada where he had learned to sail, fish and chop down trees. His mother had insisted on sending him to Great Britain for his education, but after leaving school he had been something of a rolling-stone. He had spent some time on a sheep farm in Western Australia and had sailed around the world three times, studying and writing about Marine Biology. In 1911 he had met and married Eve Thorpe, the only daughter of a London stock-broker. This had caused him to settle down to a more static life as a junior partner in his father-in-law's firm in the City. He had a warm and generous nature; people said of Jack Mitchell that he was a bit of a rough diamond but a good sort, a man who had seen life. Some had wondered whether he would not find life in London with Eve dull and uneventful. But after three years of marriage, which was sadly childless, the Great War came and Jack was able once more to indulge his passion for the sea by joining the Royal Navy.

Rosie turned her attention back to Richard. "Of course you must go, darling," she said, squeezing his arm. "Jack's quite right. The change will do you good and I shall be all right. Mother can come down and stay with me and Nanny will be here."

Jack was secretly relieved, for he had expected at least some opposition to the plan.

"How long will you go for?" Rosie asked.

"Oh, I'll be back in good time for Christmas."

"With all sorts of trophies, I expect; ivory tusks, antlers and an elephant's-foot waste paper basket."

Richard smiled and put his arm lovingly round his wife's frail shoulders. "That's right. Well, it's settled then."

"Yes, darling. You write to Jack and tell him you'll go."

Richard paused to kiss her cheek. "If you're quite sure you don't mind. You won't be lonely?"

"Of course not."

"I'll have to spend a few days in London getting my kit together."

Rosie had a sudden vision of Richard in khaki shorts, a safari jacket and a solar topee, standing proudly with his foot on the belly of some dead animal, surrounded by grinning natives. She had seen similar photographs in the *Tatler*. She felt glad that she was not going too.

They were approaching the log cabin now and Hugo, seeing them coming, ran along the lakeside path to meet them, brandishing his paint brush and dripping white paint everywhere.

"Come and see what we've done," he panted. "Mr Cooper's painting the door and I'm painting the window-sills."

It was decided not to go inside the cabin to inspect the work, owing to the prevalence of wet paint. But Rosie noticed through the window a small jam jar filled with wild flowers on the little table.

"Who picked those?" she asked pointing to them.

"Me and Nanny. And I'm going to bring some books and some toys here too, so I can play and read and . . . and . . . live in my own house . . . forever and ever."

ONE evening after it had been settled that Richard was to go to Africa the family were in the hall after tea as usual and Hugo, once again, was staring into the fire. Rosie, head bent over her embroidery, suddenly became aware that he had turned his rapt gaze from the fire to her.

"What is it, Hugo?" she asked gently.

Then, to her surprise, the child leaped to his feet, ran over to her, and buried his head in her lap. Then he looked up into her face, to ask "Mummy, you won't leave us, will you?"

What a strange question that was! – But then it occurred to Rosie that Hugo was worried that she might go away for a long holiday, like Richard, or perhaps with him. 'You won't leave us, will you?' he had asked, and presumably he was thinking of himself and Nanny.

"No, darling," she said. "I'm not going away. I'm going to stay here with you and Nanny while Uncle Richard is away."

She smiled lovingly at Hugo but for some reason he did not respond, so that she wondered what was going on inside his young head.

Had she known, she would have been distressed, for Hugo's thoughts were not running quite as she had imagined. Hearing of Uncle Richard's departure had certainly been their starting point, but thinking of his stepfather's absence and being alone with his mother reminded him that once before he and she had been alone together, although he had been too little to remember it now. That was after his own real father had been killed in the war. He liked Uncle Richard but he was not his father and he wished he had his very own proper one. But there was a worse thought; people who shouldn't die sometimes did, and he couldn't be sure that it wouldn't happen to Mummy. She had been so ill and pale when she had been in bed not long before that perhaps she was going to die, too. At that point he had asked his question, thinking how unbearable it would be if he were left with just Uncle Richard.

A few moments later, seeing that he was still looking very solemn Rosie said encouragingly "We must look after each other, when Uncle Richard is away, mustn't we?"

Immediately Hugo brightened up, to give her a beaming smile: her words spelt reassurance, warmth, and togetherness and love.

THAT night it was Rosie's turn to worry. Lying in bed in her room above the terrace, she lay watching Orion's Belt as it wheeled slowly across the sky. Her chest was hurting again; so much so, that she supposed she would have to go back to that vile sanatorium with its icy draughts, its cold nurses and its atmosphere of despair. She wept a few tears, until the facts of the case made her more practical. If she did go away, it could not be until Richard came back from Africa; she had promised Hugo only that evening that she would not leave him. But what if she was to leave him for good? Richard would surely marry again; she hoped for his sake that he would. In that case he might have a child of his own; she regretted bitterly that everyone had agreed that she must not risk giving him one. If it were left to her she would take the risk, but once Richard had been convinced by the doctors he was too obstinate to change his mind, and she had Hugo to consider. How would the poor little boy manage with two step-parents? He was such a sensitive child, more like a girl than a boy. Rosie sighed, and turned restlessly in her bed. Months before, the thought of dying had seemed claustrophobically dreadful, but now she had seen it approaching several times, and on closer acquaintance it had seemed less intimidating. After all, what was the point of going to church every week, if it did not stand one in good stead at just such times as these? No, death

23

did not frighten her; but if she died, what would become of her son? Once more she wept.

RICHARD'S old wound was making itself felt when he and Jack returned to camp after another gruelling hot day in the bush. It was towards the end of their first week in Kenya and Richard's roughly-restructured thigh had until now stood up pretty well to the long treks over rough ground from one side of the vast game reserve to the other. Now, as the safari party started down the last slope into the kraal where their tents were pitched, Richard was forced to hand over his gun and haversack to his personal bearer, a slim, grinning Kikuyu called Opa.

Jack Mitchell noticed that his companion was limping slightly. "That old leg playing you up, Dick?"

"Just a bit today," Richard admitted. "Probably some rain on the way."

Jack put a hand on his friend's shoulder. "We'll slow engines a notch or two," he said and turned to the long line of native bearers, who were strung out ahead of them, to shout out something in Swahili.

The head boy in the lead called back "Okay," and made a gesture to the others to slow down.

"Good fun though today, wasn't it?" Jack said as they continued on their way at a steadier pace.

"First rate," Richard agreed. "Only wish I'd bagged that second rhino."

"Never mind, you've broken yer duck, that's the main thing," said his companion.

After dinner that evening, a simple meal of hot broth and bully beef in the mess tent, followed by a pipe and a large whisky and soda outside under the stars, Richard told Jack he'd like to go to his tent and write some letters, then turn in early, as a rigorous schedule was planned for the following day.

"Good idea, old lad; sleep tight and make sure the bugs don't bite."

"They won't . . ." Richard left the mess tent and made his way to his own sleeping quarters, calling back out of the darkness, "unless there's a hole in my mosquito net."

Minutes later, in the dim light from a paraffin lamp, Richard was crouched over a small collapsible table writing with a fountain pen on a lined letter pad:

24

P.O.Box 15, Nairobi, Kenya, E.Africa
November 6th, 1920

My Own Darling,

I'm writing this in my tent in v. poor light to tell you that your husband managed to bag a rhino today – much to Jack's amazement and mine! He called it 'beginner's luck' and I think he was quite envious. However, I missed an easy shot at another one for which I am rather ashamed of myself. The air is wonderful out here and I'm feeling pretty fit although we trek long distances every day which can be v. tiring. We're going down to Mombasa on the coast next week where I gather we shall bathe in the ocean and go on a boat trip over to Pemba Island. Please write soon and tell me how you are and give me news of home. Is Hugo disappearing every day into the lake hut to read books? I suspect that he's going to be a brainy lad. Take care of that cough and try not to catch any chills. And please convey my best regards to Nanny and the servants. Should be home about first week in December.

Your Loving Richard

P.S. I'll send you a p.c. from Mombasa.

The same ramshackle white Ford motorcar, which Yates, the white hunter's man, drove into Nairobi twice a week to and from the camp to post and collect the mail, returned the following afternoon with a cablegram for Richard from London.

As he tore open the envelope a sudden twinge of anxiety gripped his stomach. Something told him it was bad news and as he looked at the message, printed in purple on strips of white paper pasted onto the form, his hand was shaking.

The cable read 'Rosie seriously ill. Doctors advise you return at once. Edith Brandon.'

"OF COURSE you must go. Right away," was Jack's immediate response. "We'll find out about sailings and get you on the first boat from Mombasa."

The two men were standing outside Jack Mitchell's tent, Richard clutching the cable in his right hand, which was still shaking a little.

"I'm most awfully sorry, Jack," was all Richard could manage to say; "just dreadfully sorry."

"No need to apologize, mate, can't be helped. Just hope it's not too serious."

"Perhaps you could find someone else to come out here and join you. Take over my gun, as it were."

Jack looked doubtful. "Not worth anyone coming out from England now," he said, "not this late in the season. Might find some wallah at the bar in the Nairobi Club, some chap game for a few days in the bush. I'll see. Anyway, the great thing is to get you onto that boat."

"Afraid so," said Richard. Then he added "Poor Rosie. It'll be those wretched lungs of hers, damn well playing up again. What rotten luck."

Twenty minutes later, while Richard was in his tent packing up his belongings, Jack put his head through the flap. "I've been thinking, Dick. There's a quicker way back, you know. Stephen Cook, that fellow in Parliament, used it last year to get back for some emergency in his constituency."

Richard turned from his packing. "How?"

Jack came into the tent and perched on the end of Richard's camp bed. "You can cut short the sea voyage by getting off the boat at Brindisi in Southern Italy, when the mail goes ashore. Then take a train to Rome and Paris, then to Boulogne or Calais and home by cross-channel steamer. Much quicker."

"That sounds a good idea," said Richard strapping up his trunk, "I'll take your advice."

As soon as he finished packing, Richard sent a cable to Rosie's mother at Lainby to say he was returning home at once and another to Page, the butler at Charnfield, with the same information.

That done, he drove into the shipping office in Nairobi to arrange his trip home by P & O liner. At eight o'clock the following morning Richard caught the train from Nairobi to Mombasa.

At first the long journey home was a nightmare. Anxiety over Rosemary's health marred any enjoyment Richard might have derived from being at sea, especially as he was travelling alone, without the benefit of Jack's company. Mistrusting the occasional sidelong glance from one or more of the bored colonial wives and spinsters returning home, Richard remained for the most part lying on his berth in his cabin reading an Edgar Wallace thriller. He only risked the promenade deck in bad weather when most of the lady passengers remained in their cabins or the saloon.

However, having been identified as a baronet by the purser, he was invited to take his meals at the Captain's table, and this proved more agreable than he had expected.

The skipper turned out to be a charming Australian who had a sister married to a schoolmaster at Sherborne, which was quite near Charnfield, and on one occasion Captain Macaulay invited Richard onto the bridge to witness the ship's passage through the Suez Canal, when the French pilot explained to him the finer points of navigation. This, and an occasional game of deck quoits with three British cavalry officers going home on leave, helped to keep Richard occupied, and by the time he climbed into the Italian train at Brindisi, for the long rail journey across Europe to the Channel coast, he was beginning to feel more relaxed and hopeful.

'Rosie will pull through all right,' he told himself; 'she's shaken off T.B. before now. Even if she has to go up to that wretched sanatorium in Scotland again, she'll come through somehow. Her mother's panicking because I'm abroad, that's all. Doesn't like the responsibility without Harry at her side . . .'

IT was starting to drizzle as darkness fell on a cheerless December evening, when the boat train finally pulled into Victoria Station and Richard spotted his chauffeur William waiting at the barrier to meet him.

William was a quiet man at the best of times and said nothing as he helped the porter to strap Richard's steamer trunk and large tim box onto the back luggage rack of the Daimler Saloon.

Richard slipped the porter sixpence and climbed into the back with his small Gladstone bag. William placed the rug over his master's knees before closing the car door and taking his seat at the wheel, ready for the long journey down to Charnfield.

They drove in silence as far as the London suburb of Hounslow. At this point Richard reached for the speaking tube and asked William if he had had any supper.

"Yes, sir, thank you," William answered. "Mrs Walcot put me up some sandwiches and a flask of tea before I left this morning."

Richard sat back in his seat while the Daimler purred along the Portsmouth road through Staines, Egham, Sunningdale and Camberley. The road surface was slippery from rain and William drove with special care but few other motors were encountered on the way. It was not until they were well past Basingstoke and approaching Andover that Richard again spoke to William. "How was her ladyship when you left this morning?"

The question seemed to put William on the spot. He drove on for a few seconds before answering. Then he said "I really couldn't say, sir. I understand the doctor's been coming every day this last week and Lady Brandon sent to London for a night nurse on Wednesday. A Miss Williams. She takes over from the other nurse at six o'clock each evening. Has her meals with Nanny in the nursery."

"I see," said Richard, and lapsed into silence again. He didn't like the sound of a night nurse – that usually meant serious illness. But surely, they would have cabled him again, he thought; sent a message to Victoria by William, if things had suddenly taken a turn for the worse. No, it was unthinkable. 'She'll pull through. Rosie will be all right.'

AN hour and three quarters later they finally passed through the Charnfield gates, held open by Mrs Keegan, the estate carpenter's wife, who scurried out from the lodge at the sound of the motor's horn. By the light from the headlamps Richard saw her nod respectfully as the Daimler drove through the gates and on, up the long drive towards the house. At the front entrance, through the gatehouse, Richard got out. As he stepped towards the heavy oak door it was opened by Page, the butler.

"Evening, Page," Richard said, and thought that the muttered reply, "Sir," was unusually subdued. The butler took Richard's Gladstone bag from him and stepped aside to allow his master to go through into the Great Hall.

The house was very quiet, and there was of course no sign of Rosie. "I'll go straight up," Richard murmured.

Half way up the wide staircase Richard caught a glimpse of Saunders, Rosie's lady's maid, walking slowly across the dark landing with a hankerchief pressed to her face. Becoming aware of his approach, to Richard's surprise she hurried away into the shadows.

He reached the bedroom door. As he raised his hand to knock, the door opened and Nanny came out, looking ashen.

"Doctor Frame has been sent for, Sir Richard," she whispered.

Richard pushed past her into the room. The night nurse, Miss Williams, was bending over the bed, apparently arranging Rosie's hands across her chest in an attitude of prayer.

28

"I'm back, Rosie; how are you feeling?"

The nurse turned round sharply and stared at Richard in astonishment. Then Richard looked past her and saw that as Rosie lay against the pillows her eyes were wide open but strangely devoid of expression.

The truth struck him like some heavy object landing a blow in his guts, almost felling him to the ground. His throat closed up, his face drained suddenly of blood and he felt a singing in his ears. Clutching at the bed-post to steady himself, he watched, dazed, as the nurse leant over the bed again to close Rosie's eyelids.

This done, she turned round to Richard and said almost apologetically in a soft Scots accent "I came in to wash Lady Cardwell and settle her for the night, but her supper tray had slid off the bed onto the floor. As I bent down to pick it up, I noticed she wasn't breathing any more . . . I'm so sorry. I don't think she can have suffered any pain. It was very quick."

She turned back to glance once more at Rosie stretched out in repose, like some mediaeval knight's lady lying on a stone tomb. Then she switched off the bedside lamp, leaving Rosie still dimly lit from the passage outside.

"She looks nice and peaceful, doesn't she?" said the nurse, picking up the untouched supper tray and going towards the door. "I expect you'll be staying with her for a little while."

Richard sank into a chair beside the bed, staring ahead of him in disbelief. Then he got up, switched on the bedside lamp again and bent over to place a gentle kiss on his wife's waxen forehead.

He was back in his chair, sobbing quietly, when the door opened and Nanny's voice came through to him from the darkness. "I'm sorry Page didn't tell you at once, Sir Richard, as soon as you got here. It had only just happened, you see, and he was too upset to say anything."

Richard did not turn round, unwilling to allow Nanny to see his tear-stained face. He nodded.

"I'll leave you then," said Nanny and slipped quietly away.

Richard, suddenly finding Rosie's expressionless mask unbearable to look at, stood up and drew the sheet carefully over her head. Then he sat down again, staring up at the ceiling, as the heavy rain outside beat against the windows of the silent room.

HUGO'S young mind had still not, after three days, entirely come to terms with the feeling of deep sadness and fear at the thought that he would never see his mother again, no longer sit on her bed reading to her or feel her soft kiss on his cheek at bed time. He had read in his nursery books about people dying but they were mostly wicked people: giants and cruel barons and old kings and, of course, Jesus – but that was different. It was in a sense a mercy that Rosie had spent so much of Hugo's childhood in the sanatorium or in bed at Charnfield, for his reliance was mainly upon Nanny. Nanny was a tower of strength and un- doubtedly helped to sustain her young charge over the first difficult days.

THE heavy rain of the previous week had stopped and the weather was changing, promising a sharp, clear winter's day with some sunshine for Rosie's funeral.

Nanny had found her employer far too shattered and stunned by his wife's death to be capable of explaining things to Hugo. So it had fallen to her to prepare the child for the ordeal of witnessing his mother's burial.

"When people die, their souls – well, they themselves – go to Heaven where God looks after them for ever. But their bodies, which they don't need anymore, are buried deep into the earth in boxes. They're called coffins. And after many, many years they just become part of the earth. There's your boots on now, dear; let's find you a tie. This black one will be best for today."

LADY Brandon had arrived from London the day before and, finding that Richard was consumed with guilt for having been away in Africa, enjoying himself when his wife had been taken ill, was trying her best to relieve him of such feelings.

"You weren't to know, Richard," Edith said. "How could you have? As a matter of fact, Rosie was in better health when you sailed for Kenya than she'd been for quite some time. These things happen, my dear; it's the way life goes. You certainly have no call to blame yourself for not being here."

ACROSS the river valley on the side of a hill facing Charnfield Park stood the little Norman church from which, just after 3.15 that afternoon, Rosie's flower-decked coffin was carried out.

It was a small family funeral and apart from Richard himself, Hugo clinging to his Nanny, Lady Brandon and a niece of Harry Brandon's, the mourners were for the most part estate and village people. Richard's land agent was there, and the household staff: Mr Page, Mrs Walcot, Robert, Miss Saunders, the parlour and kitchen maids. As the family gathered at the graveside, the others, including Nanny, stood back at a respectful distance. They watched with heavy hearts, for Rosie had been loved by everyone at Charnfield. The sight of her little five-year-old son, now deprived of both father and mother, standing at his stepfather's side by the grave, dressed in his Sunday best with a little black tie, caused some of the older women to bite their lips and fight back the tears.

By four o'clock the funeral was over and the mourners slowly dispersed in small groups. Richard walked back to the car with the vicar. He would have preferred to be alone but evidently the good man felt it his duty to see him and the family off properly. So the two men walked in silence, Richard with his head bowed.

Suddenly he stopped in his tracks, looked up and stared ahead of him. "One got used to men being killed in battle in the war, you know," he murmured, "but this . . ."

"Indeed, yes," said Mr Setton, diffidently taking hold of Richard's arm in a shy gesture of sympathy, as they walked on.

They reached the motor and William, who had reverently exchanged his pall-bearer's bowler hat for his chauffeur's cap, opened the door.

Richard gestured to Lady Brandon, Nanny and Hugo, who were waiting for him, to get in. Then he turned to the clergyman. "Thank you again, Vicar," he said, and got in himself quickly, anxious to be driven away as soon as possible before, as he put it to Edith, "I make a fool of myself in front of half the village."

ROSIE'S mother stayed on at Charnfield for what was to be another sad, quiet Christmas.

Despite her personal sorrow, however, Lady Brandon was determined that Hugo's Christmas should not be spoiled. She spent much of her time in the nursery, helping Nanny and the little boy to make and hang up festoons and bunting. There was a fine tree down in the Great Hall waiting to be decorated and this took up the after-tea hour on Christmas eve. There was also Hugo's stocking to be filled and his list of required presents to be checked and then put up the chimney in the hall for Father Christmas. Hugo's main request was for a fairy cycle which he could ride to the lake hut and round the grounds. His second

31

choice was a set of plasticine, which Nanny said would be messy but his grandmother decided was a good idea.

"He's an artistic little boy with a feeling for shape and form," she pronounced, "and who knows, he might take up sculpture one day." Richard agreed.

After dinner that evening Richard and Edith went up to the nurseries to find Nanny and tiptoe together into Hugo's room to fill his stocking. Hugo did not stir, and appeared to be in deep slumber. But it was anybody's guess whether he was really asleep or just pretending, as children so often did, to open one eye and get a glimpse of 'Father Christmas', thus confirming long-held suspicions as to his real identity.

Nanny assured his grandmother and stepfather that Hugo believed in the Santa Claus legend and Lady Brandon agreed that the child must not be disillusioned yet awhile. Not until he went to school where he would find out for himself.

Christmas Eve and Christmas Day proved busy days and Lady Brandon admitted to her son-in-law that she was grateful for the occupation to keep her mind off their grief.

From Boxing Day onwards it was not so easy. Hugo went off with Nanny to ride his new fairy cycle round the gardens and park and Edith was thrown back on her own resources. She wrote letters in her room, most of them replies to letters of sympathy, and she went for walks alone. Then, on New Year's day, after a week of trying her best to console and distract Richard at meals with small talk about nothing in particular, she felt it was time to tackle the matter of Hugo's future.

They were sitting in the hall after dinner, taking their coffee, when Edith suddenly said that she felt obliged to take some financial responsibility for her daughter's child. A small trust which Robert Mayne had set up before he was killed for Hugo's education would relieve Richard of the burden of school fees later on but, if the boy was to continue living at Charnfield – to which there seemed to be no alternative – Lady Brandon felt she ought to provide some sort of living allowance for him from her own pocket, in addition to the small legacy she knew Rosie had left him in her will. The only alternative to Hugo remaining at Charnfield, she pointed out, was for her to take the boy away to live with her in London.

Richard would not hear of it. "It's quite out of the question, Edith," he said at once, "to expect you, at your age, to bring up a child in a small London flat . . . No, no, he must certainly live here. Charnfield is his home."

"That's very generous of you, dear," said Edith, somewhat relieved.

"It's very generous of you to offer financial help," Richard replied. "One has considerable costs, running a place this size."

"Of course, you have. – Well, it's settled then," said Lady Brandon, "and all for the best, I suspect. A boy ought to grow up in the country, if he's lucky enough to have a country home. And he'll certainly need the influence of a man to give him some sort of discipline later on. I'm far too soft, I'd spoil the child."

"I'm sure you wouldn't," Richard said.

Lady Brandon stirred her coffee and Richard got up to put another log on the fire.

The problem of Hugo was deeply painful to Richard but it had to be faced. Neither Edith nor Nanny could say with any certainty how far Rosie's death was affecting the boy. Over Christmas he had seemed happy enough but, since Boxing Day, he had become much quieter. Nobody could guess what was going on inside his mind, for he spoke little, seeming turned in on himself, and he spent long hours alone in his little hut by the lake, reading, making things with his Christmas plasticine or carving small objects from pieces of wood with a penknife.

Nanny had continued to explain to Hugo, now five years and seven months old, that his mother was happy in Heaven and in God's care for ever and that one day he, Hugo, would see her again when he became an old man and died himself. But that was a long, long time away.

Evidently Hugo took in this information, but he showed no signs of either belief or disbelief. The general consensus was that he must not be allowed to brood or pine for his mother all on his own in a large, empty house, missing the sound of her voice calling him from upstairs, or the pleasure of her coming up before dinner, elegantly dressed and perfumed, to say goodnight to him.

Whatever the future might hold for him, what Hugo needed now, in his grandmother's opinion, was a complete change of scene and some form of distraction. This, she decided, could best be achieved if she had the child to stay with her for a few days at her flat in London. She would take him shopping at Hamleys, to the Zoo and Madame Tussauds, and Richard, relieved of responsibility for the boy for a week or two, would be free to get on with the sad but necessary business of dealing with Rosie's private papers and other matters that had to be discussed with the family solicitor. Nanny, who was anyway due her annual holiday later in the month, could get away earlier than planned to her sister in Scarborough. The change would do her good too. To all this Richard agreed.

THE morning after William drove Lady Brandon and Hugo to catch the train to Waterloo Richard went through the drawers of Rosie's desk, searching for the papers and certificates that were needed for the probate of her will. She had always written her personal letters in the privacy of her bedroom and when the embossed leather blotting pad on her desk accidentally slipped to the floor Richard noticed a half-finished letter in her handwriting that was addressed to him. It had been started when he was still away in Africa and never completed; it was dated November 31st, 1920, the very day on which she had been taken ill and retired to bed.

Richard's hand shook slightly, while he read:

My own darling,
I hope this letter reaches you in the jungle! I do miss you but I'm sure you are enjoying the change and benefitting from the marvellous African air. It will do you so much good. Everything at Charnfield is fine. Hugo adores his hut and goes almost every day, rain or shine. Nanny takes her knitting or darning down there and sits in the hut while he potters about making things and reading out loud to her. I join them sometimes for tea!
I am feeling so much better these days, just get a little breathless going upstairs but nothing to worry about. I am counting the days until your return and will motor down to Southampton to meet your boat, so let me know in good time when you are due to dock. No more news except that Jack Stapleton came yesterday to say a bullock had got through a fence into the back drive and was found in the walled garden eating the cabbages. Apparently there was no other damage but the men took almost an hour trying to . . .

And that was all.
Nobody had bothered Richard on his return with trivialities like the escaped bullock so, in spite of the poignancy of Rosie's unfinished letter, he managed a gentle smile at the thought of

Jack and the others trying to round up the determined bullock trampling all over the vegetable beds.

Then, almost reverently, he placed the unfinished letter back in Rosie's blotter and closed it.

HUGO had never been to London and for a few days the excitement of travelling on the tops of buses and in taxis around the capital and the visits to shops, theatres, museums and the Zoo helped to engage his attention and prevent his child's mind from looking back to the sadness of recent events at Charnfield.

A visit with his grandmother one wet afternoon to the Wallace Collection in Manchester Square after a morning of shopping suddenly changed Hugo's mood.

Lady Brandon had taken him to the Zoo where, although he seemed as amused as the other children in the crowded Monkey House by the antics of the apes and orang-outangs in their cages and as morbidly absorbed by the pythons and boa-constrictors in the Reptile House, he did not, in his grand-mother's opinion, show quite the enthusiasm for animals she had expected. Madame Tussauds went down rather better, for Hugo recognized in some of the historical tableaux the same kind of period costumes and wigs that he knew from pictures at Charnfield and from his precious *Child's Book Of Art*, which he studied for hours on end in his hut. But it was when Lady Brandon, who was aware of the boy's early love of art, took him to the Wallace Collection in Manchester Square that Hugo started to show real excitement and interest, although this culminated disappointingly in a measure of unhappiness and misery for them both.

They had been upstairs in the eighteenth-century French section inspecting the Watteaus, Fragonards and Bouchers, with their pretty shepherdesses and frilly girls on swings at fêtes champêtres, and were on their way down the staircase to the ground floor when Hugo stopped for a moment to gaze with intense longing at a painting of a fine Georgian house set in a park with a carriage approaching it up the drive. As Hugo looked at the picture he suddenly started to cry, not loudly but just emitting quiet sobs that shook his small frame. Lady Brandon, with as little commotion as possible, led the boy quickly downstairs to a chair in the entrance hall to sit him down and ask why there were tears.

35

"I want to go home," Hugo whispered, bravely smothering his sobs, for the quiet of the place demanded the minimum of fuss.

At first Lady Brandon assumed that 'home' meant a swift return to her flat in Artillery Mansions, possibly to relieve himself. So she told Hugo she would ask an attendant to direct them to the lavatories. But Hugo shook his head and said he didn't want to go to the lavatory; he wanted to go home. It was only as they were travelling along Victoria Street on a No. 11 bus that Hugo revealed to his Granny that he was actually homesick for Charnfield. Somehow the painting of a fine house in a park had pierced his heart with a sharp sense of longing, a yearning for Charnfield, for the house, for the park around it, the ornaments and pictures in the Long Gallery and for his own little cabin by the lake.

"GRANNY."

"Yes, dear?"

"Am I really an orphan?"

Lady Brandon was caught completely off-guard by Hugo's innocent question, which he asked in a quiet, rather sad little voice that touched her grandmother's heart.

"Where did you hear that word, Hugo?" she asked, steadying her voice and pouring herself another cup of tea.

They were sitting in Lady Brandon's rather dark mansion flat on their return from the Wallace Collection. The sitting-room was crammed to overflowing with furniture, ornaments, family photographs and paintings from Lainby. Edith Brandon was seated in a high-backed wing chair with a cushion at her back, presiding over the small folding table which had earlier been set for tea on a lace cloth by Carter, her faithful maid for the last thirty years.

Apart from the tea service with its silver kettle suspended over a little glass methylated spirit lamp, the silver teapot, milk jug and sugar bowl with tongs, there was a small silver dish with a funnel and a stopper underneath for the hot water which kept warm the toasted teacakes under the lid. There was also a plate of watercress sandwiches and a very promising chocolate cake.

Hugo was perched on the sofa opposite his grandmother, his legs dangling some way from the floor, while he munched a sandwich and kept the chocolate cake under constant surveillance, as though he feared someone might come in and remove it before he could get his teeth into a slice of it. The boy knew full well from Nanny's teaching that cake could only come after bread and butter or sandwiches and must be awaited with patience.

He looked up from the cake and fixed Lady Brandon with his wide, pale blue eyes. "Nanny says I'm an orphan. She says orphans are children who have no mother and no father."

"That's true, Hugo," said his grandmother with a wistful smile, thinking that he was now an orphan twice over. "But you have Uncle Richard instead. He's your stepfather. He takes the place of your real father who died in the war, you see. And I, as your Granny, take the place of your dear mother who died too."

Hugo nodded. The question had been answered and Edith hoped that his mind was already back on the chocolate cake. She changed the subject quickly.

"I expect you'd like a slice of that cake now, if you've had enough sandwiches."

"Yes, please."

Lady Brandon rose from her chair rather quickly and was about to cut the cake when the knife suddenly fell from her grasp and clattered onto the table. Hugo was experiencing a sharp pang of disappointment while he stared at the uncut cake in front of him, when he became aware of a violent jolt. The tea table rocked on its legs and a jam jar fell over. His grandmother lurched past him, almost knocking him off the sofa, and, with a swish of skirts, swept out of the room. A door slammed in the passage and Hugo sat quite still, shocked and rather scared.

In the privacy of her small bedroom Lady Brandon turned the key in the lock and sat heavily on her bed. With one great shudder and a gasp she gripped the brass bedhead and dissolved into floods of tears. It all came out in a great wave of weeping, all the pent-up strain and sadness of the past five years which had begun when her son-in-law, Robert Mayne, was killed at the Front; then had come the death of her beloved Harry, followed by the painful selling up of Lainby, her home for thirty-five years, and much of its contents; and finally the illness and loss of her only child, Rosie, at such a tender age. In the short space of two minutes, as Lady Brandon cried alone in her room, her mind flew back over her life. Part of her, the stoic English matron part, told herself not to indulge in self-pity at her recent sorrows. England, she reflected, had just come through a terrible war and many of the younger women with their lives before them had, like Rosie, lost husbands and sons. Life must go on now. Edith had had her fair share of happiness. Her future lay now in that little boy, her grandchild, sitting patiently on the sofa out there, waiting for a slice of chocolate cake. The thought of Hugo in the next room helped her to get control of her emotions. She blew her nose with a delicate lace hankerchief, put a quick dab of powder on her cheeks to disguise the tear-stains and returned, head held high, to the sitting-room.

She resumed her place at the tea table. "Now, unless I am very much mistaken," she announced in a firm, cheerful voice, "it's time for that slice of chocolate cake."

Hugo's face lit up with a hopeful smile.

3

AS the summer months of 1921 went by Hugo saw less and less of his stepfather and began to miss him. One night, shortly before bedtime, the boy raised his large enquiring eyes from an animal book he had been studying and asked Nanny "Is Uncle Richard dead?"

Once the poor woman had recovered from the shock and put Hugo's mind to rest on the subject, she had to admit to herself that Sir Richard might just as well be dead. As she had said that very morning to Mrs Walcot, "I've not set eyes on him for over a week. He never comes to the nursery these days. Poor man, I suppose he's still grieving for her ladyship or too busy with the estate."

Nanny was not to know that Richard was purposely avoiding contact with his little stepson because the sight of the child upset him too much. At six and a half Hugo's clear blue eyes, fair hair and firm little mouth were all too painfully Rosie's. There was also a distinct look of her when he laughed. Things might have been different had Hugo been his own son; as it was, the boy represented to Richard a living reminder of his beloved wife and was thus a source of considerable sadness and pain. To take Hugo's hand now would cause him an awkward surge of emotion which he was anxious to avoid. So Richard retreated into his study and Hugo retreated into his own private world, isolated but not anxious for company other than Nanny's or his own.

Hugo's cabin down by the lake provided a refuge from the feeling of gloom and emptiness that pervaded the house. There he could hide away in a small kingdom where he was the ruler and Nanny was his personal guard and companion. He was happy down there. Even when Richard was away, Hugo was rarely to be found other than in the hut, the nursery wing or the servants' quarters. He was no longer invited into the main rooms of Charnfield: the hall, which he avoided because of its associations with his mother, the drawing-room, billiard room, library and the Long Gallery, where Richard had once taken him to inspect the art treasures. But the memory of that early excursion remained with him. One wet July afternoon, during one of Richard's rare absences in London, Nanny returned from her own room along the corridor to the day nursery where she had left Hugo minutes earlier sitting at a table with his paints, attempting to copy an elephant's head from a book. The child was not there. Nanny called out to him but no reply came. He was not in the night nursery or the bathroom or anywhere else on the top floor.

Nanny hurried down to the kitchen, suspecting he might have gone off on his own to try his luck with Mrs Walcot, if she was baking. Hugo knew that a visit to the kitchens on such occasions meant the present of a crisp hot scone, fresh from the oven.

But Mrs Walcot was chopping parsley and had not seen the boy, nor had Doris the kitchen maid. Nanny tried the stables next, where old Keegan had his carpenter's shop, cluttered with timber planks, nails and pots of glue heating on a rusty old stove, with his workbench and vice. But Keegan, who was busy mixing paint, had not seen Hugo at all that day, and neither had Jim Cooper nor anyone in the garden.

Becoming slightly alarmed, Nanny half walked, half ran through the drizzle down to the lake, calling out Hugo's name, until she reached the cabin. He was not there either, nor was there any sign of him in the nearby woods.

In something of a panic now, she ran back to the house and alerted Page, who summoned the footman and one of the housemaids. A search was made of every room in the house. At one point it occurred to Nanny that the boy might somehow have been drawn to his dead mother's bedroom. But Page reminded her that her late ladyship's bedroom had been locked on Sir Richard's orders and the key was hanging on a nail in the pantry. They checked the billiard room, the dining-room and the library which were all dark and empty with the blinds down and the furniture covered in dust sheets. Robert searched the downstairs cloakroom and opened the coat cupboards, in case the child was hiding in one of them, but in vain. It was getting dark now and Nanny's anxiety was mounting when one of the housemaids came running out of the Long Gallery, to say she thought there

40

was someone in there, down at the far end, but she had not dared to go to look.

Nanny followed Page into the Long Gallery and there, just visible in the failing light, was a small figure in silhouette at the far end of the room. Hugo was standing in front of the Reynolds portrait of Richard's ancestor, the one with a red nose and a penchant for port. Hugo was gazing up at it enraptured. In his loneliness the little boy had come to regard as personal friends the elaborately dressed figures who looked down at him from the great canvases by artists such as Kneller, Lely, and Hoppner that adorned the walls of Charnfield. And his special friend was the figure in this Reynolds portrait.

Pent up anxiety and fear immediately drove Nanny into a fury and, for once, the woman lost control of herself enough to cuff her six-year-old charge across the head. "How dare you run away like that, worrying everybody to death? You naughty, thoughtless little boy!"

"I only wanted to see the picture again," wailed Hugo, "because I'm going to draw it with my paints."

"You're not to run about all over the house like that, do you understand? Don't ever let me catch you doing that again or I shall tell Uncle Richard. Then there'll be real trouble." With that, Nanny marched her indignant charge back to the nursery. The other servants melted tactfully away.

By bedtime Nanny had melted too, and after Hugo had told her that he was sorry and had asked Jesus to forgive him in his prayers, which he said kneeling at his bedside, peace was restored to the nursery floor.

The incident was not reported to his stepfather, for it was several days before he returned to Charnfield from London.

IN London Richard had spent more than one evening in the company of his old friends Jack and Eve Mitchell.

Jack was the best possible company for someone in Richard's state of grief. He was unsentimental, direct and the kind of friend to whom a man could confide his innermost feelings without embarrassment and yet be sure of a frank, cheerful response. Jack had decided that what Richard needed was what he called a 'whirl' around London, to take his mind off Rosie and to give him a change of scene from Charnfield which was, he said, a house in mourning.

41

"I'll take you out to a few night-clubs, my old friend," Jack said, "and get you plastered. We'll go and patronize old Kate Meyrick at the '43' and I'll tell Eve to get hold of some girls one of these evenings and we'll go out dancing in a party to Ciro's or the Kit Cat. Must buck you up, old mate, get you laughing again and enjoying yourself. Can't go on grieving for ever. Last thing Rosie would have wanted, what?"

Richard had to agree, and somehow Jack managed to restore his morale and give him hope, a glimpse, however misty, of a future without Rosie, a new life.

Early one September morning after the Mitchells and some friends of theirs had had a night out with Richard, Jack telephoned Richard at his Bryanston Square flat.

"What are you doing for lunch today, old lad?" came Jack's ever cheerful voice over the line.

"I was planning to go back to Charnfield this morning. Why?"

"Just wondered if you'd care to lunch with us at Claridge's. Someone you met last night is coming."

"Man or woman?" asked Richard, whose face was covered in shaving lather so that he was forced to hold the telephone well away from his lips.

"What's that? Can't hear you, old son!"

"Man or woman?" Richard shouted back.

"Woman," came the reply.

Richard's heart sank. For the past few weeks he had been receiving telephone calls and letters both in London and at Charnfield from women whom he and Rosie had known and some from his earlier, unmarried life before the war. There were invitations to stay for the weekend, to dine, to play bridge, to accompany them to the opera because they'd been given a box, or to a charity matinée because they were on the committee. In short, Richard was now a prey to every unattached woman in London who was looking either for a husband, a romance or just a spare man to make up the numbers for a dinner party. He was in the firing line again and he knew it.

"Who?" Richard asked, attempting with difficulty to wipe some lather from around his mouth and hold onto the telephone receiver at the same time.

"Girl called Celia Gage. You met her last night. The tall, dark one in a blue dress. Didn't you dance with her?"

"Didn't get the chance. Never spoke to her, in fact, except to be introduced."

"That's the point, mate. You didn't sit next to her last night so you can make up for it at lunch today. She's a nice girl."

"Are you by any chance match-making, you rotten old sea-dog?" asked Richard, rinsing out his shaving brush with his disengaged hand.

"That's right," said Jack. "See you at Claridge's. One o'clock. Don't be late."

"Anyone else coming?" Richard asked.

"No. Just Eve and me and Celia."

"I thought so. You *are* match-making, you old rascal."

But Jack had already hung up, leaving Richard staring at the telephone. After a moment of doubt he set about drying his face. As he glanced at himself in the mirror over the wash basin, he realised now that he was by no means disliking the idea of meeting Miss Gage and found to his slight shame that his pulse had quickened. Celia Gage was indeed an attractive young woman and he recalled his mild disappointment last night when the party broke up and the Mitchells had offered to drop her at her mother's house in Hyde Park Square, leaving him to make his own way back to Bryanston Square. If they were really bent on a bit of match-making, Richard wondered, why had he not been encouraged to escort the girl home last night? Then it occurred to him that the Mitchells meant to try out their match at lunch today and this led to a sudden pang of guilt and remorse. 'What the hell am I doing,' Richard thought, opening a drawer to get out a clean shirt; 'trembling at the thought of meeting a totally strange young woman I've met only briefly, with Rosie dead less than a year? It's obscene. Callous, and yet . . .'

He remembered Jack's words and decided the old sea-dog was right. A man cannot go on grieving for ever. Besides, there was Hugo to be considered. 'The child is only six,' he thought; 'he still needs a woman's care. One day Nanny will go and he'll have to be sent off to boarding-school. A boy must not be seen off on the school train by a nanny. He'd be teased mercilessly. He should have a stepmother to . . . well, kiss him goodbye at the station and arrange treats for him in the holidays.'

Then Richard began to wonder what kind of a stepmother Miss Gage would make. How on earth could he possibly know at this stage? Better wait and see. Anyway, what chance was there of a bright young creature like her contemplating going out with, let alone marrying, a war-weary, wounded, widowed officer of thirty-seven, many years her senior?

IN the anteroom to the restaurant of Claridge's Hotel a string quartet was playing an American ragtime tune when Richard walked in from Davies Street and crossed the grand marble hall in search of the Mitchells and their guest. He found them at a table close to the restaurant entrance. While Richard was looking round the foyer, Jack spotted him through a glass partition and signalled to him.

As Richard approached the table, Celia Gage turned round in her chair and stunned him with a dazzling smile. He saw a lovely, oval face with dancing, humorous brown eyes and a slightly retroussé nose. She was wearing a well-cut navy coat and skirt with a blouse, a pearl necklace and a becoming little hat and veil.

Jack Mitchell was quickly on his feet, taking charge. "There you are, old son, come and join the party. Eve you know, or should by now, and this is Miss Gage whom you met the other night, or almost met, eh? Sit down there, my friend, and let me order you a cocktail. What'll it be? The barman here does a pretty handsome Manhattan. Or would you prefer a Bronx or a White Lady?"

Richard asked for a Gin and It.

"Good to see you," Jack said, "and delighted you could get away from Charnfield and have a day in London, away from all your cares and worries down there. Isn't that right, Eve?" Then to Celia he added "This man needs as much variety in his life as possible."

Jack's manner was a trifle over-hearty, Richard thought. But he was like that, anxious always to be the life and soul of the party. "Not too much variety," he murmured to nobody in particular.

Eve sipped her cocktail and smiled at Richard. She was a small person, 'petite', one would say, with mousey hair but strikingly large grey eyes. Although at times she seemed almost swamped by Jack's hearty *bonhomie*, it was plain to see that she adored him. It was one of those familiar cases of a quiet, shy woman sheltering behind a gregarious man who made friends easily. Sometimes, Richard reflected, it was the reverse. More often, in fact. He knew several quiet, shy men with strong wives who did all the organizing, all the talking and took most of the action for

44

them. He did not think he could ever be happy with one of those strong, extrovert women. Rosie had certainly not been one. Like Eve, she had been essentially feminine and so, perhaps, was Celia Gage. But something told Richard that Celia would not be quite like Rosie. She seemed confident, very much in control of herself, and positive.

As Jack took a drink from his glass, a split second's pause in his monologue reminded Richard sharply of his duty to talk to Miss Gage. She was sitting next to him, very upright on her chair, her shapely legs carefully crossed, her piquant little hat and veil at a jaunty angle on her head, coolly awaiting the moment when he might chose to address an opening remark to her.

Richard took the plunge. "Never got a chance to talk to you last night."

"I know." She smiled.

"Well, there's nothing to stop us now." Jack and Eve were discussing some people they knew who had just passed them with a nod of recognition on their way into the restaurant.

"No, there isn't, is there?" Miss Gage removed the cherry on a stick from her cocktail glass and popped it into her mouth, disposing of the stick in an ashtray.

"What part of the . . . ."

"Eve tells me . . ."

Each stopped in mid-sentence. They had overlapped.

"I'm so sorry," Richard said, "please go on."

"No, you, please . . ."

"I insist," Richard said.

"Well . . . I was only going to say . . . that Eve told me you lived in a lovely Elizabethan house in Dorset. Is that right?"

"Yes. Charnfield. And I was about to ask you what part of the world you come from."

"Me? Well, I spent most of my childhood in India. Daddy was a judge out there and we lived in Simla. That's where I was born."

"Brought up by an *ayah*, I suppose."

"Yes. I loved her dearly and all our Indian servants. They were so kind and loyal and . . ."

"Colourful?"

"Yes. It was sad leaving them all when my father retired and we had to come back to England."

"When was that?" Richard was hoping to discover Celia's age without appearing inquisitive.

45

"Must have been about 1912. I was at a boarding school in Sussex by then. A gawky schoolgirl."

"I'm sure you weren't."

Richard's probing had so far yielded no exact age but now Celia provided a clue. "My father died the year war broke out, although he would have been too old to fight anyway."

"And your mother?"

"She's at home, in Hyde Park Square. Not terribly well."

"I'm sorry."

"She has a weak heart."

"But she has you."

"Well yes, I look after her."

Richard paused for a second then asked, "Did you get involved in any sort of war work?"

"Me? Yes, I joined the VAD after a young man I . . . knew was killed."

"How sad," Richard said sympathetically.

"I was only one of many, but it made me long to get over to France. Unfortunately I wasn't allowed to go overseas until 1916 because girls under twenty were considered too young."

So she was twenty-five. Richard wondered about the young man who was killed. Perhaps Celia Gage wasn't yet ready for another affair. Was he, come to that? At least they had something in common. Recent grief.

Jack Mitchell's voice interrupted his thoughts. "Come on, let's go and get our feet in the trough. Personally, I could eat a horse."

Jack and Eve were on their feet now and Richard stood up to hold Celia's chair, as she too rose and allowed Eve to take her arm and steer her into the restaurant. Jack and Richard followed at a short distance.

As the two men approached the corner table Jack muttered "She likes you."

Richard, somewhat defensively, replied "She's very young."

"To hell with that. She's past the age of consent, so don't mess about or you might lose her." Jack thumped Richard heartily on the back and they all settled down at table.

They had almost finished lunch and Jack had ordered coffee when Richard suggested that the Mitchells should bring Celia down to Charnfield for a weekend in early September.

"If it's warm enough we can play tennis. If not, there are some good walks over the downs."

"Celia's a pretty good golfer," Jack said; "has to give me strokes, don't you, m'dear?"

Celia smiled and Richard said "There's a links at West Downham, couple of miles away, if you'd like a game."

"Only if it fits in with your plans," Celia said tactfully.

"She'd love it," Jack said. "Eve doesn't play but we could rope in the pro. and have a foursome."

"So bring your clubs," Richard added.

When the lunch party finally dispersed at the Brook Street entrance of the hotel, Richard offered to escort Celia in a taxi back to her mother's house in Hyde Park Square. She accepted the offer with a charming smile. The Mitchells said that they intended to walk down to Bond Street and do some shopping.

As the taxi turned up Clarendon Street out of the Bayswater Road, Richard wondered whether he ought to invite Celia's mother down to Charnfield for that weekend, not as a chaperon for her unmarried daughter because the Mitchells would fulfil that function, but because she was evidently dependent on Celia and Richard had no wish to be discourteous.

The taxi drew up outside Lady Gage's house and Celia invited Richard in to meet her mother. "She'd be so pleased to see you."

Richard paid off the taxi and followed Celia up the steps to the front door which she opened with her latchkey.

Inside the hall a butler came forward to greet them. Richard noticed that the house, although a trifle dark and old-fashioned in its decoration was spacious and gave an impression of some affluence. There were a number of ivory objects, a large Siamese gong, oriental vases, urns and rugs in evidence, and a stuffed tiger's head on one wall: all symbols of Sir Henry Gage's long and distinguished career in the Judiciary in India.

"Come up," Celia said and led the way upstairs.

Her mother was sitting on a sofa in the first-floor drawing-room with a shawl over her shoulders, in spite of the warmth of the day. With her was a Miss Bright whom Celia introduced as "Mother's companion".

Lady Gage was small and frail with a sweet, gentle manner. Richard noticed that she had Celia's large, honest eyes. She thanked Richard for bringing her daughter home and offered him tea. Richard accepted and Celia rang the bell. A parlourmaid brought in tea and Miss Bright poured out.

Prompted by Celia, Richard told Lady Gage of his big-game hunting trip to East Africa but he did not mention the reasons for its curtailment. His hostess talked of her early days in Simla and of occasional visits to the Curzons at Viceregal Lodge in Delhi. She was a charming, rather sad woman and Richard warmed to her as he had already warmed to her daughter.

When it was time for him to go, Celia came down to the hall to see him off.

At the front door he said "Perhaps your mother would like to join us for the weekend of the 15th, and Miss Bright."

"Mother rarely leaves home nowadays. Travelling is rather a strain for her and our doctor doesn't recommend it because of her heart. But thank you all the same; it was sweet of you to ask her," Celia assured him.

Richard had liked Lady Gage so that he almost regretted this refusal. But then it occurred to him that Jack Mitchell might not be the ideal fellow guest for such a quiet, delicate person as Lady Gage. And Miss Bright's presence at Charnfield for the weekend would undoubtedly put a damper on any kind of amusement or fun. It would be as well to have Celia on her own with just the Mitchells.

"Consult with Jack and Eve and let me know what train you'll be catching," Richard said, "and I'll send in to Sherborne to meet you." He turned to descend the steps to the pavement.

"I will," Celia called after him and then stayed on the doorstep to watch him stride away down the street with a brisk, light, gait.

THERE was inevitably a good deal of talk in the servants' hall at Charnfield when it became known that Commander and Mrs Mitchell were coming to stay for a weekend, bringing with them an unmarried young lady, a Miss Gage. Page received his orders from Richard and duly passed them on to Saunders, Rosie's lady's maid who, rather than seek other employment after Rosie's death, had begged Richard to let her stay on at the same wages as housekeeper.

Saunders arranged for the Mitchells to have the best guest suite on the South Front overlooking the park and Miss Gage was to have the Blue Dressing Room on the West Corner overlooking the rose garden, with a bathroom across the corridor.

48

"THERE'S a lady in the garden with Uncle Richard."

"Yes, dear, that's Miss Gage who has come down with Uncle Jack and Aunt Eve for the weekend. They've just arrived."

Hugo's little face was pressed to the nursery window, just as it had been on Armistice night three years earlier. But on this occasion it was illuminated, not by the coloured flashes of the fireworks, but by a look of intelligent curiosity. His questions to Nanny came so thick and fast these days that she had a job keeping up with them. If anyone arrived at the front door or was heard in telephone conversation with his stepfather in the hall, Hugo needed to know who it was and why. Nanny told him on more than one occasion not to be so inquisitive but it was in the child's nature to ask questions.

Hugo did not have to wait long to satisfy his curiosity about the lady on the lawn, for Nanny was instructed to bring the boy down to the hall after tea – a practice that had lapsed since Rosie's death.

"NOW go and say 'how-do-you-do' to Miss Gage."

On entering the hall Hugo had gone straight over to shake hands with the Mitchells, with whom he was already well acquainted, and then retreated to his stepfather's side. Richard had placed both hands on the boy's shoulders and turned him round to face Celia.

Hugo advanced with confidence, extending his hand to Miss Gage who rose from her chair to greet him. Richard watched with obvious pleasure as Celia grasped Hugo's hand warmly, then said "Shaking hands is so formal; I should like to kiss you, if you will allow me to."

Hugo glanced at Richard quickly and then, with a shy smile, offered his cheek to Celia, who bent down and planted a kiss on it.

Mildly embararrassed, Hugo blurted out "Would you like to play Snakes and Ladders with me?"

At this Jack Mitchell laughed heartily, almost spilling his tea. "You watch him, Celia me dear. He's a sharp lad; take yer money off you, if you're not careful."

"Jack, really!" Eve remonstrated mildly.

Richard smiled benignly and stirred his tea.

Ignoring Jack, Celia told Hugo that she would love to play, "but not for money. We can just play for fun, can't we?"

49

"All right," said Hugo, and dropped to his knees in front of the fireplace to set up the board.

Celia sat on the floor, too, ready for the game, and Richard noticed the ease and grace with which she accomplished this. She was physically well-made, with a firm, supple body. No wonder she was a good golfer. Probably good on the tennis court too, he thought. Rosie's health had always prevented her from playing tennis but this girl, Richard sensed, would give anyone a run for their money. He would have to get in some practice.

After delivering Hugo to his stepfather Nanny had stayed by the steps down into the hall to see how the boy would behave himself in company. It was some time since he had encountered any visiting grown-ups, or children either, for that matter. Ever since his mother's funeral the previous year, Hugo's life had been one of isolation and self-dependence.

Nanny observed Celia's confident descent onto the rug on the stone floor of the hall and, satisfied that her charge was behaving perfectly, but slightly suspicious of Miss Gage's motives, she made her way up the steps and back to the nursery. 'Seems a respectable enough young woman,' Nanny thought to herself. 'He could do worse. Depends on whether she can run a house this size and deal with the staff. We shall just have to see.'

Down in the hall, Page and Robert removed the tea things and Richard took the Mitchells outside to inspect the rose garden, while Hugo and Celia still crouched on the floor, laughing happily over their game of Snakes and Ladders. Hugo was warming to Celia fast; she had a way of teasing him good-naturedly and joking with him on equal terms and he felt that he had acquired a new friend. By the time Richard and the Mitchells came in from the fading September sunshine, Hugo had invited Celia to come down to his cabin by the lake the following day to have tea with him.

"Are we all asked?" Eve enquired.

Hugo looked momentarily deflated. He had decided that Miss Gage was a special friend. He wanted to show her his cabin and entertain her as an expression of this feeling for her. 'If they all come,' he thought, 'it will spoil it.'

Fortunately the matter was swiftly resolved by Jack who said, "You'll have to count us out, old chap. Can't stay for tea tomorrow; must get back to London after lunch; I've got a bit of business to do."

"You could ask Uncle Richard," Celia suggested, but Hugo's expression remained one of disappointment.

Richard caught Celia's eye and with considerable tact said "I shall be busy, Hugo. Why not entertain Miss Gage on your own? Besides, I don't want to be a goosebery."

"What's a gooseberry?"

"Someone who gets in the way when two people want to be together on their own."

Celia flushed a little, but was secretly quite pleased at the prospect of getting to know Hugo a little better for if – and the thought was inevitably present in her mind – something came of her new relationship with this stern but charming widower, the step-child's attitude to her would be of considerable importance. So far she felt Hugo liked her. He was obviously bright. She knew that his mother had been delicate and an invalid for most of her married life but Hugo would be sure to compare her with his recently dead mother and Celia knew she must win him over. She must listen to him, answer his endless questions and provide him with companionship and moral support.

NANNY was delighted to have a Sunday afternoon to herself when Celia Gage and Hugo went down to the lake together, armed with a hamper of tea things. When they got there they gathered twigs and small pieces of kindling wood to make up a fire with the help of old newspaper in the stove.

"Will you light it, please, Miss Gage?" Hugo asked, handing his guest the box of matches. "I'm not allowed to yet. Nanny thinks I'll set everything on fire."

Celia took the matches from him. "I'll try, but I'm not very clever with matches. – By the way, you can call me Aunt Celia if you like."

"I see."

"If you want to, that is."

"Yes. I do want to. – Could you try now?"

Hugo was getting impatient. He couldn't wait to see the stove lit and to show Celia the smoke curling up into the tall trees from the little chimney on the cabin's roof; then to put the small kettle onto the open top and boil the water for tea.

CELIA struck a match but it went out. With a silent prayer she struck another and put it to the paper, which this time caught at once.

51

Hugo laughed and clapped his hands with excitement as the fire roared into life.

"Do you like being here?" Hugo asked, as they unpacked the sandwiches while waiting for the water to boil.

"Very much. What fun to have your own little house, all to yourself!"

"It was my birthday present when I was four."

"And now you're . . ."

"Seven. Well, not quite seven. I will be on . . . next May."

How sweet, Celia thought, that a small boy should add on to his age, unlike a grown-up woman who would knock off a year or two if she could get away with it.

It was getting on for seven o'clock by the time Celia and Hugo had packed up the basket and left the cabin to walk back to the house.

Celia found that the Mitchells had left and that Richard was waiting for her and Hugo in the front hall. He seemed a trifle put out. "We shall be having cold supper in half an hour, if that's all right. You've just time to change."

"I'm sorry if we're a bit late. We had such fun down by the lake, didn't we, Hugo?"

"Yes. Aunt Celia lit the stove."

"Good," said his stepfather. "Now you must run upstairs and find Nanny. She'll be wondering where you've got to. Off you go."

Obediently Hugo skipped off up the main stairs, pausing only to turn and call down to Celia "Thanks for coming to tea with me."

When he was gone Celia smiled and said to Richard "He's a very sweet, intelligent little boy. You must be very proud of him."

Richard nodded and Celia thought, too late, that her last remark had been inept. After all, Hugo was not Richard's child, even though he was resposible for his upbringing. Slightly embarrassed, she went upstairs to change for dinner into a simple tea gown in gold satin.

SITTING at the candle-lit table, alone with Celia for the first time that weekend without the Mitchells' company, Richard felt ill at ease. When Celia said how beautiful the house was and the surrounding country, he took refuge from his awkward shyness in embarking on a potted history of Charnfield.

52

"The house was built," he told her, "in 1575 by a certain Robert Cardwell. He was a wealthy merchant who was later raised to the Baronetcy by Queen Elizabeth as a reward for provisioning the ships which defeated the Spanish Armada."

"That's fascinating," Celia said, genuinely interested.

Richard went on to tell her how the gatehouse had been damaged by cannon fire in 1645 when the house was occupied by the third baronet, Sir Francis Cardwell. He had raised a regiment for King Charles Ist during the Civil War but managed to hold onto his lands by embracing the Parliamentary cause shortly after the battle of Naseby. Then Richard pointed to an oil painting on the dining-room wall. It was a portrait by Lawrence of a young woman in Georgian costume.

"That's Catherine Adams, who married Henry Cardwell, the grandson of Sir Francis. She was the daughter of William Adams, a wealthy importer of cloth from the West Indies. Just as well she brought money into the family because Henry was a gambler at cards and narrowly escaped bankruptcy . . . I say, do have another glass of wine."

"Thank you," said Celia, and Page refilled her glass with claret.

Even after the servants had left the dining-room the conversation remained rather formal. Richard was suffering from a stifling fear that Celia did not like him and this was making him nervous.

THE next morning when Celia entered the dining-room, preferring to come down for breakfast rather than having it on a tray in bed, Richard had already finished and was standing by the window with his coffee cup in one hand, *The Times* in the other.

He told her that he would not be going up to London until later in the week. "William will drive you into Sherborne to catch your train," he said, adding " there's a fast one at 11.38, if that would suit you."

"Perfectly," Celia replied, finishing her coffee.

Richard was still anxious and uneasy in her company, desperately afraid she might not be as charmed by him as he was by her and that he might be boring her. "I'm afraid's it's been rather a dull weekend for you. Not much to do."

"I've loved every minute of it."

"Pity it was too cold for tennis."

53

"Never mind. I enjoyed our golf."

"Good."

Richard was silent for a moment. Then he said "You've been so good to Hugo."

"He's a darling. Our tea together in the hut was most enjoyable."

"Yes." He looked out of the window. The sun was shining brightly outside.

"Rather a lovely day; pity you've got to go."

"I know, but I must."

After a slight pause Richard said "Perhaps we could meet in London later in the week. I've got to be up on Thursday to see my solicitors. Would lunch be any good?"

"Lunch would be very good. How kind."

"Keep Thursday free, then, and I'll telephone you tomorrow."

"Lovely."

From the nursery window an hour later Nanny observed Richard standing on the steps and waving to the car as it left with Celia for the station. He remained there for some time after it had vanished from view down the long drive. Then he turned slowly back into the house and closed the door.

4

NOT long after Celia Gage's first visit to Charnfield Richard decided to unburden himself to the one person whose blessing and support he would need if he were seriously to contemplate asking Celia to become his wife.

That he was deeply attracted to Celia was beyond doubt and there were other, more practical reasons for considering such a step, if she would have him. Richard was modest enough to question his own suitability as her husband. He was some years older than her, only recently widowed and rather set in his ways. From her point of view, he might appear to be just a lonely, bereaved man seeking comfort in sympathetic female company; someone unable to shake off his grief, still in love with his dead wife. He had no reason to suppose that Celia loved him, indeed, felt anything more for him than friendship and respect. She had seemed happy that weekend at Charnfield and had made an obvious effort to become friends with Hugo, but nothing could be taken for granted.

HAVING been to a matinée of Somerset Maugham's comedy *The Circle* one afternoon in November, Lady Brandon and Richard were taking a late tea at the flat in Artillery Mansions.

"Quite apart from my extreme fondness for Celia," Richard explained to Edith, "I feel certain she would manage things at Charnfield very well and would make an excellent stepmother for Hugo. Nanny and the servants seemed to like her and she was really quite wonderful with Hugo, playing in the nursery and going for a picnic with him in his hut. The little chap's quite gone on her." Richard paused in his eulogy of Celia, feeling rather like a barrister in court giving the defendant a good character.

"I do appreciate your concern for my feelings as Rosie's

mother, Richard dear, but it's your life and it must be your decision. Personally, I don't know Miss Gage beyond meeting her that one day for luncheon at the Ritz. But my impression on that occasion was of an extremely likeable young person. If she can make you happy and be a good wife to you, I am certain that dear Rosie – if she can see us and hear us, which I'm convinced she can – would be all for it."

"I was hoping you'd say that, Edith, and I'm really most grateful for your encouragement."

After a brief, reflective silence they went on to discuss other topics: the play they had just seen, which Lady Brandon had found mildly shocking, the Sinn Fein outrages in Ireland, Lloyd George, the Bright Young Things and unemployment.

Richard was going to the theatre again that evening, this time with Celia to see *Trilby* and afterwards to have supper at the Trocadero. He left Edith early to change for his evening engagement. As he struggled into his overcoat in the small front hall of her flat, he asked Edith if she had any plans for Christmas, because otherwise she would be most welcome to spend it at Charnfield. "I'm not having a party this year," he explained, "just some neighbours coming over for Christmas Day."

Lady Brandon, having nowhere else to go, had been hoping for this invitation and told Richard that she was deeply touched by his kind thought and accepted readily. She wondered privately whether Richard had it in mind to invite Miss Gage for Christmas, too, and wanted herself as a chaperone. If that was the case, she reflected, it would give her a perfect opportunity to find out what the young woman was like. She knew better than to ask Richard for his opinion; she did not wish to appear inquisitive or as if she were interfering in her son-in-law's life. Her own daughter was dead now and she was anxious not to alienate Richard and risk jeopardizing her future relations with little Hugo, who was very precious to her.

As it happened, Celia was already committed to spending Christmas with her mother at an hotel in Harrogate where Lady Gage could take the waters. Miss Bright, the companion, Celia had told Richard, was to have time off.

The week before Christmas Lady Brandon developed a severe cold and chest infection and her maid telephoned Richard to say that her ladyship was confined to bed and that her doctor considered it unwise for her to travel. She was sadly disappointed but would be obliged to cancel her visit. So Christmas 1921 at Charnfield was every bit as quiet as the previous one. The Mitchells, who often spent their Christmases there, had decided this year to seek warmer climes and had sailed in mid November from Tilbury in a banana-boat for Buenos Aires, where a cousin of Jack's was the British Consul.

So the only visitors were some neighbours, the Morrisons, invited for Christmas Day. Clive Morrison was a barrister who had married a cousin of Richard's. The couple lived the other side of Blandford and had no family. Sheila Morrison did her best to talk to and play with Hugo but, unlike Lady Brandon or Celia, she was not very good with children, being somewhat inhibited and awkward with them. So after presents had been exchanged and lunch was over, Hugo escaped from the hall and went off alone to the hut by the lake, to spend the rest of the afternoon reading about Leonardo da Vinci in a new book which Lady Brandon had sent him.

Later that evening, after the Morrisons had left, Richard went into his study and sank into a chair, feeling lonely and depressed. He stared at the opposite wall for some time then, suddenly resolute, he went to sit at his desk and lifted the receiver from its hook, asking for 'trunks' and a number in Harrogate.

It took the hotel receptionist on the other end some time to find Lady Gage and her daughter. While a porter was sent into the lounge and dining saloon to search for them, Richard waited on the line, impatient, anxious, and becoming more and more certain that they had gone out for the evening. In the background he could hear a string orchestra playing.

At last Celia's voice came through, on a bad line.

"Celia? It's Richard," he said, raising his voice. "Just telephoning to wish you a happy Christmas; and to your mother, of course."

Celia's voice came back rather faint and distant. "How wonderful to hear your voice. Happy Christmas! – Are you at Charnfield?"

"Yes I am, and I'm all alone."

Celia sang a few notes of a song: "'All alone, by my telephone,'" and then added "Isn't Lady Brandon with you?"

"She couldn't come. She's laid up with a cold and throat infection."

"Oh, dear, I am so sorry. How's Hugo?"

57

"He's all right. Bored, I suspect. We need you here."

"I wish I was there, darling."

"Is your mother all right, and is the hotel comfortable?"

"Mother is very well and the hotel is pretty comfortable, but a bit gloomy. There's nobody in the place under sixty and most of them are in wheel-chairs."

"It sounds grim."

"It is. Anyway, Mother's benefitting from the cure; that's the important thing."

At that point the pips went and the operator indicated that the time was up.

Before Richard could say anything more, Celia shouted "There, we must say goodbye now. Thanks for telephoning . . ."

She was gone, so Richard slowly replaced the receiver and sat staring into space. His heart was beating fast and he knew for certain that he was in love with that bright, fresh, adorable creature miles away in Harrogate, and that he must, come what may, marry her.

IT was on New Year's Eve, the dawn of 1922, that Richard's courtship of Celia Gage came to a head.

Some extremely rich and hospitable Canadians from Montreal, friends of Jack Mitchell's father, had bought a large house in Carlton House Terrace. Frank McGibbon was the London representative of a large Canadian investment corporation and he had married Polly Corbett, a musical comedy actress from the New York stage, who was fun-loving and out-going with a flair for entertaining and enough money to make her parties talked about.

The McGibbons were giving a grand New Year's Eve Fancy Dress Ball and they had invited Jack and Eve, who had just returned from South America. The Mitchells had previously planned to spend New Year's Eve with Richard and Celia, dining at a restaurant before joining the crowds in Trafalgar Square to see the new year in. But Eve was keen to go to the McGibbons' ball, so Jack decided to ask Polly McGibbon if he might bring Richard and Celia along after dinner.

Polly agreed at once. "Why dine first? We're having a running buffet. Bring your friends and come around nine, do. Besides," she giggled, "you won't want to go out to a restaurant in fancy dress; you'll get stared at."

Richard was mildly annoyed and a little embarrassed to hear that he had been foisted on complete strangers. "Celia might have preferred a quiet foursome," he muttered.

Jack would have none of it. "She'll love it, old son; you can take it from me. All women jump at the chance to dress up in fancy garb. Ring her up and tell her to start thinking about what she's going to wear. And you too; and that's an order from the bridge, my old shipmate."

Richard conceded that Jack had a point; it might be fun for Celia.

"Aye, aye, sir," he said, saluting Jack in naval style, with a dead straight face.

AT lunch at the Café Royal the day after Boxing Day Richard broke the news to Celia of the suggested change of plan for New Year's Eve.

"I'll have to dig out my old Indian sari and sandals, I suppose, and wear a veil and paint a caste mark on my forehead," she said. "That's what I usually do – not that I go to many fancy dress balls. I just hope I can find it."

"The Indian sari sounds beautiful, darling. I can just see you as the Mahranee of somewhere or other, but I'm afraid the theme is the French Revolution. Jack had forgotten to mention it until he telephoned me this morning. Everyone is to go as Louis XVI or Danton or Marie Antoinette or someone."

"Oh, I see." Celia seemed a bit put out.

"Don't worry; we'll go to a theatrical costumier and find something for you," Richard said quickly, anxious that she should not be put off going altogether.

"No, no, I can run something up to wear," she said brightly. "I've got some old bits of material and a sewing machine. I'll enjoy making a costume."

"Good," said Richard, glad to have the matter settled.

Celia was looking down from their balcony table at the gilt and plush Empire décor and the marble-topped tables of the crowded café below. Its clientele included the usual number of well-known actors, critics, painters, and journalists, drinking and talking with raucous bursts of argument and laughter.

"Look, there's Hannen Swaffer; I'm sure it is, in that huge hat."

Celia was pointing down excitedly, like a child.

59

Richard paused in the act of paying the bill and looked in the same direction. "Yes, I think it must be," he said and felt a sudden flush of excitement and a fluttering under his waistcoat at the sight of Celia's lustrous dark hair, neatly shingled, and her shapely white neck as she surveyed the scene below.

Suddenly she turned back to face Richard. "What about you?" There was a look of concern in her normally sparkling brown eyes.

"What about me?"

"We haven't discussed what you're to wear. For the ball. How rude of me; I'm so sorry."

"Not at all," Richard said, taking her hand and pressing it to his his lips. "I shall go as the chap in charge of the guillotine, with a nasty leer and a butcher's apron, drenched in blood. Sansom, he was called."

"Oh, no, Richard, don't . . . ." Celia covered her ears in feigned horror, laughing at the same time. "You won't really, will you? I shall be sick."

"Wait and see. – Come on, let's go to the Academy."

Richard had discovered that Celia painted quite well in watercolours and loved going to art galleries. So they left the Café Royal and walked arm-in-arm the short distance along Piccadilly to Burlington House, where they spent the rest of the afternoon at an exhibition of Dutch and Flemish old masters, finally repairing to Gunter's for tea in Bruton Street.

NEW Year's Eve came and Richard, wearing an opera cloak over his fancy costume, took a taxi from his rooms to Lady Gage's house to collect Celia and take her to the Mitchells', where they planned to meet for a cocktail before going on together to the ball. He had decided against a bloodied apron and settled for an ordinary eighteenth century gentleman's dress with breeches and hose, an embroidered coat and three-cornered hat.

On arrival at the house in Hyde Park Square, Richard asked the taxi-driver to wait, and rang the bell. After a moment a light came on in the front hall and the door was opened, not by Lady Gage's butler, but by a drab-looking, bent old woman with untidy hair straggling from a skew-whiff cap and a shawl. She appeared to have some front teeth missing. The thought flashed through Richard's mind that Lady Gage had given most of her staff the evening off to celebrate the new year and had left her house in the charge of an old retainer.

"Good evening," he muttered, slightly taken aback. "I've come to fetch Miss Celia.

"'Ave yer?"

"Yes. Would you let her know I have a taxi waiting?"

At that moment the old woman giggled, and Richard realised that it was Celia.

"My God, it's you . . . take your seats for the guillotine, eh? Got your knitting?"

"I fooled you, didn't I, just for a moment? – Admit it!" Celia chided him.

"You certainly did – Come on, let's give the taxi driver a shock."

They walked together down the steps to the waiting Beardmore. The driver reached out behind him and opened the door for them, evidently noticing nothing unusual, which added to their amusement.

As they drove off, Richard said "When I told Jack you might have preferred a quiet New Year's Eve with just the four of us in a restaurant, he said 'Women always jump at the chance to dress up in fancy garb'. His very words."

"And I did," Celia replied, squeezing his arm, "didn't I?"

"Yes, but I think what he meant was that women usually seize the chance to make themselves look attractive."

Celia turned to her companion with a questioning look. "Are you annoyed? Oh, Richard, am I going to let you down? I'll go back and change, if you like. I can find something else; it won't take long. Would you rather? Be honest."

"It's not what I think, Celia, darling. As far as I'm concerned you'd look beautiful in anything, sack cloth and ashes or an old moth-eaten overcoat . . . it's Jack and Eve . . . they, well, the McGibbons are their friends, not ours."

"All right, darling. If they seem to be in any way put out or disapproving, I promise I'll take a taxi straight back home and change. You can all go on and I'll meet you at the ball."

A slightly cool silence prevailed in the taxi as they drove along Connaught Street to the Mitchells' house.

"You've got me all worried now," Celia murmured, as Richard paid off the cab and rang the bell.

Wilson, the Mitchells' maid, opened the front door and uttered a shriek, which she hastily suppressed by clapping her hand over her mouth, and stared at Celia in frozen horror, until she realized who it was.

61

Richard felt a need to explain Celia's bizarre appearance as quickly as possible. "Miss Gage is supposed to be one of those women who sat beside the guillotine during the French Revolution . . ."

Celia completed the explanation: "watching the aristocrats' heads being chopped off and rolling into the basket and knitting all the time."

"Ooh, dear, Miss," said Wilson with a nervous giggle, anxious to enter into the spirit of the evening. " – The Commander and Mrs Mitchell are in the drawing-room, if you'd like to go up."

"I'm sorry if I frightened you," Celia said, with as sweet a smile as she could manage with her greasy, lined face and blacked-out teeth.

"That's all right, Miss."

Wilson made for the basement but then paused, while the new arrivals started up the stairs. She was curious to hear her employers' reactions. She did not have to wait very long. A shrill cry, followed by an outburst of male laughter, reassured her that upstairs, too, they had received quite a shock.

"My goodness me, a *tricoteuse*," cried Eve, instinctively backing away from Celia. Eve looked very fetching as Marie Antoinette and Jack was got up as a rough varlet of the Paris streets in breeches, a smock and a red knitted cap with a red, white and blue rosette.

"What a revolting sight," he said, "I'm damned if I'm going to kiss you, Celia dear; might catch something nasty."

Their laughter and a glass of champagne made Celia feel easier.

Richard, too, felt reassured, and went on to tell himself that he was extremely lucky to have a companion for the evening – and perhaps, who knew, for the rest of his life – who was not stuck up. Celia was lively, unconventional and had a marvellous sense of humour. She was not vain and conceited like so many women. There would be plenty of them at the ball, dressed up to the nines in their decolleté gowns with expensive wigs, jewels and beauty spots, anxious to show themselves off to their smart friends. Celia was Celia, an adorable, fun-loving girl, natural but sensitive. Had she not offered to go straight home and change, sensing his disappointment? She would have done so, if he had insisted. Richard was constantly aware of the difference in their ages and the last thing he wanted was for Celia to think that he was stuffy and pompous and easily shocked. Let the guests at the ball stare at the dirty, toothless haridan in a mob cap, and disapprove if they wished. After all, the theme of the ball was the French Revolution which had involved the Paris mob, the ordinary citizens, the peasants from the fields and the sluts of the back streets, as well as the aristos, the *ci-devants* vicomtesses and marquises in silk and satin. Good for Celia for choosing one of the lesser fry. Full marks for courage, originality and a healthy contempt for vanity!

"It's time we were going," Jack was saying, jerking Richard sharply from his thoughts. "Finish your champagne, my dears, and I'll get Wilson to ring for a taxi, if she hasn't died of shock by now. Come on, *mes citoyens*, let's go and join the McGibbon revels. We'll give them a rude shock, eh, Celia?"

CARLTON House Terrace was jammed by limousines and taxis, disgorging the guests who streamed onto the pavement, up the steps to the grand entrance of the McGibbons' house and into the vast reception hall.

On the great staircase to the first floor, the landing and in the spacious drawing-room stood massive vases of out-of-season carnations, lilies and roses. The rooms were filled by people in fancy costume, some seated around the parquet expanse of the dance floor, others dancing or standing in groups, talking. Overhead hung huge crystal chandeliers that shone with sparkling brilliance while more subded light was cast by ornate gilt wall sconces. The air was vibrant with the babble of voices and the rythmic thump and blare of an all-negro jazz band, brought over especially at great expense, so Jack heard, from Paris. Liveried footmen moved purposefully among the guests, serving champagne, and through the half-open double doors of the dining-room could be seen white table-cloths on the long tables bearing supper.

Richard, Celia and the Mitchells shed their cloaks and joined the long queue on the stairs, waiting to be announced. As they went slowly up the stairs they looked at their fellow guests; most of the women were wearing elaborate court dresses in embroidered silk or satin with long, full skirts, ribbons and lace ruffles, with piled-up powdered hair decorated with flowers, jewels and even in one bizarre case, a wobbling plate of fruit. The men were similarly adorned in knee-breeches and hose with lavishly embroidered satin coats and waistcoats, frilly shirts and jabots. Some carried spyglasses on ribbons and others feigned the taking of snuff from jewel-studded, enamelled boxes. Only a few people were dressed as coarsely-clothed revolutionaries and Celia stood out as the coarsest and roughest of them all.

While they waited, Jack invited Celia to dance. This struck Richard as particularly chivalrous, for Celia was looking slightly apprehensive and had probably taken fright, on account of her own costume, at the sight of the multitude of exquisitely dressed, bewigged and bejewelled ladies moving slowly on their escorts' arms up the staircase. To start by dancing with Jack would, he thought, restore her wavering confidence, especially as the Mitchells were close friends of their hosts.

As the four of them reached the top of the stairs, a tall flunkey in scarlet was bellowing "The Earl and Countess of Waring and the Lady Elizabeth Lumley-Scott . . . His Excellency, the Belgian Ambassador and Madame de la Falaise Champery."

As those who had been announced shook hands with Frank and Polly McGibbon and moved into the ballroom, the footman bent down to enable Eve to murmur in his ear against the deafening noise. Then he straightened up again. "Commander and Mrs John Mitchell, Sir Richard Cardwell and Miss Celia Gage."

As Celia extended her hand to her hostess, she thought she detected a fleeting look of surprise, but Polly McGibbon was not an ex-musical comedy actress for nothing. She laughed heartily and then said "My, but that is a really cute costume, Miss Gage. Get a look at this, Frank."

Frank McGibbon, dressed as Robespierre, grasped Celia's hand. "Why, I'm darned sure Miss Gage is a real beauty under all that grime."

"I can vouch for that, Frank, and thanks for inviting us. It looks like a great party," Jack said.

Her self-confidence perfectly restored, Celia floated away in Jack's arms onto the dance floor. Eve and Richard decided to find somewhere to sit down and appropriated a couple of gilt chairs in a corner where they could watch the proceedings. From their vantage point they caught an occasional glimpse of Celia and Jack as they flashed past in a lively quick-step. Richard noticed that Celia was laughing happily, so that her blacked-out teeth showed, giving her the appearance of one of the witches in *Macbeth* cackling over the cauldron.

The fox-trot ended with a blast of saxophones and trumpets. The dancers clapped their hands and Jack took Celia over to sit down on the edge of the dance floor to recover her breath. This gave him the opportunity he had hoped for, to find out what she felt about Richard. In truth, it had not been only an act of chivalry on his part to dance first with Celia. He had been prompted also by avid, if understandable, curiosity.

"Come clean, lass, no need to keep secrets from your old mate. We've known each other long enough."

Celia said innocently "What secrets, Jack?"

"Are you going to marry Richard?"

"I don't know." Celia shrugged her shoulders, just a fraction embarrassed, and looked out across the dance floor where the couples were beginning to dance again to a slow Blues.

"Has he asked you yet?"

"No."

"If he does, will you accept him?"

Celia turned to face Jack and smiled behind her hag's make-up. "That must remain a secret, Jack," she murmured, "even to you."

"Oh, come on, Celia. After all, we did introduce you to him," Jack said, rather pained.

Celia sighed. "I promise you on my honour that, if Richard and I ever do get engaged to be married, you and Eve will be the first to know. Absolutely the first, I swear."

"That's my girl." Jack took her hand. "Come on, then, let's show these sons of guns how to dance the Blues."

Celia got up, backed onto the dance floor and held open her arms to Jack. "We must look quite comic," she smiled, as Jack took her round the waist; "a couple of bloodthirsty revolution-aries dancing the Blues, as though we were way down in Noo Orleans."

Jack laughed and held her closer. "Richard's a lucky blighter. That's all I know, Celia my girl. Damn lucky," he said as they drifted off into the throng of dancers on the floor.

SHORTLY before midnight, while some of the guests were still in the supper room, their host Frank McGibbon mounted the band stand. A burly, slightly bald man, he raised his hand for silence.

A roll of drums heralded his announcement: "Quiet, every-body, if I may have your attention, please. We don't have many minutes left of the old year, 1921, so we're going to open the windows right now and let 1922 come on in. If it gets to be a little cold, why then the ladies might care to go fetch their cloaks or something to keep 'em warm, then get right back up here; and let's all stand together to welcome in the new year. Would someone please make a check downstairs in the supper room and have anybody still around down there come on up here rightaway? – "

The rest of Frank McGibbon's speech was drowned in chatter as the crowd closed in round the bandstand. Some of the ladies went in search of their cloaks, while a footman scurried down the grand staircase to inform those in the supper room that they were required in the ballroom.

Celia looked round for Richard, wishing to be close to him when midnight chimed.

"Are you going to be warm enough?" Jack asked her.

Celia glanced over to another footman who was in the process of opening the large windows to let in the cold night air and the year 1922.

"I doubt it," she said with a shiver in her voice and decided then and there to get her wrap from the cloakroom, asking Jack to look out for Richard and Eve. They must all four be together for the big moment. A few moments after she had vanished into the crowd Eve and Richard spotted Jack and made their way to him. He explained Celia's absence.

"Hope she gets back here in time for midnight," Richard said, anxiously looking round the ballroom.

By now the windows had been flung wide open and Frank and Polly were stepping out onto the balcony, followed by a number of guests, waiting for Big Ben to chime.

Several of the men were consulting fob watches taken from the pockets of their eighteenth-century satin waistcoats. Suddenly the first strokes of Big Ben could be heard outside and a number of people shushed for silence, listening intently. Then came an outburst of cheering and shouting. The band struck up 'Auld Lang Syne' and everyone started to shake hands and kiss and wish each other a happy new year. Richard looked round for Celia, kissed Eve and patted Jack on the back, then looked round again, more wildly. People round him were singing and cheering and joining hands but there was still no sign of Celia. He was almost in despair until, through a gap between two people, he suddenly spotted her running at top speed across the dance floor towards him. He opened his arms wide for her and, as she ran into them, he saw that she had scrubbed off her dirty hag's face, removed the black from her front teeth and made some attempt at combing her hair.

"I couldn't start 1922 looking all dirty and ugly for you," she cried as they hugged each other.

She embraced Eve and Jack and then they all joined hands with people near them to sing in the new year with gusto.

For Richard and Celia, this would probably be a year of some importance, Jack thought to himself when he squeezed Eve's hand and kissed her again.

Not long after midnight the party began to thin out. A number of elderly guests had gone home already and more were now making their way downstairs to the hall to collect their cloaks, some of them stifling yawns while retaining the set expression of feigned enjoyment that had to be preserved until they were out of sight of their hostess. Round the front door were clustered a number of liveried chauffeurs, scanning the faces of the departing guests for their employers.

When, a little later, Jack and Eve decided to leave, they found Richard and Celia in the ballroom, dancing together to a slow waltz on an almost empty floor. The negro band had given way to a small string orchestra, which was playing Strauss and Waldteufel for the benefit of the handful of romantically-minded younger couples still there. Celia and Richard were waltzing in a dream, Richard holding her firmly round the waist while they moved gently round the floor. In spite of his wounded thigh, which ached slightly when he became tired, as he was now, Richard could still manage to dance.

Then Celia spotted Eve and Jack by the door. "I expect they're leaving," she said, pausing in mid-step.

"Probably had enough," Richard murmured as they let go of each other and crossed the dance floor to the door to speak to the others.

"Do excuse us," Eve said.

"We're going home, old chap," Jack explained. "Eve's just about all in. Hope you can get a taxi."

"We'll be all right," Celia said. " – And thank you so much for getting us invited. It's been a wonderful evening."

"We thought you might enjoy it," Eve said, taking Jack by the arm.

After a couple more waltzes Richard felt his thigh beginning to nag more strongly. "Perhaps we should be on our way now; don't want to get swept out with the crumbs," he said.

Celia agreed, and within a few minutes she and Richard had taken leave of the McGibbons and were in a taxi heading for Hyde Park Square. They held hands for most of the way and spoke very little. Celia had a feeling that Richard was mentally rehearsing what he planned to say to her when they finally parted. She could not help hoping for a proposal of marriage, but although she felt sure that Richard liked her, he was perhaps not quite ready to commit himself. Besides, he was plainly tired and probably not feeling like saying anything tonight, even if he was thinking of it. In fact, she decided, he might well feel it was too soon after his first wife's death. Perhaps he wasn't really anxious to marry again anyway – her or anybody else. She must guard against disappointment.

The taxi drew up outside Lady Gage's house where Richard helped Celia out and paid off the cab, which drove away into the night. As they mounted the steps to the front door they could hear the distant sound of revellers singing and shouting all over London, reminding Richard of Armistice Night when Rosie had suffered that terrible coughing fit outside Buckingham Palace – just over three years ago.

Celia had found her latchkey in her purse and was about to insert it in the lock when Richard took her hand and drew her towards him. "Don't go in just yet. I have something to say to you."

Celia held her breath.

"I know I'm a bit older than you, darling Celia," he began, "and I've been married before, so . . . I suppose I'm second-hand goods in a way. But I do adore you, and I know now that I want to spend the rest of my life with you. It's all very selfish, because I can't face the prospect of growing old alone. If I have to grow old, as we all must, I want to do so with you at my side. So would you please consent to marry me and be my wife? . . ."

Richard gazed at Celia, anxiously awaiting the outcome. At first no answer came; she was standing looking away from him into the distance with shining eyes and her mouth open in an expression of astonishment.

"Is it such a very dreadful idea?" he asked pleadingly.

Celia turned towards him. "Of course I want to marry you,

darling; very, very much. Thank you!" She seized him in a passionate embrace, pulling his head down to kiss him feverishly on the lips. They stood there for several minutes, locked in each others' arms.

Then Richard said softly "I'll come round for you about midday tomorrow; today rather; to speak to your mother. And then we'll go somewhere for lunch to celebrate, shall we?"

"Oh, yes," Celia said, feeling a little stunned.

"Until then . . ." Richard was still holding her tight. "Now in you go, Citizeness Gage, before you catch cold. And sleep well."

"How will you get home? Will you get another taxi?"

"Sooner or later. Meanwhile I shall walk . . . on air."

"And I shall sleep on air . . . up in the clouds."

Richard let go of her and allowed her to complete the unlocking of the door that had been so importantly interrupted. She blew him a kiss and went quietly indoors.

He remained for a few seconds on the doorstep, looking up at the stars. Softly he murmured to himself 'Dear Rosie, please try to understand and forgive me. I love Celia as I loved you; my love for you will never die and I shall always feel you are close to me, whatever happens. But life has been unbearably empty since you went and I soon discovered that a man desperately needs a woman to love and to be loved by, someone to share his home and his problems. Perhaps I'm a coward but I can't face life alone. Celia loves Hugo and we shall bring him up together, as you would have wanted him brought up, so please trust us and give us your blessing.'

With that, Richard glanced back for a last look at Celia's front door and then walked down the steps. Happily humming 'The Blue Danube' to himself, he set off down Albion Street to the Bayswater Road where he found a taxi that was soon speeding towards Marble Arch and home.

By the time Richard reached his flat in Bryanston Square the first cold light of 1922 was breaking over London. Dawn was breaking, too, over the Dorset Downs where, warm and secure in his bed in the night nursery at Charnfield, Hugo Mayne lay fast asleep, totally unaware of the momentous event that had just taken place on the doorstep of Lady Gage's house: an event that was to alter the whole course of his life.

5

ONE day in January, 1922 the Engagements column of the *The Times* carried as its first item:

Cardwell-Gage. The engagement is announced today between Capt. Sir Richard Davenport Cardwell Bt of Charnfield Park, Dorset and Celia Helen, only daughter of the late Sir Henry Gage, KCSI and Lady Gage of 14, Hyde Park Square, London.

The following day a photograph appeared in the *Evening News* under the heading 'To Marry Soon', showing the happy couple posed in country tweeds on the terrace at Charnfield. The caption underneath described Celia as having 'spent much of her childhood in India where her father was a distinguished judge' and concluded 'Sir Richard, who was badly wounded in the war serving with the Grenadier Guards at Arras and whose first wife, Rosemary, died in 1920, is the seventh baronet.'

During the ensuing weeks further photographs of Richard and Celia graced the pages of the *Sketch* and *Bystander* while the *Tatler* of February 12th carried as its frontispiece a wistful studio portrait by Bertram Park of Miss Celia Gage in a satin evening gown with earrings and a pearl necklace.

This particular issue of the *Tatler* was lying open on the table in the Servants' Hall at Charnfield one afternoon early in March under the close scrutiny of Miss Saunders, Nanny and Mrs Walcot, as the three of them drank their afternoon tea.

"She takes a nice photograph, no doubt about that," commented Miss Saunders, mentally comparing the mistress-to-be of Charnfield with 'my late lady', as she continued to refer to Rosie.

"Good strong face, that," Mrs Walcot added. "Looks to me

like a young lady who'll know what she wants and see that she gets it."

"And what's wrong with that?" Nanny interposed sharply, scenting disloyalty.

Mrs Walcot covered up quickly. "Nothing's wrong with that, Nanny. I'm all for a lady who knows her own mind. Saves a lot of shilly-shallying."

With that, Charnfield's cook went off to inspect the potatoes that were boiling for dinner in a saucepan on the kitchen stove, pricked them with a fork, and came back to the Servants' Hall.

"Well, I think she's lovely," said Miss Saunders, defying contradiction. Then, more quietly, "But not like my late lady. Not . . . well, not quite the same."

There was a momentary silence as the three senior female members of Charnfield's indoor staff turned their attentions back to the photograph. Then Nanny, to whom the copy of the *Tatler* had been lent by a friend, the housekeeper at the Vicarage, reached down and scooped the magazine off the table, closing it firmly.

"Well, this won't do," she declared and went off with her magazine to get Master Hugo's tea.

IT was Celia's idea that Hugo should be a page at the wedding and Richard agreed. Nanny was delighted, and soon she and Celia were conferring on the style of costume for the little boy, studying a number of designs, submitted by Daniel Neal's shop, of velvet suits with knee breeches, silk shirt and jabots.

The ceremony was to take place at St Peter's, Eaton Square in June and arrangements were made for the servants and estate people to travel up from Charnfield for the day in a hired charabanc.

Celia opened her eyes on her wedding day, praying for fine weather, but she was to be disappointed. Leaving her warm bed in Hyde Park Square at around half-past seven to draw back the curtains, she saw only a dull, grey sky and raindrops spattering her bedroom window.

But Celia was not a young woman to be easily dejected. 'Better to marry Richard on a wet day than not marry him at all,' she reflected, as she climbed back into bed and settled against her pillows to think about the eventful day ahead.

The ceremony was to be at 12.30 and her uncle, Clive Walsh,

Lady Gage's only surviving brother, a retired university lecturer, was coming at half-past eleven to escort her to St Peter's and give her away. He was rather frail after a mild stroke and Celia hoped he would not stumble with her as she made her way to the altar on his arm.

In the event, the wedding went off smoothly. Hugo, resplendent in his wine-coloured page's suit, performed his well-rehearsed role with an air of grave dignity which amused some of the guests and charmed others. He enjoyed posing on the church steps with Richard and Celia and the Maid of Honour for the photographers. Nanny watched her charge from a distance with considerable pride, privately giving herself full credit for the boy's impeccable behaviour.

At the reception afterwards, for which Jack and Eve Mitchell had lent their house in Connaught Square, Hugo was given his first taste of champagne, and rather liked it. "It made my nose tickle," the seven-year-old reported to Nanny Webster, as she helped him off with his page's buckled shoes that night.

William had driven the two of them back from London immediately after the reception came to an end, when Richard and Celia left for Victoria Station, amid showers of confetti. They were to catch the boat train to Paris for their honeymoon.

Shortly before Hugo was settled in bed that night the charabanc with the servants and estate people returned to Charnfield. When Nanny went down to get the hot milk for Hugo's cocoa, Mrs Walcot told her they had had quite a lively trip back. Some of the staff had drunk too much champagne and had insisted on singing all the way from Connaught Square to Charnfield. Moreover, they had had to stop on the road outside Basingstoke for one of the younger housemaids to be sick. "What was Mr Page doing, allowing them to carry on like that?"

"Nothing. He slept most of the way back, snoring in the back seat with his mouth wide open – had a drop too much himself, if you ask me." Nanny looked disapproving but Mrs Walcot concluded cheerfully "Sure it was a fine old day, so it was."

BEFORE long the new Lady Cardwell was at home with her husband and Charnfield had settled down to the new régime.

RIDING had never been one of Richard's favourite pastimes and it was out of the question now, for his thigh muscles were too badly damaged by his war wound to have sufficient grip to enable him to stay in the saddle. Consequently, there were no horses in the stables at Charnfield. However, one evening at dinner, Celia, who had ridden a great deal as a child in India, asked her new husband if he would allow her to go to look at a mare she had heard of locally and, if it seemed a good buy, to have it at Charnfield for something to ride over the downs.

"Certainly, my darling, as long as you don't ask me to go with you. I never did master the art of horsemanship." Then he added "I dare say you'll need a groom."

"Oh, no, I shall look after her myself."

"Will you have the time?"

"Well . . ."

"We'll get Jim Cooper to help you. Put his wages up a bit and tell him he's a groom as well as the under-gardener. He's good with horses; used to help his father with the carriages when he was a small boy."

"So it'll be all right . . . I mean all right to buy the mare, if she's suitable?"

"Yes, darling, of course. Just don't break your pretty neck, that's all."

Although Page had just come into the dining-room with Robert to serve the next course, Celia got up and came round to Richard's chair, putting her arms round his neck from behind and kissing the top of his head. "Oh, thank you, thank you; you're an angel," she murmured.

She resumed her chair again, just in time to help herself from a dish of roast chicken. "Thank you, Page," she said, smiling.

"M'lady," Page murmured in acknowledgement, and moved on to serve Richard, although he would have liked to say more, something like, 'Good for you, m'lady; you have a horse if you want one,' for he approved of Lady Cardwell, as did the entire staff.

Celia was liked at Charnfield, treating the servants with the mixture of friendly understanding and authority that they expected from her. Even Miss Saunders had to admit "She's a lady all right, even if she was brought up by natives in India."

But it was not long before a certain tension began to develop between Celia and Nanny Webster. It showed itself for the first time on the afternoon that Celia went over to High Barrow to see the mare she hoped to buy. Returning from a walk round the garden with Hugo, Celia told the boy to hop into her two-seater and come over to High Barrow with her, leaving Richard to explain to Nanny where Hugo had gone.

Hugo thoroughly enjoyed his trip in the car with Celia, of whom he was becoming extremely fond. She was fun to be with and told him all sorts of interesting things, as well as answering his endless flow of questions.

At the High Barrow stud, he was shown a brood mare in the paddock, heavy with foal, and another with her offspring trotting beside her. Hugo was enraptured by the frail, skinny little four-day old creature nuzzling its mother.

When another mare was brought into the yard from a loose box for Celia to inspect, she explained the points of the horse to Hugo, as she carefully examined the animal's mouth, then her hocks, spavins, fetlocks, shoulders, rump, quarters, withers, mane and the rest.

"Are we going to have her?" Hugo asked finally, after Celia had engaged in a long discussion with the stud-owner and consulted some papers.

"Yes, we are, darling. She'll be coming over next week. Isn't that exciting?"

"Will she stay with us?"

"Of course. Come on, we must get home now."

As soon as they were both back in the two-seater Celia suddenly and spontaneously gathered Hugo in her arms and hugged him. It was probably a sense of excitement and joy over the new mare that prompted her. But she had already developed strong, motherly feelings for the little orphan boy, who seemed so lost and lonely in the big house with no other children of his age to play with or talk to. For this reason she had decided to try and fill the gap by making friends with him and encouraging him to confide in her and come to her with his troubles and worries.

To say that Nanny was 'put out' by Hugo's return late for tea would be an understatement. She was almost rude when Celia brought him up to the nursery and apologized for keeping him out so late.

"I'm so sorry, Nanny. I thought Sir Richard was going to tell you where we'd gone but I suppose he forgot."

"Very good, Lady Cardwell," Nanny said tersely. "It's not my business where you choose to take Master Hugo in the afternoons."

And that was that. Celia said no more but left the nursery and went downstairs to find Richard and tell him she'd bought her mare. She chose not to mention Nanny's pique; it would only worry him and he had enough problems with the estate.

She realized, too, that Nanny, for her part, was probably unsettled, suspecting that her days at Charnfield were numbered anyway, unless there was another baby. Hugo would be eight the following year and they would be sending him away to boarding-school, which meant she would probably be looking for another position.

One fresh September morning Celia's mare, Olga, arrived at Charnfield while Hugo was doing his lessons in the day nursery. With preparatory school looming the following autumn, he was being taught by a retired governess, Miss Bryant, who had been cycling over from a nearby village every day to instruct him in reading, writing and arithmetic.

Hugo had been astonishing Miss Bryant with his excellent memory for facts and his application to every subject. He was a 'well above-average' child, she judged, probably scholarship material. They were doing maths together that morning and Hugo had just completed a difficult exercise in long division when the clip-clop of a horse's hooves could be heard in the stable yard at the back of the house.

Hugo jumped up and cried out excitedly "It's Aunt Celia's horse . . . can I go and see it . . . Please, Miss Bryant. I want to see the horse . . ."

Miss Bryant glanced at her watch, and saw that it was almost midday, the time for lessons to end, and said "Oh, very well. But you must come back afterwards and put your books away."

Hugo was out of the nursery before she had finished speaking, clattering down the back stairs and out into the yard. Jim Cooper was holding the mare with Celia stroking her nose when Hugo appeared from the house like a whirlwind.

Celia turned, saw him coming and said "Come and pat her, Hugo; make her feel welcome."

Hugo hesitated for a second, not quite sure what to do, so Celia, realizing he couldn't reach the mare's neck, picked him up and, with her free hand, laid Hugo's small hand on Olga's neck.

After a while Hugo prevailed on his stepmother to let him ride Olga. Celia wanted to encourage the child, so Jim was instructed to lift the boy up. He showed him how to hold onto the animal's mane and walked her slowly round the yard. As he felt the movement under him and the sense of grandeur that came from seeing everything around him from a great height, Hugo became delirious with excitement. As soon as they stopped and Jim lifted him down again, Hugo tore off back into the house and upstairs to tell Nanny breathlessly "I rode the horse, I rode on its back . . . round the yard . . ."

It was Jim Cooper who first suggested a pony for Hugo. Helping Celia to mount for her early morning ride a few days later, Jim said "Master Hugo ought to have a pony, I reckon, so he could go out on the downs with you, m'lady. Never too young to start."

The idea had occurred to Celia, too, but she had been reluctant to ask Richard to spend more money or to give Jim more work.

Jim's willingness made a difference.

She timed her moment carefully and put the suggestion to Richard after his first whisky and soda one winter evening. It worked.

Richard was all for it. "A boy ought to learn to ride. Make a man of him."

That was it. A pony was bought for Hugo, and the necessary jodphurs, hunting cap, hacking jacket, riding crop and gloves.

Some children, especially girls, take to riding instantly and show no sign of nerves, while others persevere bravely, disguising their anxiety, because they are determined not to show that they are scared. On many a winter morning that year, Hugo managed to conceal his anxiety from Jim and Celia as he trotted beside her along the road to the downs, first on a leading rein, later on his own. But he was inwardly tense and uneasy and his heart raced when once or twice his pony, Charlie, shied at something on the roadside or pulled too hard on his bit and tried to bolt with him.

By the following January Hugo had got as far as learning to jump. It had been raining one morning but had stopped after lunch when Celia had taken Hugo out. She was watching him put his pony at some small jumps that Jim had put up in a field. The fences were only small posts and rails of timber two feet off the ground and Hugo had already jumped Charlie over all of them without mishap. Then Celia put the poles up an inch or two higher and told the boy to take Charlie round again. Hugo did as he was told but at the last but one obstacle Charlie slipped on take off and caught his foreleg on the pole, causing him to lose balance and fall, rolling over and throwing Hugo down hard on his face in the mud.

Celia ran over to Hugo, who was scared, in tears but apparently unhurt. Down on her knees on the grass, she tried to comfort the boy and reconcile him with his pony which had got up, wandered off and was unconcernedly cropping at some nettles.

"You're not hurt, darling. It's all right. Charlie just slipped . . . it wasn't his fault or yours . . . it's very slippery . . ."

Hugo soon managed to get control of his shock and stopped crying. He sniffed and brushed the tears from his eyes with his sleeve.

"You ought to mount again; it's much better to do it straightaway after a fall. Get up, and I'll catch Charlie."

"I'm afraid I'll fall off again."

Richard had appeared now from the garden and was approaching the paddock gate.

Celia called out to him "We had a little spill, that's all. No harm done."

Hugo was on his feet now, intending to walk over to Charlie where he was grazing. But as soon as he put his left foot down he cried out with pain and collapsed onto the ground again. "My foot hurts," he cried.

Celia, who had caught Charlie and was holding him by his bridle, looked at Hugo in concern, wondering if he had sprained his ankle.

Before she could get to him, Richard, who was in the paddock now, reached Hugo and pulled him to his feet. "Come on, Hugo, you're all right. Get up on that pony, otherwise you'll lose your nerve," he said.

"He's hurt, Richard, can't you see?" Celia called.

Ignoring what she said, Richard picked the boy up and carried him over to Charlie to put him firmly in the saddle.

Hugo let out a scream of pain.

"He can't ride if his foot's injured. What on earth are you doing?"

Richard took no notice. "Come on," he shouted, "ride the damned thing."

He seized the reins from Celia and handed them to Hugo.

Before she could stop him, Charlie started off at the trot with

77

Hugo hanging on grimly. Then the pony began to canter across the field and because Hugo could not stop him he shouted out again, in panic, "I can't stop him . . . please . . . stop him . . . my foot hurts."

"Go on," Richard called out to the boy, "ride him, don't be such a cissy . . . go on."

Charlie was now careering wildly round the paddock. Celia dashed over to try and catch him, calling to Hugo to hold on and pull on the reins.

It was too late. Charlie suddenly pulled up short by the paddock gate and dug his hooves in, throwing Hugo over his head. The boy crashed against the five-bar gate and fell to the ground.

Celia raced across to Hugo, where he lay quite still. Richard followed.

"Hugo!" Celia gasped, cradling the boy in her arms. As Richard came up to her, she turned on him in a fury. "Now look what you've done. He might have been killed!"

To Celia's annoyance, instead of apologising or expressing concern, Richard said nothing.

Hugo opened his eyes and looked from Celia to Richard, quite dazed. Then in a quiet voice, he asked "Is Charlie hurt?"

"No, darling. Charlie's fine. Come along; let's get you in to Nanny." Celia lifted the boy up in her arms, hissed to Richard "I hope you're proud of your achievement," and strode back towards the house, while Richard went to telephone the doctor.

That night Richard and Celia had the first serious row of their marriage. Celia accused her new husband of callous cruelty towards Hugo. Richard felt this was unfair, and told Celia he had no wish to see the boy grow up into a miserable little weakling.

This angered Celia. "Just because he's deeply sensitive and artistically inclined, that doesn't make him a weakling," she retorted. "He showed great courage today, getting back on to that pony after . . ."

"I had to put him back by force."

"What could be more brutal?"

"I am not brutal, Celia. I didn't know how badly he had hurt his foot."

Celia paused, and then reminded Richard that they were shouting at each other over a child who was neither his nor hers. "We really mustn't, darling."

Richard admitted he had perhaps been a bit hasty with Hugo, and added that he had been in some pain himself that day from his old wound. Celia kissed him tenderly and peace was achieved. But not for long.

A FEW nights later Hugo was woken up by the sound of raised voices coming from Celia's bedroom downstairs. Thoroughly scared by the sound of his stepfather's voice raised in anger and of Celia, evidently in tears, Hugo threw off the covers and crept from his bed. His heart was thumping as he tiptoed to the night-nursery door to listen. He opened it a fraction. It was dark outside in the corridor but he could see a light on in the passage on the floor below, and by peering over the banisters he could see his step-parents' open bedroom door, with light shining from it, and could hear more clearly angry voices and the sound of weeping.

"It's cruel, Richard, the child's only just eight," he heard Celia say.

"It is not cruel, Celia, it is perfectly normal. Other boys go away to school at eight; I did myself. They have a perfectly good matron there and the Headmaster's wife acts like a mother to see them through the first term . . ."

But Celia would not have it. "He's not ready yet, can't you see? He's a sensitive, lonely child . . ."

"All the more reason to go," Richard retorted. "He can make friends with other boys of his age, learn to stand on his own feet . . ."

"He'll be bullied."

"Why should he be? Anyway, Edith's all for it and I'm quite certain his mother would have been too . . . and his father, probably."

"Poor mite, that's all I can say."

At that point the door closed. Hugo scuttled quickly back to his room before Nanny or anybody could catch him, darted in, closed the door behind him and leaped into bed.

Hugo's pony remained unridden, although Hugo's ankle had soon recovered. In the spring of that year Charlie was out to grass in a paddock and was soon joined by Olga. Both animals remained unridden throughout the summer, for Celia had also given up riding.

The reason became clear one evening in July when Richard and Celia had invited some neighbours to dinner. Hugo, bathed and in his pyjamas, was watching from his window to see the guests arrive. He was clutching his usual mug of cocoa, his eye firmly on the gatehouse through which the visitors' cars drove up to the front entrance, when a delicious smell of scent assailed his nostrils, so that he turned round from the window. His stepmother had come up to hear his prayers and tuck him into bed. She was dressed for dinner in a loose, flowing gown unlike her usual evening dresses and when she sat down on his bed, Hugo thought that she seemed rather fatter than usual. In fact, he noticed that her tummy was swollen, and he told Nanny so after Celia had kissed him goodnight and left the room.

"Is Aunt Celia going to have a foal?" Hugo asked.

Nanny who already knew the truth, which was by now common knowledge in the Servants' Hall, recovered from the surprise of Hugo's remark and said soothingly "Yes, dear, but not a foal. A baby is coming, if God wills it."

Hugo thought about this for a moment. Then he started bouncing up and down in his bed. "That'll be fun," he cried cheerfully. "What will it be called?"

"That will depend on whether it's a little boy or a little girl."

Hugo stopped bouncing for a moment. "I hope it's a boy," he said. "I don't like girls." Then he started to bounce again, until Nanny stopped him.

"You don't know any girls," she said; and it was true that apart from an occasional encounter with Mrs Bennett's little girl, Rita, in the village post office, Hugo had no experience of the opposite sex of his own age.

"Well, I don't want the baby to be a girl," he insisted. With that he picked up a book called *Roman Art* with coloured pictures of temples and arches of various caesars and was soon buried in it.

"Just ten minutes, then lights out," Nanny said, and left the night nursery to tidy up in the bathroom.

A few mornings later, when Nanny took Hugo's clothes out of the cupboard and brushed his hair, Hugo noticed that she seemed quieter than usual, and when he asked her a question, she did not answer and seemed far away. "Are you angry with me today, Nanny?" the boy asked. "You didn't say anything just now, when I asked if you'd seen my red jersey."

80

Nanny found Hugo his red jersey and gave it to him with a sniff. He saw that she had been crying and was puzzled.

After lunch, which Nanny and Hugo had in the dining-room with Richard and Celia if there were no guests, Richard told Hugo to come and see him in the Library. "Something I want to talk to you about, old chap."

Hugo looked quickly to Celia for an explanation.

"It's about going to school, darling. Uncle Richard will tell you all about it," she said.

Immediately, apprehension gripped Hugo, but then he felt excitement welling up inside him. After all, going away to school sounded very grown-up. He had often heard Nanny talking to Miss Saunders about her 'Stuart boys, Jamie and Ian', the twin sons of an Inverness family she had been with just before the war and how she had packed their school trunks for Ludgrove. When Hugo asked about Ludgrove, Nanny had explained that, after they reached a certain age, most boys went away from home and lived at school, just for the term, and came home for the holidays. Recently, since hearing Aunt Celia and Uncle Richard talking about school, Hugo had asked how old he would have to be before he must go but Nanny had remained silent. But when she described more of school life and the dormitories where a dozen boys all shared a big room with their beds alongside each other and how they all sat together and worked at their desks in a classroom for their lessons, Hugo thought it all sounded good, for he often wished he could meet more boys of his own age who were not like Philip Brayson.

Celia had recently asked some neighbours, Major and Mrs Brayson with their son Philip, to lunch. Philip was a year older than Hugo and the boys had both been shy. Later, when Hugo was asked back to the Braysons, Philip had proved a bit too rough for Hugo and had given him a terrifying afternoon when they played out of doors by daring him to jump across broad streams and out of tall trees. On the next occasion when Philip was asked to tea by himself at Charnfield and the two boys were, at Philip's instigation, balanced precariously on the branch of a tall tree, Hugo had suggested going indoors so that he could show his guest the pictures in the Long Gallery. But the older boy thought that would be jolly boring and said that instead they should go to find some sticks in the woods and fight a duel. Hugo did not mention his cabin, for fear his guest might

81

in some way damage it, and since then no one had been invited to tea.

Now, Hugo hoped Nanny was not fibbing when she told him that there would be some nicer boys at Stanborough House, and that he would make plenty of friends there.

"When will I go to Stanborough House, then?" Hugo enquired of his stepfather, half way between fright and excited anticipation. He was sitting on the fire seat in the library with his thin legs dangling short of the floor.

"Next term. It starts on September 24th, in about six weeks' time. You'll enjoy school, old boy, I know you will. I certainly did. You'll make lots of friends and learn to stand on your own feet. And if you work hard at your lessons and try your best at games, you'll find it's all right. Good fun. And you'll look forward to the holidays, as I always did."

Hugo said meekly "I see," and waited for his stepfather's next remark.

Richard could not for the moment think of any more comforting information to alleviate the boy's anxiety so he said, as cheerfully as possible, "Off you go, then. Run along and find Nanny," and was quite relieved when Hugo slipped off the fire seat and ran from the room.

Nanny was inclined to Celia's view that to send a child off to boarding school at eight – especially an only child and an orphan as sensitive as Hugo – was almost barbaric. But both women knew they were up against centuries of tradition and Celia, for her part, did not feel it was appropriate for her to go on protesting to Richard on the boy's behalf. Better to concentrate on her own state of imminent motherhood and keep her opinions to herself. She dreaded another bitter row with him on the subject and she knew he would never change his mind.

Celia did, however, embark on a campaign that summer of developing her friendship with Hugo in an effort to prepare him for the possible shock of Stanborough House.

At every opportunity, when Richard was busy in his study or about the estate, Celia would go up to the nursery to see what Hugo was doing. If he was drawing pictures in his book with a pencil or filling in set outlines with his water-colour paintbox, she would sit beside him and show an interest, making suggestions and praising or criticizing. He would need to become accustomed to criticism from teachers at school, she felt, and to this end she pulled no punches. "That mast is much too tall for the ship, don't you think? I'd make it just a bit shorter, more in proportion," she might say, and Hugo would make the necessary alterations at once.

They went for walks and called at the hut by the lake, which Hugo was now treating not only as his private residence but as a private art gallery, too. Over recent weeks he had covered its walls with pictures of all kinds, stuck on with drawing pins, and there were a number of small pieces of wood on a shelf; odd bits off tree branches, curiously shaped by nature like the heads of animals or birds. Of the pictures on the walls, some were his own creations, executed both in the nursery and down at the hut; others were postcards of famous paintings, acquired from the Wallace Collection, the National Gallery and the Tate during his regular visits to his grandmother in London.

"You'll be able to draw and paint at school," Celia told Hugo one July afternoon while they were making tea together in the hut. "I expect there'll be an art master who'll show you how, much better than I can, and then one day perhaps you'll be a famous artist; who knows?"

Hugo liked the sound of that. He looked round the decorated walls of the hut. "Can I take my pictures to school?"

"I don't expect that would be allowed; not at first, anyway."

Hugo looked crestfallen, so Celia went on "I'm sure you'll be allowed to bring home the pictures you draw at school. Then they can go up on the walls in here too, can't they?"

Hugo seemed reassured.

At this point the kettle boiled on the wood-burning stove and Celia made a move to take it off. "There's our water boiling," she said but Hugo jumped up to forestall her.

"I'll do it, Aunt Celia," he said, "let me, please."

Celia was quite glad not to have to get up to make the tea in the little hut tea-pot, for she was not feeling her best that day. At five and a half months, she was beginning to suffer from the baby's uncomfortable weight and bulk, which slowed her down and made her constantly aware of the fact that she was well over half-way through her pregnancy.

AS the day drew near for Hugo's departure for Stanborough House a kind of unspoken truce broke out between Nanny and Celia. It was as though both women accepted the inevitability of

83

Hugo going to boarding-school, out of the nursery and the schoolroom now and into the outside world, leaving them both deprived.

ODDLY, Nanny never spoke to Celia about her own forthcoming child, beyond an occasional polite enquiry as to how she was feeling.

For her part, Celia knew better, too, than to interfere with the packing of Hugo's brand new school trunk and standard wooden tuck box which had arrived a few weeks earlier, both bearing Hugo's initials H.A.M. freshly painted in black.

One day when Nanny was busy in the nursery sewing Hugo's name tapes into his clothes, Celia remarked to her that the boy's initials might cause him to be teased at school. "If only we could leave out his middle name," she said.

But Nanny knew all about sending boys away to school, having done so three or four times before. "They always insist on the full initials, Lady Cardwell, in case there are boys of the same surname and christian name. He is Hugo Arlington Mayne and his initials must be H.A.M."

"Just as well he's not going to be an actor!" Celia replied.

As the first day of term approached, Hugo himself seemed surprisingly calm until, a few days before leaving home, he tried on his school clothes after tea in the nursery. As he stepped into a pair of stiff new grey flannel shorts he felt a great wave of excitement rising inside him. He pulled up his new grey knee-socks, with their sweetish smell of new wool and their satisfying suppleness, unlike the stiffness of old socks that had been washed too often or of woollly gloves that had gone for too many walks in the rain or in winter had patted too many snowmen or grasped too many icicles. As Nanny did up his tie over a pristine white shirt, he looked at himself in the mirror with a feeling of amazement. 'That little boy is *me*,' he thought. '*He's* going away to school . . .' But the boy in the glass still looked like a stranger. But Hugo raised a hand to him and the stranger raised a hand in reply. 'It *is* me,' he told himself; but a strange feeling of unreality possessed him, so that he found it hard to believe. And if anyone had asked him at that moment if he was looking forward to boarding-school, he would not have known whether to give a heart-felt 'yes!' or a terrified 'no!'

Parents and guardians of new boys had been asked to arrive by four o'clock on September 24th for tea with the headmaster and his wife. Richard had advised Celia to remain at home, as the journey to Swanage would be taxing for her. So shortly after lunch Hugo cheerfully said goodbye to the domestic staff who were gathered for the purpose in the Great Hall. They wished him a pleasant time at school and looked forward to his return for the Christmas holidays.

When it came to kissing Nanny Webster goodbye, Hugo said simply "Don't be sad, Nanny. I'll be very happy at school," which forced the poor woman to turn her head away sharply so that her charge would not see the tears in her eyes.

Lastly, as Hugo stepped into the Daimler, Celia hugged him and said "Don't forget to write to us on Sundays. And we'll write to you."

Hugo's school trunk and tuck box were strapped onto the luggage grid and he was settled on the back seat. Richard got in beside him and William placed a rug over their knees before climbing into the driver's seat. As the car started off down the drive, Hugo waved back through the rear window to the little knot of people waving to him from the front door: Celia, Nanny, Mr Page, Mrs Walcot, Robert and Miss Saunders. He did not see one of the young housemaids waving from an upper window. As the car rounded a corner in the drive and the house receded from view, he turned back to sit properly until they were passing through the lodge gates where he waved again, this time to Mrs Keegan.

As the Daimler reached the main road and headed southwards towards Poole, Richard tapped Hugo's knee and said "Well, old boy, this is the beginning of a new chapter in your life. I know you're going to be happy at school and do well in your work so that Aunt Celia and I can be proud of you."

"Yes, Uncle Richard," said Hugo. Then there was silence while Hugo tried hard to ignore a sinking feeling in his stomach that had grown into a hard uncomfortable knot by the time the car reached the outskirts of Bournemouth.

CELIA spent most of that afternoon on her bed, resting, for she was tired and emotionally drained by Hugo's departure. Lying with the curtains closed against the autumn sunshine, she began to wonder again, as she had so often wondered lately, whether her baby would be a boy or a girl. 'If it's a boy,' she mused with her eyes closed, 'I suppose Richard will insist on sending it away to school. I shall hate that. It's bad enough with Hugo but with my own . . . I'll probably have a row with him about that. Or will I agree, for the sake of peace?'

She decided she would like to have a little girl to spoil and dress beautifully and love. 'And when she grows up,' Celia reflected, 'she'll be terribly pretty and Hugo will be old enough to protect her and care for her and, when she's old enough for boys, he'll introduce her to his friends who come to stay in the holidays.'

With these thoughts going round in her mind, Celia dozed off. She did not awake until almost five o'clock. Autumn was closing in and the light was fading outside when she left her bed and made her way up the stairs to the nursery. She hoped that Nanny would be there, to offer her a cup of tea. She was confident of a warm reception, for she and Richard had asked Nanny to stay on to look after the new baby and this had made a much better relationship between the two women.

As she passed the door of Hugo's room she noticed it was ajar. She pushed it open and peered in. Her eyes went straight to Hugo's little wooden bed on which she had so often sat to read him a story and kiss him goodnight. Now the bed was tidily covered by its bedspread of animals on a blue background and at its head sat Hugo's well-worn, well-loved toy dog Pip, in mournful solitude. Tears suddenly welled up in Celia's eyes, but she swallowed hard, pulling herself together quickly. A sound outside in the passage told her that Nanny had returned to the day nursery. She left Hugo's room quietly, closing the door behind her, and wandered, as casually as she could, into the day nursery. "Hullo, Nanny. I suddenly felt like a cup of tea. Have you had yours yet?"

Nanny greeted her with a sympathetic smile. Perhaps she could guess where Celia had just come from but for the moment she avoided any reference to Hugo. Instead she said "I was just going to put on a kettle, Lady Cardwell. Come in and sit down, I'll not be a minute."

"Thank you, Nanny. – It's been quite a day, hasn't it?"

But Nanny had left the room and there was no reply. Celia looked round the day nursery, at the Hornby train set and the rocking horse. She recalled others, the toys of Hugo's infancy: a big woolly bear, an elephant, and the little horse on wheels, which had long ago been put away. 'Soon,' she thought, 'we must get them out again: all those toys will be used and loved again by my child, my own child.'

"I'M Maidment; what's your name?"

Hugo looked round, startled. He had been staring at the notice board in the school lobby, confused by all the class and dormitory lists, football fixtures for the term, instructions about fire-escapes, seating in the dining hall, times of meals, chapel services, when to see Matron, Lights Out, etc. Reading the notices was something to do on his own, a refuge from the rough and tumble of the form room where older, bigger boys might come up to his desk and start asking him awkward questions or challenge him to a fight or try to steal his books. He felt safe, standing there by the notice board. It helped him to feel he was part of the school, as though he belonged to it, but it kept him somehow out of harm's way.

A good-looking boy, quite tall and well dressed with gentle eyes and wavy dark hair, was standing beside him, also surveying the school notices but at the same time glancing sideways at Hugo.

"I'm Hugo . . . I mean Mayne . . . sorry."

"That's all right."

Hugo felt reassured. The boy seemed friendly enough, so he said cautiously "I'm a new boy; are you?"

"No. I came last term. I see you're in Lower Third; so am I."

"Does that mean for lessons?" Hugo asked, still a little uneasy.

"Yes, for everything. And we're in the same Dorm."

"Oh," said Hugo, still not absolutely sure whether this was a good thing or not. But Maidment seemed nice, despite his rather grand appearance, and Hugo wondered if he might be in the process of making his first, real school friend. What he did not know yet was that, in spite of his good looks, David Maidment, a doctor's son from the Midlands, spoke with a mild Birmingham accent, and was consequently short of friends. At Stanborough House he was looked down on, because of his difference from the others, the sons of country squires, Conservative members of parliament, officers in the Army or Navy or diplomats. All Hugo knew at that moment was that a boy called Maidment with wavy hair, who wasn't a new boy, had spoken to him. And when, on the first morning at breakfast in the dining hall, Maidment came and sat down next to him at table, Hugo's cup was overflowing. The two boys instantly became firm friends.

On the first Sunday morning at 'letter-writing' Hugo wrote home:

Dear Aunt Celia and Uncle Richard,
I am liking school very much and yesterday we played football and I am going to be inside left for the new bugs' team. There are some very rough boys in my dorm and one of them got the hairbrush on his B.T. from Matron for throwing water over another boy's bed called Spencer. I have a friend who is called Maidment he is very nice and I sit next to him in form and we send funny messages to each other when Chappo who is really called Mr Chapman isn't looking. Please send me some sweets and my book of famous paintings which I want to show to Maidment.

Love Hugo

6

ON the first day of October Richard left for London early, after hearing from Lady Carnarvon's Nursing Home in Langham Place that Celia had started labour. In his pocket was Hugo's letter which had arrived that morning. William drove him to the station where he caught the train to London. As it sped through Woking and Byfleet on its way to Waterloo, Richard wondered if the baby would have come by the time he reached the nursing home. As he pondered this possibility, his thoughts floated back to his nightmare dash home from East Africa three years earlier, only to find that he was too late, that Rosie had died. A sudden stab of fear caused him to catch his breath . . . what if Celia . . . or the baby – ? But an express on the other line, suddenly flashing past the window with a violent thud and a rush of wind, jolted him out of his morbid reflections.

In the waiting room at the nursing home, Richard sat half-heartedly flipping over the pages of a fortnight-old copy of *The Illustrated London News*, until at last, at twenty minutes past three in the afternoon, a sister came in to say that Lady Cardwell's baby had been safely delivered and would he like to come up. As they left the waiting room Richard asked anxiously if it was a boy.

Celia was lying in a room filled with flowers, pale and exhausted after fourteen hours of labour. But her eyes were shining with joy and pride. Richard kissed his wife gently on the forehead.

"It's a little boy, darling," she said simply and Richard looked down at the little bundle in her arms, at the tiny head with its short, fine hair and puckered red face, and rejoiced that this was his son.

Later, when Celia was resting, he went to his club to send off an announcement to *The Times* and telephone the good news to Charnfield and Lady Gage. He also informed Lady Brandon.

Edith's voice sounded warm over the telephone. "Oh, Richard, I'm so glad for you. You must be delighted to have an heir." Then, unaccountably, Richard thought he heard her sigh.

"Are you all right?" he asked.

"I'm sorry," she said, "I was just thinking of Rosie, how thrilled she would be for you." Then she added "Do give Celia my love and congratulations and tell her I'll pop in and see her tomorrow, if I may, when she's feeling a little stronger."

Edith Brandon put down the telephone thoughtfully. Of course Rosie would have been delighted. She knew how much her daughter had regretted not being able to give him a son, owing to her poor health. But what of Hugo? How would it affect him? He had been the only child in residence at Charnfield for some time now and was certain to resent the arrival of another. If the new baby was a younger brother and Hugo himself was in line to inherit the estate one day, a little jealousy now would not matter much; Nanny would make sure it wasn't allowed to last long. Unfortunately this was not the case, and the possibility of the new arrival supplanting Hugo in the affections of his step-parents as well as one day becoming the owner of Charnfield caused Lady Brandon to feel uneasy for her grandson's future. Hugo loved the place so much that she dreaded the day when he would come to realize it could never be his. From the way the boy talked about Charnfield she felt pretty certain that Celia had never mentioned these matters to him. Richard evidently talked to him very little about anything these days, which was a pity. Lady Brandon was tempted to mention the new situation to Hugo herself, tactfully, the next time he came to stay with her in London, but now was certainly not the moment. Better that it was broken to him one day when he was old enough to envisage leaving home, even wanting to. After all, she thought, all young people eventually spread their wings and fly the nest. At the right moment she would definitely discuss it with Celia.

It was a pity, too, that her own financial affairs were such that she could not leave anything to Hugo in Charnfield's place. Her husband's estate had been encumbered by debt when he died and there had been barely enough left for a modest income for herself, which would come to Hugo one day. But that was all.

90

She didn't imagine Richard would feel inclined to leave him anything.

Richard had meanwhile telephoned the good news to the Mitchells.

In all the excitement about the baby Hugo's letter from school was forgotten. It remained in Richard's pocket until he found it on his return to Charnfield the following afternoon, put it into a fresh envelope, addressed it to Celia at the nursing home and asked Page to get it off by the next post.

Page took the letter and paused by the door. "May I take the opportunity of offering my congratulations, sir, and those of the staff."

"Thank you, Page."

"And may one ask what name will be given to the young gentleman, sir?"

"Yes, of course you may, Page. Her ladyship and I have decided to call him Jeremy. Jeremy John, after Commander Mitchell."

"Very good, sir. May I inform the staff of that, sir?"

"You may indeed, Page, and I would like you to open a bottle of champagne, too, and invite the servants to drink the baby's health; then you can bring me a whisky and soda. On second thoughts," he added, feeling the need for a sustaining drink, "bring me the whisky first, will you?"

"Very good, sir."

As the door closed on his delighted butler, Richard moved over to the library window and gazed out across the park towards the distant downs with a sigh of contentment.

THE christening took place at the village church a fortnight after Celia's return home. The new baby was baptized on the Saturday afternoon that Hugo was playing his first football match in the new boys' team against another school.

He had been disappointed not to be allowed home to see Jeremy's christening and this feeling had revived the home-sickness that had struck him, particularly at night, during his first few days at school. Homesickness, compounded of abstract feelings of loss, loneliness and desolation with a longing for a particular place and particular people, was added to a sense of injustice that his nursery, the undivided attention of his nanny and that of Aunt Celia at certain moments, were being taken over

91

by a new infant he had not yet been allowed to see. A feeling of sadness and rejection when he woke up that Saturday morning was only slightly alleviated by his excitement about the football match. But his enjoyment of the game was spoilt when he failed to score an easy goal, missing the ball when it came to him and making a spectacular 'air shot'. This caused some amusement and jeering from his team mates, which upset him considerably. That evening at supper, however, his friend David Maidment told him that football didn't matter, anyway. It was much better to be good at work than kicking a ball into a net. Hugo was duly reassured and the two boys settled down to study a magazine, which Maidment's parents had sent, containing pictures of the treasures from Tutankhamen's tomb, discovered by Lord Carnarvon's expedition a year earlier and now on display in the national museum in Cairo.

Earlier that afternoon at the font in the little church at Charnfield Celia, looking strong and healthy and wearing a very becoming hat, had shared the carrying of her baby with Nanny Webster. When the Vicar pronounced the infant's names, Jeremy John Davenport, Jack Mitchell, who was to be a godfather, squeezed his wife's hand and winked at her with a hint of pride. He was flattered to have his own first name assigned to the future baronet.

Little Jeremy's screams echoed around the church when the water was being dropped over his head but Celia held her baby firmly, rocking him in her arms to calm him.

Jack whispered the usual comforting cliché about the devil being driven out of the child's soul; nevertheless as soon as it was decently possible Celia handed the bawling baby over to Nanny and they all left the church to face the press photographers.

WHEN Hugo came home for the Christmas holidays Nanny Webster was watching from an upstairs window for the car to drive up from the station. She saw Hugo get out and run into the house, leaving William and Robert to deal with his trunk, tuck box and Gladstone bag. 'He's filled out a little,' she thought as she moved into the nursery to glance down at the terrace below, where she had put Jeremy out in his pram. She imagined that Lady Cardwell would take Hugo straight out to peep at his sleeping stepbrother before he came upstairs. But Hugo failed to emerge onto the terrace and almost at once Nanny was surprised to hear the squelching sound of rubber soles on light shoes scampering up the stairs.

As Hugo reached the landing and ran towards the wide open nursery door, he could see that the room looked somehow different but he had time only to be aware of a great sense of happiness as Nanny came towards him, arms outstretched. She was still his nanny, he thought, she hadn't changed and must still want him, in spite of the new baby.

As he ran into her arms and hugged her she contained her emotion and simply said "How was school, then?"

In the excitement of coming home all those nights of homesickness, the fear of being bullied by older boys and the shame of bungling the ball at soccer were forgotten. "Oh, it's fun!" he said.

"So that's all right," said Nanny, thinking that perhaps she and Lady Cardwell had worried unduly that this sensitive little boy would be miserable away from home.

Hugo detached himself from Nanny, noticing that his model theatre was no longer in its central position on a table by the chimney piece and that its place had been taken by a large furry rabbit he had not seen before. 'How babyish!' he thought. He ran to open the toy cupboard where his meccano set and Hornby train normally lived, to find inside it his old friend, Dobbin, the toy horse on wheels he had almost forgotten. The sight of it, carved out of wood, painted dapple-grey with bright red nostrils and red braid tying his real horse-hair mane, made Hugo feel suddenly unhappy. Dobbin looked more battered and only a fraction of the size he remembered but he could hear once more the grating noise its wheels made as he pulled it along the gravelled terrace. He thought of his mother in a big hat, although he could not quite see her face clearly. He was aware only of a shadowy figure bending over him, slender, beautiful and kind.

"Have you seen Jeremy?" Nanny was asking him.

Hugo turned from the toy cupboard. "No. Aunt Celia said would I like to see him or you first and I said you, so she said I could see the baby at tea time."

Nanny smiled indulgently and took his hand, leading him to the window.

"There," she said, indicating the large black pram on the terrace below, where the infant lay asleep under a layer of blankets and the safety of a cat-net.

Hugo looked down but made no comment, so Nanny led him along the passage to see his new room.

Here Hugo was delighted to find all his books, paints and toys already put away in cupboards; there was an old, worn sofa and a table and chair at which he could write his letters and do his wood-carving. Soon William and Robert brought up his school trunk and Nanny started to unpack, sorting out clothes for the wash and tut-tutting over the quality of the school darning in his socks.

When it was time for tea Hugo went downstairs and Celia took him out onto the terrace and quietly over to the pram, where she eased the shawl clear of the sleeping baby's face for him to peep at his stepbrother. Privately Hugo thought he looked like a baby pig but politely kept the thought to himself and just said "Gosh".

The new baby soon became for him more an object of curiosity than a threat and, once assured by Aunt Celia that it would presently grow into a boy like himself with whom he could play, Hugo was able to put the new addition to the family out of his mind and concentrate on his list of required Christmas presents, no longer to be put up the chimney for Santa Claus but delivered to Aunt Celia by Nanny.

DURING the Easter holidays of the following year, 1924, when the weather became a little warmer, Hugo once again invited Celia down to tea at the cabin by the lake.

On this occasion, however, she brought the baby with her, and Nanny too, which spoiled things for Hugo. He was used to entertaining his stepmother on his own and her visits had always made him feel very grown-up, almost on a level with her, whom he saw more as a companion than a figure of authority. Having her all to himself, he could indulge in long, interesting conversations and plenty of jokes. Now it was different. Aunt Celia fussed about with the baby, making faces and endless clucking noises at it and Nanny did the same, when she wasn't telling Hugo when to put on the kettle and sending him back to the house for the sugar which had been forgotten. Hugo was no longer a master in his own house and he resented it deeply.

When he walked out of the hut in a sulk that day, after fetching the sugar and slamming it down on the table with very bad grace, and stood outside glaring at the lake, Celia whispered

94

to Nanny that perhaps tea at the cabin hadn't been such a good idea.

"He likes to rule the roost down here, Nanny, that's the trouble."

"I agree, Lady Cardwell."

"And he doesn't really want to share it with anyone else."

"I'm afraid someone's had his nose put out of joint . . ." Nanny said darkly.

That night at dinner Celia told Richard that she thought Hugo ought to have a school friend to stay for part of the coming summer holidays.

"What school friend?" Richard asked, without displaying much enthusiasm.

"There's a boy at Stanborough House he talks a lot about; Maidwell or Maid-something."

"Well, ask him."

"I think we ought to find out first whether Hugo really likes the boy; enough to have him to stay, that is. For all we know they may have fallen out and become deadly enemies."

"I think you're right," he said. "A school friend might get him out in the fresh air a bit more. I'd like to see him climbing trees, kicking a football around, exploring the woods, that sort of thing; not always stuck down in that hut poring over books and messing about with his paints."

"He's not a very boyish boy, darling," Celia said. "He's more the artistic type."

Richard grunted. "I'm all for him taking an interest in pictures and books and that sort of thing, as he always has since he was small, but we don't want him growing up into an effeminate kind of boy, a pansy."

"He won't. Not if we ask his friend to stay. They can go off and do the things that boys do. Climb trees and take the boat out on the lake. That sort of thing."

The next morning Celia found Hugo at the table in his room working on his model theatre. Armed with scissors and glue, he was fixing the little cut-out cardboard actors and bits of scenery into position on the tiny stage.

"How would you like to have your school friend to stay with you next holidays?" she suggested.

"Maidment?"

"Yes."

95

Hugo's face lit up. "Yes, please," he responded eagerly. Then he added doubtfully, "But Maidment's older than me. He's been at school a term longer."

"I don't think that would matter, darling," said Celia.

"All right," Hugo replied with relief.

"Didn't you tell me you were both going to be in the end-of-term play?"

"Yes," Hugo said, "it's *The Tempest* but we're not going to be told what parts we're going to be given till the end of next term."

"Then you could learn them and practise together during the summer holidays, couldn't you?"

"Me and Maidment?"

"Certainly. But not work all the time. You could go off and explore the woods and play tennis if it's fine."

Hugo nodded.

Celia went on "So, when you go back next week ask him to give you his parents' address; then I'll write and ask them if he can come. – What's his Christian name?"

"He's called David."

So that was settled. Celia would write to Mrs Maidment and hope the boy would be allowed to come and stay. Company for Hugo was indeed essential if he was not to grow up a lonely, isolated boy. Maidment sounded quite civilized. He must be suitable or Hugo would surely not have spoken of him so often as 'my friend at school'.

IN June Celia had a letter from Mrs Maidment agreeing to the visit. "So that's all right," Celia commented to Richard. "She sounds nice. The father's a doctor, by the way, in Wolverhampton."

She put the letter away with a mild degree of satisfaction that the arrangement was made and that she had persuaded Richard to agree to it. He was, she felt, one of those people who rarely initiate anything themselves but can usually be talked into a reasonable proposition.

TO begin with, David Maidment's stay was a great success. Hugo went into Sherborne with William to meet the train and was excited to see it steam in and to recognize his friend as he got out some way up the platform. The two boys greeted each other simultaneously and were soon in the car on their way to Charnfield.

"Is all this your home?" Maidment asked in wonder, as the car passed through the lodge gates into the rolling parkland on either side of the long drive.

Hugo nodded, pointing out of the car window with proprietorial pride to a rise in the ground away to the left. "We own all the land beyond that hill right down to the river and the village."

He was nine and three months now, and developing into a good-looking boy with a high forehead, intelligent blue eyes and fair hair.

David said "Gosh," and stared out at Charnfield Park in awed silence until they drove through the gatehouse arch and pulled up at the front entrance. As soon as he had recovered from the surprise of a footman taking his cap and coat from him and had been conducted into the hall to be introduced to Richard and Celia, Hugo took his guest upstairs to his room to chat to him while he unpacked his things.

"Did you bring tennis shoes as I told you and a racquet?"

"Yes."

"We have to have lunch in the dining-room, I'm afraid; that means being tidy, you know, washing our hands and brushing our hair and we have grown-up dinner some nights with the grown-ups, if there's nobody staying; if there are, we have it in the school room. I say, what do you think of this place?"

David moved over to the window. "Absolutely terrific," he said, looking out across the park.

"After tea I'll ask Uncle Richard if I can show you round the long gallery."

Over the following days the two schoolboys explored the house and grounds thoroughly, Hugo taking a special delight in showing his friend round and explaining the history of Charnfield and its treasures to him, just as he had himself been shown round by Richard when his mother was ill.

"That's a Zoffany," Hugo informed Maidment on the first evening, pointing to it as they descended the grand staircase to the hall. "It's an ancestor of Uncle Richard's. He was a Hun."

Maidment looked puzzled. "Who was?"

"Zoffany was, silly. He painted quite a bit in England but he

97

was German. We've got another one by him in the passage just outside the library"

Maidment proved a willing audience. He was also captivated by the lake hut where the boys spent long hours when it was wet, poring over a large jigsaw puzzle of Constable's *The Haywain* or painting a mural on one wall of the little sitting-room.

Hugo had acquired a bicycle for his ninth birthday the previous May and a second-hand machine had been hired in Dorchester for David, so the two of them could get about the place when it was fine.

Because it often rained the atmosphere was humid when the sun came out; as they bicycled along the tracks and paths round the estate steam wreathed from the ground ahead of them and mist lay under the dark late-summer foliage on the the trees and shrubs in the park.

"Race you to the top of the knoll," David said one evening when they were out for a ride after tea, having been kept indoors all day by the rain. "I'll give you fifty yards' start."

"Right! I'm off!" Hugo replied, pedalling furiously away, towards the clump of beeches surrounding a Grecian temple a quarter of a mile away.

They reached the top of the hill at about the same time, and then flung themselves, laughing, onto the ground under the trees where the grass was shorter and dryer than beyond the shelter of the tall bare trunks and their branches.

"I won!" said Hugo.

"No you didn't. My bicycle wheel was ahead of yours!"

"Only because it's a larger bike; my body was ahead of yours."

The two boys began to wrestle with each other, rolling over and over until they were too hot and puffed to go on, and then lay agreably intertwined, looking up at the grey and blue of the sky above them.

Hugo, with David's arm across his chest, felt a great surge of contentment. Looking down across the park to the grey house with its wings and windows and tall chimneys rising from a dozen chimney-stacks, he thought that Charnfield was the most beautiful place in the world, and that having a real friend with him made it even more perfect.

"I wish this could go on forever – having you here, I mean," he added quickly, to modify any hint of soppiness David might have detected in his first dreamy remark.

"Same here; it's topping, staying with you."

Glowing at this flattery from someone older than himself whom he liked, Hugo felt a greatly increased warmth for David. "What shall we do now?" he asked solicitously.

"Let's have a swim."

"We'll have to go back for our bathing suits."

"Don't need them. No one will see us."

Hugo was not sure that Nanny would approve, but she was unlikely to be down by the lake at this time of day. She would be busy with Jeremy while Aunt Celia and Uncle Richard were dressing for dinner.

A few minutes later the boys were in the lake, their bare bodies looking strangely pallid and frog-like through the dark water.

That night when Hugo and David were in bed they talked to each other for some time through the open doors of their two bedrooms, which were not quite opposite each other on the nursey corridor. After they had said goodnight Hugo lay awake, wishing once again that the week could go on longer. It was all perfect: but a small voice inside him said 'Too perfect'. It startled him, and at first he could not understand the remark, until he reflected that in his experience, when he loved people too much, something was likely to go wrong. His memories of his mother were already dim, but he could remember remembering, and he recalled perfectly the feelings of security and happiness and love he had known when she was alive, just like finding Dobbin in the toy cupboard last Christmas holidays and touching him for the first time for years and being reminded of her. His mother and Maidment . . . but David was only a friend, and there was something about him that made Hugo uneasy. For one thing he wasn't part of Hugo's family so he would go away and leave Hugo on his own again. His thoughts slipped back to the view of the house across the park that afternoon. Charnfield was beautiful, and it would stay there, in the same place, always. Nothing could happen to spoil it. Places didn't die. It was better to love Charnfield than people.

TWO days before he was due to leave, David said, "I say, we haven't read the play yet and we've got to learn our parts by next term. Don't you think we ought to start swotting it up?"

"Oh yes, let's," said Hugo enthusiastically.

That afternoon they took their play books down to the hut to read their scenes in *The Tempest* together and start learning the words.

Although it was a warm afternoon, David told Hugo that he thought the door of the hut should be kept closed, since he did not want their rehearsal to be disturbed by grown-ups or any other intruders such as Nanny Webster with the baby. Hugo agreed.

It happened that David Maidment had been cast in the role of Ferdinand and Hugo was to be Miranda. Young Maidment, as the older boy, naturally took control of the rehearsal.

"It all happens on an island, you see, where some people have been shipwrecked and there's this magician called Prospero who lives on the island with his beautiful daughter, Miranda. That's you."

Hugo groaned and said "I wish Chappo hadn't made me a girl, I hate girls."

"It's because you look like a girl, Mayne. You're girlish."

Hugo reacted with fury. "I'm not girlish!"

"Well, you're Miranda anyway, so let's get on with our rehearsal or we'll never know our words by next term."

"All right," said Hugo meekly.

"Now," said Maidment, "hold your book in one hand – at the beginning of Act Three – and we'll read the scene where I come on with a heavy log and you offer to help me and your father, Prospero, watches from a little way off while we sort of make love. Miranda has never seen any man except her father because she was born on the desert island and, until the shipwrecked people came, there wasn't anybody else there except an ugly monster called Caliban. That's going to be Skeffington-Reed Major but we won't bother about him. We'll begin here." David pointed to a speech in Hugo's book and began:

"Admir'd Miranda! Indeed, the top of admiration; worth what's dearest to the world! Full many a lady I have eyed with best regard . . ."

Suddenly David broke off with a gesture of irritation. "Look here, Mayne, this is stupid. I can't act this scene with you dressed like a boy. You're supposed to be a girl . . . you know, in a skirt or a dress or something."

Hugo said, rather pained, "I can't help it."

"Well, I think it would be much more real if you took off your shorts and socks and your tie and then you'd look more like a girl and we could act the scene properly."

Hugo was keen enough on the idea of acting in a play, the weather was very warm and he did not want to quarrel with his best friend, so he complied.

"That's better," Maidment said, when Hugo had shed his shorts and tie, and had been helped to unbutton his shirt almost down to his waist.

The rehearsal continued and Maidment became increasingly excited, his mouth turning dry and his knees trembling, as Hugo read out his lines in his clear, high voice: "I do not know one of my sex; no woman's face remember, save from my glass, mine own . . ."

Hugo, unconscious of anything strange about his state of undress, was only vaguely conscious of a need to please his friend and to enter into the part as well as possible. And so the two boys continued their play-acting, unaware that as it was Nanny's day off Celia was out pushing little Jeremy in his pram along the path to the lake, accompanied by Richard who had chosen to spend a warm summer afternoon with his wife and son.

"I think the boys are in the hut this afternoon learning their parts for *The Tempest*," Celia said, screwing up her eyes against the bright sunshine and looking ahead along the lakeside path.

"They are," Richard said, "I can see their bikes propped up outside."

"Have you seen their mural? It's really rather good."

"No," said Richard, "should I?"

"Well, it's quite clever. All sort of animals and birds and angels. It was Hugo's idea, inspired by a picture he saw of the Sistine Chapel in a book he found in the library. So he told me."

"Good for him," said Richard without enthusiasm.

They were a few yards from the hut now and Celia slowed down as they came alongside the entrance where the two boys' bicycles were leaning against the wall.

"Go and peep in, darling; you can see the mural from the right hand window. No need to go in and disturb them."

"Aren't you coming?"

"I'll stay here with the pram."

Celia put the brake on and waited while Richard went up to peer into the hut through the front window. To her surprise, her husband turned sharply round almost at once and came away from the window in a state of agitation.

"What is it, Richard? What's the matter?"

101

Instinctively Celia let go of the pram and moved quickly towards the hut window but her husband seized her arm and dragged her away back to the path.

"No, Celia . . . don't look in there . . ."

"What is it?" Celia asked, alarmed by Richard's tone.

He was visibly shaking. "That boy will have to go . . ." he muttered.

Celia struggled to get free but her husband held her arm firmly. "No," he said, "take the baby back and leave me to deal with this. I'll explain later. Go on, now."

Then, as she hesitated, he roared at her, at the top of his voice, "Do what you're told."

Celia stood for a moment, immobile, staring at Richard in astonishment. She had never seen her husband in such a state of fury before. Then, badly shaken, she took the handle of the pram to turn it round and push it back along the path towards the house.

As soon as she was on her way, Richard went into the hut, closing the door behind him. The sight that met his eyes was not exactly what he had seen through the window. Hugo was now struggling into his clothes whilst Maidment stood facing the door as Richard came in. The expression of guilt on his face confirmed what Richard had seen earlier: Maidment had been kneeling on the floor, his play book flung aside, stroking Hugo, who was stark naked, caressing his thighs and kissing his stomach . . .

"Get up at once, Maidment. And you, Hugo, put your clothes on. Then get out of this hut, both of you, and cycle back to the house. And when you've had your tea, I'd like you, Maidment, to come and see me in the library. Do you understand?"

"Yes, sir." Maidment had turned bright scarlet and his voice was shaking.

Richard went out, slamming the door of the hut and strode off back to the house, not sure quite how much he should or should not tell Celia.

IN the end he told her everything – just as soon as they were both back in the house and the pram was safely parked in the hall with its brake on so that baby Jeremy could continue sleeping.

In the privacy of the library Richard, with some difficulty and embarrassment, reported to his wife in detail exactly what he had seen in the hut. "Like a pair of lovers," he concluded, "but I

102

blame the Maidment boy. Hugo knows nothing of that sort of thing. Good Lord, the child's only nine."

To his surprise, Celia proved nowhere near as shocked as he was. On the contrary, she accepted the situation with sensible, broad-minded wisdom. "Boys do start to have feelings at that age, darling," she said, taking his hand, "instincts of desire. Girls do, too. It's partly the curiosity all children have about their bodies and partly a need to caress another human being . . . to touch bare flesh . . ."

"It's pretty disgusting."

"It's not disgusting at all, Richard. It's a substitute for normal love-making. They grow out of it later, when they reach puberty. Then they start wanting to caress girls."

"Some boys stay that way all their lives," Richard said grimly.

But Celia retorted, "That doesn't mean that Hugo's always going to be like that."

Richard paced about the library for a moment deep in thought. "I've a damn good mind to write to his parents," he said, "and to the Headmaster at Stanborough."

But Celia urged him to do no such thing. "That would only make things much worse," she said. "I beg you not to say anything to anybody. It's quite a natural thing to happen. I agree you should speak to Hugo later about those sort of things. But there again, I understand the boys at Stanborough House have a lecture about sex anyway, before they go on to their public schools."

"What do you call a lecture about sex?"

"Well, the birds and the bees and how babies are born, all that. And, of course, to beware of older boys when they get to their public schools."

"You seem to know a lot about it."

"You forget my cousin Lionel once taught at a prep school."

Richard grunted and stared out of the window.

Then Celia asked "What do you plan to say to Maidment when he comes to see you?"

After a pause Richard said, "Probably nothing. I shall just tell him to leave Hugo alone . . . in that way . . . or there'll be trouble. Just warn him, that's all."

"Good," said Celia, getting up to leave Richard to deal with Maidment. As she went out of the library she added, "Be nice to the boy, won't you . . . and understanding. He is Hugo's best

103

friend and they meant no harm. It's better than fighting and hurting each other . . ."

She closed the door behind her.

Richard sat down heavily in a chair and closed his eyes, where he remained until he heard Maidment tap on the door.

"YOU can consider yourself damn lucky you weren't caught doing that kind of thing at school, my boy. Because, if you had been, you'd have been expelled at once. You realize that, don't you?"

"Yes, sir."

Maidment looked thoroughly miserable, standing there in front of Richard with a sheepish expression on his face.

"On this occasion," Richard went on, "I shall say nothing about it to your parents because I have no wish to upset them; nor do I intend to say anything to the school. But you've got to promise me on your honour that it won't occur again, that sort of behaviour, either with Hugo or with anyone else. Is that clear, Maidment?"

"Yes, sir."

"Very well. Run along then and find Hugo and remember what I said."

"Yes, sir."

THE next morning was the last but one of Maidment's visit. As the two boys sat together on a hay bale at the home farm with their cycles propped against a nearby fence, David Maidment said in a pained voice "I still can't see why your stepfather was so angry. After all, I didn't hurt you, did I?"

"No. Course not. Rotten to get ticked off for nothing like that . . . Come on, let's bike down to the village shop and get some Liquorice Allsorts."

So the two friends mounted their cycles and pedalled away as if without a care in the world. But Hugo's light words had covered deep feelings.

The following morning Maidment left. "I'll miss you, Maidment," Hugo told him when the boys said goodbye.

"I'll miss you too, you rotter."

Hugo was very quiet that evening and had his supper alone in his room. When Nanny came in to take away his tray she found him trying to read a book while tears ran down his cheeks, wetting the pages.

"What's the matter, dear?"

"Nothing, Nanny."

"You shouldn't be crying, not a grown-up schoolboy like you. Can't you tell Nanny what is it, dear?"

Hugo sniffed, trying to control his tears.

"Are you missing your school friend; is that it?"

Hugo nodded then collapsed into Nanny's all-embracing arms and sobbed his heart out while Nanny rocked him gently.

'Poor child', she thought, 'they should never have sent him away to school so young. He's still a baby.'

What Nanny could not know and would never understand was that Hugo was crying not only for Maidment but because of a new loneliness and sense of rejection, caused by a feeling of increased coolness – almost of hostility – on the part of his stepfather.

WHEN Hugo returned to Stanborough House for the winter term he found Maidment changed. It was nothing very definite but the older boy seemed cool and distant. They were in different forms now, so that they no longer saw so much of each other. They still met in the lobby, in the changing room and on the playing fields and talked of every-day school matters but Hugo noticed that Maidment never mentioned his stay at Charnfield. It was almost as though the visit had never taken place. Hugo reasoned that his friend was still smarting under the ticking off he had received from Uncle Richard and had no wish to raise the matter further. It also became evident over the next week or so that Maidment was becoming friends with a boy called Skipton who was older than him and higher up the school. Skipton was a tall, handsome boy who had been cast to play Prospero in the school play. This new friendship caused Hugo a twinge of jealousy, especially now that David and Skipton were sitting next to each other at a different table in the dining hall.

Two weeks into the term, rehearsals for the school play began instead of normal prep on Thursday nights. The boys assembled in the gymn. and 'Chappo', the English master Mr Chapman, explained their relationships with each other in the play and gave them detailed moves and gestures. Hugo particularly enjoyed his scenes with Prospero, for Skipton was captain of football and a swell and evoked in Hugo a good deal of awe and admiration.

105

Mr Chapman seemed pleased with Hugo's performance at rehearsals and told him on several occasions that he was getting the hang of it very well. There were, however, one or two passages that were giving him trouble in the first long scene between Miranda and Prospero, so Chapman kept Hugo and Skipton back one evening to work on this scene. On the next occasion, however, he dismissed Skipton, informing him that he would not be needed and invited Hugo to continue work on the scene with him in his rooms. Hugo was worried that he would be late for Lights Out in the dorm and so be in trouble with Matron, but Chappo assured him that he had obtained special permission from the Headmaster for boys to work late on the play when necessary. So began for Hugo a series of evenings alone with Chappo in his room in one of the lodges, reading, learning and being coached for his part. Hugo was offered cocoa and biscuits and sometimes, after they had done enough studying for one evening, Chappo would encourage Hugo to stay on, sipping his cocoa while he talked to the boy as a friend and an equal. Chapman asked Hugo about his home and Hugo willingly told the friendly schoolmaster all about Charnfield and the pictures and ornaments in the Long Gallery there; about his stepmother and his stepfather and Nanny and the hut by the lake and the mural which he and Maidment had painted together in the summer holidays.

Every now and then Hugo would pause for breath in his excited outpourings and notice that Mr Chapman was staring at him with a fixed half smile on his face, a friendly smile, that made the boy feel warm and confident and secure. The mere fact that a master at Stanborough House was talking to him like this out of school and taking an interest in him was something quite new and unimagined, and Hugo was spellbound. Mr Chapman soon became his best friend, his confidant and the object of his affection. Before very long David Maidment faded from his mind and was no longer one of the most important elements in his life. Hugo concentrated his love and affection on Chappo and Mr Chapman knowingly and willingly took it; romantically and physically aroused, the young schoolmaster accepted total hero-worship from this beautiful, smooth-skinned, fair-haired boy of nine who was so sensitive, so filled with artistic instinct. He thrilled to the idea of moulding this boy who was so open to enlightenment on the world of art. And so desirable.

106

"I should like to see your paintings and your mural, Hugo, and your hut by the lake. And all the beautiful things you tell me there are at Charnfield," Chappo said to Hugo one evening.

"Oh yes, sir; I could show you round, if you came to stay with us. Like I did with Maidment when he came."

"That would be delightful," said Chapman with that same fixed gaze at Hugo. "If you were to ask your parents to invite me, I'll have some time free during the Easter holidays."

"Oh, good, sir," said Hugo, "I'll ask them."

After a fractional pause, Mr Chapman picked up his copy of *The Tempest*. "Now, shall we read that scene with Prospero just once more? Then you must cut along to bed before Matron starts to wonder where you are."

So Hugo found the place in his book and, sitting close beside Chappo at the small table, warmed by the gasfire in his sitting-room, began to read. As they read, Hugo felt, as usual, Mr Chapman's warm hand slide down into the top of his shorts and along his thigh towards what he ·had been taught to call his 'private parts'. It was not an unpleasant sensation; indeed, it was quite pleasing to Hugo. Its implication did not really cause him any great alarm, distress or fear. He was becoming used to it. This intimate contact was a normal occurrence at extra study with Chappo, part of the routine. It would have been strange and perhaps more puzzling, if Chappo had suddenly stopped doing it. But Hugo loved, admired and trusted Mr Chapman. He was his hero but also someone to whom he could talk. Someone who seemed to believe in him and admire him. Hugo believed it was the schoolmaster's way of expressing affection for him and he wanted desperately to be liked – especially by Chappo.

THE *Tempest* was a resounding success. For all three nights of its run on the rigged up stage in the school gymnasium every seat was filled and many parents came down to see it – including Richard and Celia.

When Hugo first appeared as Miranda, barefoot and wearing a simple white dress and a blonde wig of flowing tresses, a gasp could be heard in the audience. He looked breath-takingly beautiful and Richard found himself quite disturbed by the sight. He could not fail to be reminded of Rosie when they were first married.

Hugo received glowing praise for his confident performance which was spoken in a clear, well modulated voice. The review of the production in the school magazine at the end of the term praised Skipton's Prospero and the Caliban of Skeffington-Reed Major. It expressed reservations about Maidment's Ferdinand which it pronounced as being at times inaudible. The notice ended with these words: 'The surprise of the evening was the radiant and bewitching Miranda of Mayne, who not only spoke his lines with clarity and meaning but moved about the stage with a seductive degree of feminine grace.'

The review was signed 'L.W.C.' which stood for Lancelot Warren Chapman. The critic was modest enough not to mention the play's producer.

IT was Celia who suggested inviting Mr Chapman to stay. Hugo had been telling her how much the English master at school wanted to visit Charnfield and see some of the treasures for which the house was famous.

"He's obviously interested in that sort of thing and a visit here would encourage Hugo to go on with his painting and art studies. Anyway, he sounds a very nice man and I think we ought to ask him. Don't you?"

Richard looked up from his newspaper. "By all means. Better than having that Maidment creature around the place."

So Mr Chapman came for a week's visit to Charnfield during the following Easter holidays, arriving in time for tea in his Morris Cowley coupé with the hood down, since it was a fine April day. He was wearing a tweed plus-four suit and had, at Celia's suggestion, brought his golf clubs; she had seen the chance of a game with Hugo's English master at West Downham.

A game was arranged for the first Sunday afternoon. Hugo himself came too, riding in the dickey of Celia's two-seater so that Mr Chapman could sit in front. Arriving at the first tee, although Celia had hired a caddy for herself and her guest, Hugo was instructed to help spot any balls that might land in the rough. Celia told Mr Chapman that she hoped Hugo might acquire a taste for the game later on.

But the afternoon on the links and, indeed, the whole visit, was a disappointment to Hugo. Once again he felt a sense of rejection. For much of the time Celia showed Chappo round the house and garden herself and the two adults talked endlessly about politics, education and the theatre, unintentionally excluding Hugo from the conversation.

Only on the last day of his visit did Hugo manage to get his hero to himself. It was Nanny's day off again and Celia was busy with Jeremy, so Hugo invited Chappo down to the hut by the lake. It was his last chance to spend any time alone with his idol and an opportunity to show off his murals and pictures with which the place was decorated.

Hugo boiled the kettle, made the tea and offered Chappo a sandwich from the hamper which Mrs Walcot had packed.

"Lucky you," Chappo said, "to have a place like this all to yourself."

"I know," said Hugo, surveying his hut with pride.

"I expect young Jeremy will want to share it with you, when he gets a bit older."

Suddenly Hugo felt a surge of anxiety in the pit of his stomach. The thought of having to share his hut with the new baby when it grew up depressed him.

"Yes, I suppose I'll have to let Jeremy come in here, if he wants to. Worse luck."

Chapman noted the somewhat bitter tone of Hugo's voice and wondered how a boy of nearly ten with everything he could wish for; good looks, brains, an adoring stepfather and stepmother and a fine home to live in, could possibly be jealous of a two-year old baby.

WHEN Hugo returned to Stanborough House for the summer term he was surprised and shocked to be told on his first night back that Mr Chapman had left the school and would not be returning. The news had been given out by the Headmaster to Chapman's English class, which would now be taken by a new beak, Mr Oatley, as Mr Chapman had left to teach at another school in Devon.

Hugo further learned that Maidment in Upper Fourth had also left during the holidays, but nobody knew why.

When this news reached Celia and Richard by way of Hugo's Sunday letter, Richard, mindful of Maidment's behaviour on his visit to Charnfield, at once feared that Hugo himself might have been in some way involved. So he wrote to the Headmaster, carefully not mentioning the incident between Maidment and Hugo during the previous summer holidays, but using, as an excuse to write, the fact that Maidment had been his stepson's close friend and had stayed with them at Charnfield in the summer.

Mr Boardman replied at once.

I regret to say that the departure of both Maidment and Mr Chapman from Stanborough House were connected and not co-incidental. Chapman agreed to resign his post here after I had been obliged to speak to him severely, following recurring complaints from the Matron about his unauthorized visits to one of the dormitories after 'Lights Out'. The boy involved was Maidment and, since I felt obliged to report the incident to Dr Maidment, the latter regretfully decided to remove his son from the school immediately. I hasten to assure you that the boys, including Hugo, have not been nor will be informed of the circumstances of these departures and will in no way be disturbed or diverted from their studies by this unfortunate disciplinary matter.

I remain, Yours Sincerely, Cyril Boardman, Headmaster

Richard sighed with relief and Celia got up to go into Dorchester to shop.

At the door she paused to say "Fancy Mr Chapman being like that. You'd never know, would you? I thought him quite attractive."

AT his desk at Stanborough House forty miles away, Hugo was deep in an essay on the Italian Renaissance which absorbed him so completely that the loss of his first school-friend and his favourite master, although the cause of considerable sorrow and pain, did not seem irreparable. The review of his part in the play had encouraged him greatly and raised his self-confidence. He was determined to come out top of his class and one day, perhaps, top of the school. Then Jeremy would have to look up to him and admire him as he admired Skipton. He would show them.

So Hugo worked hard at his studies over the next three years and his report for the winter term of 1928 indicated to Richard and Celia that he would soon be moving on to the next phase of his education and a new chapter of his life. The Headmaster of Stanborough House summed up thus:

Hugo has had another excellent term. He continues to do well at all his subjects, in particular English and Art, and he should have no

110

difficulty in passing his Common Entrance examination next term. Out of school he is a quiet boy and not especially gregarious, preferring his own company and that of the masters to mixing with other boys of his age but he is by no means unpopular. Hugo is a definite asset to the school.

Celia was delighted with Hugo's report. Richard was, on the whole, relieved. He had long suspected that his stepson was clever and would do well at his work but he could not suppress a certain deep-seated anxiety that somehow Hugo's rather gentle, effeminate nature, his lack of interest in games, might one day lead him in what he once described to Celia as 'the wrong direction'. Time alone would tell.

7

"BOYEE . . . ee" came the full-throated roar from somewhere on the floor above Hugo's room, followed by the sound of opening doors and the clatter of feet running down the poky, narrow corridor past his door and up the rickety stairs. Hugo cursed as he flung down his pen. This was the third 'boy call' to interrupt his work that Sunday afternoon in October 1928 and he was beginning to resent it. He flung open his door and dashed out to join the stampede of small boys already surging in the direction of the call.

Hugo at thirteen and four months had been at the Grange, the Eton College boys' house presided over by Mr Thomas Carey Whittle, since the end of September and was beginning to get used to it. On arrival at Whittle's house, generally known as T.C.W.'s, he had found two boys he knew from Stanborough House, Paley and Matthews, with whom he 'messed' in his room. But so far, apart from them, he had not made many friends.

Racing up the stairs to the floor above, he almost collided on the landing with a number of boys coming from another direction, among them his two friends, Paley and Matthews, whose rooms were on the upper floor. They were both small and dressed in short jackets with large Eton collars, whereas Hugo was just tall enough to be in tails.

"Boyee . . . ee." The bellowing was louder now, as Hugo ran on down a dark, narrow corridor, following the others. In the doorway of a room at the end of it stood the caller, a tallish, saturninely handsome youth of seventeen with quite long, curly, black, Brylcreemed hair, an aquiline nose, and the sponge-bag trousers, braid-edged tail coat and wine coloured satin waistcoat of a member of 'Pop', the élite, self-electing Eton Society. His name was Michael Wedgwood and he was Captain of T. C. W's.

Gathered around him was the cluster of panting Lower Boys who had dashed in a frenzy from all over the building in answer to his call for a fag.

Due to his near collision on the landing, Hugo had been fractionally delayed and thus arrived comfortably last at the scene.

Wedgwood surveyed the anxious group of Lower Boys assembled before him. Normally, the last to arrive was fagged but sometimes two fags were required to run different errands, or even three. But this was a normal call.

"You were last, Mayne," said Wedgwood to Hugo, who was still gasping for breath at the edge of the group and could only just manage to nod. "Rest of you can go," he added, and the other fags dispersed.

Wedgwood looked long and hard at Hugo, then said quite formally, "Come in." Hugo followed the House Captain into his room, its walls plastered with photographs of Etonian friends, framed 'choices lists', rowing and Rugger caps and the usual Rules of the Eton Society framed in pale blue ribbon with two crossed 'pop' canes attached to it.

"You're to take a note to someone in Harvey's. Know where that is?"

"Yes," Hugo muttered, still short of breath. All new boys had to pass an exam in their first two weeks on Eton geography and Hugo knew precisely where Mr Harvey's house was.

Wedgwood went to sit at his 'burry', a kind of antiquated folding-top desk, and started to scribble on a pad while Hugo stood waiting, rather rigid, hoping that all his buttons were done up correctly and that there was nothing wrong with his appearance that could be termed a 'float'. For such minor faults could get a new boy into serious trouble. After a while Wedgwood got up and handed Hugo a small piece of paper, thinly folded in the shape of a figure four.

"Take this round to Dale-Adams. He's Keeper of Fives, in case you didn't know."

Without a word Hugo took the note and turned to go.

"And see that he gets it before Chapel."

"All right." Hugo knew full well that any failure to deliver on time would result in a tanning in the library, a form of thrashing with a wicker cane on the bottom from Wedgwood in front of the six senior boys in the house. Or, worse still, a Pop caning.

113

Hugo had thus far avoided being beaten. His only clash with authority had been during his first week when he was stopped in the street by an older boy, draped in a red and light blue Field scarf and riding a bicycle, who had fined him half-a-crown for eating a choc. ice on Barnes Pool Bridge.

Hugo reflected quickly that Harvey's house was some way out along the Eton Wick road and that, even with the short cut through Judy's Passage, it would take him about ten minutes. He'd better get a move on.

It being a cold Sunday afternoon in winter, the streets of Eton were fairly empty, most Lower Boys preferring to remain in their rooms by their fires, reading the *Strand Magazine*, doing their Sunday Questions or constructing model aeroplanes. As Hugo put on his top-hat and set out for Harvey's house, he realized that the note he was clutching in his cold hand had not been folded securely and was coming apart. It occurred to him that he would be blamed if the missive arrived open, so he stopped to try and refold the slip of paper before proceeding. But with the note open in his hand, he succumbed to the compelling temptation to have a quick look at the message. He was curious to find out how very senior boys in the school addressed each other. The note had been scribbled hurriedly but Hugo was just able to read Wedgwood's scrawl: 'Have booked a Fives Court for two-thirty on Wednesday. Meet you at School Stores after Absence. What think you of our fair messenger? Did you ever see such blue eyes and long eyelashes? Methinks Stephen Warren's days as Pop bitch are numbered. What thinkst thou? Yours, Mike.'

It took Hugo quite a few moments to realize that the 'fair messenger' referred to was himself. When he understood the meaning of the scribbled comment, he blushed and a sense of alarm swept over him, then astonishment. It seemed to him very strange that Wedgwood, who was so grand and important in the house and rarely looked at Lower Boys, let alone spoke to them except to fag them or shout at them at football practice, should write to another senior boy about his eyelashes. All the same Hugo was aware of a warm feeling inside him, and the sense that somebody high up in the school had noticed him and cared about him was gratifying. It was rather like when Chappo's hand used to invade his shorts while they read *The Tempest* together or like when Maidment, as he stroked him that summer at Charnfield, had told him he was good-looking. It was becoming clear to

114

Hugo that people admired his looks and gradually a sense of satisfaction, even of vanity began to creep over him; he knew he possessed some power over people, an ability to make other boys want to be friends with him.

As he quickly refolded and licked up the note to make it stick down and hurried on along the road, Hugo realized that his heart was beating quite fast. Reaching Harvey's house, he walked with cool confidence through the Boys' Entrance. Inside the door a short, plump and freckled youth with red hair, who was loitering by the notice board, looked round as Hugo came in. Buoyed up by the flattering contents of the note in his hand, Hugo had no difficulty in demanding of the freckled boy the way to Dale-Adams' room.

"I'll show you," said the red-headed cherub, who had nothing else to do, and Hugo followed him up a few steps, along another murky corridor to a door at the far end. The boy knocked on the door once, then ran for it. Hugo stood his ground.

"Do come in." A surprisingly soft, rather oily and effeminate voice came from inside. Hugo turned the handle and went in.

A languid creature also in 'pop', with a lean, pale face and long, untidy fair hair, was sprawled in a wicker armchair, his feet on the mantelpiece, his bottom towards the warming fire, a magazine open on his lap.

"A note for you . . . from Wedgwood at Whittle's," Hugo said.

Without moving an inch or taking his eyes off his magazine, Dale-Adams wearily held out a limp hand for the note, took it and opened it slowly. Hugo waited for what seemed an age while the note was read. After a while he thought he heard Dale-Adams chuckle to himself. Then the languid figure removed its feet from the mantelpiece and eased itself round in the armchair to inspect Hugo, who stood patiently awaiting instructions.

"Go and stand over by the window, I can't see you properly," came Dale-Adams' drawled command.

Hugo, well aware of the senior boy's reasons for such a request, complied.

"That's better." Dale-Adams gazed at Hugo for a while, then resumed his former position, putting his feet back on the mantelpiece.

"Shall I go now?" Hugo asked, imagining his mission to be ended.

"No. Wait and you can take back an answer."

115

Hugo remained rooted to the spot, standing almost to attention. It was very important, he had discovered, while dealing with these high-up swells, to behave rather like Page, the butler at Charnfield. Stand still, say nothing until spoken to and thus avoid trouble. Dale-Adams had by now found a pencil and scribbled an answer underneath the message on Wedgwood's note which he now held out, refolded, for Hugo to take from his extended hand.

"Off you go . . . By the way, what is your name?"

"Mayne, sir."

"Not sir, you stupid child. That's only for 'beaks'. Try again; what is your name?"

"Mayne," said Hugo.

"That's more like it. Pretty voice. Are you in the Lower Chapel Choir?"

"Yes, I am actually."

"Thought you might be." Dale-Adams was smiling at him now, a warm, friendly smile. "Off you go, then, Mayne."

And Hugo left, almost with regret. He would have liked to stay a while and talk to Dale-Adams, who seemed rather nice.

On the way back to his Tutor's Hugo felt compelled to read Dale-Adams' reply, so he stopped in Judy's Passage where nobody else was in sight. Under Wegwood's signature, Dale-Adams had added, 'Fives on Wednesday OK. Agree about messenger. Not bad but not quite as pretty as Stephen Warren. A. D-A.'

Hugo felt a little piqued by this hint of competition and, that evening after lock-up, was pondering what Stephen Warren looked like and where he boarded as he tidied up his own personal fagmaster's room.

Hugo was fagging for a boy called Harris, a lean, smooth, rat-faced youth with too much Brylcreem on his scanty hair.

Hugo found him fairly pleasant to fag for, not too strict and deeply interested, as far as he could make out, in what was known as 'London Society'. While most of the boys at Whittle's were sent magazines such as *Autocar*, *The Railway Magazine*, *Horse and Hound* and *The Strand*, Harris subscribed – or rather his parents did – to the *Tatler*, which came to him rolled up on Thursdays.

Harris was buried in his latest *Tatler* when Mansfield in the next-door room dropped in, as he often did to borrow a ruler or pencil-sharpener. Hugo was busy stuffing his fagmaster's sweaty, muddy football clothes into a chintz-covered ottoman when he heard Harris say to his visitor "There's rather a jolly picture in here of my cousin, Deidre Wills, at Queen Charlotte's Ball. Look."

Mansfield glanced at the page and said politely: "By Jove, yes."

"Her father's my mother's brother, you see. Lord Cravenhurst."

"By Jove, yes," Mansfield said again, and departed.

A week later Harris was sitting in his wicker armchair, flipping through the School List, a light blue publication which recorded the name, address, house tutor and parent or guardian of every single boy in Eton College. As Hugo picked up some books off the floor to put them away before boiling the kettle for Harris's tea, the former said suddenly "I say, Mayne."

"Yes?"

"Why is your parent or guardian called Cardwell?"

"Because he's my stepfather. My father was killed in the war."

"Oh. Rotten luck. So you won't be Sir anything when he dies."

"I don't know."

"Well, you won't, will you?" said Harris. "Not like Grant."

Hugo looked puzzled.

"Chap I sit next to up to old Suthers for History," Harris went on; "his name's called out as 'Sir Henry Grant' now at Absence because his proper father died last holidays and he's become a Baronet."

"I see," said Hugo.

"If your stepfather had a son, he'd be the Baronet, you see, one day."

As this thought took shape in his mind, Hugo felt a sudden twinge of jealousy and resentment. So Jem would be 'Sir' if Uncle Richard died, Hugo reflected; but he was only a baby.

Before he could brood any further over this new, rather troubling discovery, Harris said sharply "You'd better go and get our teapot, Mayne." And Hugo had to jump to it.

WHEN Eton broke up for the holidays, Hugo was to go to Granny Brandon for two nights before they travelled down to Charnfield together on Christmas Eve. Hugo loved his grandmother for herself and because whenever she had him to stay with her in London – which was quite often – she always spoiled him with treats and thought up interesting and exciting things to

117

do together. Lady Brandon was a cultured woman who loved picture galleries and museums and her influence on Hugo was considerable. She taught him a great deal more than he knew from books and helped him to develop a remarkable knowledge of the various schools of painting, drawing and sculpture. As soon as the school train pulled into Paddington, Lady Brandon found a porter and then Hugo among a seething mob of boys on the platform, whisked him and his luggage into a taxi and took him to her flat for an early lunch. After that she took him to see *Peter Pan* with Jean Forbes-Robertson at the Garrick Theatre, where they had tea on their knees in the interval. When it was over, they sat on the top of a bus back to Victoria. Hugo was rather silent on the way home, still lost in James Barrie's 'Never, Never Land', until Lady Brandon suddenly asked him if he was happy at Eton.

"I think so, Granny," the boy replied cautiously. It was early days yet. "It's rotten having to fag; that's for your first few halves until you get into the upper school. But everyone has to do it. It's not bad fun. I mess with two boys I know; they're called Paley and Matthews; they were at Stanborough House. We make our own tea and we're allowed to boil things on the gas ring like baked beans and spaghetti and things and have it on toast."

"Really, and do you know how?"

"Oh, there's a Boys' Maid to help us. Paley's people sent him a pheasant one week which he got plucked and cooked at Rowland's and we had it for tea with bread crumbs and bread sauce and crisps and everything."

"My goodness," gasped Lady Brandon. "A whole pheasant for tea!"

"There were three of us, Granny, and we were jolly hungry after football."

"I'll bet you were. And you make your own tea?"

"Yes. Like in the hut at home." There was a pause while the bus pulled up in Whitehall. Hugo was staring out of his window at the Cenotaph in the centre of the road opposite the point where they had stopped. Lady Brandon noticed this but decided to say nothing, unless Hugo asked about it. But his mind was quickly back on Eton and then, as the conductor jerked the string twice and the bus started off again, Hugo asked suddenly "Does Jeremy boil the kettle in the hut?"

118

Lady Brandon was taken off guard. But instinct told her to be careful. Celia had hinted at possible tension between the two boys, as Jeremy grew older. He was five now and developing into a pretty strong, active little boy with a mind of his own.

"Oh, I expect Nanny helps him. After all, he's only five."

Hugo relapsed into silence for some time and spoke little until they reached the Army and Navy Stores in Victoria Street where they climbed off the bus. Hugo took his granny's arm as they stepped onto the pavement and set out for Artillery Mansions.

CHRISTMAS, 1928 was not an easy one for Richard and Celia. With Hugo away at Eton, Celia and Nanny between them had been able to manage Jeremy fairly well. He was a bundle of energy, physically fearless and full of what was politely called mischief. Richard was inclined to spoil him and leave the discipline to his mother and Nanny. In his opinion, children should remain under nursery rules until they went away to boarding-school. After that, Richard admitted, it was a father's job to rebuke and punish. A fairy cycle had been bought for Jeremy for his fifth birthday and it was hoped that he might expend some of his surplus energy pedalling round Charnfield, up and down the drive, along the terrace and down to the lake.

With Hugo home for the holidays, Jeremy was no longer quite the centre of attention he had been for the last three months and it was still too early for the two boys' lives to be much involved with each other. As an Eton boy, Hugo was now treated as a grown-up and consequently had all his meals in the dining-room, with Richard, Celia and Lady Brandon, whereas Jeremy, at five, was still technically 'in the nursery'.

ON Boxing Day Hugo was due to go out shooting with the grown-up party. He now owned a 4.10 shot gun and a small cartridge bag with his initials on it – a Christmas present from Uncle Richard. His brief was to walk through the woods in the line with the beaters and 'get a shot at any rabbits or stray birds breaking back'.

"Good practice for you, Hugo," Richard had said, assuming the boy would be thrilled at the prospect.

It was not so. Hugo would have died rather than admit it to anyone but he was scared stiff of firing a gun of any sort and dreaded the noise and the recoil. Richard had once encouraged

119

him to fire one of his full-sized pair of Purdey 12-bore guns at a pigeon in a tree and the kick had almost knocked him off his feet. Another deep worry for Hugo, which kept him awake on Christmas night until two o'clock in the morning was the fear of missing an easy shot at a bird and incurring his stepfather's displeasure.

The day went well until late afternoon, when the light was beginning to go. Hugo had avoided betraying his dislike of shooting by remaining with the beaters and the two keepers for five drives. He had simply walked through the thick woods, imitating the strange clucking and cooing bird noises issuing from the mouths of the village lads who, for five shillings a day, crashed through the undergrowth, whacking the trees with their sticks to drive the pheasants over the guns. In the course of this activity Hugo had loosed off twice, once at a rabbit and once at a low-flying hen pheasant which broke back and almost knocked his cap off. He missed both targets.

As the fourth drive ended, Richard told Hugo to come and stand next to him for the last drive. He could pot at anything he saw, so long as he didn't fire head high. Hugo's heart beat with apprehension and he felt just a bit sick, as he stood anxiously grasping his 4.10 about fifteen yards from his stepfather. Jim Cooper stood by Richard as his loader. A whistle blew in the distance and Hugo could distantly hear his old friends, the beaters at the far side of the wood, begin their ritual clucking and beating the trees and fences. After a while a number of pheasants came rocketing and swerving out through the thick trees and into the open. Hugo saw several hit and brought down.

Somewhere ahead in the wood, between him and Richard, Hugo saw a cock crash down with a thump, hit in the legs, fluttering and wriggling frantically. Sickened by the sight, Hugo stared morbidly at the luckless bird as Richard's golden Labrador, Whisky, whimpered and strained at his leash, wanting to charge in and seize the bird. But the drive was not yet over and Richard bellowed at his dog, "Stay, Whisky. Stay, damn you."

Hugo was still worrying about the wounded cock when a shout interrupted his thoughts. "Over you, Hugo; quick . . ."

A fluttering, croaking sound made Hugo look up sharply, as Richard shouted at him. Hugo just had time to see a cock pheasant coming at him in a straight line, at a reasonable height and steady speed, with no tree branch in the way; a clear, easy

120

shot. He flicked off his safety catch, tried to see the bird lined up with the bead on his barrel, and fired.

The cock pheasant seemed to jerk in the air. Its wings stopped and spread out, as it went into a glide, both legs hanging down. For a moment Hugo dared not look round, for fear of seeing another struggling, flapping, wounded bird.

"Good shot, Hugo, well done. You hit him. He's a runner, won't get far . . . Whisky'll get him."

Hugo risked a look round. The drive was coming to an end now. The beaters were scrambling over a fence, emerging from the wood and assembling on the road close by. There was great activity everywhere, and dogs bounding about with retrieved birds in their mouths.

Two of the guns were in polite dispute about a bird, claimed by each. Hugo heard one, Colonel Mapleton, say to Lord Barringer, "I think you'll find that was mine, Geoffrey; that hen by the gate."

"No, no, mine, I think. You winged her but I killed her with my second barrel," was Lord Barringer's icily polite reply.

Hugo spotted the bird he had wounded, creeping about in the bracken.

At that moment Richard unleashed his dog. "Go on, Whisky, get him . . ."

The labrador galloped off and Hugo saw it chase the bird he had brought down and which, with both legs and a wing peppered, was quite unable to fly.

Whisky soon overtook the wretched flapping pheasant, gathered it up in his soft mouth and came running back to deposit it at his master's feet.

Hugo's stepfather picked the bird up by its neck and squeezed it until it stopped fluttering and was dead. Then he threw it casually down onto a pile of dead birds to be collected later by the game cart.

THAT night, when Celia came to say goodnight to him in his room, Hugo told her he never wanted to go out shooting again. "It's boring and very cruel."

"I rather agree, darling," she said, "but it's part of the tradition of country life in England. Part of Charnfield."

Together they discussed how Hugo might avoid shooting in the future without upsetting his stepfather. In the end Celia said

121

"Leave it to me," and Hugo kissed his stepmother, his eyes moist from relief and love.

The rest of the holidays passed off without incident, Hugo keeping very much to himself and finding his own amusements. At times he found himself wishing strongly that David Maidment could be asked to stay again, but Aunt Celia had avoided discussing the subject. Why had David left Stanborough without writing at least once, to say goodbye? All Hugo had gathered was that David had been sent to another prepschool in the Midlands and on from there to Rugby.

As the weather in early January was dry and fine, Hugo cycled a good deal around the Dorset countryside, armed with an old guide book, exploring churches and old ruins. On one occasion he rode his bike over to Cerne Abbas and climbed up the steep slope to inspect the famous giant carved into the side of the hill. He sat down on the hillside where the chalk outline of the giant stretched like a snake across the turf and looked out over the blue country below him, surrounded by blue sky and silence. It was broken only by the occasional 'cark-cark' of a crow or the faint reverberation of some kind of distant engine. Suddenly he became immensely aware of his loneliness, miles from the nearest human and many miles from home, and he was filled by a great longing for David's companionship. Chappo had deserted him as well as David, his two best friends; was he destined to spend his whole life alone? The thin January sun could not defeat the nip in the breeze and he shivered. Realising that he was cold, he jumped up. Chappo and David would have been left behind anyway, when he went to Eton, and Paley and Matthew weren't bad chaps.

On his next outing he went into Dorchester, where there would be people about. He had remembered, also, that Dorchester was the setting for Hardy's *Mayor of Casterbridge*, which he had read the previous term, and his grandmother had given him a leather-bound copy of Thomas Hardy's *Wessex Tales* for Christmas, so he had begun to see the country around his home in the light of Hardy's dramas.

He visited the old courthouse in Dorchester where, he was excited to learn, the notorious Judge Jeffreys had condemned hundreds to death after the Monmouth Rebellion – for this event had featured in last half's history lessons at Eton.

When it was time to return to Eton for the Easter half, Hugo went back with few regrets; indeed, although he was sorry to

122

leave home, he went with a certain degree of pleasant anticipation. He would be able to regale Paley and Matthew over tea in his room with accounts of his exploration of Dorset on his bicycle. He also wondered, rather guiltily, how much more admiration he might excite in other senior boys as the half progressed.

MIDWAY through the summer holidays of 1929 things came to a head between Hugo and Jeremy.

The two boys had only visited the hut by the lake together a couple of times since Jeremy had been allowed to ride his fairy cycle round the property unaccompanied. On these occasions Hugo had allowed Jeremy to join him at the hut for tea but had been very much in charge, rather like a schoolmaster inviting a pupil for tea in his rooms. He had showed the younger boy his drawings, pictures and objects carved in wood; and demonstrated the art of boiling a kettle on the stove and making the tea. In short, Hugo had twice entertained his six-year-old stepbrother in his own domain.

Then, one afternoon in late August, Hugo returned to Charnfield from a bicycle trip. He had been to Bridport for the day, with a sandwich lunch, his bathing things and a book. He had bathed and then lain sunning himself on the beach. Returning around five o'clock by way of the lake, he noticed Jeremy's fairy cycle propped up against the hut. Although nothing had been officially agreed with Celia, Hugo did not expect Jeremy to go to the hut on his own. Suspecting the worst, he quickly pedalled up, flinging his bike down on the grass outside, and stormed in.

Jeremy was alone, using some of Hugo's coloured chalks from an open box on the table to daub and over-draw one of Hugo's own most treasured efforts that was pinned to the wall. It was a sunset in coloured chalks with Charnfield in a fold of the downs and some birds flying high in the evening sky.

"What the hell are you doing in here, Jeremy?"

"Drawing pictures," he said simply and continued to daub the wall.

"Get out," Hugo shouted, "and don't you ever come in here again without asking me, do you hear? This is *my* hut, mine. It was given to me for my birthday and it's not yours, it's mine."

Jeremy started to cry and ran out of the hut.

123

Hugo called after him. "Go back and sneak to Nanny, go on, or tell Aunt Celia. I don't care. You were trespassing in my hut and you're not allowed to."

Hugo was beside himself with fury, trembling and shaking, as he watched Jeremy wheel his fairy cycle along the lake path towards the house, whimpering as he went.

Hugo went back into the hut and sat down to inspect his damaged drawing. Jeremy had almost completely destroyed it, so Hugo finished the job by ripping it into several pieces and throwing them on the floor. He knew full well there would be trouble awaiting him when he returned to the house. Jeremy would go straight to Nanny and Nanny would go to Aunt Celia and he would be in serious hot water for chucking Jeremy out of the hut.

"WHO the hut belongs to is not the point, Hugo. It was made for you to have somewhere to play when you were growing up, but you're not a child any longer."

Hugo's fears were confirmed. Jeremy had, of course, sneaked on him and he now found himself standing in the library facing a furious Uncle Richard. It was about 6.30 in the evening and Celia had tactfully, and not without some anxiety, taken her gloves and secateurs and slipped out to the rose garden, leaving Richard to deal with the matter.

"You're at Eton now, Hugo, and old enough not to need a hut to play in. It was made for a child, so if you're still childish enough to want it, you can damn well share it with Jeremy."

"But he didn't ask me if he could go in there . . . he should, if it's mine."

"It's part of Charnfield, Hugo, and this is Jeremy's home. He was born here; well christened here, anyway. And the place is more his than yours. Kindly remember that."

"But I'm older," Hugo protested.

"I'm not going to argue with you, Hugo. Go up to the nursery now and tell Jeremy you're sorry and I think you'll find he'll apologize to you for spoiling your drawing. Whether he does or not, I'm not going to have you boys fighting nor any bullying on your part. So you can make it up and shake hands and damn well get on together from now on. As the older . . . . boy you ought to be helping Jeremy now and . . . showing him things and setting

124

him a good example, not throwing your weight about like some school bully."

Hugo was outraged by this last remark. His tear-stained eyes blazed with fury. "I'm not a bully, Uncle Richard. That's unfair."

"I'm not going to argue any more. Just go now, will you, Hugo. Go upstairs and make it up with your stepbrother. Go on."

Boiling inside with a sense of injustice and smarting under the lash of Richard's words, Hugo left the library and went up to the nursery wing. Here, the sound of voices shouting against the noise of splashing and running water told him that Jeremy was having his bath. He went straight up to the bathroom door, opened it without knocking and walked into a steamy haze where Nanny was in the act of hauling Jeremy out of his bath to dry him.

Hugo stood in the doorway. "I've come to say I'm sorry," he said mechanically, "if I was too rough when I chucked Jeremy out of the hut this afternoon."

Nanny grasped the situation quickly. "There," she said to Jeremy, "now what have you got to say to Hugo?"

She had Jeremy on her knee now, wrapped in his bath towel. After a couple of jerks to prompt him, Jeremy, who had been carefully rehearsed, said equally mechanically and without feeling, "I'm sorry I messed up your drawing."

"And what else?" Nanny asked.

Jeremy pondered, then said, " . . . and went into the hut without asking . . . you."

"That's right," said Nanny. "Now I'm sure you and Hugo are going to be friends and not quarrel any more."

Jeremy had lost interest and was trying to bend down and fish a toy duck out of the bath.

Hugo said nothing, but turned on his heel and left the bathroom. As there was a short time before dinner, he went to look for Celia and found her still outside in the rose garden. He was anxious to tell her that he had made it up with Jeremy.

"Aunt Celia. I told Jeremy I was sorry."

"Good boy," said Celia and rewarded him with a hug and a kiss. "Now come and help me. You can take these and snip off all those dead ones while I tie this one up . . ."

Hugo took the secateurs and started dead-heading a bush of crimson roses that was past its prime. He worked thoughtfully, until he asked suddenly, "Why did Uncle Richard say this place is more Jeremy's home than mine?"

Celia's heart missed a beat and a sick feeling hit her stomach. This was a moment she had been dreading for some time. In fact she had discussed the problem more than once with Richard over the six years since Jeremy was born. They both knew that, sooner or later, Hugo would come to realize the truth about his position and be forced to face up to the fact that, one day in the not too distant future, Jeremy would inherit Charnfield: every acre of the estate, the park, the house and its treasures, the baronetcy, everything. Hugo, the orphan child, would then have no right of residence, no claim on the place that had been his home ever since he could remember and which he loved with all his heart.

Before she could start to answer Hugo's question, the dressing gong sounded in the house. This was not the time for a serious talk with Hugo now and she must put off the long and painful explanation about Jeremy and the future.

"Oh, I think he just meant that Jeremy is his own son and you are his stepson, that's all. Of course, you live here, you both do. Only your father . . . didn't live here, that's all." – 'Coward!' she thought to herself, before adding "Come on, we must go in and change, the gong's gone."

As the sun went down behind the downs Hugo walked back from the rose garden to the house with Celia, through the hall and up to his room to put on his dinner jacket and black tie.

The evening light was ebbing from the room and Celia's words had left him feeling cold and depressed. The way she had spoken to him had seemed as if she was avoiding his question, as if he didn't matter enough to be talked to honestly, and this made him feel sorry for himself. It was almost as though he no longer belonged anywhere, as though he was just a stranger who happened to have dropped in for dinner, an uninvited guest . . . an outsider. As he carefully tied his black bow tie and brushed his wavy, fair hair, he noticed his reflection in the mirror on his dressing-table, and the sight lifted his spirits. He turned his head from side to side, pushed a lock of hair back over his forehead and began to count the days until it would be time to go back to school.

BY the time Hugo was in his fourth year at Eton and had long since become an 'upper' – which meant no more fagging and time to develop a number of spare-time activities – Jeremy was seven and within sight of being sent away, in his turn, to boarding-school. For reasons of which only Celia was aware, Richard had decided against Stanborough House and had put Jeremy's name down for Upton Court, a smaller prep school near Salisbury.

By the summer of 1930, while Jeremy was having lessons, as Hugo had, from an older and slightly deaf Miss Bryant, Hugo's voice had broken and, although only fifteen, he was singing tenor in Whittle's House Quartet competing for the annual cup. Being rather too frail for competitive rowing and not caring at all for cricket, Hugo was in the habit of spending his Saturday afternoons on the river, gently paddling up to Queen's Eyot for tea with his friend Paley. He never missed a concert in School Hall or an organ recital in College Chapel and his Thursday evenings were spent as a member of the Eton College Fine Arts Society, attending lectures and reading papers on an assortment of subjects from early Byzantine architecture to Renaissance painting. He was also designing, in collaboration with the Arts Master, the settings for a production of Molière's *Le Bourgeois Gentilhomme* to be given in Upper School during the following Half. He had never been gregarious enough, nor fond enough of the ebulliently hearty, games-playing, orthodox kind of boys among his contemporaries, to be elected to Pop. Nor was he considered likely to make it to Sixth Form. But he was an above-average Etonian, leaning strongly to the academic and the aesthetic world, and it seemed to his House Tutor that he was ideal Oxford material with an eventual career in Teaching, the Arts or the Diplomatic Service.

DURING the summer holidays Hugo and Jeremy found a new companionship that was born mainly out of Jeremy's anxiety about going away to boarding-school and the need to learn all he could about it from his elder stepbrother.

Hugo, for his part, found Jeremy a little more sensible, less of a rowdy, noisy, cheeky little boy, a step nearer to his own maturity and more pliable than before.

The nursery at Charnfield had become a schoolroom now but Nanny remained in residence to help Mrs Saunders around the house, to pack Jeremy's school trunk and to live out her retirement making herself useful at Charnfield.

127

One wet summer afternoon in August Jeremy was on his stomach on the schoolroom floor, playing with an elaborate fortress he had been given for his birthday. He already possessed a large army of tanks, guns, soldiers, Red Indians and a couple of Sopwith Pup fighter aeroplanes. A big battle was being lined up and Jeremy, who had a distinct *penchant* for military matters and perused countless picture books about armies and navies at war, was planning the forthcoming battle like a kind of god-like supreme commander.

Richard and Celia were away in London for a few days and Hugo had earlier suggested to Jeremy that, in their parents' absence, he should take him on a conducted tour of the house to show and explain to him some of the pictures and furniture, vases and sculpture in the Long Gallery and elsewhere.

Jeremy had forgotten this plan until Hugo came to find him after lunch in the schoolroom.

"You needn't, if you don't want to," Hugo said, anxious not to force things.

But Jeremy was keen to agree to anything Hugo suggested during his last few weeks of freedom before incarceration at Upton Court. So he got off the floor, leaving his widely-scattered soldiers, guns and tanks. "It's all right," he said, "I'll make them fight a battle after tea." Willingly he followed Hugo out of the room.

Ten minutes later the two boys were standing in front of a large oil painting at one end of the dining-room. It was a portrait of an early Lady Cardwell by Sir Peter Lely.

"That lady," Hugo explained, "was the wife of Uncle Richard's ancestor, the third Baronet. He was called Sir Francis Cardwell and he fought in the Civil War. He raised a regiment of cavalry here at Charnfield and they took part in the battle of Naseby."

"Gosh!" said the future eighth Baronet who liked the sound of that. Battles and cavalry were very much in his line.

Then Hugo took him into the Long Gallery and, standing him in front of a priceless Ming Dynasty Vase in a glass case, explained that the vase was Chinese and 500 years old and worth thousands of pounds. That was why it was in a glass case, so that no one would break it, dusting it. "Isn't it a lovely colour?" he finished.

And Jeremy said, "Gosh" again.

128

Hugo went on: "Now I'll tell you all about the Ming Dynasty. They were the rulers of China in the fifteenth century . . ."

But Jeremy was bored and, suddenly yearning to get back to his toy soldiers, he started to walk away.

Hugo, carried away by his own enthusiasm, was surprised by this reaction, and called after him "Oh, well, if you're not interested, I won't waste my breath."

"I want to play with my soldiers," whined Jeremy.

"All right," said Hugo, "go and play with them. I'm staying here for a bit. I want to read about the bronze fifteenth century Italian coins in that other case. There's a book about them in the shelf by the fireplace . . . they're by Pisanello who . . ."

But Jeremy was already on his way back to the schoolroom, while Hugo was left alone in the dark, musty-smelling, fascinating long gallery. Exasperation made him think how stupid and ignorant Jeremy was going to be when he grew up, until his thoughts returned to antiquity and the pleasure of living surrounded by the history and treasures of Charnfield.

8

BOARDING-school evidently suited Jeremy. His happy letters from Upton Court, where he had a number of friends and became Captain of the Junior Football Eleven, pleased Richard who yearned for his son and heir to be a tough and healthy outdoor boy with a love of sport and adventure. It was a great relief that he showed no signs of becoming an effeminate, bookish creature like Hugo, who by now knew more about Charnfield and its history than he knew himself.

Celia, too, was relieved that her son was settling down at his prep school, but her thoughts and sympathies were more often with Hugo, for whom she retained deep, unspoken feelings, loving him for his physical beauty, because she found him an interesting, sensitive boy and because he seemed to be rather a sad figure. Unhappily, she could foresee difficult days ahead for him. There was another reason why Celia cared for Hugo. In the last few years Richard had become noticeably more irritable and bad-tempered. He was getting on for fifty now, his thigh was still giving him pain and, in common with almost everybody else just then, he was beset by financial worries. He had lost quite a lot of money in American stocks and shares at the time of the 1929 Wall Street crash and, like many of Britain's country landowners, had been forced to economize and make substantial savings. In Richard's case this had been achieved only by getting rid of the London flat, laying off his footman and one of the under-housemaids and by dismissing or retiring early some of the older estate people who had served his father before him.

Celia sympathised deeply with her husband's troubles but they did not make him easy to live with. Hugo's pleasant, articulate manner was all the more attractive by contrast with her husband's increasing irascibility.

One August afternoon during the summer holidays of 1932 the relationship between Hugo and his stepfather came to a head through yet another incident that took place down by the lake.

Hugo, who was now seventeen, had just left Eton after easily passing into Oxford, where a place was reserved for him in the following spring at New College. He was to read English and History. To fill in the gap before going up to University, Mr Whittle, his Eton housemaster, had recommended – and Hugo's guardian, Richard, had agreed – that he should spend six months with a German family of his acquaintance in Munich, people called von Graetz, who took in English boys and girls *en pension* to learn German and study the arts. It would be a perfect solution for the Hugo problem, Richard considered, to get the boy away on his own for a time, away from Charnfield and away from Jeremy. It would be a chance for him to practice self-reliance and to widen his horizons. Hugo himself was delighted by the plan and excited by the prospect of living in a foreign country where, apart from the chance to learn German, there were museums, art galleries and the opera to be visited.

Hugo now had a portable gramophone which closed up like a small suitcase, and a collection of classical records. He had discovered Wagner, Richard Strauss and Sibelius, *Finlandia* in particular rousing him to wild flights of fancy.

That afternoon the two boys had decided to spend the afternoon at the hut, which they now shared without argument. Here Hugo would be happy to play his records of *Lohengrin* while studying the libretto and Jeremy would mess about in the woods or try to catch minnows in the lake.

Hugo settled down to his idyllic afternoon of Wagner under the trees beside the hut while Jeremy, who was wearing his gumboots, went off on his own. A small rowing boat, which was full of water from recent rain, was tied up by a delapidated boathouse on the far side of the lake, and Jeremy, without telling Hugo, intended to take it out. Hugo wound up the gramophone to carry it through the next important passage and was at the point in Act One when Elsa and the Chorus are singing *fortissimo*, as Lohengrin appears in his boat, drawn by a swan. Despite the loud music Hugo became gradually aware of another sound competing with the Wagner. A high, shrill cry was echoing around the woods across the lake. Hugo lifted the gramophone head from the record and listened, his heart beating. The

131

shouting and the sound of splashing water were not far away. He jumped up and ran to the edge of the lake, following the direction of the sound. Looking to his left, he saw that the rowing boat had capsized some way out and was upside down in the water. Clutching frantically at its slippery, scum-covered hull was a small hand. Now he could see Jeremy's head, bobbing up and down in the water, his cries becoming weaker as he fought to keep afloat.

Hugo took a deep breath and shouted "Help!" twice, as loudly as he could, but his voice echoed through the trees and, as he expected, nobody came. Shaking with terror but driven by every instinct to save his stepbrother, he dashed to the water's edge, tore off his tennis shoes and scrambled through the thick weeds into the lake. Jeremy and the sinking boat had drifted well out in the middle now. The water felt cold but Hugo was a good swimmer and as soon as he was clear of the shallow edge and through the weeds, he plunged forward into the slimy water and struck out. It was an effort to swim in a shirt and flannel trousers and he was tired before he was within striking distance of Jeremy and the overturned boat.

While he was still some way off, he summoned what voice he could to call out to Jeremy, who was thrashing about in a frenzy, trying to clutch the boat's keel. "Tread . . . water, if you can . . . Jeremy . . . can you hear me? . . . tread water . . ."

Jeremy's head was still visible, just above the water but only just, and, as Hugo gradually closed in on him, he saw it might be difficult to get hold of the small wriggling body and hold it up clear of the water. With a final, desperate effort Hugo thrashed forward to grasp Jeremy by one arm. His attempt to turn the boy round in the water and take his other arm caused such a splashing that Hugo momentarily went under, losing sight of him. Underwater, visibility was green, thick and murky and Hugo could see nothing. Then something struck his back so that he spun round as he surfaced. It was Jeremy's body, floating close beside him, face downwards. Treading water vigorously, Hugo seized hold of Jeremy once more and raised his head into the air. The boy's face was sheet white and his eyes were closed. Slimy lake water was pouring from his nostrils. At this moment by some miracle Hugo's life-saving drill now came back to him, all that he'd been taught in the open-air pool at Stanborough House. With a great effort he rolled the heavy, inert little body on its

132

back, grasping it under the armpits. Then, lying back in the water, he started to swim backstroke by thrashing with his legs, at the same time keeping Jeremy's head clear of the surface.

Suddenly, in spite of the water lapping in his ears, he became aware of a new sound coming from somewhere behind him.

"I'm 'ere!" A man was standing on the bank shouting at the top of his voice. "Grab the rope, Master Hugo . . . 'ere, catch it and 'ang on to it."

They were a little nearer the bank now but Hugo's strength was deserting him. His legs were ceasing to function and he kept going only with difficulty, knowing that he must get Jeremy ashore somehow, as quickly as possible. It might be too late by now, for Jeremy's lungs must be full of water.

"Grab the rope, Master Hugo. By your right hand there." The voice from the shore was nearer now.

Hugo let go of Jeremy with one arm and seized a rope end that was slowly floating past him in the water. "Grab it and 'ang on tight and I'll pull you in." Although Hugo could not turn in the water and see who was shouting at him, he recognized the voice. It was Jim Cooper. Hugo grabbed the rope and held it tightly with one hand, Jeremy's limp form with the other. The rope was wet and slimy and almost slipped from his grasp but he managed to keep hold of it until he and Jeremy were finally hauled ashore by Jim. Like a couple of landed fish they slithered through the reeds onto the mud where Jim was able to lift them bodily from the water.

Hugo rolled over, panting and puffing on the grassy bank, scarcely able to breathe, let alone speak. He was dizzy and faint from his efforts and on the verge of collapse. But Jim Cooper knew what he had to do first. Quickly rolling Jeremy over onto his stomach, he knelt down and urgently pumped at the younger boy's lungs, working them furiously up and down with all his strength until some lake water began to flow from his mouth, mingled with vomit. The boy was in obvious distress; it was touch and go and Jim Cooper knew it. After a while, when no more water came out, he stopped and saw to his relief that Jeremy was still breathing, although only gurgling weakly. He let him lie still for a moment and turned his attention to the older boy.

Hugo had recovered enough now to be able to gasp weakly "The boat went over; Jeremy couldn't swim when his boots filled with water . . . Is he all right?"

"He'll be all right, Master Hugo. Lucky thing I come when I did."

Hugo nodded, still desperately short of breath.

"Just lay there, the pair of you, while I go and get help," Jim said. "Don't try and get up, just stop there and rest. Shan't be a tick."

Jim hurried off along the path towards the house, leaving the two boys stretched out on the grass beside the lake, sodden and exhausted.

After a few moments Jeremy recovered a bit and began to sob and whimper.

"You're all right now, Jem. Cheer up. Someone'll come soon and take us home."

JIM ran all the way back to the house. He made instinctively for the servants' rear area. He was frantically ringing the back door bell and shouting to attract someone's attention when Page appeared in his shirt-sleeves, disturbed from his afternoon siesta.

"Come quickly, Mr Page," Jim gasped, very out of breath, "there's been an accident, down by the lake. It's Master Hugo and Master Jeremy, both been in the water, but they're all right. Get Sir Richard."

Page informed him that Sir Richard and her ladyship had motored over to Salisbury and were not expected until after tea.

"Then come down quickly and give me a hand with the young 'uns. They're both half-drownded," Jim said, "and that weak, the pair of 'em, they'll not get home on their two pins. Have to be carried, I reckon."

Abandoning any further hope of an afternoon nap, the butler took immediate charge. First he went to find Mrs Walcot in the kitchen and tell her what had happened, advising her to warn Nanny to be ready for Mister Hugo and Master Jeremy as soon as they could be carried back to the house. Minutes later the two men were at the lakeside where they picked up the two prostrate boys off the grass beside the path, Page humping Jeremy across his back and Jim assisting Hugo, who was just able to walk along slowly, hanging on to Jim's arm for support.

As they walked, Jim told Page how he had been clearing undergrowth and collecting firewood not far from the hut. Hearing Jeremy's cries and the splashing of water, followed by Hugo's shout for help, he had thrown down his sickle and run through the woods to the spot, taking the rope he had with him to tie up the wood. "Give me a turn, seeing that boat upside down and the young gentlemen in the water."

It was shortly after three by the time Page and Jim had delivered the boys, soaking wet and exhausted, to Nanny who instantly hustled Jeremy up to the nursery for a hot bath, a good rub down, hot Bovril and bed. Hugo also had a hot bath and after changing into dry clothes, he had tea with Nanny and Jeremy. Then he went to his room to read. At about four o'clock when he heard the car drive up and voices, he closed his book and went downstairs, feeling it was his duty, as the older boy, to report the incident to Uncle Richard and Aunt Celia immediately on their return.

"HOW dare you allow Jeremy to take out a leaking boat by himself? What in God's name do you think you were doing?"

Hugo was staring at the library wall past Richard's head, smouldering once again with a sense of outrageous injustice. At first he remained silent, refusing to look his stepfather in the face.

Richard persisted, "Well? Are you going to answer me?"

Hugo took a deep breath, more like a sigh of exasperated resignation, and said, "I was in the hut, Uncle Richard, playing records on my gramophone. I didn't even know Jeremy was going to take the boat out. He never said he was. I thought he was just baling the water out of it."

"That's no excuse. It was thoroughly careless and irresponsible. You ought to know better at your age."

Celia had been listening to the conversation with mounting alarm. Now she was driven by anger to put in a word. "I do think you're being rather unfair, Richard; Hugo probably saved Jeremy's life."

"Jim Cooper saved Jeremy's life," said Richard sourly.

That was too much for Celia. She turned on her heel without a word and walked out of the library, slamming the door behind her.

Perhaps this gesture of angry defiance made Richard see a little of his injustice, for he appeared suddenly to relent. When he spoke again, his voice was softer, less tense. "I dare say you did the sensible thing, Hugo. But if Jim hadn't come with his rope . . . you might both have drowned."

This fell well short of the praise and gratitude that Hugo felt he was entitled to, and he was still trembling with inner fury

135

when he looked Richard in the eye to say "It wouldn't have mattered a damn to anyone if *I'd* drowned, would it? I don't really belong here." With that, he walked out of the Library too, but unlike Celia he did not slam the door; he went out quietly and with dignity, closing the door behind him gently.

Then he went upstairs to his room and fell on his bed, sobbing his heart out. All the pent-up horror of his nightmarish experience in the lake two hours earlier came flooding back, but he wept not only from relief after a long period of danger and intense fear; he wept also at the greater predicament of his whole life at Charnfield. He cried bitter tears of self-pity and anger at the awful realization that had dominated his thoughts and coloured every moment of every day lately, both at school and in the holidays. It was envy of Jeremy's future ownership of the place he loved, the home in which he had grown up and which he had known all his conscious life; the home that he would lose and which in years to come, when Uncle Richard was dead and gone, would never be his. Never.

AFTER a while, feeling a bit better, Hugo stopped weeping. He pulled himself together, brushed away his tears and lay on his back, staring up at the ceiling. The low, setting sun was still bright on the horizon, turning the ceiling of his room into a vivid crimson, broken up by the mottled pattern of tree branches moving gently in the light breeze. The Charnfield church clock struck six and Hugo realized he had been lying on his bed for almost two hours. Now, as the last stroke of six died away on the evening breeze, he felt a strong urge to get away, out of the house, into the fresh air, somewhere private where he could be alone for a while and brood. He had already changed into a dry shirt, trousers and a pullover. He now put on his tennis shoes and, anxious not to encounter anyone, especially not Uncle Richard, he left his room quietly, tiptoed downstairs, moved stealthily across the hall and crept out into the garden by the French windows in the dining-room.

Making sure that he was unobserved, Hugo made his way out onto the terrace, through the shrubbery and down the path that led to the lake. Within minutes, he was inside the hut, winding up his gramophone. The *Lohengrin* record was still on the turn-table where he had left it, so he started it up again, and as the turn-table started to revolve, he lowered the arm gently onto the record, careful not to scratch it. Then he sat down on the grass outside the hut and gazed up into the trees and away across the lake, while the glorious, powerful voice of Lauritz Melchior as Lohengrin reverberated and echoed round the water. He closed his eyes and once more imagined Lohengrin gliding through the smooth water in his boat drawn by a swan. He was able for a time to forget the nightmare that had overtaken him a few hours earlier out there across the water beside another, upturned boat.

As he listened attentively to Wagner's music, Hugo experienced mixed feelings of gloom and depression, anxiety and excitement. With only a week or so left of the summer holidays, he was about to go abroad on his own for the first time. When Jeremy went back to Upton Court in September, he would not be returning to Eton. That chapter of his life was over. All his contemporaries there, those who were staying on to be in next year's cricket Eleven, the rowing Eight or Sixth Form, would be making their way down the Great West Road or by train or Green Line coach to Windsor and school again. He quite hoped he would be missed by some of the boys with whom he had made a distinct conquest, especially a boy called Ryder whose mother was an actress. Simon Ryder had written Hugo a passionate love poem with a signed photograph of himself and left them in his room on the last day of the preceding half. Hugo was pleased and touched by this gesture of abnormal affection but by no means disturbed by it. He was a school beauty and he knew it. He had 'fans' like a movie star.

In spite of his social success at Eton, Hugo was glad to be leaving now. He felt pleasantly superior to all those boys and masters who had so admired his good looks, for he was going abroad, to Germany, to Munich, to the land of Wagner where he would live with a German family and learn to speak the language fluently, to converse in German. He would go out to restaurants and shops in Munich and to the opera and to concerts and Art Galleries and absorb European culture. That was really living, not hanging about Eton looking ridiculous in a tail coat and top-hat, to be gawked at and photographed by American tourists. By the time he had relaxed with *Lohengrin* and followed through his own train of thought, he felt much better and even stronger and more adult than he had ever felt before.

At dinner that evening nothing more was said about the boating accident on the lake and Richard, although rather

137

quieter than usual, was evidently making an effort to be nice to Hugo.

Celia mentioned the von Graetz family in Munich.

"Odd to think I was in the trenches shooting at those people thirteen years ago and being shot at by them. Now Hugo's going off to live with a Hun family. Extraordinary," Richard said without emotion.

Hugo smiled. "I don't feel any hatred towards them at all. I suppose I should, considering they killed my father and wounded my stepfather. But I don't. Hope you don't mind, Uncle Richard."

"Doesn't worry me," said Richard charitably. "War is war. And it's been over thirteen years, that's the point."

"You were only three when it ended," Celia remarked to Hugo with a warm, friendly smile.

Richard added, with just a suspicion of nostalgia in his voice, "When your mother and I got back from London after the Armistice, Nanny told us you'd kicked up a hell of a hullabaloo in the nursery when they let off the fireworks in the park. Screamed your head off."

"How clever of you to remember that, darling," Celia said.

"Not really." Richard sipped his claret thoughtfully. "Seems like yesterday sometimes."

There was a silence.

Then Hugo said, "By the way, have Thomas Cook's sent my tickets through yet?"

"Should come this week," Richard assured him. "You're going by the cross-channel boat from Folkestone to Ostend."

"So I gather."

"Then by train across Belgium to Cologne and down the Rhine into Bavaria. Should be an interesting journey."

"Sounds wonderful." Hugo was genuinely excited.

Celia began: "I understand the von Graetz son speaks good English . . ."

"Dieter . . . " Hugo interjected; "that's his first name. Yes. Whittle told me; and the mother speaks a bit too, but not the Baron . . . not a single word apparently."

"Then you'll get plenty of practice at meals, won't you, darling?" Celia said, getting up from the table. "Shall we move?"

Hugo got up to follow, as was his usual habit. But to his surprise his stepfather interrupted them.

"Like a glass of port, Hugo?" he asked.

Celia had been enjoying her last evenings with Hugo, before the months began when she would have to sit on her own in the hall, while Richard stayed on and on over his port. She threw down the gauntlet, asking Hugo, "Do you?"

Hugo was caught between two fires. He did not answer at once, so Celia went on, a touch sarcastically, "I don't mind; I shall go upstairs and get on with some letters."

"A glass of port won't kill you, Hugo," Richard said acidly. "Most normal boys enjoy a glass when they've left Eton. My father gave me my first glass while I was still there."

"I don't really like it all that much, Uncle Richard," Hugo said, "so, if you don't mind, I think I'll go and keep Aunt Celia company."

Richard went white in the face and slammed his fist down on the table, shouting at Hugo "You'll stay here and have a glass of port!"

There was a terrible silence. Hugo stood immobile, rooted to the spot.

Celia glared at her husband. Then she said quietly to Hugo "It's for you to decide. You're grown-up now."

"I really don't want a glass of port, thank you, Uncle Richard, so I'll go with Aunt Celia." Hugo's voice was quiet but firm.

Richard made no reply but sat at the table with his head bowed. Celia left the room and Hugo followed, closing the door.

As soon as they had gone, Richard reached out for the decanter and poured himself a glass, his hand shaking uncontrollably. He swallowed it quickly and poured himself another.

IT had been arranged for Hugo to spend two or three days in London with his grandmother before leaving for Germany. He would take his luggage with him, stay in her flat for a few days and catch the Victoria boat train on September 19th from Artillery Mansions nearby. Lady Brandon, now in her eightieth year, had been looking forward to his visit. She had always been deeply fond of the boy and they had much in common. Ever since he had first stayed with her as a child, shortly after Rosie's death in 1920, she had enjoyed his company and this affection for her grandson was more than reciprocated. To Hugo, Granny Brandon represented another world, another life: a life

139

of London, theatres, big shops, museums and grown-up conversation. For this coming visit she had reserved seats for a concert at the Queen's Hall to hear Dr Felix Weingartner conduct the London Symphony Orchestra, and for a new play, *Musical Chairs*, at the Criterion.

It came, therefore, as a cruel shock and a bitter disappointment for Hugo when, a few days after the incident at the lake, Celia broke the news to him that Granny Brandon had been taken ill with pneumonia and was in a nursing home in Harley Street. She had also suffered a fall in her flat and broken her hip.

Although Richard did not make too much of it, he was alarmed. At Edith's age, double pneumonia was dangerous. Richard, too, was especially fond of Edith Brandon with whom he had always kept in close touch since Rosie's death.

Immediately after Edith's maid had telephoned him at Charnfield with the news of her employer's illness and Lord Brandon's nephew, Hugh, had also rung to tell him, Richard caught the first available train to London to see his ailing mother-in-law in the nursing home.

Here, with Richard at her bedside, the old lady, who now looked shockingly thinner and frailler than in recent months, could just summon enough breath to speak to him in a weak, husky voice. Painfully she instructed him to go to her flat and collect the tickets for the concert and the play, so that Hugo would not be disappointed.

Richard promised to get the tickets, urged her to lie still and obey the doctors and kissed her goodbye on her wrinkled forehead. Outside in the corridor the Sister seemed unwilling to forecast any rapid recovery. On the contrary, she was plainly not hopeful that Lady Brandon had the strength to fight on very much longer.

At the flat in Artillery Mansions Richard found Carter upset but philosophical. "I reckon her ladyship's had a lot of sadness lately, sir, but it's not been all bad. She looks forward to her visits to Charnfield and to treating Master Hugo when he comes to stay with her. Shame about this time."

In view of his grandmother's illness, it was arranged that Celia would go to London with Hugo, spend the three days with him in a hotel and see him off to Germany on the 19th from Victoria. Celia had seemed to Richard genuinely delighted with the plan. Indeed, the prospect of spending three days in London with

140

Hugo, where she would have this astonishingly good-looking young man on her arm, go with him to a concert and a play and have him to herself for all that time, made her pulse quicken. It would be a break for her, away from Charnfield, away from her husband who was not proving easy to live with these days.

Richard was hardly aware of it himself but every day he was sounding more and more disapproving of Hugo and of his wife's obvious *penchant* for his effeminate stepson. The two of them seemed to him to be constantly chattering and laughing, going for long walks or working in the garden together. He felt shut out, uneasy. Could it be that he was becoming jealous, imagining that Celia saw in Hugo a lover, a young man of beauty and charm to whom she could, might lose her heart? No. It was ridiculous, he told himself. Celia was twice Hugo's age. It was unthinkable. At any rate, Hugo was not a man at all. He was more like a girl. And Celia was turning him into a pansy, encouraging him to spend his time studying old prints and flowers and furniture and music and talking to him at meals about dress fabrics and wall papers. Since that Christmas when he was thirteen, the boy had never once been out with a gun to shoot a pigeon or a rabbit on the place; he couldn't fish and he hated the outdoor life. He was a wet, girlish, precious dandy and Celia was encouraging it.

All the same, Richard was not anxious to have a row with her about Hugo before the boy went off to Germany. He resolved to keep his thoughts to himself. Hugo might change out there in Munich, in a strange city with new interests and different people. He would certainly be away from Celia's feminine influence. Perhaps the von Graetz daughter would make a man of him. He'd heard there was a girl there, Helga, aged nineteen and very attractive. Then he thought 'Why should I worry about Hugo? As long as Jeremy turns out all right, marries and has a son, the family will be all right.' He must make sure that Celia didn't make a sissy of him. He would get out Hugo's old 4.10 gun next autumn, pass it on to Jem, start him shooting, teach him to cast a fly for a trout. 'Let's hope by the time he succeeds to Charnfield there'll be an estate to shoot over, some fish in the river and enough money to mend the roof. Well, that'll be his worry, not mine,' Richard mused. 'I'll be under the sod by then.'

ON the morning that Celia and Hugo left for London Richard gave his stepson £25 spending money in German marks and wished him a pleasant time in Munich, hoped he would benefit from the experience, learn German throughly and enjoy himself at the same time. Hugo shook hands rather formally with his stepfather and promised to write.

Celia told her husband, as they got into the car, that she and Hugo would telephone the nursing home as soon as they reached London and go to see Granny Brandon together before Hugo left for abroad.

Hugo had not seen his grandmother for some time and the sight of her lying in bed, frail, thin and hardly able to speak, stabbed him to the heart. He looked at her through moist eyes, thinking of all the fun he'd had with her in his short life: the jaunts to museums and theatres, the teas at Gunter's, the shopping sprees and ice cream sodas in Selfridge's, and then the long talks in her flat when she had expounded to him her views on such subjects as life and death and sorrow and happiness. To see this wonderful figure in his life, his grandmother whom he adored, reduced to a thin, weak little bundle lying on a sick bed was deeply upsetting.

Hugo left the nursing home fighting back tears, which he managed to contain until he and Celia were half way down in the lift to the entrance. In the taxi back to Brown's Hotel, where they were staying, Celia had to put her arms round him and comfort him like a distressed child, and she found the experience far from disagreable. All her maternal instincts of gentle care and concern were mingled with her hidden longing for close, physical contact with a young, handsome male. She was moved and excited at the same time. Hugo, although not her son, seemed to her at times exactly like an older brother to Jeremy. And yet her feelings for her own son were totally different. For one thing he was only ten and very much his father's boy. Hugo was more than a stepson; he was a friend and, she had to admit to herself, someone whose company she found exciting.

The concert at the Queen's Hall was a wonderful experience and Celia noticed Hugo's expression of near-ecstasy as he listened with deep concentration to the glorious music. In the interval Hugo talked to her about Brahms, and Weber whose *Freischutz* overture had opened the programme.

They spent the second day at the National Gallery where again

Hugo was able to talk knowledgeably and intelligently about the pictures.

"This Rubens," he said at one point, "is thought to have been painted about the same time as the one at Charnfield, but it's nothing like such a good one as ours. And there's a lead-pencil drawing by Ingres I want to see, because it's very like the one in the Long Gallery at home."

On the last night before Hugo's departure, they went to see *Musical Chairs* by Ronald Mackenzie, which they found interesting and moving. In it, the elder son of a family living in the Rumanian oil fields was depicted as a sharply witty but sensitive and musically gifted but rather misunderstood young man with whom Hugo could easily identify. The part was beautifully played by John Gielgud and when, after Joseph's death towards the end of the play, his father gently closed the lid of his piano, Hugo was shattered by emotion and hardly able to leave his seat.

WHEN the dreaded moment came the next day for Celia to say goodbye to Hugo at Victoria Station she felt an empty, aching void which remained with her all the way back to Charnfield and for some days afterwards. She was reminded of that depressing, gloomy evening nine years earlier when Hugo had first gone to Stanborough House, leaving his toy dog, Pip, guarding his bed in the night nursery. It had not been the same when Jeremy went to Upton Court. He was tough, confident and eager to go. She knew that he would be all right. He was not sensitive or vulnerable like Hugo.

Now, it was not only the pain of parting from him that hurt. It was also the cold realization that he would not be at home for months to come, and that the only adult she could really talk to and enjoy being with in an easy, intimate relationship was gone.

She and Richard were mentally drifting away from each other. He was spending more and more of his time in his study or around the estate, brooding, worrying, lapsing into silences at meals, unwilling to open up and let her share his problems and worries. She had become almost a stranger in the place and it hurt her.

At nine Jeremy was already quite a handful. He was a short, stocky and physically strong boy with Celia's colouring. Otherwise he was not in the least like her. He was inclined to be lazy and arrogant, was often disobedient and not noticeably

143

brainy. She tried her best to get on close terms with him, to build the kind of relationship of trust and companionship she had enjoyed with Hugo, but it was an uphill struggle. During the holidays from Upton Court, when his reports indicated a preference for games over work, Jeremy spent much of his time with Jarrot, the keeper, walking through the woods around the place, shooting rabbits and pigeons with the small 4.10 gun, originally bought for Hugo. Sometimes he would go to the lake hut and play with his Hornby train set, making the model engines and rolling stock tear much too fast around an elaborate network of lines, sidings, junctions and points, until the inevitable derailment, when Jem would curse Hamleys for making rotten toys. On occasions Richard would take him fishing or in the car to visit one of the farms or into Dorchester to the bank and allow him to take the wheel of the two-seater once inside the lodge gates.

One morning at school during the Michaelmas term Jeremy received at breakfast in the dining hall a letter bearing a German postmark. The stamp was quickly sold to a boy across the table who was a collector. The price was the boy's fishcakes over the next three Friday breakfasts. Tearing open the envelope, Jeremy was surprised to find inside a postcard of the twin-turreted Frauenkirche, Munich's famous cathedral on the Frauenplatz, and an accompanying letter from Hugo, which he stuffed into his blazer pocket to read in private, away from the prying eyes of other boys.

In the event Jeremy read it in the lavatory, feeling rather like a spy reading some secret document in a John Buchan thriller.

> Munchen (Bayern)
> Kaiserstrasse, 23
> Sept. 29th, 1932
>
> Dear Jem,
> Well, here I am in Hunland and having a v. good and v. interesting time. The von Graetzes are terribly nice and kind and make one feel very welcome. I work in the mornings at German with Frau von G, usually in the garden if it's fine, and in the afternoons we play tennis or bathe or go to see a church or a museum. Tomorrow night we are all going to the opera – the Baron, Frau v G, Dieter, Helga and me – to see Julius Patzak sing Walther in *Die Meistersinger*. As you know how potty I am about Wagner, you can imagine how excited I am. How is everything at home? I had a letter from Aunt Celia who told me you

144

won the 100 yards in the sports at Upton Court and that you have turned my lake hut (only teasing) into Waterloo Station with trains all over the place. I'll have to sort your timetables out when I get home for Christmas. Tell Nanny I'll try to write to her, if I get a moment.

Aufwiedersehen. Love Hugo

Jeremy would probably not have bothered to reply to Hugo's letter had not Celia insisted on it a few days later when she and Richard came down to watch him play in a football match and he showed it to her.

"What a lovely letter. He sounds so happy. You must answer it."

"But there's nothing to tell him."

"Of course there is. Tell him what you've been doing, all about catching that trout with Daddy at half-term, and the jay you shot in the woods . . ."

"He doesn't like shooting."

"It doesn't matter, Jeremy, he's your stepbrother and he's taken the trouble to write to you, so you must write to him."

"Oh, all right."

So Jeremy sat down one wet afternoon soon after and wrote

Dear Hugo,

Thanks for your letter and card. You seem to be having fun. Daddy showed me where Munich is in the Atlas, so I know where you are. I shot three rabbits and a jay at Half-Term and the parents came down for our match against Halbury Hill and I got a goal.

Love, Jem

Hugo also wrote home regularly, dutifully prefacing the address with Richard's title, although what he said was intended mainly for Celia and, in any case, he doubted if his stepfather was much interested in what he had to say.

Indeed, when one of his letters arrived one morning, Richard recognized the writing and stamp and handed it immediately to his wife.

"Letter for you, darling. German stamp with President Hindenburg on it."

"Oh. thanks." Celia's heart leaped as she took the envelope. "From Hugo," she muttered, happily tearing it open.

Richard did not stay to hear Hugo's latest news but went off

145

to his study and Celia took the letter upstairs and sat on her bed to read it alone.

Dear Uncle Richard and Aunt Celia,

You may be glad to hear that most of my time is now taken up with German lessons, and with going to concerts and the opera and ice skating. There is a wonderful ice rink here and Helga and Dieter and I go twice a week. I am getting quite good now, thanks to Helga who is excellent and tries to teach me. I can do an outside edge – very wobbly – and will soon attempt an inside edge. We waltz together too but she does most of the work! I should not boast about it but Helga has fallen in love with me. She keeps writing romantic poems and little messages to me and putting them under my pillow. She is very nice but I do not want to marry her.

Dieter is learning to fly. There is an aeroplane club outside Munich and he goes every Sunday to have lessons. I think he wants to join the Heidelberg University Air Squadron and be a reserve pilot for the German Air Force, called the Luftwaffe. We joke about how one day, if there is a war, we shall shoot at each other up in the sky, like Baron von Richtofen and our Royal Flying Corps air aces such as Commander Mitchell's cousin who was shot down over France in the war. I like Dieter very much. He is very good-looking and we listen to music together in his room . . .

The rest was mainly a detailed description of a trip with the Graetz family to Oberammagau to see the nativity play theatre there and to visit two of King Ludwig of Bavaria's famous castles and some amazing Baroque churches with white and gilt interiors like wedding cakes.

Celia put the letter away with a wistful smile and a sigh. She wondered how changed Hugo would be by his stay in Germany, how independent and self-contained he would become, perhaps no longer needing her company. Time would tell. He would be back at Charnfield for Christmas but not for long. After that, Oxford and another life.

ONE afternoon Dieter asked his father if he might take his English guest over to the flying school on the pillion of his motorcycle, so that Hugo could go up in an aeroplane for his first flight. Although Dieter was eighteen and halfway through university, his father, who was a strict disciplinarian, would not countenance such a thing without his permission.

146

Baron von Graetz reminded his wife, when they discussed it, that he was, after all, responsible to Sir Richard Cardwell for Hugo, while the young man was living under his roof.

"Are you sure that Hugo is so enthusiastic to go to fly in an aeroplane?" he asked his son. He looked from Hugo to Dieter and back, as the two stood before him in his study.

Dieter assured his father that Hugo was very keen. "Ist nicht so, Hugo?" Dieter said.

Hugo nodded. "Ja. Ich moechte gern in einem Flugzeug . . . fahren."

"Fliegen," corrected the Baron. Then von Graetz turned to his son. "How shall you be permitted to take up Hugo with you when you have not yet your certificate?"

"Of course I can't, Vati; I know this. My instructor, Herr Kellner, will pilot him. He has promised already . . ."

So Hugo went up in an aeroplane for the first time in his life and experienced the thrilling sensation of bumping along, faster and faster, across the grass field with the wind streaming against his leather helmet and goggles, until at last with a final jolt of the undercarriage, the plane lifted off the earth and soared high above the countryside into the blue sky above. Hugo clutched the side of the rear cockpit and looked down. As the plane banked sharply into a steep turn, he could see the other aeroplanes on the ground and, at the far end of the field, Dieter waving beside the hangar, now both become tiny objects, like toys on a green cloth.

HUGO enjoyed Munich so much that he became sad as the days rushed by to the third week in December, when he was due to return to England. All the same, he had missed Charnfield and would be glad to go home.

In the first week of the month, when a letter came from Richard sending his tickets for the return journey, Helga lapsed into a gloomy silence. Hugo knew how she felt about him and was sorry for her.

When he remarked one evening to Dieter, as they played a record of *Parsifal* in the German boy's room, that Helga was very sad that he was going, Dieter replied acidly that his sister was very young and would soon meet another boy.

Then Dieter suddenly seized Hugo's hand and pressed it to his face. Hugo could feel the wet, salt tears on his knuckles, for Dieter was weeping.

147

"I do not wish that you go, Hugo. I shall be lost when you are gone, I will be sad and unhappy."

His years at Eton had conditioned Hugo for this sort of thing and he took it in his stride. He had become attached to Dieter von Graetz, to the whole family in fact, and he had enjoyed his stay in Germany as much as he had enjoyed anything before. But life had to go on. He was already thinking about Oxford and counting the days to his return to Charnfield for Christmas. But Dieter was not someone to be lightly cast aside and Hugo could sense the depth of his feelings. "We shall keep in touch, Dieter, always. I will write to you from Oxford and you must promise to write to me."

Dieter could only nod and turn his head away to control his tears and compose himself. "Oh, yes, we must remain good friends, Hugo. Maybe, I shall come to England one day and visit you at your wonderful home and see all the beautiful pictures and furniture and the objets d'art of which you speak."

"That," said Hugo calmly, "would be lovely."

FOUR days after Hugo's return to Charnfield and a week before Christmas the first of two cruel blows fell. This was in the form of a letter from Baronin von Graetz to Celia, asking if she would break to Hugo the sad news that their son, Dieter, had crashed his plane going 'solo' for the third time and had been killed instantly.

'I feel that Hugo would wish to know,' Dieter's mother wrote, 'as the two jungen seemed to be such close friends together and our son was so fond of him.'

This was a great shock for Hugo but a worse blow was in store. The day following the news of Dieter's death, a nephew of Lady Brandon telephoned to say that Edith had died in her sleep at the nursing home. Thus was Christmas, 1932 a sad, cold, empty time for Hugo and his spirits were depressed as never before.

Richard could not help reflecting how sad events seemed habitually to mar Christmas at Charnfield. Rosie's father had died in December, 1919 and Rosie herself only two weeks before Christmas in 1920. Now, even as the 1932 Christmas decorations were going up at Charnfield, Edith Brandon had died in her sleep in a London nursing home.

By January 28th, 1933 Jeremy had returned to Upton Court for the Easter term, so Hugo found some consolation in his

148

misery by going down through the frost-covered woods to light the stove and play his gramophone in the hut. Listening to the music, he thought of Dieter and he thought of his grandmother, two people whom he had loved and who had loved him deeply. He felt deprived, lonely and sorry for himself; but there was always Aunt Celia. With that consoling thought he put on a record containing the *Parsifal* aria he had listened to with Dieter, and gazed up into the sky, remembering Dieter in his aeroplane and imagining him up there still, flying through the sky for ever, for eternity, a pilot who had gone from earth but still existed in another life, another dimension. And Granny Brandon would be up there too, he imagined. His thoughts moved on to the interior of some of the Baroque churches he had seen in Bavaria, where beautifully-carved ascending figures in fluttering garments rose towards the golden rays of heaven. He found it harder to visualize heaven itself; the image of hordes of saints 'casting down their golden crowns around a glassy sea' was cold and repellent rather than attractive. More pleasing was John Martin's painting of *The Plains of Heaven*, with their grassy slopes and garlands of flowers aand blue distances. But heaven was ineffable; whatever it was like, however, there he supposed was his mother, almost as shadowy a figure as his picture of her lasting abode. There too, now, was his grandmother, he felt sure, one of the many who 'step by step and silently' increased the shining bounds of that place where 'all its paths are gentleness and all its ways are peace.'

Feeling a little better, Hugo took off *Parsifal*. In its place he put on a record he had been given by Aunt Celia of music from *The Cat And The Fiddle* by Jerome Kern, which was all the rage, and started to think about Oxford.

9

AMONG the throng of dancers crowding the floor that warm May evening in 1934 one couple stood out. On the bandstand Carroll Gibbons and his famous Savoy Orpheans were playing a current hit, the slow, romantic fox-trot by Rodgers and Hart, 'Blue Moon'.

It was a tall, darkly pretty woman in her late thirties who first caught the eye. She was wearing a crimson moiré evening dress with ribbon-thin shoulder straps and was dancing with her eyes closed in the arms of a strikingly good-looking young man of nineteen. This Adonis was elegantly dressed in a dinner jacket, black tie and white waistcoat. He was lean but well-proportioned with pale blue eyes and a finely chiselled profile, featuring a distinctive patrician nose, his fair, wavy hair brushed back from a high forehead. The two of them made an intriguingly attractive pair.

However, the two occupants of a large table for six by the band, Richard Cardwell and Eve Mitchell, who were sitting out that dance, were both acutely aware of – and mildly embarrassed by – the look of near-ecstasy on Celia's face, as she danced with her stepson, Hugo Mayne. The dance ended to applause and the dancers returned to their tables. Jack Mitchell arrived first, slightly puffed but triumphant, escorting his partner, a voluptuous eighteen-year old in a pink taffeta dress. She had a good, curvaceous figure but walked with a slightly rolling gait. Her brown eyes were bright and sparkling and her best feature was her long auburn hair. She was called Polly Curtis and, as they reached the table, she was laughing noisily at some joke that Jack Mitchell had cracked. The Commander, with his customary old-world gallantry, held Polly's chair for her as she resumed her seat, fanning herself with a menu.

Then came Hugo and Celia, the former making for his chair next to Polly, the latter sitting down beside Jack.

The occasion was Hugo's nineteenth birthday for which he had come down from Oxford for the weekend. Richard Cardwell's oldest friends, the Mitchells, anxious to repay him and Celia for numerous weekends at Charnfield, had insisted on giving Hugo a theatre party to celebrate his birthday. They had booked tickets for Noel Coward's Regency operetta, *Conversation Piece* at His Majesty's and a table for six at the Savoy for supper afterwards. They had also tracked down as a partner for Hugo the voluptuous Polly Curtis, who was a distant relation of Eve's.

"We must get a girl for him," Eve had said to Jack; "he doesn't seem to have anyone special."

Sitting next to Polly at the theatre earlier that evening, Hugo had found the girl's flirtatious manner off-putting. She was pretty brash, he thought, and busy playing the irresistible temptress. Before the curtain rose, she had irritated him by squeezing up close to him and asking him in an embarrassingly loud, ginny voice how often he went out with girls, what kind of girls he preferred: blondes or brunettes; and if it was true that girls were sometimes smuggled into the undergraduates' rooms at Oxford and stayed there till dawn, when they escaped over a high wall. Hugo sensed that Polly was imagining herself in just such a romantic role, climbing down a drainpipe outside his window in New College and dodging the 'bulldogs' on her frantic dash back to Lady Margaret Hall. But Polly was not destined to be sent down for the love of a young man like Hugo, nor was she an undergraduate at Lady Margaret Hall; she was the daughter of a retired General from Suffolk and worked in the gift department at Fortnum and Mason's. Hugo found her very tiresome and although he had been put next to her at supper, he had failed in his duty to ask her for the first dance. Instead, he had invited Celia onto the dance floor and left Polly at the mercy of Jack Mitchell.

"You must dance with Polly some time, darling," Celia had breathed in his ear as they moved off rhythmically to the music.

"I find her overpowering," Hugo said; "liable to devour one."

"But don't you find her madly attractive?" Celia pressed him with a mischievous tease in her voice. "All that auburn hair and so much lovely white flesh and those thick lips?"

151

"She repels me. I'd rather dance the fox trot with a boa constrictor," Hugo said crisply.

Celia laughed gently and held her stepson close. He did not resist for the attraction was mutual.

Hugo was growing into manhood and his mind was maturing fast. His physical beauty was causing male and female hearts alike to flutter wherever he went and Celia found herself more and more eager to share his life, to be with him, to laugh and make plans and exchange views with him. He was as sensitive in manhood as he had been as a child. As a companion he was intelligent, charming and always deeply interested in her life. She would often seek his advice on what to wear, in what style to redecorate her bedroom at Charnfield, what courses to order and who to invite for dinner parties. They also enjoyed gossip together – sometimes laughing together privately at some of Richard's more conventional and stuffy friends.

Celia felt a pang in her heart knowing, as they danced, that Hugo would be returning to Oxford the following day and was going abroad with a friend as soon as he 'came down' for the summer vacation. She would not be seeing much of him for the next few months. This made her squeeze his hand tight and sigh rather sadly. "Oh, Hugo . . ."

"What's the matter?"

Before she could answer the music came to an end and Celia led her partner by the hand back towards their table.

On the way, Hugo asked "Aren't you going to tell me?"

"Tell you what, darling?"

"Why you sighed like that."

Celia smiled and shook her head. They reached the table and took their chairs.

The midnight cabaret consisted of a remarkably deft Italian conjuror named Giovanni who called for a male guest to join him on the floor as a volunteer. He then proceeded, in a dazzling display of sleight of hand, to relieve the mortified guest of his watch and his braces whilst engaging him in rapid conversation.

When the cabaret was over and the music started up again, it was from Geraldo's Gaucho Tango Orchestra on the bandstand. Hugo, mainly to please Celia, took a deep breath and invited Polly to dance. In a flash she was up on her feet and waiting for him on the dance floor, her eager bare arms outstretched for her Greek God of a partner. Hugo took her round the waist with as much enthusiasm as a porter loading mailbags on to a train, and was dragged off into the dancing crowd. After a few moments Richard found himself obliged to offer Eve a dance and escorted her onto the floor, leaving Jack Mitchell with Celia.

"By jingo, young Hugo's grown into a good-looking lad, eh?" said the Commander, watching the two couples disappear into the crowd.

"Hasn't he?" Celia answered, trying her best to sound casual. Privately she was fearful that Hugo, in spite of his dislike of her predatory tendencies, might succumb to Polly's bodily charms. Then she reminded herself of the business with David Maidment that summer several years ago at Charnfield. He probably wasn't the type to drag girls into his bed. Young men like Hugo, she reflected, usually got on best with older women. And he'd told her often enough that she was his favourite woman . . . Feeling happier, she became aware of Jack's voice beside her. "Still not much of an outdoor chap, I gather," he went on; "more interested in art and all that."

Celia bridled. It was typical of Jack Mitchell not to understand, or pretend not to understand, Hugo's interest in art and taste for beauty. "He's just one of those young men who prefer painting and music to slaughtering birds with a gun. Nothing wrong in that, is there?"

"Not at all, my dear. It takes all sorts. – What do you think of Polly?"

"Isn't what Hugo thinks of her more to the point?" Celia retorted, quite sharply.

"Can't see why, old thing," said Jack stubbing out his cigar in an ashtray. Celia realized she was betraying her feelings too much and changed gear rapidly. "You're matchmaking again, you wicked old mariner. You and Eve. Just like when you asked me to lunch at Claridge's to meet Richard."

"That's right, me dear. And let's hope we'll be as successful this time as we were then."

Celia smiled, just a bit sadly, and paused before saying "I don't believe you will."

"What do you mean?" Jack looked at her closely, his eyes narrowing.

"I just don't think Hugo's ready for marriage. Anyway not yet."

"I get your meaning, old love. But I'll bet Polly could make a man of him. You see if she doesn't."

153

Celia murmured "God forbid," but the band's accordions were playing rather loudly now and Jack did not hear her.

Unable to continue conversation, owing to the proximity of the orchestra, Jack made a sign to Celia, indicating an invitation to dance. Celia smiled acceptance and rose to her feet. Soon Jack was steering her away from the table, away from the band, to a far corner of the dance floor where it was possible to talk.

"Tell me about young Jeremy," Jack asked her, as they went into a Tango. "How's he doing at school?"

"He's not exactly the blue-eyed boy of Upton Park, I'm afraid. He's been caned twice for bullying and failed his end-of-term exams. Otherwise Master Jeremy is doing all right."

"Oh, dear, that doesn't sound too promising. What's the matter with the lad? Idle or bolshie or what?"

"A bit of both," Celia sighed. "Richard seems to find it all rather amusing, his son getting caned. 'Harden him up', he says, 'make him pull his socks up.' Personally, I find it disappointing."

"Oh, I wouldn't worry too much, love. As long as the lad's healthy and gets plenty of fresh air and exercise, he'll come up to scratch. How old is he now?"

"Jeremy is going to be eleven in September."

Celia delivered this statement in such a flat, matter-of-fact tone that Jack Mitchell found himself wondering whether she was even remotely fond of her own son, her only child. For Richard's sake this thought troubled him quite a bit. There was no doubt now in Jack's mind that Celia was deeply, almost improperly, attached to Hugo, whom she seemed to prefer in every way to her own son. If Jeremy was Richard's boy, keen on shooting and sport, tough, energetic, an outdoor chap with a bit of spirit in him, then Hugo, the effeminate, art-loving, pretty boy who read poetry and talked about flowers and pictures, was Celia's favourite. Could such a divergence of affection for the two boys of Charnfield Park come between Celia and her husband? Jack was further troubled by his own considerable fondness for Celia, which increased his regrets that she should have this foolish weakness for her stepson. Jack's uneasy thoughts were interrupted by the Tango ending and by Celia applauding and taking him gently by the arm to lead him back to the table.

"You must be ready for a drink after that," she said, beaming up at him.

Forgetting his criticism of the moment before, Jack thought, as

154

he had so often thought before, 'Lucky old Richard. I did him a good turn, bringing this one into his life.' What he said to Celia was, "Lead the way, my girl."

THE summer holidays of 1934 that followed Hugo's birthday party was a time of unusual sadness for Celia.

An hour before dinner one hot August evening she was lying on the large four-poster in her elegant bedroom, wearing a light bath-robe and resting before her bath. The window was wide open and through it she could see the sun setting over the distant downs and hear pigeons cooing in the woods. She was also aware of the fragrant scent from a large bowl of sweet peas on a table in the corner of the room. Superficially, everything was right with the world. The weather was lovely, she was living in a beautiful house, surrounded by beautiful things. She had position and servants to wait on her; she had been married for twelve years to a husband who, although sleeping now by mutual agreement in his dressing-room, was loyal, reliable and probably loved her in his awkward, undemonstrative way. And she had given him a son and heir. But she was unhappy tonight, utterly miserable, in fact.

Celia, who was always something of an analyst, reflected that her depression might be due to the death in the previous March of her mother, which had left her feeling sadly deprived. But there were three other reasons for her mood, all of them male. Her son, her stepson and her husband were each of them causing her distress and worry. No wonder she felt almost suicidal. 'For two pins,' she thought, 'I'd leap out of that open window.' Then she realized that she would land from a considerable height in the herbaceous border below, if she did not become entangled on the way down in a very old, impenetrable clematis that had covered that wall of the house for many years. The thought made her smile to herself. Suicide was probably out, but things were grim, all the same.

The grimmest thought of all was that Hugo was not at home. He had left for Italy the day after he came down from Oxford, spending only one night at Charnfield to unpack and repack for his trip abroad with an Oxford friend. Part of the income from the small inheritance left to him by his grandmother, Lady Brandon, had enabled him to invest in a small car, a black Wolsey Hornet. So at the end of July Hugo had driven up to London and the two young men had motored down to Newhaven, where they and the car were to be loaded onto a boat for Dieppe. They were to drive across France, along the Italian Riviera to Genoa and on to La Spezia and Florence, where they would be based for a tour of Tuscany. Hugo had said that his friend, whom he did not name, was a fellow undergraduate who shared his love of painting and sculpture. They planned to visit Siena, San Gimignano, Verona and Padua and possibly end the holiday in Venice.

Celia envied Hugo the thrill of motoring abroad in his new car to see Italian Renaissance churches and art treasures, to bask in the Tuscan sunshine and to discover small hotels and restaurants off the beaten track. She also envied his friend, whoever he might be, for having the enjoyment of his company.

The only company Celia had for the summer at Charnfield were her husband and her son, which should be all right but somehow wasn't. Jeremy had brought back an appalling report from Upton Court in which the Headmaster had pointed out that, in view of the boy's idleness and failure in his end-of-term exams, 'it might be prudent to arrange extra coaching for him during the holidays, especially in Maths and History.' To this end a tutor had been engaged.

He had proved to be a dour pipe-smoking Scot of forty-five in plus-fours, called Mr Cameron, who gave lessons to Jeremy for two hours every morning and took him out in his car on expeditions each afternoon. On one such trip to Sandbanks, Jeremy had been extremely rude to him. When the tutor had refused to allow his charge to spend the afternoon in a cinema, Jeremy had called him a "boring old Scotchman". Mr Cameron, who meant well but was indeed a bore at meals, was mercifully leaving the next day. But that meant that Jeremy would be at a loose end again and liable to get up to mischief.

As the weeks went by, Richard kept more and more to himself. He had found the tutor irritating and fussy, holding forth at meals about mountain-climbing and wild flowers and endlessly predicting that Jeremy would fail his Common Entrance for Eton.

"That's what you're here to prevent, Cameron, isn't it?" Richard had snapped at the man one evening at dinner after Jeremy had left the room. "To see to it that he doesn't fail."

Richard had by then, Celia observed, drunk several glasses of wine and his speech was thick.

Cameron had retorted that he could only do his best. "If the

156

boy won't work or use what few brains he has, then there's little I can do."

"Then you must make him work, mustn't you? That's what I'm paying you for."

Celia was relieved that Mr Cameron was going but worried about Jeremy's Common Entrance. If he failed to get into Eton, she thought, Richard would remind her that her son was the first Cardwell not to go there for six generations and would blame her. 'He'll think the Gages are rotten stock, just because Daddy went to Marlborough. Anyway, Daddy was a judge in India and a damn sight more brainy than all those depraved-looking, in-bred Cardwells hanging from the walls of Charnfield. – I'm depressed, blast it,' Celia thought, rolling off her bed. 'Better try and soak it off in the bath'. She went into her bathroom and turned on the taps.

ONE evening in early September, while Celia was still out in the garden and Richard was up in London for a couple of days, Jeremy quietly took his 4.10 gun from the gun-room, emptied a box of cartridges into a bag and set forth into the woods to try to pot a few pigeons as they came in to roost in the pine trees near the lake. He was taking advantage of his father's absence, for Richard had ruled that Jeremy was on no account to take his gun out unless accompanied by either himself or Mr Jarrot, the gamekeeper.

As the boy trampled through the thick woods in the fading light, making for a suitable position among the fir trees where he could lie up and wait for the pigeons to come in, Jeremy heard the sound of splashing and shouting coming from the lake. The voices were those of two young men and the sound suggested that they were enjoying an evening dip in the cool water. Jeremy decided to investigate. It might be a couple of estate workers or two lads from the Home Farm. He knew most of the people on the estate by sight.

Arriving at a clearing in the trees close to the lake, he saw what he took to be two village boys, whom he did not recognize, fooling about in the water, their clothes piled neatly on a log by the water's edge.

"Who are you?" he called out to them in a challenging voice.

"Who are we? Dunno," answered the bigger of the two, a

157

hefty chap of about seventeen. He turned to his slightly younger companion. "Who are we, Len; any idea?"

"Don't know, Bob!"

At this, both lads roared with laughter and went on splashing about in the water.

Jeremy gulped with anger at being so humiliated. "Do you realize you're trespassing? – I say, did you hear what I said? You're not allowed to bathe in our lake; nobody is except the family, so you can clear off."

At that the younger one let out a great snort and, like a whale, spouted water from his mouth in Jeremy's direction.

Jeremy stiffened. "Look here, you people, you can damn well get out of that water and go back to wherever you came from or I'll report you to the police. You're . . . on my land."

"Your land?" shouted the elder boy. "Come off it, you stuck-up little squirt. We're having a dip and you can't do nothing about it."

"Oh, yes I can," said Jeremy, now quivering with anger.

"Put a sock in it," came the reply.

Jeremy raised his 4.10 gun to his shoulder and aimed at the two bathers.

"Here, what do you think you're doing; trying to scare us?" Len called out.

"You put your toy gun away, me lad, before it goes off in your face," Bob added.

"This gun is not a toy, I'm warning you!"

The elder one repeated Jeremy's remark in a high-pitched female imitation of Jeremy's upper-class accent. "This gurn is nort ay toyee. Aim wornin yew."

Suddenly a shot rang out. The older youth grabbed his shoulder and plunged down into the water. Jeremy could see blood on the back of his hand.

The younger yelled at the top of his voice "You've hit 'im, you stupid bugger! E's shot . . ."

"I warned you," Jeremy shouted.

"Come on, Bob. Quick. Run for it . . ." the younger lad called.

"Just you wait," yelled Bob as the two youths started to make for the bank.

Jeremy stood frozen to the spot, dazed and motionless with his gun hot in his hand. The two youths plunged quickly ashore, Bob still gripping his shoulder where the blood was flowing freely.

158

They snatched up their clothes and ran into the thick woods, crashing and stumbling through the undergrowth until they were out of sight.

RICHARD was still up in London and Jeremy was in the schoolroom making a model aeroplane when Page came to Celia shortly after breakfast the next morning to inform her that a police officer was at the front door asking to see Sir Richard. Celia's heart missed a beat, as she rose quickly from her writing desk. Had Richard been in a motor accident, she wondered, or had something ghastly happened to Hugo abroad . . . ?

"YOU'LL appreciate that we're obliged to investigate the matter, m'lady, considering there may have to be charges of causing grievous bodily harm or, at best, malicious wounding."

Inspector Cobb of the Dorsetshire Constabulary was addressing a shocked, disbelieving Celia. Mr Walker, the neighbouring farmer up at High Cross, the Inspector told her, had cycled to the police station early that morning to make the complaint.

Her voice shaking slightly, Celia said "You're saying that my son levelled his gun at these people and actually fired at them?"

"That is the contention of the two persons concerned, m'lady. Bob Watts and Len Harris it were, both of 'em labourers on Mr Walker's farm. It seems Watts sustained a gunshot wound in the shoulder and had to have the pellets taken out of him at the Infirmary in Dorchester late last night."

After a short silence Celia asked "Presumably you'll be wanting to question my son?"

"I'm afraid we'll need to, yes, m'lady."

Celia rang for Page and asked him to go to find Master Jeremy.

"Yes, he has a gun, a small 4.10 single barrel, given him by his father. I'm sure it's licensed," she added in response to the police inspector's next two questions.

Then a sullen-looking Jeremy came into the room. Questioned by Inspector Cobb, sulkily admitted firing his gun towards the two youths, "to scare them off," he explained, adding that he had aimed high over their heads but that a pellet or two must have hit Watts by mistake. He also reminded the Inspector that the youths were trespassing on private property, but Cobb told him sharply that trespassing did not justify shooting at people with a gun.

159

At this point Celia spoke up again. "Before this matter goes any further," she said, "I would like to go with my son and see the two young men personally. We may be able to explain things to them, you see, offer some apology and find out if they would be willing to drop the charges."

"I'm afraid it's not up to them to drop the charges, m'lady, not when an unlawful shooting has taken place."

All the same, the Inspector did agree, before the matter went any further, for Lady Cardwell and her son to visit the two trespassers. He gave her their addresses but warned her that he would still be obliged to put in a report to the Superintendent.

"Are you going to tell Daddy?" Jeremy asked after the police officer had left.

"Of course he'll have to know, when he gets back. It was a stupid, senseless thing to do, Jeremy, and I can tell you now that your father will be furious with you, and I don't blame him. It'll serve you right if he confiscates that wretched gun. As a magistrate, he might even send you to prison." She did not add that as a magistrate he would be embarrassed by and deeply disappointed in his son.

Later that same morning Celia got into her two-seater car with a glum Jeremy sitting beside her and drove up to High Cross. Here, with Jeremy lagging a few paces behind her, she explained to the farmer why she had come and asked his permission to speak to the two labourers. Mr Walker agreed.

Both of the youths were out working in a field loading turnips into a cart, Bob Watts with a bandaged arm, when Celia and Jeremy bumped down a rough track towards them.

Getting out, Celia introduced herself and Jeremy. The youths scowled at Jeremy who turned his head away from them with an expression of disgust, as though they were vermin.

"I'm very distressed at what happened yesterday," Celia said quickly, "but before you say anything, please hear what I have to say and what my son has to say." Then she set about patching things up.

Her charm and reasonable attitude disarmed the youths, who finally admitted that it had been wrong of them to bathe in the lake at Charnfield without the landowner's permission. But it was a warm afternoon and they "didn't think nobody would object".

Celia assured them that her son would be severely punished by his father for firing the gun in their direction, but he was, she

160

explained, "young and excitable and must have completely lost his head."

At that point Jeremy, prompted by his mother, said in a flat, toneless voice without a trace of sincerity, "Sorry," and with glaring reluctance haltingly shook each of them by the hand.

The apology over, Celia told the injured parties that she would ask Sir Richard to offer them something by way of compensation, if they were prepared to let the matter drop.

The youths, mildly embarrassed, nodded their heads.

Later that evening Inspector Cobb confirmed on the telephone that he had prevailed on the Superintendent to close the case and say no more about it.

Celia saw to it that, immediately on his return from London the following afternoon, Richard was informed of the incident and of his son's irresponsible behaviour.

"What do you expect me to do: send those two louts a pound each as a reward for being caught on my land?" Richard asked sarcastically.

"I certainly think we ought to make some gesture to them."

"I thought you said Jeremy had apologized."

"He has. I took him up to Walker's farm myself and made him say he was sorry and shake hands with them."

"Well, you shouldn't have apologized, in my opinion, either of you. Why the hell should you? It's damned humiliating for my wife to be seen going about my estate apologizing to bloody trespassers."

Celia was shocked by this response. "Well, we did and that's that. I have no regrets about it, whatsoever. I'm surprised that someone on the bench takes your attitude but, in any case, in my opinion it's a question of good manners."

"I trust you're not going to start lecturing me on good manners," Richard said sharply.

Celia ignored this remark and there was a silence.

Richard realized he had reacted badly to this bad news. He had been goaded by bitter disappointment in his son into clashing with Celia, who he knew had in fact done exactly the right, shrewdly wise thing, the only possible thing in the circumstances.

"So the affair is finished," he said finally, settling himself into a chair in the library to look at his letters.

"It may be," Celia replied coldly, "with a bit of luck, when Harris and Watts have been compensated."

161

"All right, I'll send them money. I'll have to if you've said I will. Dangerous practice though; you realize that, don't you? Can be taken as an admission of guilt."

"Jeremy is guilty," Celia said, becoming angry again. "He shot a farm labourer in the arm with a gun. We just have to pray to God the police don't decide to prosecute. We've only the Inspector's word for it."

"Very well, then." Richard fell silent once more and started reading one of his letters.

But Celia was far from finished with the matter. "You are going to speak to Jeremy, I take it. After all, part of the arrangement with those men was that Jeremy would be punished for what he did. You can't just do nothing."

"I'm not going to flog him, if that's what you mean."

"Of course I don't mean that, Richard. I simply mean he mustn't get off scot free. You're his father. For God's sake, punish the boy and stop being so lenient with him. You were quick enough to give poor Hugo hell when Jeremy nearly drowned in the lake."

Richard looked up from his letter, exasperated. "Are you implying that I favour my own son against Rosie's?"

"Yes, I am." Celia was smouldering now.

"Well, someone's got to take Jeremy's side," Richard replied acidly. "You certainly don't. It makes me sick, the way you smarm over that pansy, Hugo, with his wavy hair and blue eyes. Anyone would think he was your lover."

"Hugo and I have a lot in common, Richard. I'd have thought that was obvious. We both love painting and music and art and history and gardens. He's a joy to be with because he's charming and courteous and interesting to talk to, and always has been since he was a little boy."

"Why on earth doesn't he get a flat on his own in London and go out with girls, like any normal young man of his age?" Richard growled.

"Why should he be sent off to live in London?" Celia retorted. "This is his home. You know how he loves Charnfield; it's his whole life. He worships every stone of this place – or didn't you know that?"

Richard was silent, so she added "Anyway, how do you know he doesn't have girls in his rooms up at Oxford?"

"I'm prepared to bet he doesn't. Boys more likely. At

162

least you won't find Jeremy turning out like that, thank God."

Angrily, Celia crossed over to the window and then spun round to face her husband. "Just because Jeremy spends his holidays shooting rabbits and behaving arrogantly to his social inferiors, you seem to think the sun shines out of his eyes. I know he's my son, our son, and I know that, as his mother, I ought to love him passionately, but I can't; not the way he is. He's not a likeable person, Richard, and it's your fault."

"My fault?"

"Yes, because you spoil him and let him do what he likes. You of all people ought to care how he behaves, as your heir, because he's going to inherit this place one day and it's time he learned to be responsible."

"Celia, what in God's name are you saying?" Richard was shouting at her now. "Watch your tongue."

"I'm sorry." Celia decided to cool things. "I get so heated when I think . . . oh, I don't know. I just feel so sorry for Hugo."

Before anything more could be said, Celia went swiftly out of the room, leaving Richard to the rest of his letters.

For some time he merely let them lie unopened on his lap while he stared ahead of him, deep in thought, an unhappy man.

IT was an evening in late September. Jeremy had been driven back to Upton Park, having promised to work harder and try to pass Common Entrance. Under pressure from Celia to carry out his undertaking to punish the boy for the shooting incident at the lake, Richard had hit on a neat compromise which combined a punishment with an incentive. He had decided to confiscate the gun and not return it, until such time as its owner passed Common Entrance. If Jeremy pulled his socks up and succeeded in getting into Eton during the Michaelmas Term, he could be out shooting again at Charnfield in the Christmas holidays. Jeremy had accepted the challenge.

Richard and Celia were dining alone. Relations between them were still strained and Celia had to be very careful in raising any matter relating to Hugo, in view of Richard's ill-disguised disapproval of the boy. All the same, Hugo was due back from his holiday in Italy the following week and would presumably spend the remaining few weeks of his vacation at Charnfield.

Partly to placate Richard and partly out of curiosity and a

163

secret desire to put Hugo to the test, Celia had invited a girl to stay during his time at home. She had not informed him of the fact.

The girl was a pretty blonde creature called Angela Prescott, a niece of Celia's uncle, Clive Walsh, and a god-daughter of Celia's mother, Lady Gage. Angela, who was nineteen with lovely features and large, laughing eyes, had done the Season, been presented and had danced at a number of débutante balls in London. Her parents, Sir Adrian and Lady Prescott, were *en poste* at the British Embassy in Madrid, so she had been brought out and chaperoned by Mrs Walsh's older sister, Viscountess Marsden, who had a daughter of Angela's age. However, for all her classic opportunities, Angela had not yet become engaged nor, indeed, had she formed a close relationship with any of the young men she had met. She was popular, but chose to keep her independence and remain, at least for the time being, unattached.

When Hugo finally returned to Charnfield from his travels, tired but enraptured by the beauty of Tuscany and inspired by the things he had seen, it seemed to Celia prudent not to break the news to him immediately of Miss Prescott's impending visit. Better to wait until he'd had a chance to unpack, relax and get a good night's sleep.

At dinner on his first night home Hugo described the journey with the car across the Channel. "My little Hornet was hauled up onto the boat by a crane in a most undignified manner and dropped onto the deck so that she bounced on her tyres like an excited child." He went on to regale them with the horrors of driving round the Piazza de la Liberta in Florence at rush hour with enraged Italian taxi drivers "honking their horns at one from behind, if one dared to stop for some panic-stricken pedestrian running for his life."

At one point, when Hugo recounted how there had been a muddle over their hotel reservations in Padua and "my friend berated the manager in furious Italian, which he speaks better than I do," Richard asked about Hugo's friend.

"Anyone we know?" he enquired.

There was a fleeting silence, then Hugo said quickly and dismissively "No. Just an Oxford friend, someone at Balliol."

For a moment Celia held her breath, wondering if Hugo would tell them and if Richard would then open a hostile attack, but Hugo was not to be drawn and she relaxed again. 'I'll find out later,' she told herself and changed the subject.

"Did you go to Venice in the end?" she inquired, sipping her wine.

"Did we not!" Hugo said and for the rest of dinner he enlarged on the delights of the Chiesa della Salute, the Palazzo Ducale and the great works of art to be seen in that magic city.

The next morning Celia and Hugo went for a walk round the garden, which was beginning to look sadly autumnal. Leaves were falling off the trees and the shrubberies and borders were being put to bed for the winter.

"Tell me about the friend you went to Italy with," said Celia suddenly; "in confidence, of course. Is he someone you like very much?"

Hugo strolled on in silence for a while. He wanted to confide in his stepmother and confidante but he was worried that she might not be able to keep his secret from Richard and was not sure where to begin. At last he said "I will tell you, but only if you swear not to tell Uncle Richard. He wouldn't approve."

"I swear, darling. Trust me."

"He's called Charles Foley. We bumped into each other in Blackwell's bookshop one morning in my first week at Oxford. He was up at Balliol reading English and Modern Languages, so we had coffee in a shop and . . . we became friends . . ." Then he went on with a rush. "We're in love, Aunt Celia."

"I see." Celia tried not to sound too dejected.

They walked on, talking of other things, until Celia found the moment which she had been dreading but which she knew she must seize while they were alone. "By the way, Hugo, Uncle Richard and I have asked a girl to stay. She's coming next week; a very nice, pretty girl called Angela Prescott."

Celia paused but Hugo said nothing, so she went on anxiously. "We thought you might like someone to stay. It's only for a week or ten days and she really is a charming girl, loves tennis and . . . well, she is kind of family really. She's a niece of my uncle Clive Walsh who gave me away at my wedding; do you remember him?"

Hugo nodded and Celia continued. "My aunt Cecily Walsh was a Miss Prescott and her brother Adrian Prescott is this girl's father." She paused for breath, glancing anxiously at Hugo.

To her relief, he simply said "She sounds charming. I'll look forward to meeting her. – My God, look at that jasmine! It's grown enormous since I last saw it. And the pieris . . . what a glorious copper those leaves go in the autumn, don't they?"

At bedtime that evening Hugo invited Celia to his room, after making sure that Richard had gone to his. He wanted to show his stepmother some snapshots he and Charles had taken of each other in Venice, posing on the Rialto Bridge, on a vaporetto landing stage and on the sands of the Lido. Charles, wearing a beach shirt and raffia sun-hat, was a tall, angular young man with a long face. Celia looked at the photo thoughtfully. This was the face of the man, not the woman, who had started the process of taking Hugo away from her into a life and a world of his own. If Hugo had girl friends he would bring them down for parties and balls and she could meet them in London sometimes, and if he married, there might be step-grandchildren to come for long holidays at Charnfield with their parents. Instead, there was this young man whose relationship with Hugo would be sterile in its shutting-out of huge areas of normal social life; and in its prohibition, because of Richard's hostility, of any kind of real intimacy between herself and the young couple – one of whom was the person she loved more than anyone else in the world.

She went on looking at the snapshots. In all of them Hugo looked grave, while Charles was usually grinning. There was nothing there to show that love had brought Hugo great happiness: did homosexuality have an inherently melancholy tinge to it – though Charles looked cheerful enough? – Or was it that Hugo wasn't really in love?

But Celia thought Charles had a charming smile, and she said so.

ANGELA Prescott's visit to Charnfield in the autumn of 1934 could not be counted a great success. One day after tea, Hugo had invited her to accompany him up to the Long Gallery where he would show her all sorts of "interesting and precious *objets d'art*". Angela had agreed. Two hours later, as the sun began to set outside, Hugo was still in full spate, showing her precious documents and seals, drawings, prints, porcelain vases, paintings and other valuable objects, when mercifully the dressing gong sounded and she was saved.

"Must go and get ready for dinner now, Hugo," she said, trying to conceal her relief. "Thank you so much for showing me everything; it was very kind of you and so interesting." And she hurried away.

At lunch the following day, Hugo announced that he would be going into Dorchester that afternoon to take a film of his Italian trip to be developed. Celia was going to visit Nanny whose failing eyesight had forced her to retire from service and settle in a cottage in the village. Jeremy had no plans and Angela, faced with driving into Dorchester with Hugo which might, she feared, involve more sightseeing and an historical lecture, said she would stay to play tennis with Jeremy.

By mid-afternoon Jeremy, hopelessly out-played by Angela who thrashed him 6-0, 6-0, started to fool about on the court, singing bawdy songs and hitting tennis balls miles up into the air and out of the court into the bushes. Angela thanked him politely for the game and told him she would be happy to go off for a walk round the place by herself.

Not quite sure where to go but vaguely intending to look at the formal gardens on the south side of the house, she found herself mounting the stone steps to the terrace, where she decided to sit down for a while and admire the view across the park.

"All on your own?" A voice at her side caused her to start. She had not heard approaching footsteps. "I thought you and Jem were playing tennis." Richard dropped onto the seat beside her.

"We were, Sir Richard, but we've . . . stopped."

"Too hot, eh?"

"Not really," Angela said. "I think Jeremy got a bit bored because I beat him rather easily."

Richard smiled. "Do him good."

There was a silence, as Richard looked sideways at his guest and Angela, aware of his eyes on her, busily studied the view.

"Charnfield is a lovely place, Sir Richard," she ventured at last. "It was so kind of you and Aunt Celia to ask me."

"Not at all." He glanced at her, adding "I say, I don't think you need call me 'Sir Richard'; after all you are 'out' now and it makes me feel so wretchedly old."

"I'm sorry. Would you prefer me to call you Uncle Richard?"

"I should think that would do very well."

There was another silence, then Richard glanced at her again. "You warm enough?"

A slight breeze had got up and was ruffling Angela's blonde hair. Instinctively, she felt her bare arms. She was not to know

167

that, ten minutes earlier, from a window in the house while on his way to fetch something from his dressing-room, Richard had for a few minutes stopped to watch her play her game, noticing how the pleated skirt of her tennis dress twirled becomingly round her, nor that he had experienced a disturbing stab of desire at the sight of her bronzed, young legs fleetingly revealed when she moved about the court.

"I'm all right, thanks."

"Perhaps we should walk a bit; don't want you catching a chill."

Richard got up from the seat so Angela did likewise, and soon they were strolling along to the end of the terrace, down the steps into the formal garden.

They went on towards the vegetable garden. In one of the greenhouses Richard invited Angela to inspect the orchids and other exotic hothouse plants, then, suggesting she might like to sample the Charnfield fruit, he led the way into another greenhouse that was full of ripe tomatoes.

"Try one," Richard invited.

"Are you sure?"

"Of course."

As Angela leant forward to pick a round, red, shiny tomato off its plant, she felt Richard's hands suddenly grasp her breasts from behind and felt a kiss on her bare neck.

Before she could turn or make any kind of movement Richard whispered "Don't move, Angela; please don't shout out or cry or anything. It's only that you're so damnably pretty and appealing; I simply can't help myself. I know I'm old enough to be your father but I'm a man, like any other, with feelings and . . . Can you try to understand?"

Angela had managed to turn now to face him, for he had relinquished his grasp on her but was now trying to take hold of her hands. The girl was shaking and distressed, not so much from the feel of a middle-aged man's hands holding her breasts and kissing her neck but from the shock of surprise, the total unexpectedness of what had happened.

"It's all right. I don't really mind. I suppose it's rather flattering . . . from someone older. But . . ."

"But what?" – Richard wondered whether she was willing to go further.

"What about Aunt Celia?" she said quietly.

168

Richard took her hands in his. This time she allowed him to do so, and he drew her gently towards him. Angela was trembling a little, confused, partly excited and roused but fearful of where it would end.

Richard's voice was hoarse with restrained passion as he murmured "One proper kiss, darling, and I'll let you go."

Angela allowed herself to be drawn towards him until he was able to take her head in his hands and kiss her gently but with feeling on the lips. Angela responded; she parted her lips and felt Richard's tongue meet hers.

"I THOUGHT you were all playing tennis."

The voice from the greenhouse door seemed to Richard to come echoing from miles away, but it caused him to let go of Angela and jump back like a shot rabbit. The blood rushed to his head and he felt a roaring in his ears. His pulse throbbed. He gulped, managing to croak "We were inspecting the tomatoes."

"They're beautifully ripe, aren't they," Angela managed to say, but she could not disguise the tremor in her voice.

Celia strolled through the greenhouse towards them, a fruit basket in her hand. "Good. I was just coming to get some," she said coolly.

Nothing more was said. But at bedtime, when Richard paused on the landing to kiss his wife goodnight before retiring to his dressing room, Celia turned her head away, saying "If you must do it, Richard, please not with my young relations and not at Charnfield."

With that, she went into her own room, leaving Richard pounding the oak balustrade with his fist for a few seconds before going to his own room and slamming the door.

Already in bed in her room along the passage, Angela heard Richard's door slam and was afraid. But the greenhouse incident was never mentioned again. Celia kissed Angela affectionately when the girl left Charnfield two days later, and Richard bade her goodbye as though nothing unseemly had occurred.

169

10

"WELL, Richard, my old warrior. We'll soon be getting our uniforms out of the moth balls, eh? Unless we can make a pact with Hitler."

"You can't stop dictators by waving pieces of paper at them, Jack," said Richard, refilling his port glass from the decanter on the table. "Sanctions didn't stop Mussolini from walking into Abyssinia. I'm afraid we're in for another bloody war. We'll have to fight him, Jack; only way to deal with a maniac like that."

Richard and Celia were up in London for a few days and were dining at the Mitchells' house in Connaught Square. It happened to be the night in 1936 when German troops re-occupied the Rhineland in breach of the Treaty of Versailles, causing shock waves in every European capital.

But it was not the threat of a new war that Eve and Celia were discussing upstairs in the drawing-room. Since the disastrous summer of 1934 when Celia had discovered her husband in the act of kissing a girl half his age, her relationship with Richard had steadily deteriorated. It was not just the fact, Celia told Eve, that her husband at the age of fifty had felt the need to force his attentions on a young girl who was their guest, it was also symbolic of an escalation of the bitter conflict that had been developing between them over her close relationship with Hugo and her lack of love, bordering on dislike, for her own son. Added to that were Richard's more and more frequent displays of bad temper and the unpleasant scenes that always followed. She was well aware that he still felt some pain from his old war wound and probably always would, which was causing him to drink more than he should. Altogether, he was becoming more difficult to live with each successive year. Sometimes she wondered whether it was guilt on his part. In the early days of their courtship the thought had crossed her mind that Richard was only looking for someone sympathetic and capable to take him on, a widower with an estate and a stepson. But, she told Eve, she had been able to reassure herself that he was genuinely in love with her on the night of the McGibbons' New Year's Eve ball when he had proposed. He was surely a man deeply in love then, not someone on the look-out out for a sort of nurse-companion.

Eve said she, too, was convinced that Richard was deeply in love with her that night and she with him.

"And now that love is virtually dead," Celia sighed, stirring her coffee. "The incident with Angela Prescott was the final straw and, since that fatal summer afternoon, we've been living, or as Richard puts it, 'existing', under the same roof with no more than a few formal exchanges at meals and long days spent on our own, avoiding each other's company."

"It's very sad," Eve murmured; "I'm so sorry." After a short silence she went on: "Jack worries about you a lot, you know."

"About us?"

"About you personally. He's extremely fond of you . . . Hadn't you guessed?"

"How do you mean?"

"I think he's always been a little bit in love with you. Oh, I don't mind, Celia; I'm used to it and he's very good to me. I've no complaints."

Celia could not admit that she had had her suspicions. On one of the Mitchells' many summer visits to Charnfield, when she and Jack were strolling on the lawn together one warm evening after dinner, he had told her that he found her "deeply disturbing", and that he sometimes wished Richard wasn't such an old friend.

When Celia asked him playfully what he would do, if that were not the case, Jack said, only half-jokingly, "Then, my lovely lady, I would take you in my arms and carry you off into the woods."

Now she felt the need to say something reassuring to Eve that was not too smug. She murmured softly "Jack is the kindest man I know."

At that moment the men joined them and they all sat down to play bridge.

BACK at Charnfield, the problem of Jeremy persisted and, ironically, became about the only topic of conversation between

171

Celia and Richard, the only subject on which they could communicate. Predictably, Jeremy had failed to pass his Common Entrance Exam for Eton. Richard blamed Upton Court but Celia argued that he would have failed whatever prep school he went to, because "he's lazy and careless and thinks that games are more important than work."

She had been on the verge of saying "because he's been brought up to believe . . ." but just stopped herself in time. No point in having a row about the fact that in Richard's world it was preferable to be Captain of the cricket XI than to win the Newcastle Prize.

In the end a school had been found in Wiltshire nearby, called Melton Hall, which specialized in boys with learning difficulties and encouraged all forms of sport and outdoor activity: climbing, sailing and gymnastics as well as tennis and riding.

Jeremy seemed happy enough at this none-too-disciplined establishment but he remained moody, sullen and ill-mannered in the holidays and his parents continued to worry about his future. It was Jack Mitchell who hit quite by chance on a possible solution, one weekend at Charnfield during Jeremy's holidays. He had wandered into the schoolroom on the Saturday morning to find his godson and suggest that they might go down to the lake together and cast a fly for a trout.

Realizing that Jeremy had become an acute problem, Jack had resolved to try to help by exercising a good influence on the boy, talking to him as 'man-to-man' and urging him to pull himself together, respect his parents and work harder for the sake of his future.

Although he never mentioned it to anyone, Jack had an unpleasant feeling that Richard's son had decided some time ago that, as a future baronet and heir to a large estate, there was no need for him to do anything but enjoy himself and wait for his father to die and leave him his title and property.

With these thoughts in his mind, Jack strolled casually into the old nursery, now the schoolroom, and found Jeremy slouched in an easy chair, reading a rather lurid schoolboy's magazine with pictures of men in space suits travelling in rockets to the moon.

"Morning, Jem, old chap. How are you this bright morning?"

Jeremy glanced up but failed to rise from his easy chair.

"Are you going to get up when an older person comes into the room?" Jack barked at him sharply.

172

Jeremy put down his magazine quickly and stood up. "Sorry."

"That's better," said the Commander, mentally on the bridge of a destroyer at sea, bawling out an idle rating.

Looking round the schoolroom, Jack's eye came to rest on something that had caught his attention. Pushed away into a corner of the room was Jeremy's old toy fortress and two or three boxes of tin soldiers.

Jack remembered that the set had been his and Eve's Christmas present to Jeremy three or four years earlier.

"Still fighting battles with your old fort and those lead soldiers and native chaps, are you?"

Jeremy looked into the corner and shrugged his shoulders. "Sometimes."

"Doesn't look as though you've had 'em out for donkeys' years."

After an insolent pause, Jeremy muttered "It's no fun on your own. You've got to have an enemy to shoot at."

"Have you?"

"Yeah. Someone down on the floor to move the hostile pieces around."

"You mean get them into a position where they can massacre your jolly Victorian chaps in their scarlet uniforms and capture the Union Jack off the fort?"

"That's right," Jeremy said.

Jack walked over to the corner of the room and, bending down with some difficulty, for he was suffering a little from arthritis, he pulled out the fort and two boxes of soldiers, British and native. Soon he was down on his knees on the cork floor, setting out the native troops with their spears and daggers to face the British fortress.

"Come on, lad, I'll be the Mad Mahdi and we'll have a bloody battle. The trout can wait."

Jeremy said, "O.K. Uncle Jack. But remember you haven't got any artillery. Spears won't do any good against field guns."

"Any more than Heile Selassie's chaps could manage in the desert against Musso's bombers," Jack said, moving a number of lead men to a flank.

They played soldiers on the schoolroom floor for over an hour, the stiff, ageing former naval Commander and the thirteen-year old schoolboy. After a while, Jack got a bit cramped and decided he had had enough, so he scrambled to his feet and sat heavily on

173

the old, worn, much knocked-about schoolroom sofa, from which bits of spring and stuffing were visibly leaking underneath.

"Seems all wrong that we should have to go to war again, doesn't it, after all that appalling carnage of 1914," Jack said casually, "but it looks like a certainty now, Jem my boy; and our young men should be starting to think about joining up; at least doing a bit of training – just in case."

Jeremy told his godfather that Hugo had been talking about the Abyssinian crisis when he was last down from Oxford. "Hugo said he'd refuse to fight if there was a war."

"Did he?" muttered Jack.

"He's going to be a conscientious objector."

"Is he?" Jack Mitchell grunted, while examining a miniature lead artillery piece which he had picked up off the floor. After a silence he said "You ought to join the Navy, my boy; go to Dartmouth and be a middie. I can recommend the Navy. Good life."

Jeremy made an imitation of a man being violently ill and said "Oh, cripes, not the Navy, Uncle Jack; I'd be seasick. I even threw up on the steamer from Lymington over to the Isle of Wight last holidays and the sea was quite calm."

"What about the Army, then? Plenty of fresh air and exercise and sport. Learn to fire a machine-gun, stick a bayonet into some Hun's belly, wear a smart uniform and impress the girls, eh?"

There was suddenly a light in Jeremy's eyes that Jack had never seen before. It was an expression on the boy's face of excitement and hope.

"How could I get into the Army?"

"Simple, my boy. Yer father'll get you accepted for the Grenadiers. All you'll have to do is sit the Army Exam, which I'm told any idiot can pass, and go to Sandhurst. It's pretty tough there, they tell me, but if you can get through the RMC, you'll get your commission."

"When?"

"How old are you now?"

"Thirteen."

"You'll have to work damned hard for the next four years. Then try."

"It's a long time to wait."

Jack looked up at the boy with a wry smile. "Oh, I expect the war'll wait for you."

At that point Celia came into the schoolroom, looking for Jeremy to remind him it was almost time for lunch.

"We were just settling young Jem's future, my dear. He's going to be a regular soldier, go to Sandhurst and be an officer. How about that?"

And the matter had been settled almost immediately. That very evening at dinner Richard had given his blessing to the idea of his son and heir taking the Army Exam and, it was to be hoped, passing into Sandhurst, then joining the Grenadiers, as soon as he reached the right age.

However, the final agreement on Jeremy's future did not in any way solve the on-going problem of Celia and Richard's strained marriage.

In the intimate atmosphere of the dining-room that evening, when Eve and Celia had left the table with Jeremy, Richard sighed and murmured to his old friend "Celia and I will just have to go our own ways, I suppose, and try to avoid rows. Absurd to talk about divorce at our age, especially with a war looming."

AFTER coming down from Oxford with a History Degree, Hugo had studied History of Art for a year at London University and acquired a 'Master's'. This enabled him to acquire a job with the Courtauld Institute in Portman Square, where he was in his element, lecturing and cataloguing the fine collection of paintings, while expanding his already considerable knowledge of art history.

His salary was modest but he was sharing a small flat near Marble Arch with Charles Foley, which was an ideal arrangement, for it was within walking distance of his job.

Charles, who had come down from Oxford a term earlier than Hugo, had already found employment with a publishing firm specializing in large and glossy illustrated art books. It was not well paid work either, but satisfying. The two young men lived contentedly in the flat, sharing the rent, cost of food, electricty, rates and general housekeeping. At weekends Charles either stayed in London or caught a Friday night train to Chelmsford to visit his parents, while Hugo drove himself down to Charnfield. Richard thoroughly disliked the idea of his stepson sharing a flat in London with a male friend but he avoided arguing with Celia on the subject.

Celia herself badly missed Hugo's company during the week and looked forward to his weekend visits when they could go for walks together and he would talk enthusiastically about his work and his life in the bohemian art world.

If any of Richard's friends, such as Jack Mitchell, ever made an adverse comment on Hugo's life-style, Richard would say "Hugo's over twenty-one now, he's got the vote, his own car and his own job. What he does with his life is no longer of any interest to me. It's entirely his own affair." And that would put an end to the discussion.

If Richard had witnessed a scene from Hugo's private life he would probably have found it as displeasing as he expected. One Friday evening in the autumn of 1936, for instance, Charles got back to the flat from work to find Hugo packing his suitcase for the weekend. Charles was not going home to his parents because they were away in Cornwall for a wedding.

"Will you be all right?" Hugo asked. "Food, etc?"

"I shan't starve," said Charles, "but you can bring me back some caviar from your stately home in a paper bag, dear, if that'll ease your conscience."

These little jabs about Charnfield that Charles made from time to time told Hugo only too well how his friend felt. Charles had never set foot in the place and probably never would, as long as Richard was alive. Even if Celia could persuade her husband to allow Hugo to invite him down for a weekend, Hugo knew that his stepfather would make little effort to disguise his feelings, which might offend Charles deeply and would certainly cause himself acute embarrassment.

"I'll stay in London with you," Hugo said. "I'll ring to say I'm not coming down. We'll go and see a film instead."

"A sweet thought," said Charles; "but no. You go."

Hugo felt a surge of anger. "One of these days I'm going to turn up with you on the doorstep and defy my stepfather to send you away."

"Oh, for God's sake, don't do that!" Charles said with feigned alarm. "I'd be as welcome as a Nazi Stormtrooper in Petticoat Lane. Just give the lovely Celia my salaams and . . ." Charles flung open his arms and assumed a sort of quavering, mock-dramatic voice: ". . . Come back to me, dearest, when the new day dawns and succour my bleeding heart!"

He ran into his friend's arms, and Hugo, entering into the same spirit, cried out "Yes, yes, my love, I shall return to you with the dawn . . ."

176

They both shook with laughter and kissed each other. Then Hugo went back to his room to complete his packing.

A FEW weeks before Christmas that year Hugo told Celia that he and Charles very much wanted to take her to the Ballet in London one evening and on to supper afterwards at Rule's.

Celia knew at once that Hugo was attempting to infiltrate his friend into the Cardwell family circle. She was touched and pleased that at last he wanted her to meet Charles. But the thought of Richard's reactions to the idea of acknowledging his existence, let alone bringing him down to Charnfield, made her heart quail.

"Naturally, I'd love to meet Charles," she said, "and it's very sweet of you both to take me to the Ballet. But I don't think it will be easy to persuade Uncle Richard to accept him here as a guest."

Hugo put his arm round her. "I know, darling. And Charles understands, God knows. But we'd still love to take you out for an evening. He's dying to meet you."

The prospect of the de Basil Ballet at Covent Garden and supper afterwards with two handsome, interesting young men was exciting and a date was settled.

Celia told Richard a white lie – about wanting to look for some material at Peter Jones and dine with her cousin Edward Walsh – and booked herself a room at Brown's Hotel.

The evening at the ballet was a delight: Massine in *Tricorne*, Riabouchinska in *Scherezade* and Lichine in *Spectre de la Rose*.

At some point in the conversation during supper afterwards, Hugo said something to Charles about how "my divine stepmother fights all my battles for me."

Celia heard herself say with mock self-pity: "You don't need me any longer, Hugo darling. You've got Charles."

There was a momentary silence. Charles knew that Hugo concealed the nature of their friendship from his conventional stepfather and that 'Aunt Celia' assisted in this. He was now much taken with this sweet, understanding lady and consequently was reluctant to compete with her for Hugo's affection. But he believed that his and Hugo's love for each other was something that no woman could usurp.

Aware of the silence, he said something about the vivid colours of Bakst's design for *Scherezade*, and the moment passed. But it left Celia feeling oddly rejected and sad.

ONE evening in the spring of 1937 Richard returned from a long day up in London with his solicitors, looking rather grim.

Jeremy had gone off on his bike to the cinema in Dorchester, so Richard was able to draw Celia into the library after a fairly silent dinner, "to tell you of some plans I've made today on old Crawford's advice. You won't like it any more than I do, but it's something that's got to be done if Charnfield is to survive."

Celia was seated in an upright chair, her coffee on her knee, a set expression on her face while Richard paced about the room, outlining to her the solicitor's advice. It was, in a nutshell, that Charnfield should be made over to Jeremy as soon as possible, in order to avoid the crippling estate duties he would have to pay on his father's eventual death.

Celia had heard of this custom among owners of large properties. "But isn't there some business about the person handing over having to go on living for another five years, if the duty is to be avoided?"

"That's right. That's why it must be done as soon as possible. After all I'm fifty-three. Reasonably healthy, I suppose, but you never know."

Suddenly Celia felt a twinge in her heart and risking everything, she put down her coffee cup, got to her feet, and said "Oh, darling, please don't talk about you dying, I couldn't bear it . . . I'd be hopelessly lost. I couldn't go on . . ."

And, for the first time in two years, she went over to her husband who was standing staring out of the window, turned him round and drew him to her, kissing him quite passionately.

"You're not to think of dying, my darling, you're much too precious to me. Please . . ."

Richard took her round the waist and held her firmly in his arms. After a short silence he kissed her gently on her forehead. "Oh, Celia, my darling girl, I've wanted this for so long," he murmured. "Do we have to go on being . . ."

"No," Celia said firmly, putting her hand over his mouth to silence him, "we don't. Not any more, darling. Not as far as I'm concerned."

"Am I forgiven?" Richard asked tentatively.

Celia presumed her husband was referring to his little lapse with Angela Prescott two years earlier but did not wish to bring up old scores. "Everything is forgiven, dearest Richard," she said. "There's going to be a war soon and God knows what's in store for us, any of us. It's no time to go on nursing silly grievances and . . . being nasty to each other."

"Thank you, darling," was Richard's response. "You don't know how much this means to me. I need your support now very badly."

"And I need yours."

She kissed him again, and that was the moment of reconciliation between them.

ONE Sunday soon after, papers transferring Charnfield to Jeremy were signed under the trusteeship of Jack Mitchell and Mr Crawford.

Hugo had been down for the weekend and shortly before returning to London he tackled Celia about the vexed question of his friend Charles never being asked down to Charnfield. Knowing that relations between her and Uncle Richard had improved and that Richard was more affable towards himself, he hoped there might now be no objection to his inviting Charles for an occasional weekend.

"After all," he argued, "he's not a violent criminal, you know, and hardly likely to murder us all in our beds. Besides which, we do share a flat in London and he is fully aware of which knife and fork to use at meals. In fact his manners are impeccable, a bloody sight better than Jem's. He's intelligent and civilized and he's my friend and this is my home, so why the hell can't I . . ."

"Darling, darling, calm down," Celia said quietly. "You know as well as I do how Uncle Richard feels about your friend. I'm afraid nothing's changed there. If you ask him, he'll only refuse and then you'll be hurt and angry."

Hugo said bitterly "All right. For your sake, I'll shut up. But you must admit it't rather difficult having to explain to Charles why . . ."

"I know." Celia sighed. Then she said "Has it occurred to you that Jeremy will soon be the owner of Charnfield, at least on paper, when the estate has been made over to him?"

"So what?" asked Hugo.

"So, technically, you'd have to ask his permission for Charles Foley to stay, not Uncle Richard's."

"Oh, God!"

The thought sickened Hugo. Then he reflected for a moment, before saying calmly "Not while Jem's a minor. He'll have no say whatever in what happens at Charnfield until he comes of age and that's not going to be for years."

"I know, darling, but time has a nasty habit of marching on," Celia replied.

BY the early spring of 1939 restoration work had begun on the old stable block at the back of Charnfield. After a series of gloomy discussions about the uncertain future, Richard and Celia had decided to restore the building and convert it into a fair-sized residence for themselves, against the day when Jeremy would come of age, marry, have children and need to move into the big house. The stable block, with an attractive façade bearing the family coat of arms, was away to the right of the large forecourt, which was reached after driving through the gatehouse and up to the main entrance of the big house. It had been built at the same time as Charnfield and was on two floors with an entrance up three steps to what could be made into a sizeable front door; there was a small paddock at the rear of the building which would make a modest garden and the back of the block faced south, with a good view across the park. Originally comprising two adjoining dwellings to accomodate two coachmen and their families, it could easily be knocked into one house to provide a large ground-floor sitting-room, dining-room and kitchen quarters with four sizeable bedrooms and two bathrooms upstairs.

The conversion was costing money but Celia was contributing to it and, with Hugo down for weekends to advise her and help with the planning of the interior decoration, she was throwing herself vigorously into the construction of what Hugo, half-jokingly called 'The Dower House'.

"Steady, Hugo, I'm not a dowager yet," she protested, but she realized that Richard was twelve years older than her and the possibility had to be faced.

In March of that year Hugo announced that he and Charles were planning to spend the Easter holiday together on the Dalmatian Coast. If his friend was not welcome at Charnfield, Hugo had decided he would find another way of enjoying his vacation with him.

180

IN late April a postcard from Dubrovkik reached Celia.

This is a magic place. We swim every day in the Adriatic, v. warm.
Have made friends with some Yugoslavs. May go on to Tirana next
(Albania) but suspect Italian occupation may present difficulties. What
progress with the Dower House?
Love to all, Hugo

BY May the respite after Munich had given way to Hitler's
new threat to Danzig and the Polish Corridor. Richard saw
clearly that war must surely come and, although Celia remained
optimistic that the catastrophe would be somehow averted,
Richard found his blood stirring again. He began to think of his
old school friends lying dead out there in the Flanders mud and
some compulsion made him decide, without telling Celia of his
feelings, to go up to London and pay a call on Colonel Mark
Broadfield, the officer commanding his old regiment, the
Grenadier Guards.

Broadfield was younger than Richard by a few years. They
knew each other slightly and had met from time to time at
Boodle's.

"I'm afraid there could be no question of active service
overseas with a fighting battalion, Richard; not at your age."

Richard was standing by the window of the Lieutenant
Colonel's office in the Regimental Orderly Room at Wellington
Barracks. Outside on the barrack square a company of
Coldstream 'young soldiers' were suffering under a Drill Sergeant
with a voice like a foghorn. The young guardsmens' boots
crashed down on the asphalt as they halted, marked time, turned
about and marched off again with the Drill Sergeant, a ramrod of
a man with a pace-stick and a waxed moustache, barking at them
"Lef, ri, lef, ri, pick yer feet up and look up, swing yer arms, you
palsied, idle lot, lef, ri . . . lef, ri . . ."

Richard turned from the window and thought to himself
'They'll be facing German tanks in a month or so, those green,
eager boys.'

"Especially with your gammy leg. Wounded at Arras, were you
not?"

Richard came out of his reverie and realized the Commanding
Officer was still talking to him. He turned from the window.
"Oh, I didn't expect active service with a Battalion at the front,

sir; just some administrative job, I thought; training young officers or running a weapons course or something." Richard, who had been invalided out in 1918 as a mere captain, took care to call the colonel 'sir', for it was a regimental tradition that, however many years older a retired officer might be, the officer commanding the regiment was entitled to be addressed in that way in his own Orderly Room, unless the retired officer was of senior rank.

"Oh, my God yes, we shall certainly be needing people like you, Richard; experienced older officers who were in the last war. I'm sure we can find something for you. That is, if and when general mobilization is ordered."

"Right, sir. I'll dig out my uniform – just in case."

"No harm in doing that," said the Lieutenant Colonel.

RICHARD'S uniform was indeed dug out – from a trunk in the box-room in the attics at Charnfield. They found his old jacket with campaign medals sewn on, boots, gaiters, a number of khaki shirts and ties, all smelling strongly of moth balls. His old service dress cap was greasy and badly squashed out of shape, so a new one was ordered from Messrs Herbert Johnson, the regimental hatters.

By mid-May Hugo was back from Yugoslavia and the following weekend at Charnfield he announced at dinner that recent events in Europe had enabled him to, as he put it, "discard my pacifistic stance and join something in the event of war."

The news came as a great relief to Richard and a long discussion followed as to where and how Hugo could best serve his country.

Richard, mindful of Hugo's way of life and habits, purposely did not suggest the Grenadiers, for he was unwilling to risk the embarrassment to Colonel Broadfield in case the Regiment, hearing of Hugo's reputation, should feel unable to accept him as suitable officer material. There was talk about his becoming an Air Raid Warden or seeking work in a munitions factory and at one point during dinner Jeremy suggested to his stepbrother that, with his knowledge of languages and foreign countries, he ought to offer his services as a spy. This caused some laughter at the dinner table which Page was able to join in as he passesd round the vegetables.

BY lunch time on Sunday, September 3rd, 1939, Britain was finally at war with Germany again. On the following morning Richard received the buff envelope from the War Office that he had been expecting. It contained a brief notification confirming that 'the above officer's name has been approved by the Secretary of State for War for re-appointment to the Royal Army Reserve of Officers and that the officer named should report at once to the Headquarters, Grenadier Guards at Wellington Barracks, Birdcage Walk, S.W.1.'

Richard found Celia in the Stable Block measuring the windows for curtains and told her his news with a slight tremble of excitement mingled with pride, adding that he would have to travel up to London immediately. He would stay up for the night. Page was asked to pack his overnight bag and at eleven o'clock the same morning William drove his master to catch the train from Sherborne. Within a few hours Richard was walking across Green Park towards Birdcage Walk, on his way to see Colonel Mark.

Although the country was by now technically at war the traffic, including taxis, buses and private cars, was flowing normally in the streets, while up in the blue autumn sky barrage balloons were floating peacefully in the light breeze.

Richard reported to Wellington Barracks and was informed by the Lieutenant Colonel that he would be posted to the Training Battalion of his old regiment at Victoria Barracks, Windsor, to instruct the newly joined young officers in map-reading and tactics.

By November he was settled in at Windsor, rather enjoying the life of the Officers' Mess. Here a mixture of young officers and elderly 'dug-outs' like himself dined nightly by candlelight, waited on, as in peace time, by mess waiters. The regimental silver was displayed on the table and the port decanter went round several times each evening, as the officers, wearing Mess Kit, discussed the strange, anti-climactic 'phoney war' on the Western Front. The British Expeditionary Force had been sitting in defensive positions on the Belgian Frontier for weeks and not a shot had so far been fired.

Richard was able to take weekend leave reasonably frequently, which enbled him to motor down to Charnfield from Windsor, petrol coupons permitting. Arriving there one wet weekend in early November, he stopped his car just inside the lodge gates to speak to a group of three men in dark suits and macs who were standing in the drive, surveying the surrounding park. One of them was making notes on a clip board.

Richard wound down the window of his car and asked politely whether he could help them. One of them replied that they were Civil Servants from the War Office, doing a survey of Charnfield Park which had been listed as one of a number of large country houses in the area suitable for the accomodation of troops.

"You mean turn us out of the house and put troops in?" Richard asked, his voice trembling with suppressed rage.

"Requisitioned, sir, yes," said one of the Civil Servants, with a sickly smile.

Richard exploded. He told the men furiously to get off his property, then he let in the clutch and drove on at speed towards the gatehouse, shouting back at them that he would be writing to the War Office at once, to complain. But on his return to the Windsor Barracks on Sunday evening he realized that there was no chance of resisting a requisition order. One or two other officers in the Mess who were landowners had already had their properties taken over to house evacuees, girls' schools and units of the RAF.

"WE must get the stable block inhabitable as soon as possible," Richard said to Celia a few days later. "If the house is going to be crawling with soldiers for the duration of the war, we'll have to get busy and store all the valuable things in the cellars and move ourselves out."

"Perhaps we'll be a hospital," Celia ventured hopefully; "that wouldn't be so bad."

"No chance of that," said Richard with a sign of resignation. "Those chaps were from the War Office. That means troops."

In the event, a requisition order from the War Office arrived a fortnight later and Charnfield became, almost overnight, an Infantry Brigade Headquarters within Southern Command.

Richard was given three weeks to evacuate the house and grounds and told that some bell-tents would have to be pitched in the park. Agreement was reached with the authorities for him and his family to occupy the stable block as long as they observed the army's regulations as to black-out, restricted movement about the place, the posting of sentries on main gates, etc.

Hugo, predictably, was shattered by the news, broken to him by Celia on his arrival home in battledress on weekend leave early in December. He and Charles had let their flat near Marble Arch when Charles had enlisted in the Royal Navy and Hugo had been called up for military service. Hugo had taken leave of the Courtauld Institute, passed his medical and been accepted for the Royal Artillery, to be posted to an Anti-Aircraft Battery in Southampton. At least he would be reasonably near home.

"They'll wreck the place, smash everything, or burn it to the ground," he said.

Celia tried to calm him. "If they do, they'll have to pay compensation. Anyway, everyone's in the same boat."

"What's to be done with all the treasures, all the porcelain, the pictures and the furniture?"

"It'll all have to be carefully stored away where the soldiers can't damage it."

"It's a nightmare," was all Hugo could say.

For most of that freezing winter he was away from Charnfield, crouched in a Nissen hut in a park near Southampton docks, shivering and yawning with boredom until an occasional air raid alert caused some momentary excitement. Whenever he could get weekend leave, he would set to with Celia, cataloguing and cross-checking all the treasures of the house, making lists of every picture, every good piece of antique furniture and every porcelian vase, ornament or statue of value. Pictures were taken down from the walls, carefully wrapped in sacking and stored in the housekeeper's room – which would be permanently locked and out-of-bounds to the army – or in the cellars; smaller objects were packed into boxes and put away in cupboards and in the attics. The family's personal belongings would be moved over to the Stable House.

One weekend just before Christmas Hugo came on leave with a single stripe on his battledress sleeves. "It'll cost you money to talk to me now, my dears," he said, as he removed his greatcoat in the hall and pointed to his arm. "I'm a Lance-Bombardier."

"A what?" Celia asked.

Richard appeared from the Library in time to hear the news. "Like a Lance-Corporal, darling," he explained, "only it's for Gunners. It means he's been promoted. Well done, Hugo."

"Not really, Uncle Richard," said Hugo modestly. "I make

them all scream with laughter, that's all. I'm the Battery Jester and they adore me. – I say, what's for supper?"

"Irish Stew," said Celia with a grimace.

"Marvellous! Then we simply must start getting the tapestries on the landing down and stored before the soldiers arrive and start playing darts against them."

By Christmas the house was stripped down to its bare walls, the Long Gallery was cleared and locked and the Great Hall looked like a vast, empty railway station. Celia did not need to prompt Richard into realizing the enormous debt he owed to his stepson for his care and concern for the house and its contents. He could see it for himself. In fact, progress was so rapid that the three of them decided, after a short conference with the builders, that they could move into the Stable House as soon as the carpets were down. This would be about the last week in February, 1940.

Celia and Richard would occupy the main suite upstairs with the two spare rooms for Jeremy and Hugo when they were home. Celia told the boys that any guests would have to have their rooms, but only when they were not there.

In July 1940, shortly after the fall of France, Hugo announced that he was being posted abroad but was not allowed to say where or when. "I thought you were with an anti-aircraft unit, for home defence against the German bombers," Richard said at dinner.

"I was. Not now," Hugo replied. "I've transferred to something else. You mustn't ask too many questions. I'll write as soon as I can . . . from Cairo."

"Cairo?" Richard's eyebrows went up.

Celia gasped. "They're not sending you out there, surely . . . why?"

But Hugo said no more and Celia felt a wave of cold fear, deep anxiety and sadness pass over her.

WITHIN a few months Celia had to admit she was glad Hugo was in the Middle Eastern theatre of war and no longer manning A.A. guns in Southampton, which was suffering from endless air raids on the docks and the town, causing heavy casualties and much damage.

Shortly before leaving for the Middle East, Hugo had explained that, not wishing to be an anti-aircraft gunner for the rest of the war, he had applied for a transfer to the Intelligence Corps. With his academic qualifications, his ability to speak fluent French, German and Italian together with a certain knowledge of Italy and the Balkans, he had been accepted as an officer and posted to GHQ Middle East.

Richard inwardly sighed with relief. This kind of occupation would, he knew, suit Hugo with his special gifts and keep him out of Jeremy's way, thus avoiding any friction between them.

Celia had to agree, although the prospect of spending the war years cooped up in the Stable Block alone, with Richard away at Windsor and Jeremy coming and going from Melton Hall, filled her with gloom. It wasn't as though an occasional visit from the Mitchells could cheer her up now, for Jack and Eve had slipped away out of the country in August and taken ship for East Africa, where Jack had bought a property. He had always loved Kenya and felt too old to fight in another war. Better to sweat it out in a pleasant climate and help protect our colonies, he had argued. And Eve had not been at all well. Jack thought a change of climate might do her good, so they had sold Connaught Square and as Jack put it, 'Upsticks and off to East Africa.'

THE crucial autumn of 1940, with the threat of invasion and the Battle of Britain, passed by without the expected German occupation of the British Isles and the country settled down to a long, cold, hard winter with bad news every day of shipping losses in the Atlantic and heavy air raids on the big cities.

Celia threw herself into her own war work. She had joined the Dorset Red Cross and was driving herself daily, with her petrol allowance, into Dorchester to work at the Red Cross centre there, to deal with food parcels, air raid relief and other matters. At least, she felt, she was doing something, and she quite enjoyed wearing her uniform in the company of other women of like mind during the long days.

She and Richard began to get used to the sight of soldiers driving about Charnfield in 15-cwt trucks, walking about in pairs, saluting their officers, drilling on the drive, strolling about in the evenings, whistling, singing, firing their rifles on a small practice range in the park and lining up with their mess tins and mugs for their meals, which were doled out at the cookhouse. This had been established in the kitchen quarters of the house itself.

187

MRS Walcot, the cook, was the last Charnfield servant left in the place. Page and the other men on the estate had all departed to join the Forces and Miss Saunders had retired to live with an infirm sister in Devon. Once a week, when Mrs Walcot had her day off, Celia would take over the small kitchen of the Stable House and cook for herself and Richard, if he was on leave from Windsor, and for Jeremy when on leave from the OCTU at Sanhurst, where he was now a cadet training for a commission in the Grenadiers.

In spite of the boy's poor scholastic record, Jeremy had improved generally as a human being at Melton Hall, learnt some manners and gained some self-respect and confidence. Thus Richard had encountered no difficulty in persuading the Lieutenant Colonel of the Grenadiers to accept him, provided he passed out of the OCTU.

Everyone in the family was wearing a uniform now, Celia reflected on one of Mrs Walcot's Sundays out. She was peeling potatoes in the kitchen of Stable House, for both Richard and Jeremy were home on leave. Outside the troops came and went in trucks and lined up for their dinners. Charnfield, like every other stately home of England, she thought to herself with a certain satisfaction, is at war. But if only Hugo were here.

11

BY the winter of 1942 Celia was becoming used to wartime life at Charnfield. Richard came and went from the barracks at Windsor on weekend leave and was posted for a month during that year to a course at Aldershot. Otherwise his war was fairly monotonous. Whenever he was at home, he and Celia would sit down after dinner – often consisting of spam fritters, a baked potato and vegetables from the garden – and listen to the nine o'clock news. Every detail of the overseas war news would cause Richard to get down an Atlas from the shelf and look up the places mentioned in North Africa, Tobruk, Sidi Barrani, Benghazi and El Alamein. He would also consult a *Daily Telegraph* War Map, cut out from the paper and pinned to the wall in the small kitchen. Most of the news was of battles in the Libyan desert and Celia secretly worried in her heart for Hugo from whom not a word had been heard since the early spring. Even when there was talk of Rommel's desert force, the Afrikakorps, trying to break through to Alexandria and the Suez Canal, Richard never referred to Hugo's presence in Cairo and Celia sat in silence, wondering where her stepson was and longing for some word from him.

There was little cause for worry, so far, about Jeremy. He had eagerly left Melton Hall school at eighteen, done his requisite spell in the ranks at the Guards Depot at Caterham and been despatched to the OCTU to train for a commission in the Grenadiers. On his first short leave from Sandhurst Jeremy had made it by a series of trains and buses from Camberley to Sherborne where Celia had picked him up and motored him over to the comparative comfort of the Stable House at Charnfield. Jeremy was plainly enjoying military life and seemed eager to get posted to his regiment and get into the fighting as soon as possible.

"I'd like to be out there in North Africa with the 3rd Battalion now, taking on Rommel," Jeremy told Celia.

She had no alternative but to say "Don't be in too much of a hurry, darling."

"You would say that," came the reply.

"Of course, I would. I'm your mother."

THE task of keeping the flag flying through the war at Charnfield fell mainly on Celia's shoulders. Every moment free from her Red Cross duties was spent in the vegetable garden next to Stable House, 'digging for victory' with Jim Cooper, who had mercifully failed a medical test due to his poor eyesight and was exempt from military service. All the other Cooper brothers were away, engaged in some form of war work, but Jim remained in his cottage at Charnfield with his widowed mother and helped Celia to grow row upon row of of much-needed produce.

Once or twice she invited the Brigadier and some of his officers for a drink at Stable House and they, in turn, asked her over to the Officers' Mess for dinner. It was an odd feeling for Celia to be sitting in her own dining-room, eating off a trestle table in a bare room, waited on by two Mess Orderlies in battle-dress. From what little she could see of the rest of the house, it seemed reasonably well looked after, with no sign of serious damage.

One Saturday morning in February, 1943, by a curious coincidence, a letter arrived for Celia from Hugo by the same post that Richard received a brief scribble from Jeremy.

Jeremy's letter read 'Dear Dad, I've got a week's leave on March 7th. Will it be all right if I bring home a girl I've met in London? She's very nice and is called Diana Pringle. Please ask Mother if she can manage, if she brings her ration book.' Richard was about to hand his letter to Celia but saw that she was deeply engrossed in her own, so instead he asked "Anything interesting?"

"Pages from Hugo. He's been learning to parachute. Why that? He says he can't tell us much about it for the moment. Oh, God, I hope he's all right . . . sounds cheerful enough . . . I'll give it to you when I've finished . . . "

Richard grunted. "Jem wants to bring a girl here to stay. He's got a week's leave in March."

"Good." Celia was too absorbed in Hugo's long missive to give that event much thought.

190

DIANA Pringle proved to be an attractive, if decidedly tarty, girl of seventeen. She was squeezed into tight clothes which Celia considered showed off too much of her ample chest and excellent legs and wore too much lipstick, but she carried it off with an air of cool confidence. If she was impressed by the size and grandeur of Charnfield, it seemed as if she was damned if she was going to show it. When Richard was explaining at dinner about the big house being taken over by the Army, she interrupted to tell him that her uncle and aunt in Herefordshire had been landed with a whole family of evacuees from Birmimingham. She described them as smelly little kids who'd never seen a cow or a sheep in their lives. At the end of dinner, Miss Pringle, registering mild surprise, responded to Celia's signal to get up and accompany her out of the dining-room, leaving Richard with his son and a decanter of port.

In the sitting-room Celia poured a cup of coffee for her guest and asked "Where did you and Jem meet? In London, was it?"

"That's right. About a month ago. He was on weekend leave with some chappie he'd chummed up with at the OCTU and we all met up in the bar at The Troc. Do you know the Trocadero? Nice place; very nice band. Anyway, Jem asked me to dance and we sort of went on dancing most of the evening. Jem's friend and my girl friend went on to the Cocoanut Grove but we didn't fancy going on there, so we stopped where we were . . . that is, until they swept us out with the crumbs."

She chatted on about the war, rationing, the problem of clothing coupons, the secretarial college she was attending in Ealing and how she was going to try to join the WRNS. "They let you wear nice sheer black stockings, the Wrens do, not those horrible thick things like the ATS girls have or the WAAF."

Celia hoped that if Miss Pringle was aware that Jem was a future baronet and heir to Charnfield she was not planning to marry him. It was an uncharitable thought, she told herself, but surely every mother suspected every girl of having designs on her son. But probably Diana was quite a likeable good-time girl, with nothing better to do than accept Jem's invitation to stay, and no ulterior motive.

As there was no other bedroom in the house to put her in, she had been given Hugo's room and Celia suspected that there would be some nocturnal traffic between the two juxtaposed bedrooms. 'If the floorboards creak' she thought anxiously,

191

'Richard may hear and go out into the passage to catch them at it and make a scene. Let's hope he'll be understanding. After all Jem's an officer in the Army now; he's nineteen and a normal, healthy young male.'

Then a hideous thought flashed across her mind, so awful that she dismissed it as soon as it hit her. 'What if Richard likes the look of Miss Pringle himself? After all, there was Angela Prescott . . . she was meant to be Hugo's guest and yet he . . . No . . . not now surely . . . He's too old – or is he?'

"Shame having all those soldiers in your proper house; the big one, I mean, mucking it all up."

Celia realized with a jump that Diana was addressing her and answered quickly "Oh, I don't suppose they'll do too much damage. They seem a very nice lot. Mostly Staff Officers and a company of troops, signal people and despatch riders."

"Oh, I see. That's all right, then, isn't it?"

Richard and Jem came in from the dining-room at that point and the four of them settled down to spend the evening playing Monopoly.

BY the autumn of 1943 Richard had been posted from the Training Battalion at Windsor to be Commandant of a Weapons Training School near Aldershot with the rank of Lieutenant Colonel. The School was almost identical with the one he'd been at in the middle of the previous war at Pirbright, except that they now trained soldiers on the Bren gun, the 3-inch Mortar and the Browning automatic instead of the .303 Rifle, Vickers Machine Gun and the Lewis Gun.

It was probably just as well that Richard was no longer with the Training Battalion at Windsor when Jem arrived there to begin his final training as a commissioned officer. It was easier for Celia to have her husband and her son home on leave at different times, so that she could give to each her undivided attention.

Jeremy had gained in confidence since becoming an Ensign in His Majesty's First Regiment of Footguards and was thoroughly proud of his uniform. His only concern was still an almost feverish anxiety to get into action. "Two officers in my term at Sandhurst were posted to North Africa last week," he told his mother one weekend. "It'll be just my luck to get sent to one of the Battalions training in England for the Guards Armoured

Division. They'll be stuck here for years and probably never see a shot fired."

"Darling, you'll be in the fighting quite soon enough. Your father thinks the war's going on for a long time. He says we can't possibly open a second front in Europe until we've had much longer to prepare. The Americans too, of course. You'll get your chance when that happens."

"I hope so."

One damp, foggy morning in December another letter came from Hugo. Celia tore it open excitedly and sank into a chair to read it. It took her only a minute to realize with bitter disappointment that it had actually been written before his previous letter and the date proved it. The new one said nothing about learning to parachute, nor did it give any indication that he was anywhere but in Cairo.

He wrote that he was going on a rather exciting course soon which might end in some adventure into unfriendly territory about which he couldn't say more.

It's very hot here, flies everywhere. I met someone called Nigel Roberts who was up at Oxford with me. He is on Gen. Auchinleck's staff. Had a letter from Charles who is with the Navy in Hove, of all places.

In April, 1944 Hugo wrote to say that he had spent his Christmas leave in Cairo, had a good time, all things considered, and might not get UK leave for some time. He added

I can't bear the thought of the war raging in Italy now; all those wonderful churches, palazzos and museums getting smashed up by bombs and shells. I'm afraid Jem's lot had a bad time at Salerno. Hope he wasn't there but is still safely at Windsor. Will try to write again soon.

Love Hugo

The newspapers had indeed reported, only the day before, the considerable casualties suffered during the Allied landings on the beaches of the Gulf of Salerno to secure a footing on the Italian mainland and cut the German lines of communication.

AS the summer of 1944 approached Richard became daily more optimistic, and one cold and cloudy June morning Celia woke up to the news that the Allied landings in Normandy had begun. By the time the bridge-head south of Caen had been firmly established and the drive into northern France had begun Celia had heard again from Hugo in Italy:

Isn't it exciting news about the landings in France? It can't be long now. As you will see, I am in my favourite country, but not sightseeing. Far from it. We are based in Bari but will be taking part in some odd adventures of which I cannot tell you. My lips are sealed but we shall be 'messing about' with rather bizarre people, helping them to help themselves – if you know what I mean.

Love to all. Hugo.

When Celia showed the letter to Richard, he frowned and looked serious. "Not being very discreet, our Hugo, trying to tell us military secrets in code."

"What can he mean by 'messing about with bizarre people and helping them to help themselves'?"

"It sounds to me," Richard said with some authority, "as though he's operating behind the enemy lines."

"Do you mean dropping by parachute into hostile territory?"

Richard nodded. "Exactly. Like the SOE agents in France. He's probably contacting the Resistance and supplying them with wireless equipment and small arms."

"So you think Hugo's been dropping into Italy, behind the German lines?"

"It's quite likely, Celia, or it may be the Balkans, but you're not to say anything to anyone . . . for God's sake keep it to yourself."

Celia sighed. "It sounds horribly dangerous and most uncomfortable. Poor Hugo."

"He's young," Richard retorted rather sharply, "and he voulunteered for it."

"I suppose so."

"No more uncomfortable than our war was, in the bloody trenches," Richard added, and Celia went off to the kitchen to get lunch, while Richard poured himself a very stiff whisky and turned on the wireless to hear the latest news from Normandy.

ON the night of December 23rd, 1944, Celia was decorating a small Christmas tree in a corner of the sitting-room and trying to decide whether to have plum pudding and mince pies for

194

Christmas dinner or one or the other. Richard, she knew, liked plum pudding and Jem was keen on mince pies, so she resolved to do both. Jem was home already, having arrived by train earlier in the afternoon and was upstairs having a bath. It was six o'clock in the evening and Richard had telephoned to say he would try to get away early, if possible, to get to Charnfield in time for a bath and a drink before dinner. At the latest he would be there by eight.

When Jem came down, changed into a polo-necked jersey and corduroy slacks, Celia noticed, not for the first time since her son had grown into a young man but more strongly than before, his extraordinary likeness to his father. For some reason, since he had joined the Grenadiers she was reminded more and more of Richard as he had looked that day in 1921 when she first met him lunching at Claridge's with the Mitchells. It was a look about the eyes and the slight tendency to drawl when he spoke.

Jeremy had come of age the previous September, and Celia reflected with a warm feeling that he was getting on much better with his father now. They were both grown men, in uniform and serving in the Grenadiers. Richard was no longer an impatient father with a problem child.

"No Dad yet?" Jem enquired, helping himself to a whisky and soda.

"Might not be here before eight."

"It shouldn't take him long from Aldershot. Could be a bit foggy, that's the only thing."

Celia said "I take it you haven't asked anyone for Christmas? A girl or anyone."

"No. Should I?"

"Just that your father said you could, if you wanted to. There's always Hugo's room."

"Well, I haven't."

"I see." After a pause, Celia fixed another silver ball onto a branch of the tree and asked "Is Diana Pringle going home to her parents for Christmas?"

"I've no idea."

"Are you not seeing her any more, then?"

"Might. Don't know."

Celia saw an opportunity to probe a little further into her son's love life and hoped Richard wouldn't suddenly turn up before she could get anywhere.

195

"There's no one special at the moment?"

"No."

"Quite right. Much better not to get married during a war. Everything's so uncertain. Besides, you're very young still; there's plenty of time."

"Mother, I'm not planning to ask Di Pringle to marry me, if that's what's bothering you."

"Nothing's bothering me, Jem. It's up to you whom you marry. You're twenty-one now."

"Exactly."

At that point in the conversation the telephone rang suddenly and shrilly outside in the hall. Jeremy went swiftly out to pick up the receiver. Celia continued decorating the tree and, as she clipped a small doll onto one of the branches, heard Jeremy say, so quietly that she could hardly hear him. "Oh, I see. When did it . . . Yes . . . Look, I think you'd better speak to my mother . . . "

Jem came back into the room, sheet-white and shaking a little. "It's the Southampton Police. Something's happened to Dad."

Celia was out of the room in a flash and picked up the receiver. Jem followed her.

"Lady Cardwell speaking. What's happened?" After a moment she swayed and clutched at the table to steady herself. Her face drained of colour as she nodded. "I see, yes. We'll come at once. Thank you."

She hung up and made straight for the front hall, grabbing a coat from a peg. "Daddy's been very badly hurt in a car crash and they've taken him to the Southampton General Hospital . . . We'll have to go quickly . . . in my car . . . get yourself a coat . . . and a torch . . . "

Jeremy hardly spoke a word, while his mother drove as fast as she dared along the road out of Dorchester towards Wimborne. There were small patches of fog about which, combined with the black-out, forced her to peer ahead with intense concentration. They went wrong a couple of times in the outskirts of Southampton but finally found the hospital and at ten past nine swept up to the entrance. Celia reported at once to Reception, explaining who she was.

The Reception Nurse was already on an internal phone and Celia heard her say "The wife's here . . . yes. OK."

Then she hung up and turned to Celia. "Would you and the young gentleman like to take a seat? They won't keep you."

196

Celia and Jeremy sat together on a leather upholstered bench inside the main door and waited. "He'll be in good hands here," Celia muttered.

Jeremy nodded.

Soon a doctor appeared in a white coat. "Lady Cardwell?"

Celia and Jem got up. Celia said "Yes, and this is my son."

The doctor nodded and said "Come this way, please," and set off along a corridor.

Celia imagined they were being taken to Richard's bedside and asked quietly "How is he?" but the doctor seemed not to hear. It was probably due, Celia thought, to the echoing clatter of their footsteps on the stone floor.

Half way down the corridor the doctor opened a door and ushered them into a small waiting room with a table, a vase of flowers and two or three chairs. "Come in, please." They went in. The doctor followed and closed the door; then he said quietly "I'm afraid we have bad news for you, Lady Cardwell. We haven't been able to save your husband. He sustained extremely severe head injuries and a surgeon attempted to operate but . . . "

Celia knew at once. No need for the man to say more. "Oh, God. No," she murmured.

"I'm so very sorry," the doctor said. After a suitable pause, he went on "I should perhaps add that even if an operation could have removed some of the pressure on your husband's brain, he would never have been able to live a normal life; his mental and physical functions would have been very seriously impaired."

"I see." Celia turned and clutched Jeremy's lapels, burying her face in his coat. They remained locked together for a second or two.

Jeremy was stunned, unable to speak, but he managed to put an arm shyly round his mother's shoulders.

Then Celia pulled herself together and, in an almost matter-of-fact, rather angry voice, asked "How did it happen; the accident, I mean? – Are they going to tell us?"

"Yes, of course," the doctor replied. "The police will be reporting further details. As far as we know from the ambulance crew that brought him in, your husband was involved in a head-on collision with a lorry on a narrow piece of road. It was foggy at the time and they think he may have been rather too far over towards the centre line."

197

"I see." Celia took a tremendous pull on herself and said to the doctor "Thank you for what you did. I'll . . . go and see the police now."

"No need; they'll come and find you. – Perhaps you and your son would care to stay in here for a while and someone'll bring you a cup of tea."

"That would be very kind. Perhaps we could go wherever it is and see my husband if it's allowed . . . I'd like to."

CELIA did see Richard. They took her into the hospital mortuary to idenify him while Jeremy, at Celia's request, stayed outside. When the sheet was drawn back, Celia saw that above Richard's colourless, waxen face with its eyes closed, the head was swathed in bandages, so that the multiple injuries were not visible. She looked quickly, nodded and said "Yes," very quietly and then went back with Jeremy to the small waiting-room, where a nurse brought them tea.

After a few minutes a police sergeant came in, offered his sympathy and proceeded to tell them that, from an examination of marks on the road, Richard had evidently seen the lorry loom up suddenly out of the fog and jammed on his brakes too late. This had probably caused his car to skid and hit the oncoming vehicle head-on. He had been thrown violently against the windscreen and never recovered consciousness. The sergeant also explained that Richard's car was damaged beyond repair and that an accident report would be sent to the insurance company. "We shan't trouble you with the details tonight, madam; you'll be wanting to get home now. The documents will be sent on to you in due course."

The sergeant went out, leaving Celia dazed. After a while, realizing there was nothing more to be done that night, they got into Celia's car and Jeremy drove his mother off into the foggy night, back towards Dorchester and home.

A WEEK later, as Richard's coffin was lowered into the ground in the village churchyard, old Nanny Webster, who with the aid of a stick had struggled along to the funeral from her cottage in the village, remembered standing in exactly the same spot in December, 1920, holding little Hugo by the hand, as Mr Setton recited the Burial Service over his mother's coffin. Nanny could see Rosie's grave now out of the corner of one misty eye. It was a few feet away and the inscription on the stone was worn after twenty-four years of weathering, lichen and moss:

Rosemary Charlotte, widow of Robert Mayne
and beloved wife of Richard Cardwell
born March 12th 1893, died December, 1920 aged 27.

Christmas had so often been a sad time for the family, Nanny reflected. After the first Lady Cardwell, there was Lord Brandon the following Christmas, and then Lady Brandon died in London; that was at Christmas time too, of course – the year that Master Hugo's German friend was killed flying; and now this.

She glanced around the assembled family group and saw Celia, dressed from head to foot in black with Jeremy beside her in service dress uniform with his Grenadier blue forage cap and a black armband. Nanny thought how nice-looking Jeremy had become, a tall, strong young Guards officer. She remembered how difficult he had often been as a child; spoilt, bad-tempered and disobedient. She hoped he would now marry a nice girl. Someone suitable, who would give him an heir to the Baronetcy. Someone who could help him to run Charnfield. Then Nanny noticed Commander Mitchell among the handful of mourners at the graveside, Sir Richard's oldest friend, standing by himself. She wondered why Mrs Mitchell wasn't with him, then remembered that the Commander and Mrs Mitchell had emigrated to Kenya at the outbreak of war. Nanny imagined that Mrs Mitchell would have stayed out there and not come all the way back from East Africa for the funeral. He would have had to come over, though, because he was a trustee of the estate with Mr Crawford, the solicitor. He'd be needed now . . . with Jeremy succeeding and everything.

A FEW days after the funeral Celia and Jack Mitchell lunched together at the Berkeley.

"It was so kind of you to come, Jack. Such a long journey; you must be exhausted," Celia said.

"Good Lord, girl, he was my mate. Couldn't let them shove Dick under the sod in my absence. Dear me no."

Celia managed a smile though her eyes were wet with tears.

"Besides, I reckoned you might be in need of a shoulder to blub on."

Celia reached out instinctively for Jack's hand, which was willingly given. She squeezed it, then he withdrew it in a gesture of slight embarrrassment.

"Holding hands in a public restaurant, tut-tut. And with another chap's wife – "

"Widow," Celia corrected him, managing another faint smile. There was a short silence, as the waiter brought their coffee. Then Celia went on "I'm so sorry Eve isn't well. Is it anything serious? You didn't say when you arrived."

"I didn't think it was a good moment, just before Richard's funeral. But I will tell you now, my dear, but you're not to be upset. Promise."

"Oh God. What?"

"She has cancer," Jack said quite simply, "in her tummy. She wasn't strong enough to travel. I suppose the old sawbones out there know what they're talking about. She's been having treatment but they don't give her too long. She doesn't know, mustn't ever know."

"Oh, Jack, I'm so sorry. Poor Eve, it's so . . . cruel."

"I wanted you to know, but keep it to yourself. Don't spread it around."

"As if I would!"

"Could be weeks, months, even years; but I reckon it's a matter of months." Jack sat back in his chair and stared up at the ceiling, as if he were fighting to control his emotions.

Celia, tactfully, said nothing for a while. Then: "When will you be going back?"

Jack came down to earth and smiled apologetically across the table. "Sorry, my dear. Still can't get quite used to it."

"I know."

Jack now took Celia's hand, a bit tentatively, and said "If I may be so bold as to grasp the hand of a recent widow, may I be so bold as to tell that recent widow that there is nobody in all the wide world; and I've travelled a bit as you know; that I'd rather share my anxiety and sadness with? Celia, my dearest child, you know how very fond I am of you, do you not?"

"I think so . . . It's mutual."

"Good. More coffee?"

"No, thank you."

"You asked when I was going back to Kenya. Well, the answer is the day after tomorrow. I'd have liked to stay longer but the

Union Castle haven't got another sailing for ten days and I don't want to leave Evie alone for too long."

"I wish you could stay longer." Celia sighed. "I'm so worried about Jem inheriting and all the complications with the house and money and taxes and everything."

"I know. Poor old Richard died a few years too early to get the better of His Majesty's Inland Revenue."

"He did. And Jem's going to need good advice from his trustees."

"Quite. Well, we'll keep in touch by letter. Meanwhile old Crawford'll advise you well. You listen to him, but write to me if you have any special worries."

"Oh, I will!"

"Does young Jeremy intend to stay on in the army?"

"I don't know. I somehow doubt it. But he'll be very disappointed if he doesn't see any action."

"And peace-time soldiering would bore him to death, eh?"

"I'm afraid so. I just hope he'll be able to get a decent job after he's demobbed. He must try and earn some money. As it is, he'll never be able to afford the cost of opening up the house again, even if he wants to."

"When do you get it back from the army?"

"Soon, I expect," Celia said. "The troops have moved out now and there's no sign of any others coming in. So I'm going over to see if there's any damage and start clearing up a bit."

"But you'll stay on in the the Stable House?"

"Have to, for the time being."

JACK telephoned Celia at Charnfield to say goodbye to her the night before he sailed. She asked Jack to convey her love to Eve and hung up, wondering vaguely whether she'd ever see either of them again.

IMMEDIATELY after Richard's death Celia had cabled to Hugo to break the news and followed up her cable with a long letter.

A couple of weeks had gone by since Jack's departure for East Africa. Most of the time had been spent in clearing out cupboards, disposing of Richard's personal belongings and in endless meetings with Mr Crawford, who was trying to sort out the complications of Richard's will. Hugo's absence made the dreary task of clearing up all the more depressing.

201

One day Celia went across with the keys and let herself into the big house for the first time since the Brigade Headquarters had left, shortly after D-Day, for Normandy. In what had once been Page's pantry, with her head in a cupboard containing a green baize apron and another of white cotton twill, a pot of silver plate powder, a bottle of methylated spirits, assorted cleaning brushes and clothes, and other similar items, Celia burst into tears. She moved over to sit at an oil-cloth covered table under a barred window, and had her first good cry since Richard's death.

After a while, as she dried her eyes, she noticed a cobweb in a corner and the shabby state of the green dado round the cream walls. Gone was the cheerful bustle of the servants downstairs and the leisurely, privileged life upstairs that had depended on their devoted service. She remembered how she had lain on her bed one summer evening years ago, out of sorts with herself and the world, and thought now how lucky she had in fact been. But she had been unhappy then because her marriage was going badly: in recent years she and Richard had come together again. She missed him now, she thought, for his practical common-sense as well as his company. How could she manage to clear up this great place without him? She supposed that Jeremy would give what support he could, but at the best it would be limited by his lack of interest in the house, lack of experience and lack of *rapport* with herself. She sighed. If only Hugo were here! His company would have done more than anyone's to help her through this difficult time. But he was abroad on some dangerous mission, and goodness knew when he would get back, if ever. This bloody war had carried off too many of the young. 'But still,' she told herself; 'he's sure to come back; he's got to!'

By the end of February no word had been heard from Hugo and a letter Celia had written to the War Office resulted only in a vague reply that 'Lieutenant H. Mayne, Intelligence Corps, has been transferred from Cairo to the Balkan Theatre of Operations and his whereabouts are unknown, although there are no reports of the officer being reported killed, wounded or missing.'

Jeremy had been granted two weeks' compassionate leave to attend his father's funeral and various meetings with the trustees in connection with his succession to the estate. No decisions could be made as to the future of the house until it had been derequisitioned by the army and an assessment had been made of

202

its structural condition. All that was certain, as Crawford made very clear to Celia and her son, was that there would not be much money left after death duties to keep up the place and there were serious problems ahead.

By March 1945 Jeremy had been posted from the Training Battalion at Windsor to a Reinforcement Unit on the South Coast. The news on April 1st that the Guards Armoured Division had crossed the Rhine and was pushing its way towards Bremen and the Ruhr made him boil with anger and frustration. He feared the war would be over before he could see any action, and by May his fears were confirmed. The land forces of Nazi Germany surrendered on Lüneburg Heath and it was all over.

By 1945 Celia was living alone in Stable House with only Mrs Walcot for company. Richard was dead, Hugo was floating about somewhere in the Balkans and Jeremy was still in the Grenadiers but now, stationed at Chelsea Barracks, was spending most of his weekends and leaves in London, rarely coming home.

And there stood the big house, Charnfield itself, the Cardwell ancestral home, now the property of 2nd Lieut. Sir Jeremy Cardwell, Bt, cold, damp and empty, its vast rooms denuded of furniture or pictures, with drawing-pin marks on every door and wall where maps, signs or notices had been pinned up by the army.

One morning a letter came from the War Office to say they would be derequisitioning Charnfield Park shortly and the house would be handed back to its owner.

"It'll be in a right old mess," Mrs Walcot said grimly.

"Bound to be," Celia said, "but we must pray there's no major damage."

As good as their word, the War Office had officially handed back Charnfield by the last week in June and Celia insisted on Jeremy accompanying her a few days later to Mr Crawford's office in Lincoln's Inn Fields to discuss the future of the whole estate. The meeting had been heated and the outcome un-satisfactory.

"I'm not going to live in a great barn like that," Jeremy announced vehemently. "It's an absurd idea and impossible, anyway. You'd need to be a multi-millionaire to keep up a place like Charnfield now. There's no future for these great big sprawling stately homes any longer. Even if we get the Socialists out, it'll still be too expensive to run the place. I'm for selling up, lock, stock and barrel and buying a place in the South of France."

What Jeremy didn't say was that he visualised spending his leaves and the money from the sale in the sun, enjoying good French food and wine and gambling in Riviera Casinos.

His announcement of his determination to sell was greeted by a short silence. Crawford fiddled with his papers and cleared his throat, glancing over to Celia as though hoping she would comment, but instead she said quietly "I think we should ask Mr Crawford for his opinion, Jeremy. After all, he is a trustee and you must listen to his advice, especially in Uncle Jack's absence. What do you think, Mr Crawford?"

Crawford was a lean, elderly man with thinning grey hair and horn-rimmed glasses. He wore a bow-tie and had a habit of screwing up his eyes as he spoke, as though he was peering through driving rain. He turned to Jeremy. "There are, of course, serious financial problems and certain responsibilities, too, which go with your inheritance of the property. There are indeed, as you say, grave difficulties today and many landowners such as yourself have to face them. Charnfield is a fine house of great historical and architectural interest and the contents are, as you must realize, of considerable importance and . . . value. Possessions that have been in your family for nearly four centuries."

"I know all that," said Jeremy, rather abruptly.

Celia bridled. "I think what Mr Crawford is trying his best to explain to you is that it would be a great tragedy to duck your responsibilities and throw it all away, without at least considering some alternative ways of preserving Charnfield."

"Even if you can't see yourself living in the house," Crawford ventured, "you may marry and have a son and . . . wish to pass the property on to him. There is revenue, of course, from the tenanted farms and from your late father's investments but . . . "

"Not enough to pay the Death Duties and keep the place up," Jeremy said quickly. "It can't be done. We'll have to sell up. The ancestors can turn in their graves, if they like. They haven't got to live in this country under a Socialist government that's bent on ruining people with inherited wealth and forcing them to abandon their ancestral homes, so they can buy them cheap and turn them into holiday camps for the workers."

204

"All the more reason to fight, I would have thought," Mr Crawford murmured, not wishing to overstep his duties.

"You like a good fight," Celia took up the argument. "Surely this is a cause worth fighting for?"

"To win a fight, you need weapons," Jeremy interjected. "For this fight the weapons are money and we haven't got enough."

The conference was inconclusive, with Jeremy continuing to insist that Charnfield should be put on the market immediately, until Celia wrung from him a reluctant promise to give the matter more thought before making a rash decision which he might one day regret. With that the meeting ended.

OVER the next few weeks Jeremy stayed in London with an army friend and pursued his life of pleasure. This was facilitated by a provisional sum of money from his father's will, advanced by Crawford for his immediate living costs.

It was soon clear to Celia that her son was getting through his money fast, taking girls out to theatres and nightclubs and betting fairly heavily on horses. On one occasion Celia took a call for Jeremy from his bank manager, while the former was up in Scotland, spending a week's leave with another army friend near Inverness. The manager of the bank in Dorchester simply asked if a message could be left for Sir Jeremy Cardwell to telephone Mr Wickham at the bank to 'disuss his account'. Celia knew she could not ask for any more details but promised to pass on the message.

When Jeremy came back from Scotland, she mentioned the bank manager's call to him at supper – after Jeremy had knocked back his third glass of port. As soon as Celia broached the subject, her son's upper lip curled into a sort of snarl and he told her to mind her own business.

"Don't speak to me like that," Celia snapped back. She had had enough. "I'm simply telling you that your bank manager wants to speak to you about your account; that's all. If you've spent all that money that Crawford advanced to you on gallivanting about to nightclubs, that's your affair. Just don't expect to get any money from me, because I haven't got any."

With that Celia left the dining-room and went into the kitchen to help Mrs Walcot with the washing-up. Then she went to bed without seeing Jeremy again. But she heard his car drive off at about eleven o'clock. He was returning to Chelsea Barracks without having come up to her room to say goodbye.

As she lay in bed, lonely, upset and miserable, Celia thought of Jack and Eve, those good, kind old friends, and of how shocked they would be at Jeremy's behaviour. Then she thought of Richard and wondered whether her son had inherited his father's temper, but reminded herself that Richard had not always had a temper – only in his later years. He had spoilt Jem, though, because he had been so thrilled to have a son and heir. The word 'heir' made her laugh cynically to herself. 'Heir to what?' she asked herself.

Then her thoughts turned to Hugo. 'Pray God keep him safe, and bring him home soon,' she muttered, although she hated to think how distressed he would be if Charnfield were sold. Maybe he could make Jem see sense, although it seemed a doubtful possibility, given Jem's present recklessness.

The next morning brought a letter from Kenya. Celia tore it open quickly and sat down to read it in the kitchen. A letter from Jack Mitchell seemed like a ray of light in the gloom. But her heart became heavy as she read:

My darling Evie died in my arms yesterday at the hospital in Nairobi. She put up a good fight but lost it, smiling and joking to the end. She had known for some time she hadn't much more cable to pay out but never showed any fear. We buried her out here, because she loved this country. I feel a bit lost and blown off course. I plan to visit London in a week or so, by air if poss., to arrange a few matters with Evie's lawyers. Hope to see you then.

                    Your old, affectionate mate, Jack.

When Jack arrived, Celia spent a week in London, staying at his hotel in order to see as much of him as she could in that time. He had so many matters to deal with in town that visiting her at Charnfield would have been impossible.

ON the Saturday evening of that very week Hugo returned to England, looking emaciated, unshaven and scruffy, after a long journey from the Albanian mountains, via Belgrade to Brindisi and then home in an RAF Dakota. At RAF Northolt he tried the telephone number of his flat, just in case Charles was back in London and had managed to repossess it, but as he had expected, he could not get through. In any case, his London life with

Charles seemed at the moment like an episode lost in the past. It was partly fatigue that made Charnfield and Celia seem of far greater importance but it was also because he had recently received Celia's letter telling him of Uncle Richard's death.

He next tried telephoning Stable House, not wishing to give Celia a shock by arriving home suddenly in the middle of the night. But there was no answer from the stable block. Hugo wondered if Celia and Jeremy had moved back into the big house, so he tried that number too, but still nobody answered. He was not to know that he had chosen a time to return when Mrs Walcot had gone home to her cottage next to Jim Cooper's and Celia was in London, dining that very night with Jack Mitchell at Quaglino's.

There was nothing for it, Hugo decided, but to make his way down to Charnfield and surprise them. He managed to cadge a lift into London from a Gunner Colonel who was met off his plane by a staff car and then he caught the last train from Waterloo to Exeter that stopped at Salisbury. When Hugo got out there, the station clock stood at five minutes past midnight. There were no taxis, nobody about save one porter and a ticket collector. After a brief consultation with this helpful official, Hugo was put in contact with a local taximan, self-employed, and a friend of the ticket collector. He was prepared to drive the gentleman to Charnfield for twenty-five quid. Hugo had fifty pounds on him, so they set off into the night, heading for Blandford.

Hugo was dog tired, rather emotional and deeply apprehensive when the taxi at last, at half-past two in the morning, approached the lodge gates of Charnfield. He was reluctant to wake Mrs Keegan to open the gates for him. Perhaps Keegan himself would be home by now, demobilized from the forces, although Hugo knew he ought to rouse his weary limbs to get out and open the gates himself. Then, as the headlights swung off the main road towards the lodge, he saw to his surprise that the gates were open. The lodge itself was in darkness with its windows shuttered, as though nobody was living there.

Once through the Gate House, Hugo stopped the taxi a short way from Stable House and paid the driver, thanking the man with his voice lowered, not wishing to disturb anyone until he was in the house.

Expecting the front door to be locked and bolted, Hugo

207

glanced around for some way of getting in. He tried the front door, just for luck, and was astonished to find it unlocked, so he went in quietly and closed it behind him. It was pitch dark in the hall and he hesitated to put on a light, so he got his torch out of his valise. If he could make his way up to his room and get himself to bed, perhaps leaving a note on the landing outside Celia's room to say he'd arrived, she would find him in the morning.

'Quite a dramatic homecoming,' he thought with some satisfaction, as he crept up the stairs. He might even get breakfast in bed. He could tell Celia in the morning, and Jeremy, about his Military Cross, which would please them, and show them his parachute badge, also sewn onto his tunic. It was sad Uncle Richard wouldn't be there in the morning, he thought. He would think his stepson had done something to be proud of at last, by being decorated for bravery.

As he reached the landing, much to his surprise, Hugo became aware of a strong smell of cigar smoke and scent, as though someone had been giving a party. He tiptoed along to the door of his room and stopped suddenly, as the beam of his torch caught a number of familiar things stacked in a recess against the banister rail. There was a pile of his civilian suits, jackets, shirts and other garments, with his old school trunk, two cases and a heap of books which he had moved down to Charnfield when the flat he shared with Charles had been let.

It did not take Hugo long to discover the reason for this evacuation of his belongings from his room. Turning the door-knob gently, he went in and flicked on the light. He stared with astonishment at what he saw. Tucked up in his bed were two people, a young man and a girl. As the light hit them, they woke up simultaneously and sat up; both were evidently naked.

"Who in God's name are you?" Hugo managed to croak in a strangled voice.

"Are you a burglar?" the girl said nervously.

"No I'm not," Hugo retorted, recovering his voice. "I'm Hugo Mayne and I happen to live here and this is my room. Who are you?"

The young man spoke up now. "I'm Harry Fawcett, a friend of Jem's; in the regiment actually; and this is Sarah Brooking."

"How do you do," Sarah muttered, clutching the bedclothes

closer round her. "We're staying here for the weekend, as guests of Jem's . . . Jeremy Cardwell's."

Hugo could think of nothing to say so he went out, turning off the light and banging the door shut. He tried the handle of Celia's room, quite prepared now to waken her and protest, but her room was empty and her things were in place. She was obviously away. Not liking to invade her room, Hugo went downstairs to the hall and found a motoring rug and two overcoats which he carried into the sitting-room. Here, too tired to care, he flopped onto the large sofa, covered himself with the rug and the coats and was soon asleep.

Upstairs in his own room Sarah was asking her sleeping partner "Who was that?"

"Jem's step-brother, I suppose. Chap called Hugo Mayne. He's been out in the Middle East, doing cloak-and-dagger stuff I believe. Queer as a coot."

"I thought he was," Sarah said and snuggled down in the bed, reaching out for Harry and turning him round towards her. "How very awkward," she giggled, "we're in his room and in his bed."

"Jem wasn't to know his step-bro. was coming back at this hour of the night," Harry said.

"He'll tell Lady Cardwell and we shan't be asked again."

"Can't be helped," said Harry and drew Sarah to him.

Hugo was mercifully asleep by the time the sound of bedsprings creaking rhythmically could be heard coming from his own room, directly overhead.

209

12

HUGO was still asleep when Mrs Walcot came in to open the curtains and tidy up, before getting breakfast for the young guests. As far as she knew there were four of them in the house: Jeremy, his friend Harry, Harry's girl-friend Sarah, and Jem's current *amour*, a little revue actress called Zoe Baker.

Jeremy had set up the house party when he realised that his mother would be away for a whole week in London.

"Holy Mother of God . . ." Mrs Walcot gasped, clapping her hand to her mouth and staring in horror at the bulk sprawled awkwardly under an overcoat on the sofa, with one leg sticking out.

Hugo had only been dozing when he heard the door open. He sat up quickly. "It's all right, Mrs Walcot. It's only me."

Mrs Walcot gaped at him, then her face lit up with a smile. "Master Hugo, thank the Lord. I was thinking it was a dead body I was seeing. All slumped over the sofa you were, like a corpse in a murder on the films."

"I'm sorry if I scared you, Mrs Walcot. It's just that I got back late last night, to find two strange people sleeping in my bed."

"Don't speak of it, sir; these youngsters, up until all hours, playing the gramophone, dancing and drinking! Well, I suppose with the war and all, they've a right to enjoy themselves but to be sure it'll be with her ladyship away in London. When the cat's away . . ."

"Yes, but I'd rather the mice didn't play in my bed. I've got cramp and a stiff neck."

"To be sure it was a deceitful thing for Mister Jem to be doing, sir, as soon as his mother's back was turned . . . I mean Sir Jeremy, beggin' his pardon . . . to bring his young friends down here from London for a hooley."

210

"Well, I got home from abroad late last night, exhausted, to find strange people in my bed."

"It's a disgrace, Mister Hugo."

"I also object strongly to finding all my belongings strewn about on the landing; great piles of my clothes and books and God knows what."

"I was given orders to clear out your room, sir, for the young guests. Sir Jeremy told me to take everything from the cupboards and the chest-of-drawers and there was nowhere else to put the stuff."

"That's not your fault, Mrs Walcot."

"Will I be getting you a nice cup of tea, Mister Hugo?"

"That would be wonderful, thank you."

As soon as Mrs Walcot had left the room, Hugo got up from the sofa, feeling cramped after sleeping heavily in an awkward posture. Having no dressing gown, he put on his overcoat and sat down to consider the situation. A few minutes later he was relishing a welcome cup of strong tea while Mrs Walcot filled him in with all the family news. There was no sound from upstairs, so the Irish cook-housekeeper was able to take the time to tell him about Commander Mitchell coming over for Sir Richard's funeral.

"Oh, it was a terrible shock that was, poor man, and her poor ladyship . . . having to see Sir Richard dead in the hospital and all in the middle of the night . . . his car was smashed to pieces, they said; it was all in the papers, and the police reckoned he was driving on the wrong side of the road in the fog, so he couldn't see the lorry coming towards him . . . "

"Yes, I know," Hugo said patiently, for he had heard all the grim details in Celia's long letter.

"And then Mrs Mitchell, poor soul, dying out there in Africa."

This hit Hugo like a sledgehammer. "Mrs Mitchell died; when?"

"Did you not know about it?"

"No. I did not. Oh God, that's terrible! When did it happen?"

"That would have been gone a month or so now. The Commander went back to Africa directly after Sir Richard's funeral and Mrs Mitchell died soon after his return, poor soul."

"Oh my god, Eve . . . dead. Was she ill or what?"

"Cancer," said Mrs Walcot, knowingly nodding her head and crossing herself.

211

Hugo had been particularly fond of Eve and felt very sad. She had been a good friend to him, he reflected, rather more so than Jack, who had always held and showed unmistakably strong disapproval of his chosen way of life. But they were Uncle Richard's and Celia's oldest friends; almost part of the family.

Hugo soon discovered from Mrs Walcot that Celia was staying at Brown's Hotel in London to be with Jack Mitchell, but decided it was too early to ring her. Instead, he took his shaving kit and toothbrush and went into the downstairs cloakroom to wash and shave. He would have liked a bath but had no desire to get involved with the members of Jeremy's house party who might start getting up and dressing upstairs.

After washing himself from head to toe, a procedure he had grown used to in the partisans' camps in the mountains of Albania, he found in his valise a clean shirt, socks and underpants, got dressed and presented himself in the kitchen where Mrs Walcot had breakfast ready for him: bacon and scrambled eggs on toast with as much coffee as he wanted.

After breakfast Hugo telephoned Celia from the sitting-room and heard her voice trembling with excitement on the other end of the line. "Where are you?"

"At home. At Stable House. But I think I'll come up to London today, if you're not coming back yet. I must see you."

"I'm up here for a few days with poor Jack Mitchell. Eve died, so he came over to deal with her affairs and I'm keeping him company on his last night here. He sails back tomorrow."

"Yes, Mrs Walcot told me the sad news."

"Do come up," Celia said. "Jack would love to see you. We'll get you a room in the hotel for tonight, then the three of us can dine together and I can drive you back to Charnfield tomorrow. How about that? There's so much to talk about. Oh God, I'm so thrilled you're home and undamaged . . . you are undamaged, aren't you?"

"Physically, yes. Mentally, I'm not sure."

"You're joking."

"Not altogether. I've seen and done some fairly gruesome things lately, but I'll tell you about it when I see you."

"Oh, darling!"

"It's all right, Celia, I'm not unhinged. Just desperately tired."

After months of fear and strain the relief of being home and hearing Celia's warm, loving voice on the telephone brought a

212

lump into Hugo's throat. He hung up quickly and choked back a violent sob. The tears filled his eyes but he bit his lip and turned away from the telephone, fighting to get control of himself. Then he looked into the kitchen to tell Mrs Walcot not to worry about lunch. "I'll get something on the train. I'm going up to join her ladyship in London. We shall motor back tomorrow afternoon."

"That'll be nice," said Mrs Walcot.

Next he decided to visit the big house, so he took the keys from a drawer in the hall table and set out, with some apprehension, across the forecourt by the gatehouse to the main entrance.

The huge, old-fashioned key turned with a slight grinding sound in the lock of the heavy oak door which swung open, revealing the porch that led into the Great Hall.

It was a weird feeling for Hugo, within weeks of physical hardship, fear and discomfort when he was operating behind the German lines in Albania, to be walking alone through the great house that had been his home since he was three years old. His footsteps echoed on the uncarpeted stone floors and up the bare staircase to the upper landing.

As he walked, he felt the ghostly presence of the figures in the old portraits, his childhood friends, of Page the butler and Robert, the footman, and up in the comfortable nurseries, dear Nanny; all the people who had kept the house running as a kind of paradise on earth. *Ichabod*! The glory was indeed departed. He went to a window to look out over the park. Flower beds and lawn had disappeared under hideous Nissen huts and there was an untidiness abaout the edges and corners of what was left that would have caused Keegan the head gardener anguish and mortification, had he seen it six years ago.

Hugo turned his attention back to the house. There were still a few posters on walls and doors and a large battered ping-pong table had been left behind in the library by the troops, but there did not at first sight appear to be any serious damage. All the mouldings, wood carvings and wall papers were intact and the only mildly offensive element to bother him was a strong smell everywhere of beer, blanco and rifle oil.

He knew they had been lucky to have a Brigade Headquarters at Charnfield, with the house occupied mainly by officers who were staffing offices, not engaged on field exercises and coming in to score the floors with hobnailed boots and transfer the dirt from their clothes and weapons to the walls and doors. The

213

signallers and other auxiliary troops had been mostly accommodated in Nissen huts in the park.

'All the same,' Hugo thought, 'it will be a mammoth task to get everything back to normal, to clean and scrub the floors and walls and restore all the furniture and the pictures and so on to their rightful places. Above all,' he thought, as he finally left, closing and locking the front door, 'the place will need to be thoroughly aired and fumigated to get rid of the smell of the army.'

"YES, it must," Celia agreed, "and we'll do it together, you and I. After all, you know where everything belongs and I doubt if Jem will raise a hand to help."

They were driving back together from London after Hugo's visit to Brown's Hotel for the night. Celia drove rather carefully, and Hugo wondered if it was because of Uncle Richard's fatal crash. She talked a lot about Jack Mitchell and how shattered he was by Eve's death and how lonely he would be, stuck out there in Kenya all alone.

As she talked, Hugo felt she was preparing him for something. Every reference to Jack was tinged with admiration, compassion and concern.

Then it came, a few miles short of Blandford. They had driven in silence for a while when Celia suddenly said "Would you be terribly shocked if I told you that Jack Mitchell has been in love with me for years?"

"It's not true, Celia! Why didn't you tell me?"

"Are you shocked?"

"Well, no. Not really. I know that it was the Mitchells who first introduced you to Uncle Richard, he and Eve; you told me that ages ago. But . . . "

"I honestly didn't know how he felt about me, I swear, Hugo; not until he told me the other day, over lunch. He said he felt it was high time he 'came clean'; his exact words, because we were both widowed and suddenly alone in the world. Well, I suppose we are in a sense."

Hugo stared ahead at the road, then said "Do you love him, really? I mean, could you spend the rest of your life with Jack Mitchell . . . in Kenya?"

"Oddly enough, darling, I believe I could. I've always been especially fond of him; he's a good, kind man and he's been a

214

wonderful friend and somehow a person I feel safe with; he's protective and strong and reliable."

"You make him sound like an insurance policy."

"You don't approve, do you?"

"Well, it's your life, Celia. You know I shall miss you like hell . . . I mean, all the way to Kenya . . . if you'd said you were going to shack up with Jack in a cosy little cottage somewhere in Surrey, I could just about bear it. But all the way to Kenya . . . with all those hungry lions and tigers. Not to mention the decadent society ladies in the country clubs, jumping in and out of bed with the white hunters and black servants. Is that really what you want?"

"I have no future here, darling," Celia said, laughing at this picture of Africa. "If Jem gets married and decides to move back into the house and have children, I shall sit in Stable House for the rest of my life, a miserable widow in a dower house, getting in my son's way, probably disapproving of everything he does and being of no use to anyone."

"That's ridiculous."

"It's not, you know. Far better to throw my lot in with Jack and end my days in the African bush. After all, I did grow up in India, so hot countries hold no terrors for me and it's a good, wholesome outdoor life."

"What in God's name would you do all day?" Hugo asked, his voice betraying despair mixed with a modicum of disbelief.

"Help with the farm, drive into Nairobi twice a week to shop, swim in the Indian Ocean in the summer at Malindi, probably photograph wild game and perhaps write a book."

"It sounds like a living death to me."

"Eve did it, and she was as happy as a clam out there for four years."

After another silence Celia continued, "Anyway, if I decide on it, I shan't go until we've got Charnfield on its feet again. I told Jack and he said he could wait, but not for too long. He is sixty-four."

"It's a horribly sad and depressing outlook, that's all I can say."

"One last thing. Don't say anything to Jem about it. I don't want to tell him until it's settled, one way or another."

MERCIFULLY, by the time Celia and Hugo reached Charnfield, Jeremy had left for London with his friends and the house was

215

empty, but for Mrs Walcot who was tidying up, making beds and grumbling about the mess.

Hugo and Celia went straight into the sitting-room where, to Hugo's surprise but not displeasure, she suddenly clutched him to her and dissolved into floods of tears. It was as though she had been holding them back all the way down from London in the car. Now it all came pouring out.

"Hugo, darling, I've missed you so much . . . you've no idea what hell it was, having to deal with Richard's . . . accident and everything without you to help me. Jem was very good, he did all he could, but I needed you with me . . . especially afterwards."

"I'm not sure I could have been much use to you," Hugo said, leading her to a chair. "I've been having rather a lot to do with violent death out in Albania, and I find I'm not very good at it, either."

Celia pulled herself together. "I'm so sorry, it's coming back here with you. I can't quite get used to Richard not being here and I keep thinking how bloody I was to him . . . over that Prescott girl and so many . . . other . . . things."

She nearly started crying again but Hugo took her hand and held it tight.

"I'm sorry, I'm being selfish. After all you've been through in the war, what am I thinking of, crying for myself?"

Hugo said nothing, but just went on holding her hand.

"Tell me, what it was like out there? A ghastly nightmare, I imagine. Were you terribly scared?"

"Sometimes. Not all the time. There were good moments; funny moments as well as grim ones. I was with a wonderful band of characters and we laughed a great deal. The only thing that's going to stick in my mind and give me bad dreams for years is . . . was . . ." He hesitated.

"What?" Celia asked, quietly.

Hugo moved over to look out of the window. After a moment he said "I had to kill a man . . . in cold blood. Stick a knife into his back from behind. Rather a short man, a partisan, actually. One of our own people, or so we thought, who'd been giving away our positions for money. He looked like a porter on an Italian railway station. He just had to be stopped, very quickly, before he could betray the whole operation, so . . . it was a horrible feeling. I'm sure he had a wife and children in the next village where he lived."

Celia was listening, tense and wide-eyed. "Don't tell me any more, please."

"There's nothing more to tell. We just wrapped his body in an army blanket and tossed it into the river." He went on staring out of the window for a while, until he said more briskly "Oh, one strange thing – " He stopped abruptly. He had been about to say to Celia 'I bumped into David Maidment in Cairo', but had thought better of it.

BEFORE Hugo was parachuted into Albania he had been in Cairo for some months. One evening while there he was drinking at the bar in Shepherd's Hotel when he saw David Maidment coming through the crowd.

David, who had become a Staff Officer with the 8th Army, evidently saw him at about the same moment; they recognised each other immediately, although they had not met since they were boys. It soon became apparent that each was equally pleased to see the other.

They spent the evening together and then David went back to Hugo's billet in a private house; its owner was away, the two servants came in daily and they had it to themselves. That night, in David's company, Hugo realised that he had probably loved him since that summer holiday at Charnfield, years earlier. Not seeing him again and not hearing from him, combined with Uncle Richard's intense dislike, had made him bury his feelings in the belief that they would only cause him unhappiness. Now, face to face, his suppressed emotion burst into flower.

In retrospect Hugo saw that as the happiest night – or day – of his life; at the time, his happiness was so great that he was constantly aware of it, as strong and as real in its different way as the sensation of pain. He said so to David, adding "I wish it could go on longer."

David, who had earlier talked a great deal but was more silent the following morning, did not reply. Soon afterwards, he had gone, taking Hugo's address with him after saying vaguely that they must meet again.

For the next few days Hugo lived in a dream. It seemed as if on that night his love for David had burst into flower like some kind of desert cactus that erupts suddenly into splendid blossom when rain comes after a long drought. 'Probably one of the sort that blooms only once in its lifetime,' he reflected sadly. David

217

had been very loving; there could be no doubt about that; but his suggestion of meeting again had been no more than cool.

Then Hugo was dropped into the Albanian mountains on his first mission, and no longer had time to think about David.

Now that he was home, he supposed that David would have forgotten him again. And Celia might be about to disappear from his life, too. He sighed. But it was no good brooding; for one thing, Celia would not approve!

He would have to pick up the reins with Charles once more, and make the best of it. He had already applied to the Courtauld Institute for his his old job.

He turned from the window to face Celia. "I say, when are we going to start work on the house?"

"Tomorrow," said Celia, glad of the change of subject. "If that will suit you."

"I'll have to go to London one day next week," Hugo said, "to find out how soon we can get our flat back. It's been let, you see. Charles told me in his last letter, some months ago, that when the end came, it might take him some time to get out of the Navy. I haven't heard a word from him yet, so I'll have to deal with the flat myself."

"Of course," she said, "but tomorrow we'll start Operation 'Scrubbing Brush'."

HUGO had managed to get his job at the Courtauld back and had been granted four weeks demobilisation leave, which he reckoned would be just time enough to get on top of the job.

They started the next morning on schedule, at nine o'clock sharp, Celia dressed in a boiler suit and Hugo in his oldest clothes. Armed with brushes, dustpans, buckets and floor cloths, they went into battle.

Mrs Walcot came over to help, as soon as she had washed up the breakfast, and a couple of women from the village, who knew and loved the place, had volunteered to help scrub floors, wash down walls, brush carpets and polish brass for a small reward. Hugo devoted most of his time to bringing out of store and unwrapping the valuable paintings and prints and some of the more precious ornaments. As each room of the house was declared cleaned and ready, Hugo went in with a ladder, spare picture wire, nails and brackets to re-hang the pictures and, with Celia, Mrs Walcot or occasional help from Jim Cooper, to move back rugs and items of furniture. It was a long, laborious task but, gradually over a week or so, Charnfield Park began once again to resemble an inhabitable stately home.

Jeremy came down once or twice, on one occasion to take some of his heavier belongings over to the big house. But he never stayed for long and usually dashed off back to London, leaving his task half-finished.

ONE warm June evening when the cleaning and refurbishing of the house was all but completed, Celia, Jeremy and Hugo were finishing dinner. It was still light and Celia wanted to go out before it became too dark to see, to pick raspberries in her vegetable garden.

Jem chose that moment to drop a bombshell. "It'll be my twenty-fourth birthday in July," he said, "so I've decided to give one hell of an orgy in the big house, to celebrate."

Much of what Jem said was empty, wild talk and his intentions no more than pie in the sky, and Celia did not wholly take in the implications of his announcement. All she said, as she left the table to go out by the French windows, was "And who's going to pay for that?"

She was half way to the raspberry cage when Hugo asked Jeremy if he was serious.

"About what?"

"Having 'one hell of an orgy' in the big house."

"Certainly. Why not?"

"How horribly common," Hugo snapped, getting up from the table.

"What?"

"You heard what I said."

Jeremy raised his eyebrows with cool arrogance and poured himself another glass of port. "I'm sorry, Hugo," he said, "but it's my house now and I shall do what I like in it."

This was too much for Hugo. He was still tired, war-weary and bitterly resentful. "Oh, I'm sure you will," he said in a menacingly restrained voice. "Go ahead and desecrate the place and all the beautiful things in it . . . trample about all those historic rooms with your screaming, empty-headed friends. I expect you'll have 'jolly good fun' later on smashing up all the porcelain in the glass cabinets and throwing the Renoirs and Monets and the Forello Athenae out of the window onto

219

the lawn. You never cared for that Forello sculpture, did you?"

Jeremy scraped back his chair and stood up, trembling with anger. "Now look, Hugo, I know you're tired and you've probably had too much port but I'm not going to put up with much more of this bitching and bickering. I'm sick to death of it; and, while we're on the subject, there's something I've been meaning to say to you for some time, and now seems to me a suitable moment to say it."

"Say what?" Hugo challenged him.

"You won't like it."

Jeremy walked across the dining-room and started to fiddle nervously with the curtains. "I'd like you to find somewhere else to live in the future. Or rather, somewhere else to spend your weekends and holidays."

"Oh, would you!" Hugo said. His stepbrother's remark had hit him like a thunderbolt, but he intended not to show it.

Jeremy knew the moment had come to have the whole thing out in the open. He took a deep breath and plunged on. "After all, you are thirty-one now. I know you're not married or anything, but it's going to be damned awkward for me, if I get married, especially if I start a family. My wife and I might rather like to have some privacy in our own home, like any other married couple."

Dazed, pale and shaking slightly, Hugo stared at Jeremy. "So you're getting married, are you, and moving into the big house?"

"I didn't say that. But I might marry soon; probably will, and whether I live over there or stay here is . . . "

"You've said yourself that you won't be able to live in Charnfield, not with a Socialist government taxing us all out of existence."

Jeremy gave a sigh of exasperation. "Watever happens in the future, Hugo, I need your room here, in this house, for my weekend guests."

"I see."

"I hate doing it, Hugo, but it's not unusual; it's the way things are . . . "

Hugo stared up at the ceiling, trying to suppress tears of rage and humiliation. "After all I've done for Charnfield, all these years, writing up its history, listing its treasures, cataloguing every single bloody book in the library, caring for the place . . . "

220

"Nobody asked you to do those things, Hugo. It wasn't yours, it never has been."

"Charnfield is my home," Hugo replied quietly, "I've lived here for thirty years, almost all my life, since I was three years old. Now you're chucking me out like some unwanted servant."

"It's not my fault, Hugo, it's just an accident of birth. The old hereditary system."

Hugo got up and went slowly out of the dining-room, followed by Jeremy.

At the foot of the stairs, Jeremy stopped. "I didn't want to mention it tonight, but you rather pushed me into it."

Hugo made no reply but leant against the banisters, burying his head in his hands.

Jeremy tried again. "Look, you could have the West Lodge, perhaps; it could be fixed up for you, I suppose, one day when old Mrs Green – "

"I've got a perfectly good flat in London, thank you," Hugo said, and went resolutely upstairs to his room, slamming the door.

Ten minutes later, when Celia came in from the kitchen garden with a bowl of raspberries, Jeremy told his mother what had happened.

"There seems little point in arguing about Charnfield, because neither of you could afford to live here, in any case," Celia replied sadly.

The following morning Jeremy went back to London to take a girl to lunch at the Berkeley. Celia and Hugo went for a long walk down the drive, through the woods and up onto the downs. It was a beautiful, warm day and they sat on a grassy bank on the edge of a wood from which they could see Charnfield spread out below them: the park, the lodge, the village and, partly visible through a belt of tall trees, the house itself.

"It's dreadful news, I'm afraid, about Charnfield. Probably more upsetting for you than for Jem."

"Tell me the worst," Hugo said, pretty certain of what he was about to hear.

"I had a long, depressing meeting with Crawford last week. I didn't want to tell you until we could discuss it together, just you and I, peacefully and uninterrupted by – "

"Yes," said Hugo, avoiding Jeremy's name.

It was indeed a sad story that Crawford had told her. It seemed that, even though Richard had been dead for over two years, the final probate of the estate had only just been agreed with the Inland Revenue and there were, as she had feared, massive, crippling taxes due, which must be paid. The cash situation was extremely serious; many of the stocks and shares in Richard's personal portfolio were at rock bottom and there was a large overdraft at the bank.

In short, there was no possibility of Jeremy being able to live at Charnfield in the future and there appeared to be no alternative to his selling the place, as he had often said he wanted to do.

"Selling Charnfield?" Hugo could hardly believe that this was coming from Celia. "Selling a place that's been in the Cardwell family for three centuries?"

"I know, darling; it seems criminal," Celia agreed; "but what alternative is there? I'm afraid a lot of lovely old family homes are going to be lost now, and turned into schools or hotels. It's a new era. The days of families living in places like Charnfield with masses of servants are over. It's sad, but it has to be faced."

A WEEK later Celia received a long, rather pathetic letter from Jack Mitchell, asking her if she had changed her mind and no longer wished to go out and share his life in East Africa. Celia knew that she must now decide her future and begin making arrangements at once, if she was to go off into the blue, into a new and possibly the last chapter of her life.

She felt in duty bound to say to Jem that she would stay if he needed her but the thought of living somewhere near him, when his way of life was likely to cause her negative feelings ranging from irritation to distress, was not appealing, and even less so if they were not to live at Charnfield. She would be sorry to be far from Hugo, but he had been away at the war for so long that she had got used to his absence, and now that he was a mature adult she would not in any case have much of a place in his life. She was getting old, and a safe haven with dear Jack seemed a very comforting prospect.

"Good God!" said Jem. "Uncle Jack wants to marry *you*?" He looked as astonished as if she had said she was planning to fly to the moon.

"Is it so very odd? Older people do get married sometimes, you know."

"I suppose so," Jeremy muttered, giving away his dislike of the idea that anyone more than about ten years older than himself should have any interest in the opposite sex.

Then he brightened up. After all, it would be pleasant to have Stable House to himself and to be able to lead his own life without interference.

He rose to the occasion, as an adult young man of twenty-four should. "The only thing that matters is your happiness," he told her. "I'll manage all right. And I'll write to you and keep in touch."

It only remained for Celia to tell Hugo that she had made up her mind, and to him it came as no surprise. But the scene with him was more difficult and painful than with Jem. Hugo understood her reasons for going but said it would be like losing his mother all over again. Rosie had died when he was only five and he'd always looked on Celia as a mother. "You're the most important thing in my life, ever since you married Uncle Richard. I can't bear to think you'll never be around again to help me and back me up and love me . . . I know you'll be happy out there with Jack but I'll be hopelessly lost without you."

After they'd both had a good cry, Hugo pulled himself together and said he was just being selfish. All that mattered was that Celia should be happy. "Send us masses of lovely postcards of rhinos charging about, and don't get bitten by a snake."

SO Celia, with her conscience clear, booked a flight for September with BOAC to join Jack at Lagos via Casablanca, Dakar and then Accra.

Hugo and Jem saw her off from Croydon. As the two young men watched the large, clumsy Handley-Page Halton aircraft bear her off into the clouds, perhaps never to be seen again, Hugo experienced a deep and painful sense of loss. As they drove away from the aerodrome in Hugo's car, back into central London, Jem asked to be dropped at Waterloo, where he would catch a train for Charnfield. Hugo went on to the flat behind Marble Arch, now back in his possession, and on the way thought about Charles, wondering where he was and how long it would be before he was released from the Navy. Hugo realised, now that Celia had gone, that he was dependent on his friend for any kind of 'family' life, and hoped they might be reunited in time for Christmas.

After he got back to his flat he rang Charles's parents' number and presently heard Mr Foley's voice.

"It's Hugo Mayne," he said. "I'm ringing to ask if you have any news of Charles."

"Hold on, I'll fetch my wife," came the rather faint reply.

There was quite a long silence, which made Hugo begin to feel uneasy.

Then Mrs Foley came on the line, very subdued, her voice shaking a little. "Hullo, this is Charles's mother . . . I'm afraid he . . ." Then silence.

"Mrs Foley, are you there?"

The distraught woman managed to pull herself together for long enough to say "I'm afraid you may not have heard the news . . . that . . . Charles's ship was torpedoed, off Murmansk . . . quite a while ago now. The Red Cross tried to get news of him from the Russians but there was no trace of him . . . he's been posted missing, believed . . . Well, we didn't know where we could write to let you know . . . "

Hugo felt a deep void in his stomach; a strange numb emptiness. But in the split second that it took him to grasp the news of his friend's almost-certain death at sea, he knew he ought to feel worse than he did. He put it down to years of living with death in Albania and a kind of remoteness which the war years had put between them. "I'm so sorry. Thank you for telling me," was all he could manage to say.

Minutes later, Hugo was hit by a shattering, aching depression and a feeling that life was no longer worth living. He could see no future at all. He was an orphan with no living parents to turn to. Although Celia had not gone out of his life forever, she was too far away to comfort him. Charles was probably lying drowned at the bottom of the Atlantic Ocean, David, whom he had loved most, had obviously thought of himself as no more than all right for a casual affair. He had dropped him at school, going off without even saying goodbye, and almost the same thing had happened in Cairo. Hugo was not used to being treated casually by the people whom he liked, so David's rejection hurt him all the more. And Charnfield would soon be sold, with all its treasures, and turned into something dreary like a home for delinquent children.

He thought of Dieter von Graetz, of his stepfather, even of his mother, although his memories of her were very faint. And he

224

began to envisage, as he had done at the lake hut soon after Dieter's death years ago, all the people he knew and loved who were now, he hoped, in heaven, living gloriously in a beautiful and happy place. After thinking for some while, death itself, the idea of a final release from life and an end to the weariness of long, grinding misery, seemed like something not to be dreaded but longed for. As he sat there in the small sitting-room of his flat, high up above Montagu Street, he could hear the rush hour traffic rumbling round Marble Arch. People out there were going home from work, back to their husbands and wives and families. But they all belonged to someone or somewhere. They were the lucky ones.

Hugo's eye alighted on the small gas oven just visible through the open door of the kitchenette. To end it all . . . the idea drew him with magnetic power, and he rose wearily from his chair. He pulled off his tie and loosening his shirt collar, like a man going to his execution, he moved slowly into the kitchenette and closed the door behind him.

ABOUT five minutes later, after moments of agonizing indecision, Hugo's shaking hand turned on the oven switch; at the same moment a taxi was rounding Marble Arch and heading up Montagu Street. It stopped outside Hugo's block of flats. The passenger got out, paid the driver, looked up at the tall building and then made for the entrance.

Hugo was losing consciousness fast and his thoughts were no longer coherent, while the gas was filling the small kitchenette. It would happen soon; very quickly now . . . just oblivion and total peace . . . And then a shrill but dimly distant sound penetrated Hugo's almost deadened brain. The door bell was ringing. At first Hugo thought that he did not want to answer. But the bell rang and rang, penetrating his dwindling consciousness with the idea that it was about something important. Clinging now to one last conscious thought, Hugo knew that somehow he must answer it. He tried to move towards the door but found that he was too feeble to change his position. Suddenly he was gripped with panic. The human instinct for self-preservation was overtaking his desire to die.

He struggled harder, wanting to get up and onto his feet. Next to the oven was a rather unbalanced little tripod on which stood saucepan lids. Hugo managed to grasp it, hoping to pull himself up. Instead, the thing swayed, and then tipped over, sending the saucepan lids onto the floor with a deafening crash.

As the noise died away, Hugo heard a voice shouting outside "Is anyone there?" It sounded familiar – gloriously familiar, so that Hugo was jerked into momentary coherence.

"Yes!" he shouted back, but the sound came out only as a faint croak.

Then the voice came again: "My God . . ."

OUTSIDE the flat, David Maidment had felt a presentiment that someone was inside, which was why he had gone on ringing for so long. As he did so, an uneasy feeling had grown on him that something was wrong. Then came the sudden crash from inside, which made him stoop down and open the flap of the letter box, to peer in. There was an unmistakeable smell of gas.

David raced down the stairs to the basement to find the porter.

"That's gas, that is," said the man, as the ascending lift stopped at the fifth floor. "Can't you smell it, sir?"

"Yes, I can," shouted David, who was already wrenching open the lift gates and running like hell along the corridor, "it's coming from that flat. We may have to break down the door."

Hugo had managed to slither out of the kithenette into the sitting room to grasp the telephone. The receiver was still in his hand and he was gasping for breath, retching and almost vomiting, when an almighty crash and a splintering of wood was followed by the sound of windows being hurriedly slid open and a voice shouting "Turn it off quickly . . it's the oven . . . can you get an ambulance and a doctor?"

The sounds became faint droning echoes in Hugo's ears, as he finally lost consciousness.

"THAT was a very silly thing to do, my dear. Really." David was sitting beside Hugo's bed in a public ward at St Mary's Hospital. On the bedside table were a dozen roses that David had brought. Apart from David himself and his parents, whom he had not yet seen but had informed by telephone of his safe return home, nobody in the wide world bar the hospital staff knew of Hugo's plight.

The ward sister had assured David that his friend would be all right and that no lasting damage to his lungs had been sustained. He would probably be allowed to go home in a couple of days.

"You're not to lecture me, David. I've already had a hospital chaplain in here giving me an encouraging 'pep' talk about the value of life – which I gather is a standard procedure for bungling, failed suicides like me."

"Why did you do it?"

With a deep sigh, Hugo said "Because Charles is dead, miles down in the Atlantic, sitting on that idiotic locker with Davy Jones and I never expected to see *you* again . . . "

David squeezed his friend's hand. "Why ever not?"

Hugo smiled, for the first time since he had been in hospital, and suddenly felt much better. David asked the nurse for some glasses and opened a bottle of champagne he had brought with him.

In the next few weeks a lot of explaining went on. David had never written to Hugo after he was expelled from school because he was afraid his letters might get Hugo into trouble. Also, he said, he had seen no possibility of meeting Hugo again; Hugo had been only thirteen at the time and would be under the control of his step-parents for many years to come. From the superior age of sixteen, David could not imagine that the younger boy would remember him by the time he was grown up and able to make his own decisions about who his friends would be.

In Cairo, he had not said much about hoping to see Hugo again because he was afraid that history always repeated itself; and Hugo had Charles, so that David could not see where he himself might fit into the picture.

Early on the day that Hugo came out of hospital David moved into the flat, ready to give him a warm homecoming. In the next few days they packed up Charles's belongings together and sent them back to his parents. When the railway van that came to collect the baggage departed they watched it from the sitting-room window as solemnly as if it was Charles's funeral hearse – which in a sense it was – representing Hugo's goodbye to his friend.

HUGO and David spent the next few weeks sorting out their own belongings and redecorating the flat, which had suffered badly from a long let to a couple from the US Embassy. David's old job was no longer open to him and he found it hard to find anything that he wanted to settle down to. After about two years of chopping and changing by David, Hugo decided to give up the

Courtauld Institute. The two of them seriously considered starting up an interior decorating business in Chelsea. Their two gratuities from the grateful armed forces, if put together, could capitalize them, provided suitable premises could be found. But before any such decision was taken, fate intervened in the shape of a telephone call one evening from Jeremy who was most anxious, he said, to meet Hugo and discuss the vexed problem of Charnfield.

THUS, one wet, misty day in November 1947, Jeremy, who had just resigned his commission in the Grenadiers, set out for London from Stable House for the lunch he had proposed with Hugo at a little Greek restaurant in Percy Street. To Hugo's relief, Jem said he would be amenable to any suggestion that Hugo could put forward which would give him some cash to live off, and relieve him of the responsibility of keeping up Charnfield in the future.

"As a matter of fact, Hugo," he said, attacking a plate of moussaka, "if you really want to know my plans, I'm cooking up a scheme with a friend of mine, a chap in my regiment who's as browned off as I am with this bloody Socialist country. There's nothing here but fog and rain and high taxation. So we're going to raise a bit of capital and bugger off to sunny Spain, start up a restaurant there. Clive Mason-Scott – that's my future partner – knows the Costa Brava well; he says you can buy property out there pretty cheap at the moment and he thinks there'll be a boom in British tourism to Spain, once the Conservatives get back and put an end to these idiotic currency restrictions."

Hugo asked how much capital he would need to start up his restaurant.

"Don't tell me you're going to finance us," Jem said with a grin.

"You've got a hope," Hugo said with a thin smile. Then he told Jeremy that he'd been talking to some people at the Courtauld Institute about big country houses in general and Charnfield in particular. "I don't know how you feel about it," he said, "but there is an organization called The National Trust. It's financed by the Treasury and its function is to take over historically important properties, which their owners can't afford to keep up. They restore them and open them to the public, like museums, so people can pay to go round the rooms and see all the pictures and art treasures."

228

"That sounds pretty good. Would they buy Charnfield off me?"

"I'm afraid it doesn't work quite like that, Jem. If you offer the house to the Trust, you have to endow it. In other words, you have to provide a capital sum that will bring in enough income to subsidise the running of the place. Just having an entrance fee and a teashop and selling catalogues wouldn't be enough."

"So what are you suggesting?" Jeremy sounded disappointed.

"If you're prepared to let me go with you to see old Crawford about it, there might be a way. There's plenty of valuable land at Charnfield; two untenanted farms for a start; which could be sold to raise quite a bit. After all, it's the house and gardens that count. Losing a bit of land wouldn't matter, if it meant the National Trust could take over and run the place. Don't you agree?"

"Yes, I do," Jeremy said. "But what about me? I shall need some capital."

"If you sell enough land, that shouldn't be a problem."

"Then let's go and see Crawford and get his advice."

"Good idea," Hugo said. "I'll make an appointment straight away. How are you fixed for next week?"

THE summer of 1980 proved to be something of a boom in British tourism. Many of the great places of interest showed record takings that year. The dollar rate was favourable to the Americans and, apart from the ever-popular Tower of London, Windsor Castle, Hampton Court, Greenwich and other such historical sites, the stately homes of England did well too. Beaulieu Abbey, Woburn, Blenheim, Belvoir and Haddon were all well attended and, among the larger houses in the South West such as Longleat, Stourhead, Minterne Abbey and others, Charnfield Park in Dorset attracted its quota of visitors. Every day coach-loads of Americans, Germans and Japanese tourists as well as many English enthusiasts and parties of ladies from Womens' Institutes and members of the rapidly-expanding National Arts Collection Fund, could be found moving in groups up the grand staircase from the Great Hall towards the Long Gallery.

One afternoon that summer one of the guides, Mrs Wetherby, was delivering her set piece about the elaborate coat-of-arms over the great fireplace in the Long Gallery. She knew it by heart, every word of it, but tried her best to make it sound fresh each time. Moving away from the fireplace, she turned to draw the attention of her guided party to the painting of a man in Georgian costume on the panelled wall opposite. "That is a portrait by Sir Joshua Reynolds," she announced.

At that moment a slightly precious elderly man's voice was heard from the back of the group: "It was painted in 1789, the year of the storming of the Bastille. He was Sir William Cardwell, the fourth baronet, and High Sheriff of the county. Look at his red nose; much too fond of his port, you see."

The tourists laughed and turned round, to see that this extra detail had been provided by a tall, frail, elderly man who had attached himself to the group. "I'm sorry to interrupt you, Mrs Wetherby," he said. "Just happened to be passing and I'm so very fond of that Sir Joshua. It's one of the first paintings I ever saw, you know, as a child, many years ago . . . it holds some memories for me. Well . . . there it is. Do please carry on, Mrs Wetherby."

With that, the man went on his way to one of the other rooms, to check the state of some very old brocade curtains that were in dire need of repair. His eyes behind thick glasses looked sad and his face was lined, but it was finely chiselled and distinguished, the face of a man who had been good-looking in his younger days.

As he moved away down the Long Gallery, a woman in the crowd asked the guide who he was. "That's our curator, Mr Mayne. He's been here for many years. There's nothing he doesn't know about Charnfield. I believe he's some relation of the Cardwells, the family that used to own this place."

Satisfied that the brocade curtains in the Blue Bedroom upstairs would last another season before money would have to be spent on them, Hugo slipped out of the house, noting with satisfaction the crowded car park. He walked across to the stable block, which housed the National Trust office, the tearoom, gift shop and his own private flat upstairs.

Here he collected a bunch of roses from a bucket in the kitchen, wrapped them in paper and set off with them to the village churchyard. Reaching the lychgate, Hugo made straight for the small graveyard where he paused by two adjacent headstones, Uncle Richard's and that of his own mother. When he reached a third grave, a few yards further on, he knelt down

230

and gently placed the roses in a small vase against the stone, which was engraved with the words:

David Gerald Maidment, born Sept. 5th, 1914
died at Charnfield, June 12th, 1973
'But if the while I think on thee, dear friend,
all losses are restored and sorrows end.' William Shakespeare

AFTER a moment Hugo Mayne rose from his kneeling position and left the churchyard to return to Stable House. It was time for his tea, which he made for himself in a thermos flask, putting it in a small basket with a few biscuits and a plastic cup. Thus equipped, he walked down through the woods, as he invariably did in the summer months, to the lake. Reaching the little hut standing in the trees by the water's edge, its paint flaking off and the door loose on one hinge, he entered it almost reverently, placing his tea basket on the rickety table. Minutes later Hugo was sitting at the door, sipping his tea from the plastic cup, staring out at the still waters of the lake, his mind filled with many sweet and bitter memories but also a comforting sense of having come home.

Also by Alfred Shaughnessy

Dearest Enemy tells the story of a retired High Court Judge searching both his conscience and modern Europe to find the love he left behind in Germany in 1945.

At the end of the war Captain Jack Hamilton, who had fought with his regiment through Northern Europe and had his fill of the horrors of fighting, encountered a beautiful girl swimming in the Rhine, and instantly fell in love. But it was an offence to fraternise with the enemy and the resulting subterfuge, blackmail, and Jack's own errant behaviour were to test their relationship.

'A solidly constructed romance by Alfred Shaughnessy . . . this smoothly readable story cuts back and forth from the days when a young officer had a love affair with a beautiful Lorelei . . . to the present. What happened to her during the long years of separation gives him and the reader a well-deserved surprise.'   *Daily Telegraph*

'Based on a true story . . . Today there is no bitterness in the heart of the woman who wept such bitter tears.'   *Daily Mail*

'A touching, erotic novel.'   *Daily Express*

'This sensitive, unpretentious love-story rings with authenticity . . . suspenseful and psychologically penetrating device as the retired judge, now a widower, sits in judgement on his own youthful, arrogant behaviour . . .'
                    Publishers' Weekly, USA

'How very well he tells a story. It flows beautifully, it rings true.'   Fay Weldon

'Thoroughly entertaining from beginning to end.'
                    Sir John Mills, CBE

'A delightful and moving novel; the atmosphere of post-war Germany is beautifully caught.'   John Julius Norwich

Hardback £12.95. Paperback £6.95. 255 pages

Also by Alfred Shaughnessy

Dearest Enemy tells the story of a retired High Court Judge searching both his conscience and modern Europe to find the love he left behind in Germany in 1945.

At the end of the war Captain Jack Hamilton, who had fought with his regiment through Northern Europe and had his fill of the horrors of fighting, encountered a beautiful girl swimming in the Rhine, and instantly fell in love. But it was an offence to fraternise with the enemy and the resulting subterfuge, blackmail, and Jack's own errant behaviour were to test their relationship.

'A solidly constructed romance by Alfred Shaughnessy . . . this smoothly readable story cuts back and forth from the days when a young officer had a love affair with a beautiful Lorelei . . . to the present. What happened to her during the long years of separation gives him and the reader a well-deserved surprise.'   *Daily Telegraph*

'Based on a true story . . . Today there is no bitterness in the heart of the woman who wept such bitter tears.'   *Daily Mail*

'A touching, erotic novel.'   *Daily Express*

'This sensitive, unpretentious love-story rings with authenticity . . . suspenseful and psychologically penetrating device as the retired judge, now a widower, sits in judgement on his own youthful, arrogant behaviour . . .'
Publishers' Weekly, USA

'How very well he tells a story. It flows beautifully, it rings true.'   Fay Weldon

'Thoroughly entertaining from beginning to end.'
Sir John Mills, CBE

'A delightful and moving novel; the atmosphere of post-war Germany is beautifully caught.'   John Julius Norwich

Hardback £12.95. Paperback £6.95. 255 pages